2-12

D0340428

THE
SILVER LOTUS

**Center Point
Large Print**

**This Large Print Book carries the
Seal of Approval of N.A.V.H.**

THE
SILVER LOTUS

THOMAS STEINBECK

CENTER POINT LARGE PRINT
THORNDIKE, MAINE

This Center Point Large Print edition
is published in the year 2012 by arrangement with
Thomas Steinbeck and The Palladin Group.

This is a work of fiction. Names, characters, places, and
incidents are the product of the author's imagination or
are used fictitiously. Any resemblance to actual persons,
living or dead, is entirely coincidental.

The text of this Large Print edition is unabridged.
In other aspects, this book may vary
from the original edition.
Printed in the United States of America
on permanent paper.
Set in 16-point Times New Roman type.

ISBN: 978-1-61173-342-6

Library of Congress Cataloging-in-Publication Data

Steinbeck, Thomas.
  The silver lotus / Thomas Steinbeck.
    p. cm.
  ISBN 978-1-61173-342-6 (library binding : alk. paper)
  1. Merchants—Fiction. 2. Trading companies—Fiction.
  3. Pacific Area—Fiction. 4. Large type books. I. Title.
PS3619.T47615S55 2012
813′.6—dc23
                                                    2011044454

This book is dedicated to my beautiful and gifted wife, Gail Knight Steinbeck.

Proposing to her has proven to be the only truly ingenious thing I have ever done.

In the far off Kingdoms of the Eastern Sea
The Silver Lotus sings for me.
And in the night, when dream's alight,
I'll hear her songs once more.

J. M. II.

THE
SILVER LOTUS

1

THE WEALTHY, influential, and much admired Master Chu-Woo Yee was considered one of the most astute and clever grain factors in Canton. In fact, he dealt in a great many varieties of exported and imported goods, but for all intents and purposes he preferred to be known as a simple grain merchant, an act of false modesty that all pretended to believe for the sake of good manners. It was said by some that Master Chu-Woo Yee was so canny in affairs of business that he could, by virtue of his wide network of mercantile correspondents and traveling associates, predict the market price of numerous goods many months in advance of their availability. This was especially true of grains and minerals. He often traveled great distances to see things for himself, to talk to farmers and miners and anyone else who could be relied upon for accurate intelligence concerning matters of interest. He once sailed all the way to Java to procure a rich cargo of medicinal herbs, and then went on to Madagascar to trade for precious minerals, pearls, and those exotic elements so prized by Chinese pharmacologists and doctors. Rarity had a virtue all its own in this trade, and Master Yee possessed an instinct for such things. He returned home with his cargo loaded into three sturdy Arabian ships, and safely warehoused his goods until after the end of the trading season. When the typhoons and winter storms closed the shipping lanes, and scarcity raised prices, Master Yee gradually released his goods onto the market at the best prices and made a considerable fortune again. It was well-known that even the imperial household physicians, renowned medical scholars known for their professional discretion, were counted on his books as valued clients.

However brilliant Master Yee's prognostications were in the course of business, his ability to foretell the future within the sanctity of his own home was almost nonexistent. Evidence for his lack of foresight could be found in the fact that every time his wife was with child, Master Yee predicted sons, and on each occasion his beloved wife presented him with a daughter. But these were no simple girls to be raised for strategic marriages. Indeed, Master Yee found to his utter amazement that he had sired three of the most talented daughters in the empire. All three girls were considered great beauties, but above and beyond appearances, they were each profoundly gifted in a number of talents. The oldest was New Moon, who at the age of eighteen was a most accomplished musician, singer, and composer. The next daughter, Winter Light, was a marvelous and inventive poet who composed beautifully complex and intriguing verse. She also gained a firm reputation for her magnificently elegant calligraphy. Even the imperial governor applauded her talents and respectfully commissioned several of her unique scrolls for his private library. But it was his youngest daughter, Silver Lotus, affectionately known in the family as Lady Yee, who proved a constant source of wonder and consternation to her parents, teachers, and friends. Every time her father returned from one of his long journeys, it was to discover that his youngest daughter had added another accomplishment to her quiver of remarkable talents.

By the time Lady Yee was seven years old, she could already speak, read, and write in both Mandarin and Cantonese and could calculate extensive lists of numbers on her abacus with absolute precision. It proved a little disconcerting when it was discovered that she could do her calculations twice as fast as her father, or any of his regiment of clerks. Sometimes she would make a game of challenging her father's chief steward to tests of speed and accuracy in mathematics, and it soon came to pass that she never lost a competition of this kind to anyone, regardless of his experience or ability. And that wasn't the least of the surprises Lady Yee had in store for her parents.

When Master Yee returned from a five-month trading journey to India and Madagascar, Lady

Yee had just celebrated her fourteenth birthday. He returned to discover that his youngest treasure had mastered passable English and very good French, and was beginning to study Italian under the tutelage of her father's warehouse master, who had served the Italian consul in Hong Kong for ten years in the same capacity.

In her brief fourteen years, Lady Yee had also managed to learn a great deal from her older sisters. She could play several musical instruments quite well, sing wonderfully, and compose lovely poetry in her own right. Her calligraphy lacked a little grace, and her sisters said she brushed her characters like a street scribe, but the copious notes she made relating to her studies and numerous interests caused her to write rapidly, and it was a habit she found difficult to break except when writing formal letters or poetry.

Lady Yee's sisters were much sought after as prospective brides, and they were soon married to men of prominence, influence, and wealth. Only Lady Yee resisted the idea of being married off. She had, since infancy, been in the habit of making up her own mind about everything, and Master Yee had come to love her too much to thwart her aspirations in anything that gave her joy. He wisely let the question of prospective husbands lie unspoken. He assumed that if anyone was going to choose a husband for his daughter, it would most likely be Lady Yee herself. This, of course, went against all tradition, but Master Yee knew that some customs had to be adapted to fit extraordinary circumstances, or at least configured to coincide with Lady Yee's requirements, which were much the same. Thus, as the saying goes, is a doting father ensnared by the love he bears for a brilliant and beautiful daughter.

If the truth were known, Master Yee was not all that pleased with the idea of losing his beloved daughter. She was the last and most endearing of his treasures, and he couldn't imagine his life without her wit, laughter, and generosity of spirit. Master Yee wasn't the only one who harbored deep affection for the Silver Lotus of Yee. There wasn't one member of Master Yee's extensive business family of agents, factors, stewards, and clerks who, having once known the incomparable child, wouldn't have given his life to protect the beautiful and wise Lady Yee from all adversity. Master Yee once quipped that if he really required his company to focus all its efforts on one goal, all he needed was to have Lady Yee make the request as a personal favor, and every man jack of them would have surrendered all his waking hours to please her. Master Yee would shake his graying head in amused contemplation and admit that his daughter had the ability to charm a rock to dance to her tune. So compassionate and modest was her nature that none could sense even the slightest flaw except, perhaps, her driving ambition to learn and know everything she could. This was a most unusual character trait in a young girl, and one that almost always intimidated the young men she came in contact with.

In Master Yee's extended household, there were those few jealous souls, hungry ghosts as it were, who thought that Master Yee had indulged his daughters beyond the bounds of tradition and decorum, but most wisely kept their sentiments strictly to themselves. The last individual that mustered the audacity to openly voice a critical opinion of Master Yee's indulgences was his great-aunt on his mother's side. She paid the price when she suddenly found herself living on a mulberry plantation in the provinces a month later. Yet it was Lady Yee who wrote her long, newsy letters about the family, and sent a constant stream of little gifts of exotic fruits and the special sweetmeats the old woman was so fond of. And it was Lady Yee who earnestly petitioned her father to bring the aging lady home, where she was happiest. It took a while, but Master Yee eventually relented. As it turned out, in the end Master Yee's great-aunt became one of Lady Yee's staunchest proponents and confidantes. When she died two years later, she left a will bequeathing Lady Yee her treasure of beautiful jewels. Master Yee said that her collection of rare emeralds and her twelve large star sapphires were worth more than two thousand ounces of fine gold, and the antique ivory casket she left, which contained two hundred large matched pearls called quail's eggs, was worth perhaps as much again. This made Lady Yee wealthy in her own right, but that fact didn't seem to impress her very much. The first thing she did was finance an endowment to ensure that her benefactor's grave was perpetually tended by an established brotherhood of Taoist monks whose business it was to look after the venerable dead. This act was considered a remarkable sign of devotion and gratitude from a sixteen-year-old girl.

Master Yee, being a man of wealth and influence, had acquired his fair share of detractors and enemies, but he had always been able to evade the snares and pitfalls his adversaries had devised to bring him down. This was hardly unusual in the highly competitive atmosphere of international trade with the Eastern and Western barbarians. He had survived many attempts to undermine his influence and power, and he had evaded the axe by practicing two rigid principles. First, he insisted that all his business dealings, whether with the authorities or with foreign traders, be as scrupulously honest and transparent as possible. He made sure that all his books were balanced and open to examination by the authorities at any time. Second, he absolutely refused to deal in contraband or smuggling of any kind, and studiously avoided associating with those traders and ship's captains who did. But like many in his line of work, the very fact that he entertained the foreign devils in his own home opened Master Yee to floating speculations that he was somehow in league with the round-eyes. This was ridiculous, of course, but hardly unheard of. There were always a number of traders who would do almost anything for gold. The opium trade, despite the devastation it had caused to the empire, had attracted numerous categories of criminals and bandits who suffered virtually no qualms about enslaving their own people to the insidious power of the drug.

Master Yee had always been a creature of high moral principles. It was part of his nature. He often said that had he been alive at the time, he would have most definitely fought on the side of the Boxers in their fatal attempts to expel the foreign drug merchants. He had watched his own beloved grandfather slowly surrender to the netherworld of opium. The venerable old man had taken to using the drug to alleviate the excruciating pain caused by a lingering injury resulting from a fall. By the time he realized that he had become hopelessly addicted, it was too late. The poor gentleman was so consumed with self-loathing and remorse as a result of his actions that he took his own life rather than burden his family with the shameful consequences of his predicament. As a result, Master Yee had come to the conclusion that opiates in the hands of a qualified doctor were one thing, but opium in the hands of the patient was a recipe for disaster, and inevitably a measured course toward a reprehensible and unnecessary death. Master Yee inculcated his beliefs in all those who worked for him, as well as his family, and even funded a clinic for those poor souls trapped in the tentacles of the drug. His feelings on the matter were so strong that he strictly refused to do business with those companies that had once been responsible for the opium trade, and in some cases were still involved in smuggling the insidious drug into China disguised as other products, and did so with the connivance of corrupt state officials who took money to betray their own people. These shameless officials were also his enemies, for they knew only too well that Master Yee would happily betray them to the courts if he ever got his hands on evidence of their involvement. They also knew he would reward anyone who came forth with such evidence, and they lived in fear that one of their number would supply it, if only to save his own neck from the block. These men would have rejoiced to discover that Master Yee had been bested by one of his competitors, and substantially reduced in wealth, respect, and influence, but none had managed to snare him as yet, and it was highly unlikely they would manage it anytime in the near future. Master Yee had always cultivated his relationships with honest and dedicated officials, and he counted many prominent scholars and administrators as friends, and occasionally even colleagues in one venture or another. But if it could be said that there was one particular driving force that encouraged Master Yee to hold a moral and upstanding course in all things, then one need look no further than the pride, love, and respect he cherished from his daughters, in particular Lady Yee. It was Lady Yee, who had by now read all the most important translations of Buddhist texts, who sometimes reminded her father that there was often greater power in total transparency than the shaded substance of subterfuge, especially when one is surrounded with jealous rivals eager to whisper dangerous aspersions in the ears of authority. Master Yee, in a moment of amused paternal pride, had once confided to a judge of his acquaintance that if Lady Yee had been born a male, she would have already taken first place in all her civil examinations and be well on her way to becoming a figure of authority on her own.

2

OF ALL THE FOREIGNERS, and there weren't that many, who were allowed the privilege of being entertained under Master Yee's roof, the one that fascinated and intrigued him most was a young Yankee ship captain who traded on his own behalf and was as vigorously honest and forthright as Master Yee himself. He was handsome, for a round-eye, with long curly auburn hair, which he oiled and clubbed at the back in the style of British tars. His name was Captain Jeremiah Macy Hammond, and he was one of the last of a long line of the great Nantucket seamen. He was heir to a great tradition of whalers, but whale oil being no longer in fashion for fuel, those Macys who still clung to the sea went into trade with the distant ports that were already familiar on their charts. But Captain Hammond was unique in many respects. Not the least of his peculiarities involved his mode of trade and transport.

In an age when steamships had started to dominate transoceanic trade, Captain Hammond still transported his cargos under sail. He had made enough money in the first few years to purchase a small fleet of older wooden four- and five-mast gaff-rigged schooners. What they might have lacked in speed, they more than compensated for by their dependability, generous cargo capacity, and economy of operation. The crews required to sail these great ships were a fraction of what was required to man the great square-rigged clippers of an earlier generation, and they carried every bit as much cargo. Accepting the utility of the age, when Captain Hammond refurbished his ships for the Eastern trade, he equipped each with a gasoline-powered cutter that was powerful enough to service the ship as a small tug to help it enter and exit port if necessary. They could also tow the mother ships when the winds went slack, or when faced with a dangerous lee shore and contrary winds and currents. But in any event, Captain Hammond was saved the expense of feeding gluttonous steam engines tons of fuel from spacious coal bunkers. The space that the large steam engines and coal supply occupied might otherwise be better used to carry cargo. His schooners had one other substantial advantage: The chances of boiler explosions and fire were substantially reduced; subsequently his insurance costs were held to a minimum.

Captain Hammond also stuck to a traditional Yankee method of making profits under the axiom of "a penny saved is a penny earned." He carried only relative nonperishables and sold his cargos at reasonable prices. Yet he still made better profits than his steam-powered competition, and without the added expense of having to sign on a gaggle of engineers, mechanics, and stokers to run his ships.

In some cases these engineers made better wages than most ship's officers, and for doing less work.

The captain was also a very pragmatic and insightful trader. He carried into China only those goods the Chinese really wanted, and in that regard he became well-known for his cargos of medicinal goods so prized in Chinese pharmacopeia. For instance, when he discovered the highly prized value the Chinese doctors placed upon an herbal root called ginseng, and was told that a wild species of the plant grew deep in the deciduous forests of eastern America, he decided it must become a staple of his trade. So he sent his cousin, Jonathon Macy, east as a purchasing agent to make bargains with various eastern Indian tribes to hunt, gather, and dry the wild roots. Captain Hammond put forward a generous offer of five dollars a pound paid in silver or currency. It cost him twenty cents a bushel to ship the ginseng by rail to San Francisco, and another dollar a bushel to ship the cargo all the way to China. The captain paid little or no export duties because the American customs agents deemed the product useless, and valued it as such. The captain might have realized substantially more money on Mexican bird guano, but the malodorous guano lingered and polluted the holds with a cloying stench that permeated all other cargo long after the guano sacks had been off-loaded. And nobody in his right mind would lay down hard cash for a cargo of fabrics, spices, or anything else that smelled like guano.

The captain studied his subject well, and even made inquiries of noted Chinese pharmacists. He was told that the wild ginseng plant is a crafty master of invisibility. When seen from above, ginseng looks like a most unremarkable little plant. Nothing about its structure, leaf shape, or color stands out at all; even its diminutive flowers are difficult to see because they only bloom late in the day and blossom fully into the night. Morning light finds the buds closed again. To hunt these innocuous little plants requires that the searcher focus closely on the ground in dense and overgrown forests, no easy task at the best of times, especially in the lengthening shadows of twilight.

By the time Captain Hammond's cousin returned from his first trip back east, he had done a good deal of research on his own. He wrote that though it was called by several different tribal names, there were some eastern American Indians who also used wild ginseng in their own medicines. The natives said that in some places the root was plentiful, and would remain so if not overharvested, but it was time-consuming and difficult to hunt and gather. Great care had to be taken not to damage the tuberous root, for that was where the treasure lay.

American ginseng roots were smaller than their

Asian cousin, but what they lacked in size they more than made up for in profit when sold in the right Asian market. The first year's cargo was modest in weight, only 890 pounds, but all of the best quality. And when it came time to sell his cargo in China, Captain Hammond was just as canny. Rather than flood the market and lower the value of his cargo, he stored the bulk of his ginseng in one of Master Yee's warehouses and had him sell it off a few pounds at a time at the best possible prices. After all expenses, duties, and commissions had been paid, Captain Hammond still realized a profit of 280 dollars a pound. The following year he did even better, for he shared the wealth and increased the price he was willing to pay the Indian gatherers to fifteen dollars a pound.

On the Arabian coast he traded iron tools for frankincense and other exotic resins, and did the same in Madagascar for rare hardwoods, baroque pearls, and medicinal compounds concocted from rare jungle flora, and in some cases fauna as well. One Chinese physician even asked for dried Indonesian fruit bats and emerald tree lizards. Captain Hammond regretted that he was unable to fulfill this request, but he did manage to make quite an impression with a half ton of candied Jamaican ginger and twenty-five barrels of very dark sweet Jamaican rum he purchased in San Francisco from a steamship captain whose vessel had been badly damaged in port by fire. The Chinese physicians who purchased the cargo used the rum to create tinctures of normally unpalatable oral medications, and the candied Jamaican ginger was a popular remedy for seasickness and morning distress in pregnant women. By always allowing Master Yee to broker his cargo to the right customers, Captain Hammond usually realized a profit of 600 percent after expenses. It wasn't until much later that he discovered that Master Yee had the rum and ginger repackaged with Chinese labels, which made it far easier to sell to the normally suspicious markets in the provinces. The profits were far better than expected, and Captain Hammond saw to it that Master Yee was rewarded beyond his expectations.

For a barbarian, the captain was insightful enough to realize that being able to cultivate a trusting and equitable relationship with a successful Chinese commercial agent was extremely problematical for most foreign traders. Such arrangements between Western and Eastern commercial factors had a tendency to lean toward the adversarial, with one element or the other working with an eye on one-upmanship. However, for Captain Hammond, having once established such a lucrative relationship, maintaining its impartial and candid foundation was imperative to success. Besides, it was the only way the captain knew how to conduct business. He once laughingly told Master Yee that having been raised by strict religious moralists, his ability to dissemble with any skill whatsoever had been discouraged. So naturally, in a pique of childish rebellion, he came to embrace a strong ambition to become a famous pirate. Unfortunately he never got the encouragement he needed from his family, so he settled for a more mundane and transparent vocation. He smiled and said that it wasn't that he couldn't tell a lie, but that he'd never had enough real practice to do it with any confidence, which for all intents defeated the purpose of the exercise. It was sentiments of this humorous and self-deprecating caliber that so amused and delighted Master Yee, and it came to pass that Captain Hammond soon became one of his preferred dinner guests.

Of course it was inevitable that Captain Hammond would eventually be introduced to Master Yee's phalanx of beautiful daughters, and though deeply impressed with what he saw, he hadn't the slightest inkling that the youngest, most luminous, and loveliest of the three was charmed by the handsome Yankee captain upon the occasion of their first meeting. In fact, no one knew of her feelings for many months. The details of her growing affection remained at all times within the bounds and constraints of propriety. Lady Yee, though strong-willed, was not about to test the boundaries of tradition at the cost of her father's reputation and peace of mind. Like the training given to a fine horse, Lady Yee very patiently used her considerable skills of persuasion to slowly introduce her father to the idea that his youngest daughter harbored a secret wish to be married to the handsome Yankee barbarian sea captain from the other side of the world. Master Yee knew Captain Hammond to be a man of wealth and principle, and yes, he could easily acknowledge that Captain Hammond was a dashing figure graced with good manners and civility, and the very model of a successful trader, but he was a round-eye barbarian after all. And the fact remained that Master Yee was not yet ready to be parted from his Silver Lotus. And when she did marry, her father would have nominally insisted that the groom be from an influential clan, be well educated and wealthy in his own right, be of modest and dignified deportment, and above all else, be Chinese. Unfortunately, though Captain Hammond qualified in several important categories, the last particular hurdle would prove almost insurmountable, even for someone as talented as Lady Yee. Needless to say, though Captain Hammond was indeed attracted to, if not smitten with, Lady Yee, he knew better than to betray even the slightest sentiment in that regard. And though his generous nature often inspired him to bring exotic presents when he came to call, he made sure that his gifts were equally shared out with all members of the family, showing no particular preference for one over the other, especially when it came to Master Yee's daughters. In fact, due to Lady Yee's well-practiced and perfected air of polite and demure ambivalence, Captain Hammond never had the slightest inkling that he already stood foursquare center in her sights.

However, about this time a festering political conflict born of ancient rivalries erupted unexpectedly, and Master Yee, despite his best efforts to stay above the fray, suddenly found himself between the proverbial hammer and the anvil. Accusations had been spread that Master Yee was in the habit of smuggling portions of his cargos upriver to avoid port duties. And though these claims were completely spurious, no matter which way Master Yee turned he seemed to find political havens of refuge mysteriously closing to him. It soon became obvious that his old adversaries and competitors would soon make the best of every opportunity to assist in his downfall and disgrace. Even Captain Hammond had been secretly approached, as had other Yankee traders; each offered inducements to change their trading allegiances away from the house of Yee.

It was a deeply concerned Captain Hammond who spoke to Master Yee about this dangerous situation and, being a friend of some standing, took the opportunity to suggest that the only way to avoid the impending destruction was to secretly exit the field of conflict as soon as convenient, and hopefully take as much of his portable fortune with him as possible. He reminded his good friend that discretion was always the better part of valor. There were certainly other cities and countries where he already enjoyed substantial business contacts and affiliations; locations where he might set himself up comfortably and wait for the winds of the this present intrigue to blow themselves out in the usual vortex of political self-destruction, a cultural inevitability which always seemed to come to pass in Chinese affairs. Captain Hammond reminded Master Yee that the only certain way to avoid becoming either a partisan or a victim was to absent himself, his family, and his wealth as quickly as possible. Special care must be taken with his ledgers, of course. In an enemy's hands they could be easily forged to reflect the substance of the charges made against the house of Yee. Captain Hammond respectfully suggested that there would be plenty of time to prove his innocence at some reserve, and at a later date. He could then return as a totally vindicated figure of respect. The captain noted that men in prison who have been stripped of all their worldly possessions rarely find the wherewithal to employ respected legal advocates to speak for them. Master Yee was free to employ the best legal representation even at a distance. Hammond smiled and winked. "And if matters turn really sour," he said, "then it is preferable that a lawyer or two go to block, rather than their innocent employer." Captain Hammond paused to gauge Master Yee's response, then added a codicil: "With your permission, Master Yee, and strictly for illustrative purposes, mind you, I would equate your present unpleasant situation with a duel of heavy artillery. It is by nature a dangerous military exercise, and best practiced at very long distances. Hopefully from behind thick walls." Master Yee smiled broadly for the first time in weeks.

To that end, Captain Hammond said he presently had two ships in harbor unloading cargos of Indian wheat, mined salt, coconut oil, and high-grade copper ingots. He put both vessels at Master Yee's disposal with the promise that he would secretly transport the whole Yee clan, as well as his household servants and all his portable goods and wealth, to any destination he liked.

At first Master Yee truly believed he could weather the political and economic crisis, so he politely but very gratefully declined the offer. But quite soon his fast-eroding political influence, and the strained circumstance forced upon him by the gnashing ministers of trade and duties, changed his way of thinking. He soon bowed to Captain Hammond's timely and munificent suggestion.

It took eighteen long days and nights of very secret business manipulations, numerous clandestine household maneuvers, and a long train of nocturnal porters—who were paid well for silence—to accomplish everything that was necessary. With Master Yee's predators smelling blood, only days from the proverbial gates, early on the foggy morning of June 5, 1896, Captain Hammond's two stout ships sailed out of Canton harbor with the entire Yee clan and their faithful servants except the two older married daughters, whose husbands were fully equipped to protect their safety and honor. The Yee family and all their moveable wealth were comfortably stowed away and invoiced as Captain Hammond's private property, thus exempt from inspection by treaty. For all intents, the Yee family just vanished like the morning fog. Their disappearance would soon become a mystery spoken of in every quarter, which was just as Master Yee and Captain Hammond had planned.

Per a private agreement, the two men kept their ultimate destination a secret from everyone until after they'd departed Canton, but it had already been decided that Singapore was the best possible choice to service Master Yee's present circumstances, as he had always maintained well-established trading offices and business associates in that busy port. In that he'd invariably entertained and honored all the right people, his relative safety in Singapore was a foregone conclusion.

Though it sometimes seemed the odds against success were almost beyond hope or prayer, Master Yee and Captain Hammond somehow managed to effect their departure from Canton without Master Yee's enemies being any the wiser for days. In fact, Master Yee, determined to have his revenge even at a distance, arranged his affairs in such a canny fashion that it appeared to one and all as though his sudden disappearance, and that of his family, had been the object of a deadly plot on the part of his political enemies. Only Master Yee's chief clerk, who had loyally stayed behind to cover his master's tracks and look after the warehouse business, knew the truth, and he was encouraged to say that he believed Master Yee and his family had been done away with, and all their goods stolen, for there was no other rational explanation for their sudden disappearance.

Lastly, Master Yee could not help himself against natural instincts that were overtly vengeful, so he set a deep hook in the bait. He created an elaborate but obviously fraudulent bill of sale for his own house and named his most caustically outspoken and dangerous adversary as the new owner. This done, Master Yee had his chief clerk sloppily forge his master's name and add a badly carved copy of Master Yee's chop to seal the document. Even a first-year student of law could have spotted it as a forgery. As a last twist of the barb, Master Yee sent his clerk to secretly insert the document into the tax files of the office of government records. There it would be found when the inevitable investigation took place, or when the tax assessor came for his money. Whichever came first, Master Yee's bomb had a long and elegantly plaited fuse, and it went off in the face of his enemies exactly six months later.

By the time the authorities in Canton were informed that Master Yee was still alive and quite well in Singapore, it was too late to save the reputations and fortunes of his adversaries. The forged bill of sale still hung in the air like a floating recrimination, and Master Yee's many friends in Canton were more than willing to believe that he had only escaped to Singapore to save himself and his family from certain destruction at the hands of highly placed conspirators, which was the truth.

Nonetheless, no one ever thought to ask Master Yee how he had managed his spectacular disappearance, and certainly Captain Hammond's participation in the scheme was never divulged. This left the captain free to come and go to Canton on trading voyages and, with the help of Master Yee's chief clerk, stay abreast of news and business information so necessary for Master Yee's continuing success.

These strained and unusual circumstances

placed Master Yee under great obligation to Captain Hammond for any number of private kindnesses as well as loyal business considerations, and Lady Yee privately rejoiced at the knowledge that her father was now under no illusions concerning his own social status. For despite his wealth, as a political refugee he had none. Without Captain Hammond's timely aid, the family would have been ruined and left destitute. Captain Hammond was in a position to ask for anything he wanted.

3

THE VOYAGE FROM Canton to Singapore was not without its hazards. Hammond's ships ran afoul of an unseasonal monsoon off the coast of China, which drove the vessels many miles off course and left almost all of the passengers weak from seasickness. The only person who seemed to thrive under the strain was Lady Yee. She thought the whole experience a wonderful adventure, and though she had never been to sea before, she expressed every confidence in Captain Hammond's abilities to get them to Singapore safely.

Over the long days aboard ship, Captain Hammond and Lady Yee were much in each other's company. She took her meals in the officers' saloon and spent much time on deck when the weather permitted. She was always brimming with intelligent questions about the ship and how it was sailed, and she boldly asked her questions of anybody at hand. She was especially fond of the ship's carpenter, Ho-John Woo, who was Chinese, but born in San Francisco.

Lady Yee was always most curious about everything nautical, but her pleasant manner and modesty soon made her a favorite with the crew, and they often vied with one another to please her in little ways. The French sailing master gave

Lady Yee a beautiful fan made of whalebone that he had purchased for his own daughter, and some of the more gifted seamen carved scrimshaw boxes and decorative combs for her hair.

Captain Hammond, who had always been very attracted to Lady Yee, but of course at a very respectful distance, now found her in such close proximity that everything about her person, her presentation, her wit, and her broad intelligence seemed to entice him even further down the road of secret romantic speculations. Pluming even that enticement, the olfactory lure rested in the fact that Lady Yee always distinctly smelled like a cross of spring tea roses and night-blooming jasmine, and on occasion, when the sea winds blew hot and sultry, she also smelled of coconut-roasted cinnamon. The poor captain was most vulnerable while he stood night watch on the stern, because he could always smell Lady Yee's subtle perfume even before she arrived from the companionway on the deck below. She seemed to enjoy witnessing the change of watches at all hours, but most especially in the dead of night. It thus began to occur to Captain Hammond that Lady Yee had taken on the meter and pulse of his ship with true insight and compassion, and with that began a true friendship from his quarter.

Lady Yee spent much of her time looking to the comforts of her family. The storm's ferocity had overawed the power of candied ginger, dried papaya, and ginseng tea to stifle the agonizing symptoms of seasickness, but happily, aside from a slight residual weakness brought on by a lack of nutrition caused by nausea, the whole Yee family recovered nicely. Captain Hammond had generously given his stateroom to Master Yee and his wife, while he and the first officer moved in together with the purser so that Lady Yee and the chief maid might have a cabin to themselves. This only worked out because the three officers served on different watches and napped in the pilothouse when they could.

A few days after the conclusion of their journey, Lady Yee acknowledged the three officers' chivalry by giving each a large baroque pearl set in gold and crafted into an elegant tiepin. She presented the captain with the largest pearl of the three, but aside from innocent motives of gratitude, the underlying significance of the gift escaped Captain Hammond altogether. Having little or no experience of feminine machinations where romance was concerned, he naturally believed that she had presented the gifts on behalf of her family. His lack of familiarity with such strange sensations insulated him from realizing that he had inadvertently fallen deeply in love with Lady Yee, and he became confused and disoriented by the maelstrom of emotions that assailed him every time he saw her.

Lady Yee, on the other hand, instinctually knew

exactly what was afoot, and did everything she could, within the bounds of propriety, to stimulate his condition, hopefully to a point where he would be encouraged to take some overt steps in the desired direction she had already marked out in her own mind.

Lady Yee and Captain Hammond spent time together whenever there were a few leisure moments to spare. They read to each other from their favorite books in English, and when the other family members recovered their equilibrium, the captain and Lady Yee kept up the readings for their amusement. Lady Yee would read to her father in Chinese, and sometimes even translated Chinese texts for Captain Hammond, which he very much enjoyed. He found Chinese commentaries about pirates very edifying, as they remained an ongoing scourge. Merchant captains in the China trade, especially those who still used the economy of sail, were wise to voyage well armed and alert to every detail of their own security. By all accounts, Chinese pirates were an audacious breed, and they had been known to take ships many times their size for ransom. Lady Yee read one entry that talked about a pirate crew that captured a vessel while it was anchoring in the roadstead within sight of the authorities in Shanghai. Nothing could be done to save the ship in time.

Once Master Yee and his family had been safely

ensconced in appropriate quarters in the Chinese quarter of Singapore, and his worldly wealth was securely stashed away, Captain Hammond purchased lucrative cargos for his two ships, took his leave, and quietly sailed away. Though she showed no outward signs of distress, Lady Yee grieved at the captain's departure until her father informed her that Captain Hammond would be returning to Singapore to retrieve a special cargo in approximately two months' time.

Recovering her composure, Lady Yee became determined to substantially affix her own future happiness at the next feasible opportunity, regardless of any and all traditional obstacles. To that end she began to lay her plans and make her lists. She believed in lists—they helped her think in an orderly fashion—and at the top of her list Lady Yee had written the characters for "Prime the Celestial Well," by which she meant laying the necessary foundation to gain her ends. Beneath the first entry she wrote, "Cue my beloved toward courage and empathy."

Lady Yee might have saved herself all the concern and effort for the slight nubbin of good it accomplished. For while Captain Hammond was far away trading palm oil, rice, dried fruits, and building tools for prime Russian pelts, resin, and amber, something totally unforeseen transpired.

As sometimes happens to men habitually harnessed to the gnawing loneliness that comes with a life at sea, Captain Hammond awoke one day and somehow patently decided that he was indeed already deeply in love with a woman of phenomenal intellect, charm, and flawless compassion, and that woman was Lady Yee.

Being a creature accustomed to competition, he immediately concluded that it was time for him to move forward and, despite the obvious cultural difficulties that were sure to arise, take on the object of his growing adoration and press his suit before someone else, most likely a gentleman with far more impressive credentials, vied for the same goal. Soon the heart-struck captain was wandering the decks at night practicing courtly versions of his introductory speech to Master Yee. After all, asking such an important, powerful, and possibly dangerous man for his daughter's hand in marriage wasn't like bargaining for a cargo of copra or cowhides. His presentation had better be clear-hearted, authentic in all particulars, and totally convincing. Yet there were other times on the windswept poop deck, though he blushed to think about it, when he practiced what he believed were grand romantic sentiments to be addressed to his intended, words hopefully composed to turn a girl's head in the direction of his affection.

When Captain Hammond at last sailed back into the roads of Singapore, he thought himself as prepared as crude nature could make him for the emotionally dangerous task ahead. In all modesty, he well knew he lacked the cultural sophistication so prized by educated Chinese, but he hoped his failings in that regard might be overlooked in favor of his strength of character, his joss, his complete lack of racial chauvinism, his obvious wealth, and his reputation for unimpeachable loyalty, not to mention his growing and unassailable adoration for Lady Yee.

Little did the captain know that Lady Yee had arranged to be the only one awaiting his arrival at the Yee company pier, and she too had come armed, like Cupid, with an emotional quiver of her own expectations and hopes. For even as her father suspected, she had in fact been deeply enamored with this handsome and gentle barbarian for more than three years. Her approaching womanhood had only solidified her instincts and given them even greater substance, foundation, and justification.

When the couple finally met again on the pier, the captain suddenly stepped out of character and took Lady Yee's hands in his, but after a long searching moment he found he had lost his voice altogether. Lady Yee seemed to comprehend his predicament, for she squeezed his hands in warm reassurance, nodded, and then, standing on her toes, kissed him gently on the cheek. The captain was somewhat taken aback at such affection demonstrated in public, especially when instigated by a highborn Chinese daughter of a man who could have the captain's head for the price of a sweet melon and a measure of rice. However, there was a clear, almost crystal quality about her moral certainty and courage that was intrinsically infectious, and before he knew what he was about, Captain Hammond drew Lady Yee's hands to his lips and gently kissed each in turn several times. Then he removed his grandfather's wedding ring, which had been made from a hundred-peso gold piece, and still without words, placed it in her palms and folded her fingers over it. She could feel his body heat still radiating from the pure gold. Their unspoken expressions of tender, loving consideration, melded with a growing passion, drove all the captain's schemes and rehearsed speeches away like dried leaves in an autumn breeze.

The details of the nuptial negotiations with Master Yee, who was hardly caught off guard by this time, and the formal betrothal rites and ceremonies that sealed the arrangement came and went like a frenetic blur of mysterious and colorful traditions. Master Yee proved truly a gracious father-in-law once Lady Yee gently convinced her father that he really had no choice in the matter. He owed Captain Hammond his life, his family's honor, and the security of his wealth. Added to that was the sum of his daughter's explicit wishes in the matter, and Master Yee soon found it expedient and far less distressing to bow to matters as they stood. If his daughter had her heart set on becoming Captain Hammond's bride, then the gods would have to see to the details of fortune, because he no longer had the power to petition the gods for anything. They had already kept their part of the bargain, and if his youngest daughter, the incomparable and beloved Lady Yee, was the price of their favor, then so be it. Besides, as Lady Yee so pointedly remarked to her father, he was gaining a whole shipping company at the nominal cost of just one insignificant girl child. Any upstanding Chinese gentleman of business would have boasted of such a lucrative exchange.

Master Yee eventually bowed to his daughter's logic, but his private tears stood mute testimony to the fact that his Silver Lotus was far more to him than just another girl child. She was proof that he had fathered a creature of beauty, compassion, and genius, an intellect worthy to study with the great sages of her race. But now, as the fates would have it, she was to become the wife of a barbarian. An honorable, honest, and courageous barbarian to be sure, but a barbarian all the same. Master Yee could hear the gods laughing, and he bowed his head in humble submission. One was never too old to practice humility in the face of heaven's will, or at the very least acknowledge that Lady Yee had once again played him like a liuqin with a broken string.

Lady Yee's mother, who normally chose not to venture an opinion on such subjects, admonished her husband that if he'd really wanted nothing more than complete obedience from his children, he should have sired boys. They were easier to intimidate than girls, but far less affectionate, and certainly less gifted in the main. Again Master Yee was forced to acknowledge an unavoidable truth. A father with clever daughters was never master of his own fate, much less his own house. His wife smiled and said that sometimes the mandate of heaven was a little justice for women to balance the scales of fortune.

Captain Hammond, in the meantime, had been making his own arrangements for the future. He sold his two smaller schooners to his cousin John Macy, who already held command of one of his ships, and then purchased a larger five-mast schooner that had been built in North Bend, Oregon, three years previously. She could carry twice the cargo of the smaller schooners, and with very little addition to the number of crew required to sail her. But her most attractive feature was the captain's accommodations. The previous owner had taken his wife and children to sea with him, which at that time was not an uncommon practice. The large captain's suite therefore reflected much that would please a woman's taste for comfort and convenience. In Singapore these amenities were beautifully enhanced and decorated to accommodate Lady Yee's Chinese sensibilities, and two small adjoining cabins were also reconfigured to lodge Lady Yee's maid, wardrobe chests, and cook.

Captain Hammond retained the services of his best officers and crewmen, and since they already knew and revered the beautiful Lady Yee, they too set about making small changes to the vessel that were calculated to please her. Mr. Hanks, the chief bosun and sailmaker, even stitched and rigged a collapsible canvas enclosure that sheltered the stern of the ship like a tented veranda. In this manner Lady Yee could enjoy taking the air in pleasant sailing weather, or when in port, without having to endure the gaze of prying eyes. Captain Hammond had never seen anything like it, but he agreed that it was a thoughtful and remarkably inventive addition to the ship's comforts. He rewarded Mr. Hanks with five pounds of the very finest tobacco he could find. Lady Yee's gift of thanks was an ivory-mounted meerschaum pipe, the bowl of which was elaborately carved to resemble a Turk's head knot. It came nested in a handsome ivory box decorated with flying bats and rampant dragons and was lined with the finest maroon velvet. From that moment on, Lady Yee enjoyed the complete adoration and loyalty of Mr. Hanks.

After coming to an equitable understanding and arrangement with Master Yee, Captain

Hammond was forced to endure two weeks of elaborate prenuptial celebrations, which included a number of clan feasts that almost laid the captain low. The captain next shouldered a ceaseless round of ceremonial interviews from Taoist priests and scholars whose function it was to examine the prospective groom for moral and spiritual suitability. This was more rooted in ancient tradition than anything else, but it served its purpose, which was to place the prospective groom under some degree of social stress and see how he behaved. As an aside, Lady Yee had warned her love in advance to guard against people maneuvering him into drinking too much strong wine at the various feasts, as this too was a tactic by which people would judge his suitability as a groom. Chinese wines, she said, could be subtle to the palate and yet surprisingly potent. She cued him to sip these offerings only ceremonially to be polite, but to avoid serious consumption at all costs. His liver would bless him for the discretion. Besides, she laughed, a groom who couldn't stand up easily on his own, or could not walk in a straight line unaided, eventually became a figure of ridicule and an embarrassment to the bride's family. Lady Yee needn't have worried, as Captain Hammond had never been overly fond of hard liquor in any fashion, though like most of his crew he enjoyed dark beer and porter with his rations.

The wedding ceremony, though modest in physical dimensions, proved cunningly elaborate in every detail of festive decoration and ceremony. Exotic flower arrangements filled the house with color and perfume, and numerous liveried servants attended to every need. There were only sixty-five invited guests, most of the Yee clan having remained in Canton, but what the gathering lacked in numbers it made up for in the elaborate luxury of their costumes and the lavish quality of their gifts.

Lady Yee, who looked as though she had just stepped off a temple altar, was presented by her father last of all. She was magnificently veiled in the finest white silk, and her brow was surmounted with a jade-encrusted diadem that supported multiple looping chains of matched pearls that framed her veiled head on three sides. She was richly cocooned in yards of the finest silver brocade embroidered with heavy gold thread to simulate a lotus flower pattern. The garment bloomed pearls everywhere. Near the hem of her robes, two small golden carp with amethyst eyes peeked up through the silver brocaded waves as if in greeting.

To note that Captain Hammond was astonished by the sight of his bride would hardly flavor half the truth. He was truly speechless once again. It seemed to him that Lady Yee veritably shimmered with a kind of celestial light; she appeared as from a dream, looking exactly like the artistic characterizations he had so often seen of the Chinese moon goddess, Ch'ang O. The only thing missing was the goddess's symbolic rabbit. However, he later discovered that a small silver hare had been deftly embroidered into the long train of Lady Yee's robes, and it could only be seen in a cross-light as she walked away. The captain thought this gesture most propitious, and very much in key with his bride's sense of satire and respect all in one gesture.

When Captain Hammond commissioned a brand-new and smartly tailored uniform to be married in, Master Yee got wind of this and gently took him aside. Using his most respectful tone, and being extremely polite and forthcoming, he attempted to convince his soon-to-be son-in-law that though he respected the gesture, it was his considered opinion that Western military-style attire, as handsome as it could be on most occasions, would artistically clash with the traditional Chinese ceremonial decor. He feared this would create a cultural imbalance that some guests might find slightly unsettling, or even disquieting. Master Yee said that the officiating Taoists priests could get very prickly when they sensed that all the spiritual elements ceased to appear in a state of natural equilibrium. In conclusion, Master Yee humbly begged that the groom bow to tradition, and that the captain allow himself to be attired in appropriate Chinese fashion. Master Yee said it would give him great pleasure to commission the robes and accoutrements personally, and he even offered to pay for the uniform, which was to be set aside until the ceremonies had concluded and the guests departed.

Master Yee was slightly shocked when Captain Hammond suddenly rose from his seat as though preparing to depart in a fit of pique. It had suddenly occurred to the captain to have a bit of fun with his prospective father-in-law before their relationship changed forever to one of father and son, when such things would seem improper. The captain stood over Master Yee and coldly asked if he was seriously being denied the dignity and apparel of his rank. He made it sound as though he were being forced to lose face.

Master Yee muttered for a moment, looking this way and that for a way to salvage the situation. Then Captain Hammond turned on his host and laughed. "My dear Master Yee," he said with charm, "my fine old friend, if you requested that I should drape myself with the fresh-killed hide of a mountain goat as the price of being wedded to our beloved Lady Yee, I would set out this very minute to hunt one down and butcher it with my own two hands if need be. I should hardly care to shame my bride's family with barbarian insensitivity at so early a date. There will be plenty of time for all that later. You may rest assured, Master Yee, that I shall proudly wear whatever garments you deem proper. And not at your own expense, but at mine."

Master Yee beamed with sincere pleasure. At last he'd gotten something his own way.

And so there he was, a Yankee captain clothed in richly crafted black satin robes trimmed in embroidered white shantung silk. He even wore the traditional embroidered black silk hat. And then, as if suspended in an ornate fantasy, Captain Hammond pledged his troth at the foot of an elaborate floral altar dedicated to the doe-eyed Guan Yin, goddess of mercy. For one hour Captain Hammond experienced emotional delights he had never known possible. He had been transported in time and space to a realm of ancient lights of immortality. And for the first time in his life, Captain J. Macy Hammond felt as though he belonged to something far greater than himself. He wondered what his distant relatives back in Nantucket would make of all this. He harbored a mostly vacuous hope that they might be happy for him, but in the end he had to admit that the Nantucket Hammonds, and even the Macys, weren't really those kinds of people. They were in the main hard-boiled Methodists, and as such mistrusted happiness and contentment as signs of self-indulgence and lazy thinking.

The wedding feast was like nothing Captain

Hammond had ever experienced before. All the food was delivered in small arranged portions, and served in exquisitely decorated dishes and bowls. But it was the endless variety and ingenuity of the presentations that truly impressed. It was impossible to keep count, but the groom estimated that in three hours of feasting he hadn't seen a single dish pass him twice. Every course consisted of numerous variations on a theme, and all were prepared and decorated in such a way as to appear like something else altogether. Pickled fish came to the table looking like floating clusters of wildflowers. Crab dumplings were craftily made to look like baby golden carp. Ginger-cured salmon was sliced almost to the point of transparency and then fashioned to look like Persian roses. Lean pork, veal, and chicken were ground, seasoned with exotic herbs or dried fruit, and then hand-molded to look like small fish or turtles before being steamed or baked. Captain Hammond had no idea that there existed such an infinite variety of ways to serve rice, not to mention stuffed buns, dumplings, custards, and pastries of every conceivable description. The wines were numerous in variety and obviously expensive, but the captain had taken Lady Yee's warning to heart, and except for ceremonial toasts and pledges he drank only tea and rose-scented water.

Master Yee was delighted with the proceedings, and very grateful that his new son-in-law had seen fit to carry off his part with such finesse, modesty, and dignity. For a barbarian, the captain was most amenable to the esoteric traditions he was compelled to study and perform. As a reward, Master Yee had rented a lovely house across the road so that for the first few weeks of their marriage the couple could be well cared for by loyal family servants, thus giving the bride and groom plenty of leisure time to get better acquainted and enjoy each other's company. And they took total advantage of the opportunity, rarely being out of each other's sight for more than a few minutes at a time. The captain and Lady Yee went on numerous excursions to local sites of beauty or historic interest, and after giving his crew orders that all was to be placed in trim order and polished bright if it didn't move, the captain took his bride out to the anchorage to inspect his ship.

Before the wedding, Lady Yee had closeted her future husband and her adoring father and politely insisted upon only one nonnegotiable stipulation to the marriage contract. If her husband chose to go back to sea, she would sail with him and make her life and home by his side. Lady Yee insisted that she had no intention of getting married to a man that was only rarely at home to watch his children grow. No amount of wealth could compensate her for the pain of longing and loneliness such a life entailed. Then, to Captain Hammond's mild surprise, Lady Yee quoted the famous biblical lines from the book of Ruth.

Master Yee wasn't all that pleased with his daughter's firm stipulation, but he knew from experience that she was dead serious, and strong-willed enough to get her way. Captain Hammond, on the other hand, was absolutely overjoyed with her decision, and counted himself blessed to be acquiring a wife who demonstrated such confidence and courage.

TWO WEEKS LATER, Captain Hammond's new ship took on a mixed cargo to trade in Malaysia for dressed coconut and coconut oil, clarified palm oil, and any and all spices and medicinal plants if the prices were right. He was also in the market for rare hardwoods prized in furniture making, and he hoped to find an ongoing supplier of aloeswood oil for his new father-in-law. The ester of aloeswood oil was much in demand for the manufacture of certain scents. It was said that even the Buddha believed that aloeswood oil smelled like nirvana. But highly placed testimonials aside, Master Yee knew how to realize a sizable profit from the oil, and Captain Hammond was only too happy to oblige the father of his new wife.

As a further sign of his devotion, Captain

Hammond went to the considerable expense of repainting the whole ship in Lady Yee's favorite colors: emerald green with pale yellow trim outlined in black. And then he went against custom and rechristened the ship. In the future the vessel would be titled *The Silver Lotus* in her honor. In this he had the full support of his officers and crew. It would prove a fortuitous choice on more than one occasion.

Then, on a day appointed by the family astrologer as most propitious, Captain Hammond and Lady Yee sailed away on their first trading venture together. And though he worried that such a life would soon distress his new bride, he needn't have wasted the concern. Lady Yee loved everything about her new way of life and took total interest in everything to do with her namesake, her crew, and her cargo.

Captain Hammond soon discovered that his young wife was far more adept at keeping precise accounts and invoices than he was. Her skill with mathematical calculations was faster and more precise than his, her eye for detail more accurate, and her skill at bargaining for supplies unsurpassed. She also learned to make comprehensive log entries, but hers were more detailed and legible than the entries her husband was used to keeping. It seemed to happen almost organically, but by the time *The Silver Lotus* returned to Singapore eight weeks later, Lady

Yee was chief purser and purchasing officer of Hammond & Co. in all but rank and title.

The Silver Lotus only remained in Singapore long enough to disembark Master Yee's consignment of exotic lumber and aloeswood oil, allowing four days for Lady Yee to visit with her family. Her relatives were all surprised to see how fit and healthy she looked. Like most families experiencing the departure of one of their own, some thought doom and gloom would result from Lady Yee's choices, but all were caught wrong-footed by the bloom in her cheeks, the sparkle in her eyes, her self-assured poise, and the affirmative texture of her voice.

Master Yee certainly marked the dynamic change in his daughter's demeanor and asked the reason for her obvious happiness. With a burst of blushing pride, his daughter replied that she now possessed every woman's treasured dream. She was loved, respected, and needed. But, she said, what made her new life even more remarkable was the fact that her husband, his officers, and his crew invariably treated her as an equal, but with the added patience not afforded their own ilk. Her opinions and knowledge were sought after and addressed with serious attention, and as acting purser she was allowed great latitude to conduct the business of purchasing stores and rations as she saw fit. Captain Hammond proudly told his new father-in-law that since Lady Yee had taken over the ledgers, accounts, and expenses, operating costs had gone down by almost 15 percent, and the quality of the stores had improved markedly. He had every expectation of even greater savings once the brilliant Lady Yee mastered the regional intricacies of maritime finance. As an aside, the captain told Master Yee that his daughter already enjoyed the complete loyalty and affection of the crew, who came to her like chicks to a mother hen for every little thing that ailed them. Her knowledge of Chinese medicine, though limited in a professional sense, was delivered with a confidence that was very reassuring. Her attention and sincere affection served the men's health and sense of well-being better than most ship's surgeons, who were in most instances little better than apprentice apothecaries themselves. She also insisted on adjusting the crew's diet with the aim of improving their general health and comfort. And though she had no objections whatsoever to the crew's daily ration of spirits, she did suggest that rather than diluting the alcohol with plain water, the ration should be portioned with strong black tea made in twice-boiled water and dressed with a bit of fresh ginger. Though mildly skeptical at first, Captain Hammond tried it and was totally surprised when his men claimed to find it more appealing and rejuvenating than the normal tar's ration they had become used to over the years. In the crew's mess, where honest objections usually brewed, the concoction was honored with the title "elixir." Captain Hammond proposed that at no time in maritime history had a gut-raw-rum grog ration ever been referred to as an elixir. The crew immediately requested that their spirits always be prepared the same way in the future. Within a few years, scuttlebutt transmission being what it is, Lady Yee's recipe could be found on any number of Western ships working the Asian trade. The captains who supported this budding fashion did not overlook the fact that black tea and ginger proved to be a strong stimulant. The brew gave strained backs and sore muscles the will to continue. On celebratory occasions, the crews sometimes dressed up their rations with fresh fruit juice and mint, or served it hot with nutmeg and cinnamon on cold and stormy nights. Sometimes, when circumstances required prolonged endurance and diligence, even the captains and officers forsook their finer vintages in favor of some version of Lady Yee's elixir.

After taking on a cargo of hand tools, farming implements, and industrial beeswax to replace what they had delivered to Master Yee, Captain Hammond and his bride said their farewells and sailed off for Ceylon and Pondicherry on the coast of India. From there on, available cargo and market demands would determine the ship's course and destination.

It would be almost two years before they returned to Singapore, and by that time Lady Yee's father and family had returned to Canton. Master Yee's adversaries had eventually been discredited, disgraced, and driven from all positions of influence, but it was also noted by one and all that Master Yee had never once raised a hand against his tormentors, which again served only to make him appear more enlightened and honorable than his enemies. He not only recovered his previous position as a preferred trader, but his customer lists doubled in less than six months. He was now even wealthier and more important than he was when he went into exile.

4

CAPTAIN HAMMOND and Lady Yee sailed together under lucky stars. Their partnership flowered in devotion, respect, and passion. The absence of children sometimes caused Lady Yee slight distress, but Captain Hammond said he really had no wish to become a father as yet. He pointed out that their way of life, though pleasing to them, was dangerous for pregnant women and newborn babies alike, and the lack of proper medical care at sea didn't make matters any easier for either of them. Besides, he said with a grin, she was already looking after twenty-six hapless children aboard ship. One more child would just make all the others jealous.

Lady Yee always allowed her husband to believe that he could humor her away from her concerns, but she still longed for children of her own. But she too now bowed to the will of heaven, and for the present remained content to look after her tar-stained, stubble-faced brood of odiferous swans, and they in turn watched after her like the sea queen she was.

Once they had set upon a course of long trading voyages, Captain Hammond had an opportunity to witness Lady Yee's native genius firsthand, and much of what he discovered gave him pause to reflect that amazing things sometimes came from unlikely packages. To begin with, Lady Yee was far more accomplished at negotiating for cargos in Asian and Indonesian ports than Captain Hammond, and after some practice, she learned to handle the old guard English, Dutch, and French traders as well. But her husband was truly surprised to find that she could also charm any cutpurse Yankee grain trader out of his socks and still elicit the fairest prices for all parties concerned. It soon became apparent to Captain Hammond that his talented Chinese princess was, to quote the Irish carpenter's mate, "as tough as pig iron, slicker than snail spit, and sharper than a cartload of Trinity dons."

Hammond soon discovered that his wife's practical skills were keyed to a hauntingly precise and perceptive instinct. Lady Yee could sense a falsehood, whether spoken or written, and do so with unerring accuracy. When sitting across from any trader bargaining quality and prices, she could immediately tell the moment he became deceitful, and could usually intuit the reason why. It was most unnerving, and the word soon got around that practicing duplicity with Lady Yee was a waste of invention, breath, and time.

When such instances did occur, Lady Yee had a habit that her husband said was rather like the rattles on the tail of a poisonous snake. She would cross her arms defiantly, cock one brow in doubt, and begin to drum her elegant fingers on her elbow, as though counting the seconds until an expected explosion. Then, pinning her prevaricating interlocutor with a riveting expression, she would say, "Please forgive me, sir, but perhaps I misunderstood. Would you say that again?" Her opponents usually withered after a few moments, cleared their throats once or twice, tossed off a few "ums" and "ahs," and then presented a more rational evaluation. In the words of Mr. Juno, the cargo master, "Lady Yee inevitably pinned the lying freebooter to a board like a June bug, and in the end he thanked her for the privilege." That last factor was the most amazing facet of Lady Yee's sociability. She could rake a duplicitous rubber trader over the coals one day, and the next he'd send her gifts of fruit and flowers, with notes professing undying respect and friendship. One flinty Dutch trader even gifted her with a bolt of fine French blue velvet, and included ten yards of rich Flemish lace just to secure her future business. At the same time, Lady Yee's own reputation for fair and honest dealing, as well as a timely attention to debts, made Hammond & Co. very popular among brokerage and trading houses everywhere they sailed.

To acknowledge her growing contributions to their success, the captain registered a change in his company's name. From then on, *The Silver Lotus* sailed under the house pennant of Hammond & Yee. He presented his talented wife with a full partnership and the new house pennant on the occasion of their third wedding anniversary. The flag was centered with a silver lotus flower upon a green field, and flanked by the initials H & Y. Not to be outdone on the occasion, the crew gave her a beautiful mahogany deck chair inlaid with whale ivory. They had created it piece by piece in the fo'c'sle away from prying eyes.

As was said before, Captain Hammond and Lady Yee sailed under lucky stars, but this didn't mean they weren't beset by mortal danger on any number of occasions, both from the sea and other more calculating sources. Though the great nineteenth-century Cantonese pirate fleets of Cheng I Sao were a thing of the past, there were a few small triad-controlled fleets still haunting the more rugged coasts of southern China. With the advent of steam power, these divergent gangs of freebooters were generally chased down and suppressed, but a few still clung to the old ways. For the most part, these brigands had been reduced to scavenging what they could from ships in distress, or vessels that unhappily found themselves beached after harsh storms. Lookouts in the hills would signal their confederates at sea, who were ostensibly fishing just offshore. Then the fleet would up-sail and dash off to descend on the hapless victim like a ravenous pack of mongrel dogs. There were rarely any witnesses to tell the tale to the authorities, and those who did escape to shore were usually hunted down by the lookouts just for sport and booty. If some victims were rich enough, they might survive to be ransomed by their families, but this increased the hazard to the kidnappers, and so the pirates usually just killed everyone to be on the safe side.

Captain Hammond had this in mind when the terrible Chu Bay monsoon almost sank *The Silver Lotus* near Hainan Island off the southern coast of China. *The Silver Lotus* had been driven far off course, and subsequently suffered a fair degree of damage to her sails, gaffs, booms, and rigging. The decks looked like a bomb had gone off in the rope locker, and at least half the crew were suffering from exhaustion, and the other half wished they had it that easy. The seas had been so treacherous and perverse that just moving about the ship proved an exercise in challenged mortality. Conditions were so dangerous that Captain Hammond issued orders that Lady Yee and her maid were to be secured in their berths with canvas straps to prevent them from being thrown about the cabin every time the ship pitched or yawed violently, or was hammered, bow down, by waves that crested thirty feet and more above the decks. But when Lady Yee heard that two of her men had been seriously hurt by falling tackle, she cut herself free from her restraints, grabbed the surgeon's case, and somehow made her way to the fo'c'sle to tend to their injuries. She stayed with them through the worst of the storm, and tended to the abrasions, cuts, and contusions of all that came to her for help. Perhaps it was the fear of imminent destruction and death, but somehow all these hard-boiled seamen, who'd normally twist the devil's tail on a wager, suddenly became like distressed children seeking the comfort and safety of their mother's care. They never forgot her courage and generosity. Captain Hammond wasn't too happy that she had risked her own safety, even in such altruistic pursuits, but he knew better than to voice his displeasure. As it stood, he knew that if he called her to account for her actions, the crew would have probably beached him in favor of serving under Lady Yee, and he later said as much to his first officer, who smiled but reluctantly agreed with his captain's assessment.

Captain Hammond and his men finally found a sheltered cove on the south end of Hainan Island that was just large enough to accommodate the ship, but with little or no room to maneuver her safely, they were forced to kedge the ship stern-first into the narrow cove. Despite laying out every anchor the ship possessed, and from all quarters, it still seemed that the next set of giant swells or waves would beach her on the rocks below the cliffs at any moment. However, by virtue of the crew's vigilance and constant readjustment of the anchor cables to keep the ship centered over her anchorage, total disaster was somehow avoided until dawn. Then, as if in answer to fervent prayers, the tail of the monsoon suddenly softened and then quietly moved to the north. At this point the crew were so spent that some of them simply fell asleep at their stations, and Lady Yee discovered her husband all wet and worn, fast asleep on a coil of cable outside the pilothouse.

About noon the captain and the crew had recovered enough energy to assess the damage and begin planning for repairs. In all, things looked worse than they really were, but both the gaff and boom on the foremast had been dangerously sprung and cracked, and would not carry sail without being first braced and fished, or totally replaced. But until such time, *The Silver Lotus* would have to depend on her headsails and a jury-rigged, loose-footed lateen arrangement on the foremast.

The crew spent the rest of the day making repairs. Their anchorage was so isolated by the rugged nature of surrounding cliffs that it precluded all habitation, so none of the islanders ever appeared, not even out of curiosity. Suddenly one of the men effecting repairs high on the foremast called down to the deck to say that a small fleet of junks were slowly patrolling back and forth just offshore. Each flew a small red pennant from the mainmast, but aside from that there was no telling who they were, or what their intentions might be, but for the present there was no way for them to enter the inlet with *The Silver Lotus* occupying most of the channel.

Captain Hammond came on deck when he heard the call from the trees and took up his glass to examine the visitors more closely. Lady Yee soon joined her husband and asked to have a look for herself. They came to the same conclusion. Their visitors were Pearl River pirates from Guangdong, and their red pennant was the standard of the Wong Chi, the largest of the maritime triads. The pirates had somehow spotted the wounded behemoth, and believing she'd be easy prey, all bottled up as she was with no line of retreat, they began to quietly patrol back and forth like sharks awaiting seals. Captain Hammond immediately unbolted the arms locker and handed out double-barreled shotguns and large navy revolvers to a dozen men. He told them to arrange themselves around the deck so as to keep the ship covered on all quarters. Then he sent four men up the trees with heavy-caliber rifles and told both sets of guards to fire upon any junk that came within fifty yards of the ship, but to shoot just over their heads and shiver their sails and rigging. If possible, he wished to extricate his ship from this sticky situation without recourse to bloodshed, but he wanted the Wong Chi to see that he was adequately armed and willing to fire. Then he had the small signaling cannon taken forward and aimed over the bow. He told his men to give the diminutive howitzer a double charge of powder and to load it to the muzzle with broken glass, but no metal.

There was a great disparity in the size of *The Silver Lotus*, which was two hundred feet long with forty feet of beam, and the Pearl River junks, which were mostly less than forty-five feet in length. With *The Silver Lotus* in place, the channel would admit only one small junk at a time, which was not how the Wong Chi liked their odds. And since there was nowhere to land, it was impossible for the pirates to launch an attack from the landward side, so for the moment all the pirates could do was wait for their quarry to break from cover and then mob the ship like crows before she could fully get under way and escape. This tactic had worked before, so the Wong Chi fleet confidently settled down and cruised just off the entrance to the channel. Some of the junks simply lowered their sails, anchored in place, and passed the time fishing. The Wong Chi, like all scavenging predators, had long since learned the virtues of patience. They were certainly impoverished, uncultured, and uneducated, but they were neither stupid nor rash, and if called upon to do so, would sell their lives at an exorbitant price indeed. The poor rarely showed signs of cowardice; their lives were worth so little as it was that little was lost if they died defending them. There was always another hungry mouth to take the place of the fallen. On the other hand, the rich could always think of a thousand reasons not to put their lives in jeopardy.

Captain Hammond called a council of his top men to the wheelhouse. He asked for suggestions on how to extricate themselves from their present dilemma. Since Lady Yee was present, most of them put a bold face on their responses and suggested fighting their way out sometime after sunset. There would be little or no moonlight, depending on the clouds, which would make it more difficult for the pirates to organize a concerted response. A few might be injured, but only if they failed to make fast work of their escape on the next outgoing tide.

Lady Yee, who had been standing in the corner, politely cleared her throat to gain attention. She had come to know the ways of men, and was always amused when they incessantly chose the same ill-considered and brutish responses to problems that could easily be solved by other means.

Captain Hammond turned to his wife, and with a knowledgeable smile he declared that, as a company officer, she had every right to make a better suggestion. It was then that Lady Yee posed a most marvelous and audacious suggestion. She began by pointing out that there was only one thing that really frightened bullies, thieves, and murderers, whether ashore or at sea, and that was to convince the discourteous beggars that you are the penultimate bully, thief, and murderer. Lady Yee went on to say that it was just a matter of dressing the part, and then scaring their notoriously superstitious adversaries half to death with a totally unexpected display of some dumb-show barbarity. Native fear and insecurity would do all else required.

There was a complete, drop-jawed silence from her audience, but Lady Yee could see at once that she had their complete attention. Even her husband stood in rapt admiration, so she continued. She said that for the most part, at a distance there was little that differentiated a ship of evil purpose from one of peaceful intentions; even the flags could be confusing. So it would be necessary to advertise the ship's bloody intentions in such a way that the pirates could see it at some distance, and would thus be in no doubt of what to expect if the situation came to blows.

"To accomplish our intention," she said, "and truly convince the Red Flag Wong Chi that *The Silver Lotus* means bloody business, we must dress up some of our crew like Chinese pirates, and then hang perhaps three or four by the neck from the foremast gaff and let them swing there in the wind."

The look on the faces of her husband and the other men was just as Lady Yee had supposed. The hanging men, she explained, would be a complete illusion created by top men wearing canvas harnesses under their clothes and sporting fake death knots around their necks. With flour-caked faces, wild greased hair, and coal-smeared eyes, they were to perform the exaggerated gyrations and struggles expected of a man being slowly strangled at the end of a rope. While this was going on, she said, other members of the crew were to bang incessantly on pots and pans, or anything at all that made a din, while still others blew whistles and horns. Since they could only depart on the morning tide at five o'clock, and as it was expected that offshore winds would assist their departure anyway, Lady Yee suggested that sand-filled fire buckets be loaded with burning sulfur and placed in the bows, to create a noxious cloud and so add verisimilitude to the illusion that the Wong Chi were about to face the deadliest pirate-killing ship from the bowels of hell. And rather than shoot guns at the pirates as they emerged from the inlet, she said, they should fire their red and green signal rockets horizontally and directly at the sails of the Wong Chi fleet. She admitted that the chances of hitting anything were remote, but the fire, sparks, and explosions would put the Wong Chi at a disadvantage. A rocket fired in the air was a relatively benign illumination, but when that same ball of fire came arching directly at a human target, it held another implication altogether. Even the fire caused by a direct hit might be easily extinguished with a few buckets of seawater, but in the fear and confusion *The Silver Lotus* might easily pass right through the Wong Chi fleet without suffering injury to a single soul. As a confirmed Buddhist with a firm grounding in all the important Confucian precepts, Lady Yee believed that the greatest victories were accomplished without bloodshed, and it seemed that every man in the wheelhouse was happy to agree.

Lady Yee went on to say that the Chinese traditionally held great store by the importance of flags to denote rank and purpose. Large flags of rich color held power, smaller pennants showed allegiance. Then there were flags bearing titles and proud slogans that were meant to intimidate opponents like the raising of a lion's hackles with bared teeth. The roar was still to come. She suggested that if the Wong Chi were flying small red pennants, *The Silver Lotus* should let fly a red banner the size of a bedsheet, and then hoist another large banner on which she would paint Chinese characters that communicated a terrifying threat: "We have come to eat the traitors to the Wong Chi. None shall enjoy further life or prosperity." This intelligence, shocking as it would seem, just might encourage the pirates to suspect that for some unknown reason they'd been betrayed, perhaps by their own triad. But it mattered little what they thought as long as the resulting confusion allowed *The Silver Lotus* to sail through the pirate fleet with negligible damage being suffered by either side.

The carpenter's mate ran about the ship collecting anything that looked remotely like a big gun, then painted it black and lashed it to the railings so it could be seen at a distance. The cook brought out every pot, pan, and ladle on deck and handed these out to those men assigned to create the unholy din when the ship got underway. The bosun's mate, who rather liked the idea of hanging some of his mates, climbed out on the foremast gaff to brace and lash the split with wet rawhide straps and rope. When he'd determined that the sprung gaff could take the weight, he drew up four tackle blocks one at a time and then carefully spaced and tied them off along the gaff. One end of the line was secured to the backs of the harnesses the boatswain had rigged up from canvas strapping reinforced with heavy leather. The other end was laced through a second block shackled to the deck, and then used to haul the man up into the air to swing under the gaff. A mock hangman's rope was affixed around the man's neck and tied off with light thread where it met the lifting line. If there were to be an accident, at least the volunteer wouldn't really hang for his courageous efforts.

The condemned men outdid themselves in attempts to look fearsome, gruesome, and dead, while the rest of the crew, including the cook, cabin boy, and carpenter, joined in on their own. They all put together outlandish costumes and made up their faces with flour, red lead, and coal dust. Mr. Lundy, who hailed from London, said it reminded him of an elaborate Guy Fawkes prank.

Captain Hammond took personal charge of the pyrotechnics, and following Lady Yee's philosophy of a bloodless assault even had the armed men remove the buckshot from some of their shotgun shells and reload them with extra powder and sulfur pellets so as to make a more theatrically impressive display of increased noise, smoke, and fire. Just the men armed with the rifles were told to keep their loads, but they were only to fire if some of the Wong Chi managed to make it on deck. The captain took charge of mounting the two launchers for the distress rockets on either side of the ship. He had only eight red and eight green rockets, so he chose to launch them in alternating colors from either side of the ship. If the surrounding junk fleet moved in too close, he hoped it might have the desired effect, because the exercise was almost as dangerous for the people firing the rockets as it would be for the people being fired upon. If his ship caught fire in the process of self-defense, it would be a tainted victory at best. To cover that eventuality, he used wet canvas to erect a couple of dreadnought screens behind the launching tubes, and then had buckets of water stationed nearby in case his calculations proved in error. He had seen distress rockets prematurely explode just feet out of the tube. The resulting injuries could be terrible, so he decided that when the time came he would fire off the rockets himself. Lady Yee had brushed the appropriate characters on one canvas banner, but the red flag had to be painted as there was no red banner in the flag locker. Both flags were flying by three in the morning. The fire buckets, now half-filled with sand and topped with oil-soaked rags, were top-loaded with large nuggets of sulfur that, when burned, would create great noxious, ocher clouds of smoke. This process had been used for centuries to fumigate ships belowdecks, but except for encouraging the more sensitive rats to take up residence elsewhere and creating a terrible stink that, like oil, clung to everything for weeks, it was only marginally useful for its intended purpose. Captain Hammond believed the practice came from the ancient belief that if something smelled absolutely dreadful, it had to be dangerous, if not deadly, and in a number of instances that was true. On the other hand, when encouraged by the presence of gunpowder's heat, pressure, and flames, the results could be spectacular. In that same vein, Captain Hammond decided to pull the charge of broken glass from the signal cannon. He was right in assuming it would have little or no effect except at very close range with a stationary target, and with the Wong Chi crew standing shoulder to shoulder on deck. He laughed when he thought of the odds. Instead he concocted a mixture of gunpowder, saltpeter, sulfur nuggets, and the contents of one of the red distress rockets that had been damaged in transit. He poured his mixture into a bag made from an old linen shirtsleeve, and after loading the cannon with a double charge of powder he slid his infernal machine down the barrel, tamped it hard in place, then drove in a protective plug made of rags soaked in hot beeswax. He rightly assumed that if nothing else, there would be one hell of a colorful explosion, with a rain of red fire descending everywhere. By four-thirty in the morning all the preparations were in hand.

At about five-fifteen the incoming tide went slack, and everything was made ready. The offshore winds would gain strength soon, but in the meantime they were blessed with a dense coastal fog that came up out of nowhere. Captain Hammond was reassured that the Wong Chi were now just as blind as he was. However, he took the covering fog as an opportunity to raise all possible sails on his three working masts.

The captain had kept his ship in place by the judicious use of three anchors, one at the bow, one to port nearest the shore, and one off the stern. As the tide turned, Captain Hammond called the deckhands to haul in the port anchor, and to do everything as quietly as possible. Then, as the offshore breezes began to push the fog to sea, he paid off the stern anchor cable and slowly crept up on the bow anchor, which he also ordered hauled up as quietly as possible. As the power of tidal race increased, and the breezes steadied from the land, the captain ordered the mainsail booms hauled out wing to wing to catch as much of the wind as possible. The sails slowly billowed with strength and a desire for momentum. The men could hear the low moans and chirping sounds caused by the extraordinary stretch and strain on the heavy stern anchor cable, but still the ship hung suspended against the forces of wind and tide like a giant spider about to drop on an unsuspecting cricket.

Lady Yee, now attired in black oilskins, stood alongside her husband outside the pilothouse. The fog would soon blow to sea, and it was imperative that they move at once. If their charade was going to work at all, the half-light of dawn was imperative to complete the effect. Besides, the deck watches on the junks would just be changing, and, it was hoped, this would only add to their confusion.

Captain Hammond walked Lady Yee to the foremast, where she was lifted up to take a seat on the furled foremast sail. From there she would conduct her percussive chorus of pots and pans, and with the help of a megaphone, exhort the Wong Chi to stay where they were and die like the traitorous slaves they were, for the Red Flag of *The Silver Lotus* had come to end their days and make widows and orphans of their families. It was a war cry that she had composed and rehearsed. Captain Hammond wasn't sure of the effect it would have on the pirates, but he honestly said it certainly scared him, and he spoke only limited Cantonese. But it also set him to wondering how such a demure creature as Lady Yee could come up with such bloodcurdling language, much less shout it at the top of her lungs.

A moment later the captain was informed that with the sails full, the stern anchor cable was likely to part under the strain any second. Suddenly orders flew like arrows, and Lady Yee's real-life Chinese opera began in earnest. Captain Hammond cued Lady Yee to begin the pot-banging chorus to cover the sound of two men chopping the stern anchor cable free. He could always get another anchor, or return later and recover it himself. While this was happening, the four hanged men were carefully hoisted halfway up the height of the mast and left to swing in the wind.

Suddenly the anchor cable parted with a loud splash and *The Silver Lotus*, for all her length and tonnage, seemed to shoot forward like a bull elk. Lady Yee encouraged her chorus to beat at a precise tempo as loudly as possible. Soon everybody with a free hand picked up the rhythm and started pounding away on anything made of metal, with whatever was at hand. It began to seem as though the ship itself were making the din.

As *The Silver Lotus* exited the fog bank, the captain left instructions with the helmsman, and then made his way forward to the bow, where the signal gun had been lashed in place for its one glorious roar of defiance. This would soon be followed by the screech of colored rockets and Lady Yee's bloodthirsty promises of a future in hell for all those who opposed the will of the Red Flag of *The Silver Lotus*. Captain Hammond waited until he judged the wind coming from astern strong enough to blow the smoke ahead of the ship, and then had the fire buckets ignited. The sulfur immediately sent clouds of ocher smoke billowing ahead of the ship. The smoke mingled with the fog to create a most unusual atmosphere that smelled like the breath of hell, but Hammond had taken the precaution of tying a wet bandana over his nose and mouth to keep from breathing in the cloying fumes. Even then, the unpleasant odor was enough to gag the devil himself.

With the help of the tide and the wind, Captain

Hammond estimated the ship was moving at a good six knots, more than enough speed to stave in the sides of any junk that happened to be in its path. He hoped it wouldn't come to that, but he'd suffer little or no remorse if it did. He waited patiently in the bow near the signal gun.

The Wong Chi pirate fleet had most certainly taken note of the mysterious clanging sounds coming out of the fog and was waiting with sails set as *The Silver Lotus* suddenly came lurching out of the fog like an animated canvas mountain. As soon as he was sure that the pirates had gotten a good look at what was coming after them—hanged men, capering red-faced devils, and all—Captain Hammond fired the cannon. Like everyone else, he was stunned by the effect. With an ungodly explosion that left ears ringing, the cannon delivered a great arc of fire that leapt from the barrel and rained burning sulfur and red stars down on everything ahead for two hundred yards. Without resting on his laurels, the captain then fired off both port and starboard rockets. They exploded very colorfully just feet over the junks, setting some of their sails alight. In the meantime the slow metered clanging continued, while Lady Yee stood on the boom with her megaphone screaming in Chinese at the Wong Chi fleet to lower their sails and meet death with dignity so as not to shame their ancestors.

Captain Hammond hadn't as yet taken notice of the Wong Chi's response. Then one of the armed seamen stationed high in the ratlines shouted down to the deck to get his captain's attention, and then pointed at the pirate fleet just ahead. Captain Hammond rushed to the port railing and watched in stunned disbelief. What he saw was a scene of mass confusion. The sails of some of the junks that had been stationed just ahead of his ship as it came out of the fog had been set afire by the burning sulfur, and their crews were trampling each other in futile attempts to extinguish the flames with buckets of seawater. Meanwhile, those frantic junk crews that were closest to the ship, and faced the greatest perceived hazard, chose the better part of valor and jumped into the sea to avoid imminent destruction.

The alarm spread as the Wong Chi helplessly called to one another for help, but nothing useful came in reply, and none ventured closer to help their comrades. The captain watched the scene in amused surprise. Suddenly, like an electric shock shared by those holding hands, the entire Wong Chi fleet took flight and, using their long sculling oars in a panic, abruptly turned in place and scattered in all directions like a covey of quail surprised by a fox. Then *The Silver Lotus* sailed majestically through the abandoned remnants of the pirate fleet, and Lady Yee silenced the tin-pan chorus. As the speed increased, all went quiet aboard ship, and they traveled on without further disturbance or threat.

The captain immediately ordered that the smoldering contents of the fire buckets be thrown into the sea and the hanged men be lowered to the deck. He then helped Lady Yee down from the boom, and as they walked together toward the stern a spontaneous cheer went up from the crew. They hailed their beloved mistress as the queen of the Eastern Sea and the mortal dread of the Pearl River Red Flag Wong Chi. She accepted their adulation with becoming modesty and quietly asked her husband if the crew might not be allowed an undiluted ration of spirits to celebrate their victory. He bowed to her wishes, of course, but only after the ship had been trimmed up, cleaned up, and set on a proper course for Viet Nam.

5

IN THE COURSE of their many journeys together, Captain Hammond and Lady Yee sailed to every port in the Pacific Ocean worth a cargo, including Hawaii, Mexico, and California. Lady Yee's keen observations concerning these destinations were recorded in her daybook. She was unimpressed with the port of San Francisco and held unflattering opinions concerning the inhabitants. Lady Yee, who had met Americans in China, and liked them in the main, found Americans at home in California a very disquieting species indeed. She tried to set aside the fact that they were culturally averse to bathing regularly and paid little attention to the cleanliness of their clothes, or to their houses for that matter. She was tolerant of their general lack of education and sense of culture, and she could endure and forgive their thoughtless manners and total absence of tact, but she simply could not abide the American concept of what constituted civilized food. She refused to partake in anything as barbarian as large animal parts roasted on a spit, or blood-rare beefsteaks, or vegetables boiled or roasted to near-pulp. Corn on the cob was impossible to eat with any finesse, and what passed for pastry and confection wasn't worth discussing. Lady Yee's food had always been prepared by qualified, if not renowned, chefs. And the one stipulation she settled upon before following her husband to sea was the employment of an experienced Chinese cook named Ah Chu for herself and her maid, Li-Lee. Captain Hammond, who was very partial to several schools of Asian cuisine, readily agreed, and soon even the crew came to be of the opinion that the rations aboard ship were much improved under the guidance of Lady Yee's chef. But once in San Francisco, and discovering that Ah Chu could not follow her to a hotel and wait upon her there, Lady Yee refused to leave the ship for the pleasures that the best lodgings in the city might provide. To her way of thinking, bad food, rude service, bedbugs, used linen, and open chamber pots were not statements of civilized luxury. She pointed out that she lived far better aboard her ship, with her own maid and her own cook, than anyone in a city hotel.

It was also perhaps Lady Yee's pointed distaste for mass alcoholism, and the subsequent street violence of the city, that made her feel ill at ease there. When her husband once escorted her to a fashionable milliner's emporium in the city, Lady Yee counted fifty-seven busy taverns in a three-mile carriage ride, and on the way back to the ship, after spending an evening with a few of her husband's friends, she witnessed three drunken brawls, a stabbing, and a number of public altercations that involved the loud use of provocative language totally composed of profanity. And if that weren't enough to disturb Lady Yee's sense of civility, then certainly the treatment of her fellow Chinese, now residing in "the land under the Gold Mountain," obliterated all desire for Lady Yee to make herself feel at home in San Francisco. She was certainly aware that in the Americas she would always be looked down upon because of her race and her gender, but that didn't preclude her fervent desire to make a life for herself that disdained those conventions. Aboard *The Silver Lotus* she had status, responsibility, respect, and honest affection. As part owner of Hammond & Yee, and quite wealthy in her own right, she also had the power to influence many aspects of her own life that were, in effect, quite above and beyond the privileges and prerogatives allowed most women who lived ashore, no matter what their race, station, or lineage.

It should be noted that despite her youth, Lady Yee maintained very liberal and open-minded sensibilities. She avoided making broad judgments based upon information or experience drawn from limited samples. It was usually her habit to take on humanity one person at a time, and make her evaluations accordingly, regardless of superficialities, fortunes, or titles. So of course she knew that the legendary California so often described to her by her husband must be somewhere else, because San Francisco Bay as a harbor was just the same tidewater snake pit as any other big harbor around the world, including Canton or Shanghai, and it attracted and nurtured exactly the same species of vice, violence, and crime. With this in mind, Lady Yee could see no reason to try and feel comfortable ashore. Besides, the money she saved on frivolous entertainments and expensive hotels went into making constant improvements to the daily comforts both captain and crew enjoyed at sea or at anchor. This made a berth on *The Silver Lotus* very desirable by any measure.

On one of their voyages to California, Captain Hammond journeyed north from San Diego to Monterey Bay. They sailed close enough to shore for Captain Hammond and Lady Yee to discover some stunning stretches of coastline. In many places the mountains ended their progress in rockbound cliffs, as the crashing ocean waves had cut away all footing. Captain Hammond had never taken a cargo out of Monterey before since it was a fishing port, and he didn't carry perishables. But on this occasion he had been commissioned by his father-in-law to purchase a large cargo of dried squid for shipment to Canton. The squid were caught, dried, placed in salt, and packed in reused tea chests by Chinese fishermen who worked the bay. These courageous boatmen and their families lived in ramshackle villages constructed from anything at hand, including driftwood. Like cliff-bound seabird nests, these haphazard dwellings clung precariously along the rock-strewn shore at several locations around the bay.

By his own estimation, the captain judged the weight of the salt as at least a third more than that of the weight of the squid, but it mattered little to him as long as Master Yee was standing security for the agreed price. Though he took every opportunity to oblige his father-in-law, there were limits, and in cases of business the limit was always set at price per ton upon safe delivery.

Because *The Silver Lotus*, at present holding two-thirds of her return cargo, drew too much water, loading the squid from the commercial pier was deemed impractical, and it was decided to take on this last bit of cargo at anchor, using the Chinese fishing junks as lighters. It would take longer to hoist and load, to be sure, but it gave Captain and Mrs. Hammond the opportunity to enjoy a small excursion through the countryside around Monterey and Pacific Grove, and then down the coast to Carmel. The captain was very taken with the area and told Lady Yee that because it was a fishing community, it reminded him somewhat of his birthplace on Deer Island in the state of Maine. Lady Yee thought the land around the bay quite lovely, but above all other considerations, she secretly believed the place had great commercial potential as well, and encouraged her husband to think about buying property in the vicinity as an investment. Since she was never wrong about such things, he gave the matter serious consideration, and the next day decided to open a sizable bank account in Monterey. He encouraged the bank to lend him assistance in finding suitable property, and the bank president, Mr. Hodges, who was only too pleased to have Captain Hammond, and his twenty-eight thousand dollars, as a new client, bent every effort toward being of assistance. To show his appreciation, Mr. Hodges informed the captain that they had recently received an order from the estate of the late Mr. Liam O'Sheen to place his town residence on the block. His heirs preferred living on their ranch in Big Sur and no longer wished to support the expense of the property.

Mr. Hodges said he had known Mr. O'Sheen for almost twenty-eight years, and having been his guest many times, he knew the property well. He told the captain the house was quite large, with five bedrooms and all the amenities, including a cook's quarters, a large laundry room, and modern plumbing throughout. The ground story was constructed of heavy stone, and sat over a generous stone root cellar. The second story was constructed of stout timber and frame in the Dutch fashion, and overhung the ground floor by two feet all around the building. The large barn was constructed in like manner. There was a stone water tower attached to the house that also contained a dovecote below, and a lovely observation deck on the roof. Both the tower and the second-story bedrooms shared extensive views of Monterey Bay. The house was surrounded by extensive walled gardens and sat on fifteen acres of partially forested land. Besides the fine barn, the property boasted a carriage house and four acres of mature fruit and nut trees in a separate walled orchard. Mr. Hodges said that Mr. O'Sheen had spent a great deal of money enlarging and improving the house for his wife and children, and no convenience had been overlooked when it came to their comfort.

The residence was to be sold with or without its contents, but Mr. Hodges stated that the remaining furnishings were of the best quality and should be examined before disposal one way or another. The banker offered to give the captain the use of one of his clerks as escort and to open the house for inspection. The captain, who was intrigued by the descriptions, said he would return at two-thirty that afternoon and avail himself of the kind offer. Then he went off to confer with Lady Yee.

It had been the captain's intention to gather up his wife, tell her what had transpired at the bank, and take her to see the property so she could make her own judgments. They had only two days before they were scheduled to sail west to Canton and then to the Philippines. If any business was to be accomplished at all, momentum was required.

However, Lady Yee had already thought out several matters that pertained to buying property in California, and one of them was based on the obvious discrimination practiced against the Chinese, though they weren't the only minorities to feel the toe and heel of white cultural insecurity. Her awareness of the racial tensions, as well as her business instincts, inspired her to tell her husband that if she accompanied him to see the house, and it became known to the bank that he had married a Chinese, the price of the house would go up, if only to hinder a purchase by the "wrong" sorts. She told her husband to avoid an auction for the same reason. If he really thought the property a sound investment, then he should purchase it on that basis alone. She pointed out that since they were hardly going to move in at once, if ever, what the bank didn't know was, in fact, best for everybody. Lady Yee advised her husband that if it came down to doing business on the fly, he should bypass all talk of auction, find out what the heirs wanted for the property, and pay it. Or better still, have the bank finance the property and deposit just enough money to cover the mortgage, tax, and maintenance for at least five years. If the captain later changed his mind, so be it. If the property was all Mr. Hodges said it was, they could always sell it on. But if they decided to keep the property, by then it would be far too late for anyone to muster financial interference, or even voice prejudiced objections that would matter to anyone.

Lady Yee reminded her husband that for most narrow-minded people the world over, there was nothing like the impressive plumage of a healthy fortune to soften most bigoted sentiments or objections. Americans, no less than any other breed, were always willing to amend their prejudices in the presence of great wealth. Even among cultured Chinese, great fortune denoted power because the first could only be acquired through the skilled application of the second. But for the present, Lady Yee demurred from the idea of giving people more information than they needed.

By eleven-thirty the next morning, Captain Hammond walked out of the bank as the new owner of a fifteen-acre property overlooking Monterey Bay. He smiled to himself as he pocketed the keys and went back to gather up Lady Yee. For sound reasons of her own, Lady Yee later accompanied her husband to see the house dressed as her own maid. She said that as a servant, people would look right through her without making any assumptions whatsoever, and she was right.

Lady Yee was very taken with the house, the property, and especially the extensive walled gardens and the orchard. Except for occasional visits by the heirs, the house had been essentially empty for eight years, and though he'd purchased the house partially furnished, almost no maintenance had been done to the property. Lady Yee saw at once that the gardens and orchards needed immediate attention, and the house itself a thorough cleaning and care. A new coat of paint all around would brighten things considerably as well.

Captain Hammond agreed, and after some judicial inquiries at Watson Hay & Feed, he hired a highly recommended Japanese nurseryman to set the orchards and gardens in order. Through the helpful offices of the bank, he found a contractor who would see to all repairs and repaint the house, barn, and outbuildings, and a bank representative would pass on all the work before payment was made. They were happy to do so, as Captain Hammond was now their fourth-largest single depositor, and they were certainly aware that his sizable deposit represented only a small portion of his wealth. They hoped to embrace more of his business in the future, and the captain led the bank to believe that would be the case if matters worked out to his satisfaction.

On the morning tide the next day, with the ship's additional cargo loaded and secured, Captain Hammond and Lady Yee sailed out of Monterey Bay. It would be quite some time before they returned again. Fat little wars prosecuted by fat little despots were breaking out everywhere, and this always meant a boost in trade for basic supplies like grain, iron, copper, rubber, and other necessary staples. There were some in the trade who valued quick profits above all else, so much so that they would ferret about in the illegal trade of arms and explosives, but Captain Hammond well understood that this was possibly the fastest way to have your ship seized, or sent to the bottom of the ocean. It was one thing to sacrifice wealth with a confiscated cargo, but it was another to place the ship's crew in jeopardy. A man could always buy another ship, but a sterling reputation for honesty and good sense could not be purchased at any price.

In the past the captain's ships had been boarded for inspection too many times to count. He found it always very helpful to order up a service of ham sandwiches and good coffee, sometimes laced with a little brandy to ward off the elements. Otherwise, he kept his books and his hatches open and his mouth closed. If he knew the inspecting officers, and in many cases he did, then he opened the spirits locker as well. In Muslim countries he served sweet tea, candied fruits, and honey-laced pastries. The captain's consideration and understated hospitality were always well remembered. The fact that his crews were always very well behaved while ashore also lent credence to his reputation as a captain who maintained steady discipline and kept his crews free of criminal elements.

But as the conflicts in Africa, India, Malaysia, Indonesia, and southern China increased in intensity, so too did the inspections, harassment, and occasional confiscations, which had all the earmarks of out-and-out piracy. After two sanguine years of pointless military conflict and confusion, profits no longer compensated for all the sailing delays and legal complications. And insuring cargos destined for areas of conflict was becoming a very expensive proposition indeed. Only gunrunners and freebooters were realizing true wealth, but they didn't bother insuring their illicit cargos anyway. One successfully penetrated blockade could pay for three ships lost. But Captain Hammond didn't fancy the odds either way, so he and Lady Yee decided to leave the China trade for the more peaceful haunts of South America and Mexico. However, the blight of cross-cultural violence and intermittent revolution had spread there as well.

It was Lady Yee's firm opinion that the stars had now aligned against their interests. For years all their dealings and voyages had transpired with relative ease, and they had both realized great profits and shared remarkable adventures together. But having thrown the coins and noted the readings, Lady Yee had a sense that they should think about a different mode of living for a while. Ships were a great expense when not employed in trade, and employment was becoming more hazardous and unsure all the time. She suggested that they fit out for one more journey to India and China, and purchase a cargo of luxury goods on their own account.

With half-penny military conflicts popping up like poisonous mushrooms everywhere, these items would, by virtue of the cresting waves of social and political instability, soon become very hard to come by at any price. This would be particularly true for quality exports like fine silks, velvets, refined linens, and polished Indian cotton goods. She also mentioned art porcelains, fine bone china, rich furnishings, and even jewels if they were offered at rational prices. Lady Yee was particularly fond of pearls and believed that a last trip to Madagascar might prove rewarding in that regard as well. She suggested they could warehouse their cargo in the Americas somewhere and sell it off slowly as the market prices gradually increased, as they most assuredly would. In the meantime, they could put their ship in the lumber trade on the West Coast of the Americas and go ashore for a couple of years of well-deserved rest and modest luxury. She pointed out that *The Silver Lotus* was nearing her end of useful service in the Asian trade, and stood in need of a major refit, which would be expensive if effected all at once. Better to put her on light duty in the coastal trade and keep her close to home. Repairs could be accomplished as needed, and she could retire from her arduous Pacific voyages. Her sailing master was more than qualified to take over command, and everyone would continue to profit, albeit on a smaller scale, but balanced by lower costs as well.

Captain Hammond was always pleasantly surprised by his wife's grasp of business, especially its place in the context of political events. It wasn't so much that she could predict precisely what was going to happen next, although at times it appeared that way, but rather she possessed a profound sensitivity for distant and sometimes obscure wisps of information. However, the consummate skill and logic with which she pieced together a picture of the whole issue from mere scraps of intelligence were as precisely extrapolated as a mathematical equation, and she knew the critical nature of X, Y, and Z would usually bring her within a hair's breadth of the truth.

Lady's Yee's particular powers of observation and evaluation were buttressed in part by an insatiable appetite for newspapers and periodicals. These she devoured in Chinese, English, and French. Whenever they entered a port, she'd pay the deck boy, Billy Starkey, to get her all the current newspapers. They were usually the first items brought aboard ship after the customs inspector departed.

She also had a habit of asking pointed questions of officers from other ships. She wanted to know where they'd been, what cargos they carried and why, who was in power on such-and-such an island, and what kinds of duties were demanded for certain goods. If it hadn't been for the fact that Lady Yee was extremely attractive, cultured, and very personable in three languages, these hard-boiled old salts would have closed up tighter than clams at low tide, but for Lady Yee they would talk themselves blue in the face, and then thank her for the privilege of her company. Fortunately for the captain, she usually focused her keen efforts on more pragmatic targets like grain factors, ship chandlers, rubber brokers, teamster foremen, and the occasional customs officer.

Captain Hammond, after much deliberation and some discussion with his officers, came to the conclusion that Lady Yee's assessments of their trading prospects in the near future were correct. He knew from experience that what she had said about the ship's condition was essentially correct as well. Even the crew was a little jaded about the Asia trade and longed for something closer to home, and with less time at sea. The captain also agreed with Lady Yee that there was at least one rich voyage left in *The Silver Lotus*, and it would be a shame to leave those rich waters empty-handed. If the profits held as projected, there would be plenty of money left over to refit the ship for the lumber trade.

Since this would be their last voyage in Asian waters, the captain said that those crewmen who wished to purchase cargo and trade in their own right could petition him to advance their wages in cash to make any legal purchases they wished. To lighten their burden, the captain promised to insure their investments with his own cargo manifest. He told them that if they chose their goods carefully, they could easily double or triple their investments. Of course, having few skills in such matters, those men who chose to dabble pooled their funds and went to Lady Yee and asked her to make their purchases for them. They gave her the freedom to choose whatever she thought would be most profitable at the end of their journey.

Captain Hammond felt somewhat slighted that they hadn't requested those services of him, but he had to admit their choice hosted less of a gamble in the long haul. Lady Yee possessed impeccable taste, which he admittedly did not, and all were aware that she would also guard her crew's investment like a mother bear, and it was that notable instinct that guided the men's ultimate choice. Lady Yee told her little pack of salt-caked investors that she would share the risk by only purchasing goods for them that she was loading on her own behalf. If she found fifty bolts of fine silk for herself, she would contract for a further five bolts on their behalf, and so on. This seemed to please them greatly. She suddenly became their lifeline to an easier future, perhaps a bid for a modest farm, a grocery, or a tavern, and of course, the chance to enjoy families, either existing or planned.

After a trading voyage of seventeen weeks, *The Silver Lotus* made for Canton before setting a course for Hawaii and the western ports of America. Captain Hammond wanted to top off his cargo with quality porcelain, fine bone china, and the kind of rich Chinese furnishings so popular in an American culture that simultaneously disavowed the validity of the Chinese that served in their homes, tilled their fields, and did their dirty laundry. Even for someone raised, as he most certainly was, in the racially conservative Macy tradition, the captain found the counterpoint between the mindlessly paranoid prejudices of the laboring classes and the sophisticated aesthetics of the wealthy way beyond sane comprehension or comment. After years of taking heed of his wife's Buddhist sentiments, it now seemed that both parties were profoundly, if not mortally, confused, and therefore eons short of enlightenment. According to Lady Yee, the only tactic left that morally applied was the application of patience, compassion, and forgiveness, because no power on earth could possibly correct these lingering weaknesses without centuries of enlightened adaptation.

Captain Hammond might never have considered the harsher realities quite in that context if he hadn't been married to the "iron butterfly" of perceived reality. As far as Lady Yee was concerned, there were no accidents. Every certainty, be it light or dark, came with promising alternatives and likely opportunities. Only cultural value judgments stood in the way of true harmony, so it was important to take these aberrations into consideration and proceed with caution. Captain Hammond was amused to recall that, according to a prudent Chinese tradition, a man who falls into a fast-flowing river is wise to swim with the current, and Captain Hammond found the same canon applied to his life with Lady Yee.

6

CAPTAIN HAMMOND kept his ship in Canton for three weeks, partially for the refurbishment and replacement of sails—an expensive exercise everywhere but in Canton, where being Master Yee's son-in-law substantially reduced the cost—but additionally so that Lady Yee could spend time visiting with her family. She also wanted to make specific purchases of matched pearls. Using the good offices and reputation of her father's company, she was confident she'd get the very best pearls for the most equitable prices, and of course she did. A portion of her purchase was made on behalf of the informal consortium made up of the crew, and they were notably impressed.

However, dangerous and violent times had once again come to the gates of Canton, and as soon as he had loaded his heaviest cargo at quayside, the captain hired a steam tug to move his ship to anchor in the offing just beyond the harbor. There he joined a score of other ships that had chosen discretion over bravado. The streets and harbor were relatively safe during the day, if you overlooked normal street crimes, but at night the hatchet men belonging to competitive triads roamed the shadows robbing and killing at will, and generally taking revenge for one thing or another. Captain Hammond told his crew that after sunset a Yankee sailor caught in the streets or alleys around the docks of Canton had the same odds of survival as a fat lobster in his mother's kitchen. Nonetheless, he did allow small parties of four men at a time to go ashore between the hours of 10:00 AM and 4:00 PM, but only with the understanding that they stay together for protection and never allow themselves to be lured to any establishment housed in an obscure alleyway. Captain Hammond knew his crew to be men of sense and prudence, so he was not surprised to find that very few chose to accept the offer of shore leave. Most contented themselves with purchasing what they wanted from the flocks of bumboats that visited the anchorages daily.

The captain had little fear for his wife's safety, as Master Yee lived in what might be styled an urban compound of buildings and warehouses that were well protected by armed guards. Nonetheless, Captain Hammond felt obliged to stay with his ship and share his crew's days of personal chores and ship's maintenance. Some afternoons, Chinese magicians and acrobats would approach in the bumboats and offer to come aboard and entertain the sailors for an hour or two. The captain thought this a fine idea, and paid the modest costs of these entertainments from the ship's purse. It was cheaper than bailing his men out of dangerous encounters with local triad bullyboys. On two occasions he commissioned a bumboat to bring him cooks and fresh provisions to feast his whole crew, and then brought aboard a troop of Chinese jugglers to entertain them while they ate under a tented pavilion hoisted over the deck for shade.

The crews on other anchored ships nearby got wind of these entertainments aboard *The Silver Lotus* and pestered their own officers to do the same. A few captains realized the rationale behind Hammond's thinking and, to keep their bored crews from mixing in mischief, copied the idea with equal success.

But on the afternoon of the second feast a man arrived by boat with a written message from Master Yee countersigned by Lady Yee. It said that the political situation ashore had deteriorated markedly in the last twenty-four hours, and it was advised that he prepare his ship for sea at once before the authorities impounded it for ransom. It was a quick way of raising cash from hapless trading captains, and a tactic that had spread to various tin-pot island kingdoms of late. The note added that Lady Yee and her maid and cook would rejoin the ship with the last of the cargo at dawn. She pointedly suggested that they be under way on the outgoing tide at 6:08 AM without delay.

Captain Hammond debated with himself as to whether or not to immediately inform the other captains anchored in the offing about this threat. He didn't want to surrender his own surprise departure before Lady Yee came aboard, and he feared the sight of so many ships getting under way would panic the authorities ashore into doing something rash. The ships most in jeopardy were the steamers. It would take a long while to bring their boilers up to pressure, the smoke giving ample warning and leaving plenty of time to be boarded by armed men of dubious authority. The big schooners were in a minority, but they could haul in their cables and be under full sail in twenty minutes or less. The captain compromised and took the lesser of two evils. He composed short notes to his fellow captains anchored nearby. These notes warned of imminent political danger ashore, including assaults upon or detention of all foreigners found in the streets, foreign sailors being a choice target for abuse. He stated that confiscation of ship's papers and cargos could be expected to follow, possibly leading to the impounding of the ships themselves. He suggested a strategic withdrawal until the chaos quieted, or at the very least to set preparations in gear for a timely departure should the authorities decide upon confiscation or worse.

Lady Yee and her servants came aboard later that afternoon. She brought with her six wax-sealed chests of goods purchased through her father. They were immediately stored away in the captain's section of the hold. Lady Yee also brought the news that matters were getting worse in Canton. It appeared that certain highly placed officials had been caught in the act of committing fraud and conspiracy on a large scale. But rather than surrender to the courts and forfeit their powers, they had gone to the triads and hired heavily armed hatchet men to take over the city government. It had happened before. To get cash to pay their gangs, they would certainly extort funds from every possible corner, especially the harbor with its wealth of warehouses and goods. Lady Yee was assured that her father and family were safe and well guarded for the near future; however, she did suggest that their ship not wait for the morning tide, but raise all sail and depart immediately. Captain Hammond was more than happy to agree, but fulfilled his promise to himself by paying one of the bumboats to distribute his notes to the captains of the nearby ships. After that, he set a course east-southeast, sure that the bad news would inevitably spread with plague-like momentum. After that it was every ship for itself.

The captain's notes must have had some impact, for by the time *The Silver Lotus* had reached the horizon, the smoke of a half-dozen steamers could be seen curling into the sunset clouds as they fired up their boilers, and at least four sets of sails could be seen following *The Silver Lotus* in trail not ten miles off the stern. *The Silver Lotus* sailed on toward the east to complete her last transpacific voyage.

• • •

IT WAS BILLY STARKEY, the sailing master's deck boy, who at 5:08 the next morning informed a sleeping Captain Hammond that the barometer needle had just dropped like a headsman's axe. He was told to report that the weather to the broad south-southeast was looking none too amenable, and also that to starboard cumulus clouds were stacking at an alarming rate, and below that a wall of black weather banded the southern horizon from east to west.

There was no indecision for Captain Hammond. He thanked Billy and instantly gave orders to change course to north by northeast and fly all possible sail. He ordered all watches on deck and called for close attention to secure the storm sails and batten the hatches down with an extra ply of waxed canvas. Half the men he sent into the cargo holds to secure any loose cases or barrels with rope netting. He had the cooks prepare rations for three days of cold fare. After that he had the galley fires extinguished and the galley gear secured against the storm.

With the wind now freshening on his starboard stern quarter, Captain Hammond hoped that he could outrace the storm just long enough to fully prepare his ship for the trials to come. He knew he would eventually have to turn and face the approaching monster, and stripped down to little more than storm jibs and small triangular staysails lofted on the other masts to stabilize the ship and hopefully keep her pointed into the wind and under moderate control.

There was one other detail in the captain's favor: Portland-built four- and five-mast schooners were famously well founded, almost overbraced, and very sturdy in every respect. According to legend, the greater the cargo load, the more stable the hulls became in serious blows. The captain prayed that this robust reputation would hold true for the next few days.

Lady Yee, in the meantime, was hard at work with her maid Li-Lee and Billy Starkey stowing everything moveable in the captain's furnishing locker just below the main cabin. Then she rigged the canvas straps for the bunks. These held the occupant in place at angles that would normally toss the sleeper across the cabin and cause serious injury. Lastly, she made sure she had food and fresh water in the cabin, and that all the medical supplies were easily at hand. When all was prepared, she called her husband to his supper, then sat to one side making detailed entries in the ship's log as he dictated them over his hasty meal.

Captain Hammond prided himself, perhaps sometimes erroneously, in the belief that he knew and understood his wife rather well, but that was to be expected after everything they had been through together. But Captain Hammond couldn't shake the sensation that the Lady Yee who came aboard ship off Canton was not the same person he had left at Master Yee's house two weeks before. There was some new, haunting aspect about the woman's very presence that was real but beyond definition. He had no reference point from which to form a question, yet his wife had become something altogether brand new without changing one noticeable detail of her demeanor or personality. He wanted to question her, but he didn't know what to ask, or how to ask it. She now exuded unquestionable confidence in everything she set her mind to. She seemed to glide on a plane of self-assured precognition. She knew beyond doubt that all would be well, and others magically became inoculated with that same conviction when in her presence. For all that Captain Hammond presently influenced, when it came to the morale of the crew, he might just as well have turned the command of the ship over to Lady Yee and have done with it. The fact that this observation amused him was one of the reasons Lady Yee cherished her big Yankee, and ultimately why the crew believed in his command as well. In all things, the rigid rules of the sea aside, they sailed under the flag of a strong and fortunate captain, who in all points and principles was a man just like themselves in many respects, but as captain and owner, functioning without excuses or alibis where his wife was concerned. Captain Hammond always managed the good grace to acknowledge superior thinking. The fact that a majority of the more creative solutions came from Lady Yee might have wounded the pride of a lesser man, but Captain Hammond seemed to rejoice in talking about his wife's brilliance and discerning perceptions. Sometimes he would privately wonder just why such a brilliant and beautiful woman would have anything to do with a tar-barrel Nantucket Yankee like himself. But so as not to jinx his good fortune, he made a point of never asking his wife just why she loved him. He was content with her assurance that this was so.

With but a few precious hours left before the inevitable clash of elements, Lady Yee insisted that her husband lie down for a short rest. She reminded him that he would get little enough in the days to come. Once tucked down, the captain was soon asleep, then Lady Yee went up on deck to judge matters for herself. With a sturdy wind driving taut sails on all four masts, the ship was running clean and fast through long regular swells. When she looked directly overhead, the night sky was luminous with stars, but when she turned to look aft, Lady Yee was surprised to see a great boiling wall of blackness that reached from the horizon to the heavens, and where they met there were no stars. She went to the pilothouse and found the sailing master poised over his charts and instruments. Every so often he would tap the barometer glass, mutter to himself, and shake his head. He turned to Lady Yee and spoke as though she had been present for a while. He said he was grateful the men had done such a superior job of sealing all the hatches with heavy waxed canvas, for he feared that with the holds fully loaded, *The Silver Lotus* was going to be spending long hours plowing her head beneath some very steep seas.

It was now 10:28 PM, and the sailing master told Lady Yee that he expected severe storm conditions by midnight. At eleven-thirty or thereabouts, he intended to turn the ship into the wind, put two sea anchors off the bow, lower all main sails, loft the storm sails, seal all the cabin hatches, and get down on his knees and pray.

Lady Yee asked after the men, and was told that most would stay strapped in their bunks unless called on deck by some emergency. She was advised to follow their lead. A tight ship's berth was the safest refuge for the foreseeable future, though she would derive little comfort from it. Having been told that the captain was resting, the sailing master politely requested Lady Yee to wake her husband before the time committed to turn the ship into the wind. She agreed and went back to the cabin. She was pleased to find her husband still sound asleep. She sat down next to him and quietly watched the meter of his breathing. After a few moments she reached out and gently touched his hand. Though most certainly asleep, he sighed as though relieved of some private burden and a gentle smile came to his lips. Lady Yee looked lovingly at her husband and thought of the trials he had yet to face.

It would take years to compile the total numbers, but it was said that the great monsoon, later named Nike-Chi, killed well over fifteen thousand people in six countries and destroyed coastal property and maritime interests valued at many millions of English pounds sterling. Thirty-nine major cargo vessels had gone to the bottom, and no one had bothered to keep count of the smaller ships lost. In some cases entire fishing fleets simply disappeared, and whole towns were washed out to sea. The bloated bodies of their inhabitants floated on the waves for days, but there were none to gather up their remains for burial, so the creatures of the sea received the bounty.

Within thirty minutes of the first blow, Captain Hammond began to doubt the ability of his ship to survive the ever-increasing size of the endless phalanx of giant waves that crested over the bow. It sometimes felt like one of them might just cleave the ship in half like a stale loaf of bread. It appeared the double-sheeted sea anchors were holding securely, but the whole match depended upon the strength of the keel and its ability to endure radical stresses not normally asked of such a critical member. He had heard of heavily

111

burdened ships simply breaking in two when their sterns were suddenly forced out of the water by a wave sinking the bow in a trough and then not releasing it in time to relieve the stress on the keel. In his mind's eye, Captain Hammond could visualize this eventuality with every new wall of seawater that broke over the bow, and so could every experienced seaman on board.

This torment went on for three days and nights, sapping all energy and strength from the crew as well as the ship. It was as physically exhausting to lie strapped in one's berth as it was to move around, and only a little less dangerous. Hammond felt blessed that the damage caused by the gale-force winds and towering sea had not so far been too critical, but he expected the fatal blow any minute, and the strain of that anxiety was beginning to show in his features.

As exhaustion set in, some of the crew suffered accidents, which Lady Yee insisted on treating herself. The bosun had reported four men down: one with a broken foot, another with a broken wrist, a third man with a badly cracked head, and a fourth who had been brutally dashed against the ship's gunwale by a giant wave that almost took him overboard when it left. He was knocked unconscious, and stayed that way for two full hours while blood slowly seeped from his ears. When he came to his senses he appeared well enough, but soon discovered he could no longer keep his balance to walk or even sit up for any length of time without suffering from severe vertigo.

The winds had taken a toll on the rigging, and Captain Hammond supposed that even if they should survive the storm, it would take two or three days floating around the swells to effect repairs sufficient to loft sails safely again. It surprised him to discover that the ship's drift rate, as it was driven back before the winds, was almost eight knots. And though the course of the storm was moving generally west-northwest, the cyclonic winds were driving the ship east-southeast, with the eye of the monsoon moving somewhere off to the west.

When the gales at last cast his ship free of the vortex, *The Silver Lotus* had survived three days and nights of near-death torment. Her decks looked like they'd been raked with gunfire, and what was left of the storm sails hung in rags like a beggar's laundry. The crewmen were almost too spent to move. They hadn't had a hot meal or any worthwhile nourishment, and the cooks were no better off than the rest of the crew.

Captain Hammond had been on deck for eighteen hours when the storm broke free and moved on. He was so tired that he collapsed on the bunk locker in the pilothouse and slept for three hours. In fact, nobody aboard could do much of anything for the ship for eight hours, and even when they managed to rouse themselves, they moved around the ship like the walking wounded, grateful to be alive to be sure, but maimed all the same.

When Captain Hammond awoke, he went on a tour of inspection and made a list of repair priorities. He next looked to the crew and their needs and lit the galley fires himself. He told the cook to brew up a rich beef soup with whatever vegetables he could find. He was told that Lady Yee had braved the elements to come to the aid of the injured sailors. With the help of Billy Starkey she set their bones, bound their wounds, spoke soothing words, and then dosed their pain with enough laudanum to put a bull elephant to sleep. It was the best she could do until professional help could be found.

Hearing this, Captain Hammond suddenly realized that he hadn't seen Lady Yee for quite some time. Something dark twitched in his brain, and he suddenly went off to his cabin. The moment he entered that dark thing twitched again. Lady Yee lay on her berth with eyes closed. Li-Lee stood over her mistress cooling her face and forehead with damp compresses, and Billy Starkey stood nearby almost in tears. There was no sign of response from Lady Yee. The captain rushed to his wife's side and looked down to notice a long, bleeding bruise on the left side of her beautiful face and a large blue-green lump above her left temple. Her left wrist had also been bandaged. When the captain demanded to know why he hadn't been called when his wife was injured, Li-Lee told him that Lady Yee insisted he not be bothered with trivialities. When he asked how the accident had happened, Billy Starkey wiped the tears from the side of his nose and said, "Sir, Lady Yee was thrown off her feet by the pitching of the ship. She and I were returning from the crew's quarters, and while coming down the companionway she fell headfirst to the deck below. She was unconscious at first, but somehow I managed to get her back in her berth, and her maid here and I managed to lash her back in place. Her left wrist appears sprained and swollen, but her maid signed there was no serious damage beyond that." In the simplest Chinese, Li-Lee confirmed that Lady Yee was sleeping comfortably now, under the influence of willow bark tea laced with Chinese brandy.

Captain Hammond dismissed Billy Starkey to his other duties with a firm handshake and sincere sentiments of profound gratitude. Then he turned to Li-Lee, nodded, and smiled to reassure the maid that he wasn't angry. Then he asked to be left alone with his wife. When Li-Lee had gone, Hammond drew a stool close to the berth and sat quietly watching over his sleeping love. He reached out to touch her hand and was pleased to find it warm and alive. But then a dark cloud

115

settled on his heart as it occurred to him how sparse and sad his life would be without her. Perhaps it was because he was still too tired and couldn't resist the emotion, but suddenly Captain Hammond found himself openly weeping in gratitude for her safety. He silently promised himself that he would never place her well-being in jeopardy again. Sitting there, Captain Hammond suddenly felt very old and raw-boned. Every muscle in his body begged for relief, and his eyes felt as though they were lubricated with sand. Because he was past fatigue and vulnerable to self-doubt, he blamed himself for everything that had gone wrong. He fell asleep on his arm while holding his wife's hand. The last thing that floated through his thoughts was a proverb he'd learned in school. He drifted off reciting it to himself. "For the want of a nail the shoe was lost. For the want of a shoe the horse was lost. For the want of a horse the rider was lost. For the want of the rider the battle was lost. For the want of the battle the kingdom was lost. And all for the want of a horseshoe nail."

Lady Yee awoke to find her husband asleep, head on arm, and holding her hand. He looked like an exhausted little boy who had spent the afternoon getting as dirty as nature allowed. She smiled and then winced in pain. The left side of her face was badly bruised, and the clotted blood on the lacerations didn't allow much room for facial movement without discomfort. Then she became aware that her chest hurt badly every time she took a deep breath, and that the pain in her left wrist was caused as much by the swelling of blue flesh against tight bandages as it was by the injury itself. But the one thing that most concerned her was the one subject she refused to even contemplate. The will of heaven would prevail, and she sailed under a lucky star. Even the famous Buddhist astrologer that her father had called in before she departed Canton predicted that Master Yee's daughter would enjoy a long span of years, be blessed with robust health, and be successful in all things of true importance. Then he said something odd. He looked at his charts and tables again, then foretold that her presence would be as food to the hungry, clothes to the naked, and shelter to the lost. She would foster a thousand souls and nourish the ignorant with wisdom.

Afterward, as the old astrologer monk was departing the house, he turned to Lady Yee and bowed. He said the reason heaven had granted her long life was that she had such a great deal to accomplish before she died. His expression turned serious when he said the charts were not in error. They indicated that she was born to be a tool of heaven's will, and thus she would remain all her days. She need not understand, just be who she was with confidence. The rest would take care of itself in time. However, the way she was feeling at the moment precluded all other desires except the "robust health" part of the prediction. She was slowly becoming aware of how much of her body had been traumatized by the fall. She felt like she'd been placed in a barrel and rolled down a mountain, a punishment usually meted out to petty criminals by angry village bailiffs.

The captain woke with a start, and for a moment believed he was still in the wheelhouse. He called out for course and heading, then realized where he was, looked about, and found his wife smiling at him despite her discomfort. She could see where his tears had washed channels down his dirty face, and her heart went out to him.

When asked, she smiled and told him she was feeling much better, which wasn't true, but she asked for Li-Lee to come and adjust her bandages. Then she shook her head and feigned a frown. It amused her to order her husband to clean himself up, look more like a captain, and go up and attend to his men and his ship. She said she had no wish to float aimlessly around the ocean for the next month while people decided what to do first. But she especially wanted word from Billy Starkey on the condition of the injured crewmen, and approximately how many days it would be before they could expect professional care in some convenient port. Lastly she asked that Billy Starkey be shown some mark of favor for his bravery and loyalty. "I don't know what would have happened if he hadn't been there to save me. He deserves professional recognition. For a young man making his own way, that's all that matters, before or after the mast."

Captain Hammond promised to look into all these matters in turn, then he gently kissed his wife and went into the adjacent cabin to wash up, shave, and change his clothes. He felt much refreshed for having done so, and ordered the ship's cook to heat plenty of water so the men off watch could do the same. They had collected plenty of fresh rainwater during the storm, and the captain believed that washing the salt off their hides and out of their clothes would put them in a better frame of mind.

Though it came as something of a surprise to everybody who had witnessed the jumbled chaos on deck, *The Silver Lotus* was back under full sail in eighteen hours. There were a few temporary patches nailed up here and there, and a few parts had to be fished together with cord and tar, but in the main she was still sharp, and held her course to the point. The cargo master was quite pleased with himself when he reported that in all those long days of dangerous marine gymnastics, not one barrel or crate shifted or broke its lashings, and as far as the ship's carpenter was concerned, all seams were still as tight as a banker's wallet, and the deck caulking sound. The bosun's mate reported that after pumping the bilges fore and aft only four to six inches of water remained, which was standard under normal sailing conditions, but after considering what the ship had been through he counted it as a veritable miracle.

After calculating their present position, Captain Hammond visited his injured men and announced that though the ship had been blown way off course by the storm, they were now approximately six days east-northeast of the Hawaiian chain. He promised to have his men ashore and in a clean hospital as soon as humanly possible. In the meantime he ordered the cook and galley boy to see they had all they needed, and he contributed a beaker of fine rum to be mixed with their evening coffee to help them sleep despite their injuries.

The next afternoon, at six bells, when the watches changed, Captain Hammond called all available men aft. When they'd assembled and been called to ranks by the bosun's mate, the captain came forward and called on Billy Starkey to step front and center. Billy looked gob-stopped, but did as he was told. Then in front of the crew, the captain announced that for services of bravery and loyalty, Mr. Starkey was henceforth rated as an able seaman, with all the privileges and heartaches that go with the rank. The men chuckled with recognition and with pride. Billy looked like he'd been branded with a poker. The captain stepped forward and continued. "Able Seaman Starkey is to be further rewarded with a gold sovereign from the ship's chest as a mark of gratitude from the owners." He handed Billy the heavy gold coin. The boy's blush could have lit up a harbor. With a grin on his face he advised Starkey to punch a hole in the coin and wear it about his neck before his new mates went to borrowing it now and then for groceries. The crew laughed and a call went up from the back. "Three cheers for our new Tuna, Able Seaman Starkey. God bless him as a true friend, a trusted mate, and a bad hand at cards." The crew cheered and laughed, and Billy Starkey almost exploded with pride as two of the crew lifted him to their shoulders and semi-ceremoniously carried him forward to his new home with them in "the shudders" before the mast.

Lady Yee was very pleased by the news, but she could not hide how ill she looked or felt. Li-Lee finally went to Captain Hammond and informed him, against her mistress's wishes, that she feared Lady Yee was developing a high fever. The captain immediately went to his wife, and like a yearling retriever, young Billy attached himself to his captain as a personal runner. He even slept outside the cabin door so the captain could continue with ship's business or any special needs without being disturbed beyond having a note from the sailing master slipped under the cabin door.

For his part, Captain Hammond sat by his wife

for the better part of three days and nights. She was unconscious most of the time, and it was a trial to ensure that she consumed as much fresh water as possible. The captain administered the standard complement of medicines called for in cases of high fever, but neither he nor Li-Lee could speak to a cause for the problem. The captain decided to employ some medicines that his wife had taught him to prepare. She always traveled with a chest of medicinal staples, such as the bark of various trees, the dried berries of numerous plants, and all manner of herbs, ointments, and tinctures. She had even added labels in English for her husband's convenience. While Billy dashed about the ship like a powder monkey under fire to retrieve whatever was needed from ship's stores or the galley, the captain, Li-Lee, and the cook Ah Chu, who was well practiced at such things, double-boiled and distilled water to brew the appropriate ingredients, then strained the mixture, let it cool, and mixed it with a dash of fresh citrus juice. Whenever opportunity allowed, they gently spooned the concoction into the patient's mouth and prayed for her relief.

There was no question that Captain Hammond feared for his wife's health, as did the rest of the ship's company. And there were moments when he thought she was slipping away and began to suffer the pangs of an insufferable remorse. If

Lady Yee died, it would be his fault, and beyond that his only horizon would be interminable grief. But even during the worst of her battle there remained an unquenchable ember of strength and endurance that refused to be extinguished. He could see it in her eyes whenever she came out of her stupor. She would notice her husband seated next to her berth, smile slightly, and pat his hand to comfort him, then drift off again into a world of shadows. Sometimes, late at night, Captain Hammond could even hear Billy outside the cabin door gently weeping, then saying prayers imploring mercy and grace for Lady Yee. The captain learned to like the boy more and more for his earnest devotion to Lady Yee.

On the evening of the fourth day, Lady Yee's fever broke, and though she said she was feeling slightly better, she remained very weak. Her husband had spent every possible moment, while not on duty, sitting by her side and applying cold compresses to her head and face. He hadn't enjoyed much sleep, and in fact looked more haggard than she did. Being most solicitous of her emotional health as well, he had decided not to stress matters by mentioning the incident that had led to her injury. Husband or not, he was still captain of his ship, and he had every reason to expect his orders to be obeyed. She should have stayed strapped in her berth as he instructed. But he kenneled those criticisms in light of her condition, and determined not to mention them again.

A few days later, when she could hold her voice without stress, Lady Yee squeezed her husband's hand for reassurance and spoke as though she knew exactly what he'd been thinking. "You must not be too angry with me, Captain Hammond," she said. "I have no excuse to offer, of course. I disobeyed your orders and put others in jeopardy as a result of my actions. But by way of explanation, I can only say that it simply appeared that the need for my services forward overrode my better judgment in this case, and I'm truly sorry for it. And you can't fault young Starkey, for he has been my greatest help when dealing with the men's health. He's the one that cleans their wounds properly, changes their bandages, listens to their complaints without comment, feeds them, and then empties their chamber pots. He is going to make some woman a prize husband one day."

Captain Hammond stroked Lady Yee's pale hand, and smiled in turn. "Well, no soul alive could ever fault either of you for the depth of your compassion, my dear, or your dedicated sense of duty to our men, which I'm sure is always much appreciated. But what would have happened to us all if we had lost you over the side like an old coil of tarred rope?" Hammond half laughed to himself. "As far as this crew is concerned, you're more indispensable than I am. They would have gone into deep mourning if you had so much as broken your little finger. Though I suspect they are aware already, I haven't let them know anything officially concerning the extent of your injuries, or your subsequent fever." The captain laughed. "Principally out of fear of mass mutiny. I can only hope that you won't break the spell by showing yourself on deck just yet. It would sadden and dishearten the men to see you so bruised about the face. Your beauty is something they take great pride in, my dear, and brag about. It is part of the joss of this ship to them."

Lady Yee ceased smiling and pinned her husband's gaze. "My dear husband, that's not quite what I meant when I said that I had inadvertently put others in jeopardy. There was also present an innocent soul that I haven't yet mentioned, but who had the most to lose from my lack of self-discipline and forethought."

Captain Hammond looked confused for a moment, and then thought perhaps Lady Yee was pulling his leg to lighten the mood. "I do hope you are not referring to that half-mad savant Ah Chu you hired as our cook. Or your Li-Lee who swears she's born of Mongol royalty and always demands more respect and fermented mare's milk. For the sake of heaven, where does one find ready supplies of fermented mare's milk in the middle of the Pacific Ocean?"

Lady Yee laughed slightly, and appreciated her

husband's attempt to hobble the tension, but she also felt obliged to tell him the truth. "No, in point of fact I jeopardized the life of our child, little Macy."

There was a serious interval when Captain Hammond looked as though he had just been coldcocked with a belaying pin. His eyes almost rolled up into his head, and for a few moments he was the one with serious vertigo. When he regained his power of speech, the first thing he said was tinged with incredulous emphasis. "We are going to have a child? Are you serious, my dearest girl?" The future father blinked like a toad on a hot rock. "And you have already given our little blessing a name? I suppose you already know whether it will be a boy or a girl."

Lady Yee grinned to reflect a private insight. "Macy will be a girl, a very intelligent and talented girl. And she will help care for the son that is to come next. Trust me. A mother needs all the help she can get raising a little boy, and an older sister makes a perfect foil and proctor. Besides, Macy is a reasonable name for either a boy or a girl. But as it stands, I'll wager my finest black pearl that the first to arrive will be a girl, and what's more she will look just like you, and without doubt she will grow to become the love of your life."

When she looked up at her husband, Lady Yee suddenly witnessed something that she never thought she would ever live to see. Though he smiled with the angelic sweetness of a child, a cascade of fat tears came streaming down the captain's face and dripped on the counterpane. Lady Yee reached up and wiped away his tears with her handkerchief. "I sincerely hope, my dearest friend," she said with a wan sarcastic smile, "that this is not how you're going to behave every time I announce that we are going to have a child . . . At the very least you'd stand to hazard all credibility with your crew as the insensate, raw-boned Yankee swashbuckling martinet that they have come to love and respect. And more pointedly, if you do stake a habit of wandering about the decks weeping like a lost child, the men will commit you to an institution just to save their own investments."

The stunned future father gave forth with an embarrassed and deeply self-conscious grin. He slowly wiped away his remaining tears with his sleeve. "I'm afraid, my dear Lady Yee, you'll have to take this old martinet just the way you find him. But you should count yourself fortunate that I kept my emotions in check the day we were married. For even then I felt these same torrents of joy when you parted your veil, and I suddenly realized that I was about to be wed to the most beautiful and brilliant creature I had ever known. But now to know you are physically sound and will also present us with a child, you might be asking for a bit more self-control than even a Yankee barbarian might be expected to display."

With this last sentiment Hammond drew his wife's hand to his lips and kissed her fingers. After a moment, he leaned forward and kissed her brow.

"Becoming your husband is possibly the only truly enlightened thing I have ever done." Then he paused as a thought occurred to him, and a look of mild surprise brightened his expression. "I can't imagine what our crew is going to get up to when they find out. I'll be fortunate if they don't toss me to the tuna and then make you captain."

Lady Yee smiled at the compliment. "But there is really no need for them to find out anything just yet. So far, the only people who know are you and I, and my maid."

Captain Hammond laughed. "My dear girl, you've been at sea long enough to know that there are no such things as secrets aboard a ship. And if Li-Lee knows, then you can bet Ah Chu knows, and if he knows, then I can almost guarantee that the whole crew will know all about it by three bells tomorrow, if not sooner."

And so it came to pass just as Captain Hammond said it would. Though no one mentioned a word within the captain's hearing, of course, the crew's conduct spoke of its knowledge. The first thing the prospective father noticed was how quiet the ship had become.

Suddenly there was no shouting of orders, and the men working in the rigging signaled each other with whistles and hand gestures. Some top man who was on duty in the crow's nest even invented a way of getting the attention of the deck officer by throwing down a bolt washer tied with a long strip of red flannel and blowing a single note on a bosun's whistle while it fell to deck. Once contact was made, the man in the crow's nest indicated the bearing and distance to his sighting with hand signals. By common understanding, the crew even agreed to avoid the stern of the ship so that Lady Yee would not be bothered by their footsteps and voices overhead. They also assigned one man on each watch to tend a stout trolling line deep off the port beam in the hope of hooking a fat tuna or dolphin fish for her table. Even the ship's cook, Mr. Gill, set aside his professional bias and made sure Lady Yee's chef had the first choice of any fresh fruits and vegetables that remained on board, and in gratitude Lady Yee's cook taught Mr. Gill how to make Chinese noodles and dumplings, which the crew heartily enjoyed as an alternative to potatoes and broth-soaked hardtack.

The captain and crew were reminded daily of their recent ordeal. They were cued to the memory by the incredible amount of flotsam and debris they spied floating on the passing swells. They identified parts of ships as well as parts of houses. At one location they passed a whole tree with two dead monkeys still clinging to the broken branches. They spotted a few bloated corpses of animals and people floating amid miles of drifting debris of every description. It was like the whole world had been torn to small pieces and scattered over the ocean. Then there'd be nothing for two hundred miles or so, and then another floating field of wreckage with different hints as to its origin would cross the bow. The lookout spotted four broken ships adrift. Two were swamped to the gunwales, one was broken clean in half with the bow and stern still sticking out of the waves, and one large ship was found completely capsized. None showed the slightest sign of survivors, but squadrons of sharks were easily spotted from the crow's nest as they patrolled the litter of ship's wreckage that floated around each broken hull. But Captain Hammond was most surprised by small islands of shattered vegetation so far from any shore. One afternoon they came across just such a patch of floating greenery. A small flock of yellow finches had taken refuge in the branches of a shattered tree drifting among the vegetation. The moment *The Silver Lotus* came close the birds deserted their temporary refuge for the more substantial safety of the ship. The men were charmed and fed them breadcrumbs, broken grain, and fresh water, and the birds rewarded their generosity by tamely taking food from their hands and perching on their shoulders and caps. Three days later, as the ship slowly approached the northwest of the Hawaiian Island chain, all the birds save one took their leave and flew off. The remaining bird seemed quite content with its present company and decided to stay, so the cook created a lovely little cage from green bamboo, and the crew presented the bird to Lady Yee as a memento of their mutual good fortune in surviving the monsoon. Because Lady Yee had always enjoyed a Chinese fondness for songbirds, she was most touched by the gift and kept the bird close by her. She named it Joss, and it soon became so tame that it spent most of its time perched on Lady Yee's shoulder.

Captain Hammond had insisted that his wife stay in bed until a proper doctor could be consulted. He worried that she might have sustained internal injuries and was unwilling to let her move about the ship until a full diagnosis could be made. However, he came to visit often through the days, and brought her every bit of news, including the fact that they had rescued a lone Dutch sailor who was found adrift in a shattered lifeboat from one of the lost ships. He was near death when they found him and was as yet unable to talk.

Two days later the lookout reported sighting the leeward islands of the Hawaiian chain off the starboard quarter. The next evening Kauai and

Molokai came close into view, and the next morning Maui and Hawaii appeared out of the mists. And by six that evening, Captain Hammond's injured crewmen were being cared for at the merchant marine infirmary in Pearl Harbor.

7

LADY YEE and her baby were another case altogether. The captain sought out the best physician he could find and paid him a bounty to come aboard ship to examine his wife. If she needed better care ashore, he would have her taken to the best hospital on the island.

Happily, the doctor told Captain Hammond that he believed Lady Yee was on the mend, and he didn't think that the fetus had suffered any injury, for he discerned a small but steady heartbeat in that quadrant. Nonetheless, the doctor said that Lady Yee needed a few weeks ashore to recover her strength. He said her health required fresh foods, springwater, plenty of fruit, sunshine, and rest. He smiled knowingly, and suggested that her condition required care in the future, but as far as he could tell she had not suffered any serious internal damage, and her other injuries were healing very nicely thanks to the care of her maid.

The doctor felt obliged to use his influence and connections to help the captain find a pleasant cottage to rent in the cooler mountain air. He also arranged for servants to take care of their needs while ashore. Lady Yee was so overjoyed by the prospect of a real bed that Captain Hammond arranged for everything at once.

The ship was another matter. Having nothing

perishable in the sealed holds, the captain decided to apply for an anchorage in the harbor for one month. Keeping only a rotating maintenance crew aboard, he allowed his other men time ashore and kept them all on full sea pay as a sign of his gratitude for their efforts during the storms. The injured men were doing as well as could be expected, and only one of them remained in hospital. However, their spirits were buoyed by constant presents of fruit, fresh pork, and beer sent aboard the ship as gifts from Lady Yee.

With his wife resting in the cooling breezes of a tropical veranda, Captain Hammond decided to visit the mercantile exchange. He was anxious to have more news from the East since the monsoon. He knew that an extensive interruption in trade, or destruction of sources, would drive up the prices of some goods from Asia. Rubber, copra, tea, palm oil, teakwood, nutmeg, and other spices sometimes sold for many times their original purchase prices. And luxury goods requiring great labor and expensive materials, or of fashionable antiquity, often did even better. The auction prices offered at the Hawaiian/American exchange, where information from the western Pacific would be freshest, could indicate what prices to expect in the futures markets of San Francisco, Seattle, or even Mexico.

The captain visited the exchange every other afternoon and made friends with the brokers. He was affable to all, treated some to coffee and cigars, and listened carefully to everything said in his presence. He also made a point of seeking out the Chinese traders on the island, as they maintained their own exchange. When the captain let it be known that he was the son-in-law of the renowned Master Yee of Canton, all doors were thrown open to him. He was told details of the extent of the monsoon disaster that none of the other traders knew. These canny old Chinese factors, who were as sharp as pins, were presently busy buying up certain goods in bulk before word spread about possible future shortages. They politely inquired what the captain was carrying in his holds, and whether he was interested in selling any portion of his cargo in Hawaii. His responses were very polite, of course, but he revealed as little as possible, just as his hosts expected of a son-in-law of the cunning Master Yee.

Nevertheless, making the acquaintance and gaining the trust of various important Chinese traders brought forth unexpected bounties. To begin with, when these venerable gentlemen discovered that Lady Yee was indeed on the island, and recovering from a dangerous mishap at sea during the height of the monsoon, they began to send along an endless train of exotic flowers, candied fruits, rare teas, expensive Chinese medicines, silk pillows stuffed with fragrant herbs, and all manner of Chinese confections. One very rich old gentleman, who claimed to have known Master Yee in Canton, sent over his prize chef to help her own cook prepare special meals for Lady Yee. He had received instructions to purchase the best of everything necessary to guarantee a healthful diet for as long as Lady Yee remained on the island. But his efforts almost proved unnecessary. So as not to be outdone, when word got out, all the trade barons sent along handsome letters of condolence, and politely appealed for permission to visit her in person if matters permitted. And still more gifts kept arriving each day. Fresh fish, dressed duck, freshly butchered and cleaned chickens, live crabs, shellfish, sweet Chinese sausage, the finest polished rice, and Chinese vegetables only hours from the soil were delivered with daily regularity. Captain Hammond swore to his wife that he'd never eaten better.

One fastidious old trader, hoping to ensure favor from Canton, even personally delivered a whole suckling pig, roasted in caked salt and stuffed with coriander and almond-flavored pineapple. Lady Yee, who ate little meat, thanked the gentleman with great sincerity, but then had the gift secretly sent along, with her compliments, to the men working aboard *The Silver Lotus*. She also sent along a two-pound tin of the best Virginia tobacco her husband could find. Since the watch crews were also laboring to effect necessary repairs to the ship, the captain thought the gift appropriate to their efforts, but he also sent along a butt of locally brewed beer and baskets of fresh baked bread so the crew wouldn't immediately switch their allegiance to his wife and beach him for crimes of sentimental insufficiency.

The Chinese merchants also gifted the captain with secret trading connections in the western Americas that were heretofore unknown to Yankee shipping princes. In effect, the Chinese merchants abroad ran their own separate economy under the very noses of governments powerless to regulate exports deemed of no value, and imports supposedly only valued by a poor minority population. In reality, both markets were priceless to the wealthy elite of both East and West, and in particular those brokers who set the prices. Captain Hammond, because of his privileged relationship with Master Yee, was presented with introductions to the very agents in America who would ultimately secure and increase his wealth for the next ten years. He gilded his reputation and honored his Chinese benefactors by never divulging their confidences to anyone except his business partner, Lady Yee. She would become his guarantee as well as his credential when it came to dealing with Chinese trading companies in foreign ports. The most prominent among these in America were agents for a San Francisco conglomerate with the mysterious title of the

Three Corporations. Besides being the richest Chinese businessmen in America, they were the largest labor brokers in the country, and as such, closely associated with western railroads and public works in six states.

Five weeks to the day after anchoring in Hawaii, *The Silver Lotus* sailed on for Oregon and California. Health had been restored, damage repaired, paint freshened, and spirits renewed all around. The ship enjoyed steady winds and strong currents flowing east-northeast. Best of all, Lady Yee showed herself in excellent health, only slightly larger in the midriff, and even this would have gone unnoticed beneath her robes.

The crew's gratitude for all they had enjoyed while in port was focused on Lady Yee. Captain Hammond paid their wages and commanded the ship, and in all things maritime he was a highly respected figure of authority. But as far as the crew was concerned, it was Lady Yee who commanded their hearts. They remembered every little kindness and gift that she had bestowed, as well as her selfless attention to their health and well-being. She became a symbol of their good fortune, and there wasn't one among them who wouldn't have sacrificed their last breath in her defense. Captain Hammond told his sailing master that Lady Yee had inadvertently created the best-behaved ship's crew ever conceived of, but that it had to be seen to be believed, as no other blue-water captain would credit the story on good faith alone.

Their first destination was Portland, Oregon, where Captain Hammond took on supplies and made arrangements for his ship to return to the yards to be refitted with an auxiliary diesel engine, and then modified for the lumber trade. The sailing master would return to Portland with the ship in two months and supervise the refit.

The next port of call was San Francisco. Here the captain housed his wife in the very best accommodations, and then paid court to various Chinese businessmen to whom he carried introductions. They helped him to find secure warehousing for his own cargo, and even purchased the crew's portion of goods at a very handsome price.

On their second night in San Francisco, as they sat down to a lovely supper for the first time in weeks, Lady Yee decided it was time to remind her husband that there was a new captain expected on deck in about seven months, give or take a few days. He sat back in his chair and stared off into the distance. After a silent interval he came down to earth again, looked at his beautiful wife, and said, "You know, I must thank you again, dearest lady, for such an inspiring gift." He did point out, however, that her happy, heaven-sent condition precluded any further journeys by sea for several years to come, if ever. That being the case, he asked her where she would like to live and raise her children. He confidently assured her that their present circumstances would allow her to choose a fine mansion anywhere in San Francisco, or all of California for that matter, and she might employ as many servants as she pleased.

Lady Yee acknowledged her husband's generosity, but she said that she preferred to live with him, even if that meant sailing away again. The captain laughed and said he had no intention of sailing away and leaving her behind. He had more than enough capital to trade on his own behalf without going back to sea for quite a while. And, barring ill fortune, *The Silver Lotus* would continue to realize decent profits for a few years to come. By any measure one cared to use, they were wealthy enough now to retire from business altogether if she so pleased.

The captain's wife smiled and declared that she would never allow her husband to sacrifice anything that gave him real pleasure, but children, she said, rarely make such allowances, and are selfishly prone to favor the presence of both parents. Captain Hammond promised to fulfill his role as a confused parent as soon as Lady Yee was pleased to make delivery. Until then, he suggested they find a fitting place to live before they were forced to emulate Joseph and Mary.

Lady Yee had no idea what he was referring to, but she smiled and suggested there was no reason to search for something they already possessed. She said the house in Monterey served their purposes directly, and they presently warehoused enough handcrafted furnishings to dress the place out ten times over. She bolstered her suggestion by saying that after their child was born, they could move on if the captain wished to. But for the moment, Lady Yee, who professed to dislike the abiding filth, noise, and constant bustle of city life, pleaded for the serenity of a small town, the peaceful refuge of her own gardens, and the salubrious influence of gentle ocean breezes. Captain Hammond, who had long since surrendered all instincts to say no to anything his wife suggested, immediately saw the logic in her thinking, and promised to make all the necessary arrangements at once.

The day after *The Silver Lotus* was dispatched back to Portland for her refit, Captain Hammond, his wife, her maid, and her cook left San Francisco by train. They arrived at the depot in Monterey that same evening. The captain had wired ahead to his bank to say he was returning to live in his house. He requested that the bank use its good offices to hire a wagon and two strong men to meet them at the depot. The captain had removed all their possessions from the ship before it sailed, and was surprised to find that their property in total filled eight packing crates and four hundred-gallon barrels. Their personal luggage was another matter, and ultimately required the services of a mule cart, along with a surrey to carry the household.

Considering the scale of his deposits, and the chances of ingratiating themselves into further financial considerations, the captain's Monterey bank sent along one of its clerks to see to it that its client's requirements were satisfied in a timely fashion. His name was Jacob Oaks. He was twenty-three and almost at once he became totally enthralled with the house of Hammond. It was young Oaks who accidently gave rise to the undying rumor that Captain Hammond was married to a very wealthy Chinese princess of the old imperial household. What Mr. Oaks had in fact said was that Captain Hammond was married to a beautiful Chinese woman who looked like a rich fairy-tale princess. Still and all, once the rumor clicked over a couple of times, the engine started right up and continued humming along, gathering momentum all on its own. Soon Lady Yee discovered that nothing she could do or say would convince people that she wasn't in the least respect related to any imperial family and, despite her husband's acts to the contrary, she wasn't a princess of anything larger than her household, and her father was only the emperor of six warehouses and three loading piers in Canton.

But the rumor only dug in its heels with denial. As it passed from one to another, and possibly challenged by a listener, people would simply say that Lady Yee was a person of infinite modesty and decorum, and a person that would never have allowed address as a titled personage in America. And still, no matter what Lady Yee did to disabuse people of this absurd story, it continued on, though part of the problem could be laid at her husband's door. His insistence on always referring to his wife as Lady Yee cemented the general belief that she must be of royal blood. Still, it was Lady Yee's serene, sophisticated, and regal deportment, plus her facility with foreign languages, which locked down the community consensus that Monterey was now home to an authentic Chinese princess. The fact that her husband was a wealthy, handsome, and dashing sea captain only enhanced the romantic image they had come to prefer. To the local population, whose middle-class tastes defiantly leaned toward the romantic side of periodical fiction, the Hammonds were like exotic characters that might have been invented by Thackeray, Brontë, or Hawthorne.

Lady Yee, however, found the whole business personally and culturally very distressing, and more like a bizarre Lewis Carroll fantasy than anything else. On the one hand the Americans treated the local Chinese very poorly, and generally thought of them as little better than beasts of burden, whereas she was always regarded with the greatest deference and respect. It took Captain Hammond to point out that in China, as well as most other parts of Asia, clan and family provided the vehicle to success and the paths to power, but in America it was only wealth. In America, any fool could rise to prominence with only one dubious credential to his or her name: stacks and stacks of greenback dollars. The captain impressed on Lady Yee the understanding that money was the American god, the American philosophy, and the American creed all in one, and that people high and low bowed to its majesty. He told Lady Yee that it was her wealth that truly instigated people's respect. If she were truly poor, whether Oriental or Occidental, no one would have bothered giving her the time of day, and her beauty would have only been an invitation to men of dark purposes.

Though she had always been taught that this was possibly true about most Yankees, Lady Yee took special note of her husband's particular lesson, principally because it seemed to interlock in an odd way with her father's favorite dictum that every disadvantage could be made to serve a good purpose if one didn't take the circumstances too personally. He had once told her that what people believed to be the truth, despite all evidence to the contrary, remained the truth in their eyes, and it was possible to make this work to one's own advantage.

By way of example, he told his daughter the story of a poor Taoist monk who was famous for his compassion, generosity of spirit, and good works. As it happened, there was another man in the next province who carried exactly the same name, but who made his way through the world as a vicious bandit and murderer. Somehow a rumor got started that the two men were one and the same. Despite the rumor's complete and total implausibility, when the story became widespread, the authorities decided to investigate. When they discovered that the connection between the two men was indeed only a name, and broadly published this fact, it did nothing to hobble the groundless speculation that the kindly monk was in fact a truly dangerous and cunning villain who had even fooled the authorities.

The poor modest little monk was so distressed by this turn of events that he even entertained thoughts of suicide to clear his name, that is, until one day when he noticed something odd. Now when he went about begging for money to help the poor, people had a marked tendency to be far more respectful and generous than they had been before the ridiculous story had taken root.

Of course, they all called him the "bandit monk" behind his back, a pointless slander he was well aware of, but with the funds he raised over the years, he built three hospitals for the poor, endowed a temple and residence for the

Taoist nuns who worked in the hospitals, and with the help of a rich and enlightened (if somewhat fearful) patron, built a medical school and sanitarium dedicated to the study of mental disorders and madness. Later in life the little monk would laugh and confess that, taken altogether, if it hadn't been for the confusion surrounding his name, none of what he'd accomplished over the years would have been possible.

Like the Taoist monk, Lady Yee became determined to make use of her situation. It seemed, the captain observed, that all of Monterey really needed and wanted a rich, beautiful, and secretive Chinese princess living in their midst and, barring all apparent reality, or cogent arguments to the contrary, that Lady Yee had drawn the short straw. She would have to make the best of things as they lay. And though he was much amused, the captain was in no way surprised when he discovered not only to what purpose Lady Yee had used her disadvantage, but how she had augmented this now popular image in the very subtlest of ways to better serve her own purposes.

ALL SUCH PETTY nonsense thankfully melted into the background as California prepared to celebrate what was hoped to be the birth of a new and prosperous century. Everyone had something to say about the portents of the year 1900.

As usual, there were always those of morbid and pessimistic predilections who foretold the end of the world for any number of moral or biblical reasons, but for the most part people ignored all that with their own plans for elaborate festivities to celebrate the future greatness of their state in a grand style. Every civic ladies' club, fraternal organization, local Grange, state college alumni association, firehouse marshal, and military veterans' group of every ilk and conflict had realigned its entire focus toward celebrating a lucrative future.

With this distraction in mind, Captain Hammond decided to introduce himself to, and ingratiate himself with, the town fathers, and do so in the best possible circumstances. Thus Captain Hammond, using Lady Yee's best testamentary and calligraphically artistic skills, wrote and arranged to have his Chinese connections in San Francisco send him six hundred pounds of assorted fireworks and rockets, all of the best quality. These crates he had delivered free of charge to the mayor and city council of Monterey, but in care of the sheriff's office. For reasons of safety and security, the captain just assumed the sheriff would know how to keep such a potentially dangerous cargo out of harm's way. A few days after the shipment arrived by train, Captain Hammond received an elaborately stylized letter of gratitude from the mayor on behalf of the citizens of Monterey. It was cosigned by every member of the city council as well as the sheriff, and came with an invitation to be the honored guest to light the very first fuse on the appointed night.

This invitation pleased Lady Yee, for being Chinese she well understood the intricate language of fireworks, and the spiritual connotations and purposes behind every cluster, arrangement, and color. And though she was quite sure the locals would follow their own agenda in such matters, fond as they were of deafening brass bands, thunderous bass drums, and crashing cymbals, Lady Yee would still enjoy the fireworks and chrysanthemum rockets for their own sake. Her father, Master Yee, had always employed a professional display team to celebrate her birthday every year, so it was something of a family tradition. Captain Hammond happily kept up the practice, though on a more modest scale when they were at sea.

Amid all this local backslapping, toasting, planning, and organizing, and while she was well into her fifth month of pregnancy, Captain Hammond began to notice that something very strange and eerily unique had begun to influence Lady Yee's insights. She just blushed in a maternal fashion, and said she assumed it had something to do with her condition, but the good captain, being of ancient New England stock, was just superstitious enough to believe that his wife was now possessed of a mysterious, and potentially disquieting, ability. He listened in rapt amazement as she would solve complex problems out of thin air, and with little or no information to guide her to a solution. Soon nothing in the house could be lost or misplaced for long. It was most remarkable, but she always knew where everything was, no matter how improbable the item or location, or whether she'd seen it or not in the past. It was most disconcerting for the captain to come to terms with the knowledge that his wife even knew how much money he carried in his wallet, and whether a sock—hidden by a boot—had a hole in it.

Then one day in late November, Lady Yee read in the newspaper about a man whose body had been found floating in the bay off Moss Landing, and despite the indisputable fact that the man had drowned, he was discovered wearing a rope with a hangman's knot around his neck. However, there were no medical signs to indicate that the dead man had ever hung from the rope. The police were confused and unable to categorize the incident one way or the other.

Lady Yee handed the short article to her husband to read, and when he'd finished a few moments later, he looked up to see his wife nodding as if she knew the answer, and she did. She calmly told the captain that the man had been murdered on his wife's orders for habitual infidelity. She also believed there was substantial money involved. Captain Hammond raised a brow and nodded indulgently as though this kind of behavior was an everyday occurrence, which was true. Then, like any number of strange things that had happened of late, he forgot all about it, and went back to his accounts.

Two weeks later the same newspaper printed another article that stated the police were actively searching for the whereabouts of one Mrs. Moira Blackrock on suspicion of commissioning the murder of her husband, whose body was lately discovered floating unceremoniously in Monterey Bay. The reporter stated that the police believed the motive was revenge for infidelity and the proceeds of a life insurance policy worth five thousand dollars. The paid assassin had been apprehended after bragging to a prostitute that his was the more lucrative line of work, as he had just been promised twenty-five hundred dollars for ten minutes' labor. Afterward, without mentioning the murder, he complained of not getting paid for his services. The prostitute, knowing that Moira Blackrock had been an acquaintance of her client, and that her husband was missing, put the parts together and went to the police with her suspicions.

When the captain, now quite surprised by the outcome, went to Lady Yee with the article, she couldn't remember anything about it. She didn't even recall reading the original gazette entry. And then later that same day, when a broker acquaintance in San Francisco wired Captain Hammond with an offer to sell a healthy block of railroad shares that were going up in price all the time, Lady Yee calmly told her husband to wait until after news of the scandal had spread, for the prices of the shares would most certainly come down.

When the captain asked what scandal she meant, she responded with the news that one of the directors of the railroad had embezzled considerable funds from the company and had run off to Brazil with the wife of a state senator.

The captain, who by custom read financial periodicals religiously, had not scanned the least breath of scandal from that quarter. Since Lady Yee could not quite remember where she had obtained the information, the captain let the matter slide by without comment. Still and all, taking past experience to heart, he made no move to buy the offered shares. Ten days later all the papers put out banner headlines reporting the fraud of the decade. The particulars of the crime were just as Lady Yee had said they would be, but by then she had forgotten all about it. The next day Captain Hammond picked up the very same shares for a fraction of the price first quoted. He didn't bother mentioning this to his wife on the plausible assumption that she'd probably known all about it before he made the purchase.

Even for a town as small as Monterey, the new century was celebrated with spectacular enthusiasm and expense. There were dress balls being hosted by all manner of organizations, and fiesta-like celebrations where food and drink were the primary focus, but all was handsomely plumed at midnight by a spectacular fireworks display launched from Lover's Point under the supervision of the police department, and a nice little Chinese gentleman the captain had hired from San Francisco to supervise the display. His name was Mr. Cheng Na Wa, and his clan had been making fireworks displays for five centuries.

It was said by some that Monterey County didn't sober up for a week, but that wasn't true in the least. The Methodist population of Pacific Grove held some odds on sobriety, which kept a balance, but the majority of people were too short of funds to celebrate that seriously, unless the spirits consumed were homemade, which was more common than one might suppose. Everybody else just went back to work the next day and talked about the fireworks, and how strange all the rich folks looked and behaved.

As the weeks rolled by and the fetus grew larger, so did Lady Yee's sense of perception, and ultimately prognostication. One day she insisted that her husband not take the train to San Jose on business. He bowed to her wishes grudgingly but was impressed and relieved when he heard that the Salinas River rail bridge had collapsed that same day. Recent heavy rains had scoured away so much supporting soil that the bridge simply collapsed on its own. Happily, no one was hurt because the train the captain would have occupied was late leaving Monterey due to a slight labor malfunction. It was reported that the brakeman had been found drunk and disorderly at his post, and was replaced with a crewman from another train. The captain visualized an inebriated brakeman and a weakened bridge and immediately went to his wife and thanked her for the timely warning. She again claimed to have no idea what he was talking about, so again he let the matter drop.

Captain Hammond was not a man easily intimidated or disoriented by unexpected events, but his pregnant wife's newfound clairvoyance and subsequent lack of recall were beginning to make him truly uncomfortable. He worried about her health, and at times even her sanity seemed in question. But there always remained the cloying reality that, recalled or not, she was always disinterested and always correct, and wherein could one possibly find fault with that?

One day matters came to a head when a telegram arrived from the sailing master of *The*

Silver Lotus. It was a truly sad communication that spoke of the death of Able Seaman Billy Starkey, who, by all appearances, had fallen overboard sometime after the refurbished ship had set out for trials. A passing trawler found his body two days later. The message said that the boy's papers and personal effects had been sent on for Captain Hammond to sort through and send on to his relatives. It also affirmed that Hammond & Yee owed Starkey 168 dollars in wages, and a death-at-sea bounty of two hundred dollars payable to his heirs. His grandmother's address was included in the message.

The captain decided not to tell Lady Yee about Billy's death, as the boy had always been a great favorite in her considerations. And knowing the stress she was already under with her first child, the soon-to-be father chose the lesser of two evils and remained silent. But one day when the captain was away on business in town, a Wells Fargo freight wagon delivered a common sea chest. It was addressed to Captain Hammond, but the name carved into the wooden lid was that of Billy Starkey, and below that was carved the name of the ship, *The Silver Lotus*.

Lady Yee had no compunction about opening the chest. She knew the moment it came through the door that death lingered in its presence. A covering letter from the sailing master explained the cause of death and the circumstances surrounding the accident. But after examining the contents of the chest only superficially, Lady Yee knew instinctually that the covering letter, though hardly an attempt to manipulate the facts, was incorrect in several particulars.

Later that afternoon, when the captain returned home, Lady Yee took him aside, showed him the sea chest and the letter, and discussed the matter with him. The captain was surprised to find his wife very calm and methodical. She told him that, in spite of all the evidence indicating an accident, young Billy had ended his own life by leaping overboard when no one was watching. Lady Yee acknowledged that it was an act of willful self-destruction, to be sure, but one with brassbound motives for a poor unsophisticated sapling of twenty who'd been at sea since he was eleven years old.

When her husband patiently asked what had led her to believe this to be the case, Lady Yee showed him a photograph of a man and woman standing behind three children. Billy could be identified as the oldest child. There was a black mourning ribbon affixed around the corner of the picture, and a note on the back indicating a date eight months prior. A card of condolence from the funeral home came attached to a newspaper obituary that mourned the passing of Mr. and Mrs. Starkey and their two youngest children from the ravages of a typhoid epidemic that took twelve lives in Pine Island Cove, Massachusetts. Then Lady Yee brought forth a poorly written letter from a girl in New Bedford telling of her upcoming nuptials to Billy's cousin, Stanhope Starkey, and hoping that Billy would understand that she didn't feel right about waiting for him to return any longer. And lastly, Lady Yee showed her husband a large vial of mercury pills prescribed by a French doctor in Pondicherry for an undisclosed ailment. However, it took little imagination to deduce just what that ailment might be. In Asia, at least, such a dangerous prescriptive could only indicate symptoms of syphilis, leprosy, or worse, in any event mortal diseases that were, despite exotic and dangerous medications, incurable in the main, and spiritually debilitating to endure. Even Lady Yee confessed that she would choose poison over lingering decay and madness, and so she saw no reason why Billy should not choose a more dignified departure for himself as well. She encouraged her husband to imagine the shame, humiliation, and sense of loss that must have inspired such a deed, and then to employ compassion. She suggested that the pills and the girl's letter be removed before the chest was sent on to Billy's grandmother. She also suggested that a personal letter of condolence from the boy's captain would go a long way toward softening the blow for other relatives, and she was sure Billy's back pay and bounty would be well received. Her husband agreed with everything and, for Lady Yee's sake, he had a bank draft drawn up for five hundred dollars, which he included with his own letter. These he placed in the sea chest before it was secured and sent east by special freight.

Six weeks later a packet arrived for Captain Hammond. Inside was a note from his sailing master saying that the enclosed letter had been discovered under Starkey's berth only recently. The sealed envelope was marked for Captain Hammond, but there was no address, which seemed to indicate that when the time came, the missive was to be delivered by hand. When the captain opened the envelope he found a short letter written in pencil. In it Billy sincerely apologized to his captain for deserting the ship without notice. He hoped Captain Hammond would not see this as a reflection on his command or a result of any dissatisfaction. Rather, Billy pleaded that the recent passing of his family, and his own rapidly failing health, left him with little choice but to leave the ship without notice. He said he realized that in doing so he forfeited all rights to back salary, but that couldn't be helped under the circumstances, and he said he harbored no ill will as a result. Besides, he said, the money was too little to do him much good where he was going. In closing, Billy especially asked to be remembered to Lady Yee as a person he regarded with the greatest respect and affection. He requested that the included gift be passed on to her as a token of fond remembrance and loyalty. The article, wrapped in old tissue paper, turned out to be Billy's cap ribbon, with the name of the ship printed in silver paint. Billy, like all sailors, preferred dressing well when ashore, and he always wore his cap ribbon with pride.

It only took a moment for the captain to decide not to show Lady Yee the letter just yet, if at all. And since it was certain that time would hardly alter matters, he felt it could easily wait until after she had delivered her child, and had happier things to contemplate. And yet he couldn't help but be deeply impressed with his wife's powers of deduction, and her ability to sense the truth of a situation even at a distance. She had always been an insightful person, but with the advance of her pregnancy she had become downright clairvoyant, and that, he could confidently presume, would present its own set of difficulties in time.

8

LADY YEE at last gave birth to a beautiful baby girl who, in spite of inheriting her father's blue-gray eyes, auburn-blond hair, and sardonic smile, was the very image of her mother. Captain Hammond wandered around with a stupid grin on his face for days. He fell instantly in love with his new daughter and was hardly surprised when Lady Yee introduced her as Macy Yee Hammond. She was so small and jewel-like that her father nicknamed her Wee-Yee by way of a bad Irish pun, and somehow the name stuck until she was four. Then one day she demanded to be called Macy and refused to answer to anything else.

Captain Hammond adored his baby daughter. He veritably doted on her whims, and took every opportunity to spend time entertaining her regardless of the game. It would be fair to say that Macy adored her father in turn. No matter what the cause of the tears, he could always make her laugh and smile. Sometimes he would take Macy for little adventures in the gardens, and Lady Yee would later discover them fast asleep on the grass in the shade like a couple of exhausted puppies.

There were several factors that helped to influence the captain's decision, of course, but one day while he and Lady Yee picnicked among the dunes of Del Monte overlooking the bay, which shimmered like blue steel, the captain told his wife that, after long deliberation and personal reflection, he had decided to retire from the sea altogether. Lady Yee was rather surprised by this offhand revelation since she had no idea her husband was even entertaining such thoughts. He went on to explain that he had recently been offered a very lucrative full partnership in a fine new Portland-built steamship. However, the arrangement was predicated on the proviso that he take full command of the vessel and manage the Asian trading relationships for at least five years. He said the arrangement was liberally generous with bonuses and bounties, and he could carry a portion of cargo under his own manifest. In all, the offer was extremely attractive.

Lady Yee fully expected her husband to immediately ask her opinion of the proposition, but he didn't. Instead, he just told her that he would never go to sea again on business, but the offer had inspired him to think about making a similar offer to his own sailing master, so he could reduce company costs and liabilities.

When Lady Yee, now somewhat taken aback by her husband's disclosure, asked what had motivated his decision, Captain Hammond hemmed and hawed and seemed shy about giving a direct answer. Then Lady Yee cocked one eyebrow, indicating the seriousness of her question, and again asked what had influenced his choice.

Captain Hammond rose from his place and paced for a moment trying to decide what to say. Just then little Macy came toddling into view a few feet ahead of the pursuing maid. She was a veritable bouquet of giggles and flapping arms, and she immediately ran up to her father and embraced his leg as if it were the trunk of a tree. Macy instinctually knew her father was safe ground, where nothing remotely unpleasant, like an impending bath, could get at her. She squeezed his leg and giggled away with the delight of an escaped fugitive. Captain Hammond shook his head and looked over at his wife with a perplexed expression. He felt like a fox caught between two dogs.

Then he glanced down at his beautiful daughter and smiled. After a moment he looked back to his wife and said he wasn't going back to sea again because Macy had said he couldn't. When his wife laughed and asked how long he'd been taking sailing orders from his daughter, Captain Hammond mocked wounded pride and declared that he had always listened to the best advice of his business partners. He reached into his breast pocket and withdrew an envelope with a flourish, and presented it to his wife.

Lady Yee read the enclosed document with surprise and smiled. Her husband, quite unbeknownst to her, had restructured their business to include a new partner. The company stationery now read Hammond, Macy & Yee. The captain picked up his bubbling, doe-eyed daughter, and mocking a stage whisper, told Macy that this was the first thing he'd done in years that her mother hadn't predicted beforehand. He said he felt rather good about that. With a chuckle, he openly surmised that perhaps his wife's prognostic tendencies were fading with the passing of time.

LADY YEE MADE A POINT of not going about the town in any social capacity, or to trade at the grocery and dry goods emporiums like the other women. She was astute enough to realize that her wealth was enough to admit entry, of course, but any attempt to fit into the common weave would most likely be misunderstood and frowned upon as being far too familiar for someone of her exalted station. For most of the people of Monterey, she was ever the mysterious, exotic, regal, and diffident Lady Yee, respected and even occasionally revered at a distance by the local citizenry. Rather than strain against the halter of social ignorance and biased mythology, Lady Yee suddenly realized a profound opportunity was now at her disposal. It was far easier to fulfill public expectations. If Monterey wanted to believe Lady Yee was some fairy-tale Chinese princess, swept off her feet and saved from some ancient barbarous practice by the dashing and handsome Captain Hammond, then so be it. If the good people of Monterey County wanted an aloof Chinese princess, then that's just what she would give them, Oriental imperiousness in spades.

Besides, Lady Yee immediately realized that she could affect far more by utilizing her financial prowess remotely through a third party, specifically a figure of her own invention. It was thus that the Macy Trust was born. With the captain acting as agent, Lady Yee employed a young and reputable San Jose attorney named J. W. Bishop to act as the public face for the trust. Then, when all business coefficients had been neatly racked into place, Lady Yee plumed her publicly perceived role by retiring behind her beautiful walled gardens. And there, unbeknownst to all except her husband, she worked her philanthropic machinations through the culturally neutral face of J. W. Bishop, Esq., and the mysterious Macy Trust.

As might be expected, the first target of Lady Yee's benevolent machinations centered on the impoverished conditions manifest in the lives of the local Chinese fishing communities of Monterey Bay. To that end, she sent her brilliant but misanthropic cook, Ah Chu, and her maid, Li-Lee, out on missions that were disguised as shopping excursions. They'd purchase Chinese vegetables at one market, Oriental dry goods at another, and fresh fish from any number of

Chinese stalls. At each location they were to make friends of the proprietors, haggle only where appropriate, and listen to everything said by the people around them. If called into conversation by local merchants, they were to ask questions and never voice opinions. In short, Ah Chu and Li-Lee were to discover what the fishing villages needed most in the way of basic services.

Captain Hammond knew that the only reason she posed the question was to have her own pre-drawn conclusions verified. They both knew, from experiencing coastal Chinese enclaves all over Asia, that her personal evaluation was dead on the mark. The three weakest elements for the laboring poor were competent medical care, basic education, and a system of internal financing and monetary support for small business ventures. Obviously the poor Chinese in Monterey lacked a chartered bank to look after their best interests. And such financial novelties, even if Chinese owned, were usually suspected by the poor as being too Western, so they shunned them out of fear of the local tongs, who in turn feared any rivalry to their own power and influence. If there were to be money made by loaning out funds at interest, they would be the ones to do it. Which was all very well, except for the sad condition of their treasuries. The local tongs were as penurious as their constituents but too proud to admit the truth even to themselves.

Lady Yee saw this rather bleak situation as a marvelous opportunity. Rather than compete with the prosaic and blinkered old burghers who ruled the tongs, she would find a way to make them work for her. And Captain Hammond had no doubt she could do just that if she set her mind to it.

Lady Yee mapped out a campaign that took several months of logistical planning to bring about, but the result was a scheme meticulous in every detail, and insinuating to the point of invisibility. Her first moves entailed a program of informal, though very pointed, publicity. She encouraged her agents, Ah Chu and Li-Lee, to begin circulating subtle rumors, all of them truthful in the main, concerning Lady Yee's esteemed family background, her influence with the most powerful traders in Asia, and her unlimited power to affect anything in which she held a proprietary interest. Setting aside all modesty for the greater good, they were to suggest that their mistress possessed wealth beyond measure, and power beyond reckoning, while at the same time letting it be known that Lady Yee was a person of enlightened habits, scholarly piety, and modest demeanor.

Ah Chu, being a creature with artistic as well as theatric instincts, took even greater pleasure embroidering gruesome tales about Lady Yee's defeat of the Pearl River pirates of the Red Flag.

To hear Ah Chu tell it, every corsair on the coast of China now went in mortal fear of crossing pikes with Lady Yee and her great ship, *The Silver Lotus*. Ah Chu's performance was a delight to witness. He would begin by luring in the grocery man, or the spice vendor, with some lurid and tantalizing image of his famous mistress, and then pretend he had spoken out of turn, and that his slip of the tongue should be ignored. Natural curiosity, like gravity, did most all the work. While feigning reticence at every turn, Ah Chu grudgingly and gradually gave way to inquisitive appeals, and theatrically unveiled the whole marvelous chronicle of the celebrated sea battle of Hainan Island, and the heroic leadership displayed by the incomparable and indomitable Lady Yee. Chinese tradesmen, like people everywhere, always savored scintillating, heroic tales, and this account, thanks to Ah Chu's colorfully augmented interpretation, was pretty grand in every dimension. As might be surmised, the entertaining narrative made the rounds of the local fishing villages faster than typhoid fever strips a prison ship of inmates.

On the other hand, Lady Yee's maid, Li-Lee, had been encouraged to spread remarks reflecting her mistress's all-abiding concern for the well-being of those in her employ, her credentialed heritage, and her broad philanthropic concerns. Lady Yee was correct in her assumption that this posture would encourage the village people to talk more freely in Li-Lee's presence. It was only natural for working folk to seek sympathy for everyday tribulations, disappointments, and complaints, and Lady Yee told Li-Lee to lend a thoughtful and patient ear to every such conversation, and to report them accurately if the sentiments expressly merited further consideration.

With the help of her faithful servants, Lady Yee soon compiled a fairly accurate picture of the lives led by the Chinese fishermen on the bay, as well as information about a good number of other people in Monterey. She knew what they had, what they lacked, and what they needed to make their lives more bearable. She was also aware of something else. She knew that nothing would or could be done to improve their condition without the wholehearted collaboration of the elders who directed the village tongs. These grizzled old burghers guarded their prerogatives jealously, and they maintained a traditional belief in the righteous dominance of their gender. Allowing a strange woman, albeit a wealthy and prominent woman, to direct matters for their village constituents was not a matter that would garner support, no matter how philanthropic the motive or viable the endeavor.

Lady Yee was well aware that a very tenuous line of demarcation separated success and failure when it came to dealing with the social insecurities expressed by the poorer classes of Chinese, but this had always been so. No one, regardless of station or wealth, wished to hazard reputation and status by taking instructions from a woman, so Lady Yee chose a course by which the tong elders would find it in their best interest to cooperate. And the best way to accomplish that was by letting the tong elders believe the whole business was their idea in the first place, but stalking that elusive horse would take careful planning and very subtle execution.

It was Captain Hammond who suggested that Lady Yee take a leaf from her father's lexicon and invite those tong elders with the greatest seniority and influence to an elaborate feast to mark the summer solstice, or some other celestial anniversary the Chinese were so fond of celebrating. Then, he said, his wife should unleash the incomparable Ah Chu and let him work his magic on the old gentlemen, for it was a sure wager that none of them, either in China or California, had ever experienced anything like the culinary genius of Lady Yee's cantankerous but brilliant chef. The captain observed that it was always far easier to call upon a man's better nature when he is well and happily fed. He went on to suggest that a fine bottle of brandy might be well received. It would warm old toes and perhaps old hearts as well.

Once the elders had been sated with fine food

and wine, Captain Hammond believed the tong elders could be influenced to acknowledge reasonable means for the sake of their constituency, especially if they were allowed to save face by assuming the mantle of credit. Lady Yee agreed, of course, and began to lay her plans to win over the tongs' ancient dragons.

Lady Yee's research had unearthed two particular and pressing needs shared by all the fishing villages along the coast of Monterey. First, though the Chinese had some access to traditional folk medicines and a few apothecaries who acted as doctors, they had virtually no facilities to treat serious injuries, communicable infections, or childhood diseases. They also lacked all but the most rudimentary form of education for their children, and many would grow to adulthood in America with only a limited ability to understand or utilize the English language. In most cases, pidgin English was the best that could be expected, and this limitation only harnessed people to lives of stoop labor and social inferiority. There was an exception to this rule, however. Though the Chinese had distinct difficulties with the English language, which was understandable considering its irrational grammar and pronunciation, she came across any number of her countrymen who spoke very passable Spanish. Lady Yee ascribed this to the fact that the Mexican population of California was far less racially biased than the Yankees were, and in some cases intermarriage and cultural assimilation followed, as they had in other parts of the world.

Lady Yee harbored no ambitious designs for building hospitals or schools. She knew that such manifest ostentation would be frowned on by every party concerned, even above and beyond the expected objections from the more conservative elements of both races. However she chose to influence the situation for the better, it was imperative that any substantive changes be almost indiscernible at first, at least until people gradually became used to the novelty, and that would take time.

The most important element Lady Yee had to address was the medical problem. She knew that no local Western doctor would set aside his practice to care for poor Chinese fishermen, but on the other side of the dilemma, Occidental physicians knew nothing of the benefits derived from Chinese medicine, which in some instances was far superior to Western medical practices. What was needed was a Chinese doctor trained in Western medicine as well as Chinese pharmacopeia, and that was an almost impossible order to fill in California.

Lady Yee decided to call upon her father for help. She wrote him a long letter describing the problem, asking him to assist her in finding a Chinese physician trained in Western medicine who was also preferably qualified in Western surgical practices. She understood that there had once been a Western medical school in Hong Kong run by an English missionary service, but she wasn't in a position to make any inquiries on her own behalf. She said that she was willing to sponsor a Western-trained Chinese doctor to come to California under contract to work for the Macy Trust for five years. If the doctor happened to be married with children, the trust would sponsor his family as well. The candidate would be given a house and a base salary of a thousand dollars a year, and his patients would, in turn, pay what they could in cash or kind. All medical supplies would be provided, and a clean infirmary established at a location convenient for his patients. If the doctor were educating a qualified apprentice, as many Chinese doctors did, the apprentice would also be welcome as long as the doctor agreed to help educate local Chinese apprentices as well. Lady Yee requested her father to finance the search, for which she would recompense him in Yankee gold, or Western exports if he preferred.

Finding Chinese schoolteachers who could speak viable English was no easy matter either, and Lady Yee asked her husband to use his San Francisco commercial contacts to initiate a search.

The captain said he would be happy to be of assistance. It was Lady Yee's money, and she could do with it as she pleased. But he cautioned his wife that she should avoid anything premature where the various tong elders were concerned. He suggested that it might be best not to mention anything about her plans for the present, as this would give power-jealous people too much time to fashion obtuse objections and thus create hobbling impediments. The captain observed that to put all the elements in place might take a year or more. Housing for the medical staff and teachers would have to be seen to, and a location for an infirmary secured and adapted to fit its purpose. These complex arrangements would take time, and it would be best if they were kept secret for the present. If matters turned sour, it would be best not to be caught wrong-footed with promised obligations impossible to fulfill.

When it came to tactical thinking in business, Lady Yee always bowed to her husband's insightful perspectives, and she observed that it was one of the things about her handsome captain that made him more Chinese than Yankee. She listened carefully when he suggested that the time delay should be made to work in her favor. While she secretly made all the physical and business arrangements, Lady Yee would be best served by discovering what incidental needs she could serve on behalf of the tong elders specifically. Many small but timely considerations, if presently dispensed with enlightened disinterest, would make firm allies for her later endeavors. Once everything was in place, she could unveil her contribution as a fait accompli, giving possible opponents no time for obstruction. And if she desired complete support, Lady Yee should modestly claim that the greatest credit rests with the tong elders. In this manner, now wreathed in local prestige, the elders could be encouraged first not only to civically support these institutions, but second to protect them as well to save face as tong administrators. But the captain advised her to move cautiously and, as much as possible, anonymously. By way of referring to her possible opposition by certain elements, the captain laughed and said that old men, like old dogs, needed very special attention. It took them longer to get used to strangers, and one pushed their circumspect schedule at one's peril. It was best to approach them inconspicuously, like a harmless snail. In time, if she remained prudent and patient, a small kindness here and an acknowledgement there would have the old burghers wagging their tails whenever she approached.

Lady Yee took everything her husband recommended to heart, and began to model her diplomacy accordingly. While waiting for a convenient opportunity to arise in which to be of some service to the tong, Lady Yee went quietly in search of properties to suit her purposes. And for this she utilized the services of her penny-wise lawyer, J. W. Bishop.

The first priority by way of property was a location for the infirmary. It had to be a building large enough to house twelve beds on a split ward, as well as all the medical space required. It had to be close enough to the Chinese communities to be convenient, and innocuous enough to the rest of the community so as to be almost invisible. The property had to be a good investment on its own merits, and relatively easy to convert and improve upon for the purposes intended. With instructions in hand, Lady Yee sent Mr. Bishop out to fill her needs as unobtrusively as possible. Her personal connection to any transaction was to remain a secret.

Her second consideration was housing for her future employees. The doctors would need modern, comfortable accommodations, within reason of course, and so would the teachers. Both groups would also require their own transportation, necessitating barn space and someone to look after the horses and rigs. In this quest, Lady Yee was almost immediately satisfied.

Captain Hammond's bank informed him, by way of a courtesy, that a handsome nine-acre property, obliquely adjacent to his own lot to the northwest, was up for sale. There were two modest houses on the property, three and two bedrooms respectively. Both were well founded and less than ten years old. The property included a full barn with six stalls, a dry hayloft, a water tower with dovecote, a large chicken house, and a goat shed.

The owner, a successful Italian nurseryman named Franco Bellini, had shared the property with his cousin. Bellini's wife and cousin had recently passed away, and the nurseryman was retiring and returning to Florence to spend his latter years and his considerable wealth among the relatives who said he'd never make good in America.

The houses aside, though they were sound, well maintained, and worth the price asked, the five acres of beautifully pruned fruit trees were what convinced Lady Yee that she might just know a way to get one half of the property to carry the annual expenses of the other half. She easily convinced her husband to buy the property as a company investment on that basis alone, notwithstanding the beauty and the views.

Lady Yee then hired four talented Chinese craftsmen to make whatever interior changes were deemed necessary to accommodate Chinese occupants comfortably. Handsome tiled ovens replaced open fireplaces, and the kitchens were rebuilt with iron stoves designed to accommodate Chinese cooking practices. The same considerations were also applied to the laundry rooms and the sanitary facilities. She employed the same Japanese gentleman who had taken care of her own orchards to oversee the new property. Mr. Bellini had planted apples, pears, plums, and lemons, all very complementary components if dried or sold as preserves. To ensure the ongoing fertility of his trees, Mr. Bellini had also set aside an additional half acre for his ten beehives. Lady Yee delighted at the possibilities the mutual properties possessed to produce income while satisfying personal needs. On her conceptual abacus, she could extrapolate potential remuneration that would ripple out over her financial landscape and satisfy numerous requirements, like a fan of modest but dependable beneficence. Captain Hammond resigned himself to the role of bemused observer. When it came to the Chinese transacting business with other Chinese, he had long since learned to keep his head down and rely on benign disinterest to save face, contention, and money.

Lady Yee received a response from her father with a promise to spend his best efforts to accommodate her wishes, but he warned that the particulars were by no means easy to come by. Western-trained Chinese doctors with a competent understanding of Eastern pharmacopeia were about as common as clams' teeth. The rarity alone would influence costs, but if Captain Hammond would send along legally notarized documents stating his financial sponsorship of the people in question, it might go a long way toward greasing the cogs of authority.

Until now, Captain Hammond had allowed Lady Yee to do just as she pleased. He believed in her goals, and since she was financing everything with her own fortune, he saw no reason to insinuate himself beyond the contribution of friendly advice here and there. However, Lady Yee rightly worried that in the present atmosphere of severe immigration restrictions aimed at the Chinese, her husband might not find it politic to be seen as one breaching popular sentiments on the subject. She waited to pose the question, but she needn't have worried, as her husband was quite amenable to the idea. He said that, in the main, he agreed with a policy restricting the import of illiterate Chinese peasants for the purposes of stoop labor. On the other hand, people of education and purpose, who could contribute to the well-being of the whole community, should be welcomed with open arms. He believed it was Cato who had once said that a nation's greatness could only be judged by the accumulated wisdom of its citizens. Sadly, the captain reflected that venal self-interest had a way of eroding the best of intentions for most people. But despite his dark appraisal, the captain stood by his word, and two days later he handed his wife the appropriate papers, countersigned and notarized by Judge Kimmerlin personally.

In the midst of all this quiet chaos, little Macy insisted on being a part of everything her parents did. Though under the ostensive care of Li-Lee, whom she loved and considered a playmate and sister, Macy far preferred to sit quietly in her father's lap while he read his newspapers out loud. She didn't understand what was being said, but the fact that she was being read to was enough entertainment. She also loved to sit by her mother while she worked out sums on her abacus. Sometimes, when she was feeling playful, Macy would move the beads about when her mother wasn't looking. This caused some problems until Lady Yee purchased a small abacus for Macy to play with. She loved to push the beads back and forth in imitation of her mother, and soon prided herself on being able to copy her mother's every move, though she really couldn't count above her own five fingers. But thanks to her mother's interest and sought-for approval, Macy was soon doing very well at simple math, and by the time she was old enough for formal schooling, Macy could compete mathematically with children twice her age. And thanks to her father's habit of reading to her from newspapers and business periodicals, little Macy had also developed a very interesting and unique vocabulary and a rather sophisticated way of speaking English. However, she far preferred speaking Chinese with her mother and Li-Lee, especially if she was really happy about something, and conversely when she was truly angry. The rest of the time she was content to jabber away in English. It sometimes occurred to Captain Hammond that perhaps his daughter would turn out to be an autodidactic polymath like her mother. Two of the same breed in one family was sure to prove most interesting, if not somewhat daunting.

FIVE WEEKS LATER, Mr. Bishop came to Lady Yee with what he believed might be a perfect location for her proposed infirmary. It was a disused sea salt warehouse that stood one hundred yards west of the coastline railroad tracks on the edge of the dunes, and it was a short half mile northwest of China Point. The warehouse complex included three outbuildings and sat on a fair-sized six-acre lot. The land alone was well worth the investment even if the buildings were pulled down, but the location had the advantage of relative isolation, and since it had occupied the same site for twenty-six years, it would hardly draw attention to itself even if slight improvements, like a fresh coat of barn paint, were applied. There were no dwellings of consequence nearby, and therefore no neighbors to complain about who came and went. Mr. Bishop believed that if it were quietly put about that Hammond, Macy & Yee intended to use the property for business purposes, not an eyebrow would be raised either way. And by the time the truth became known, it would be too late for naysayers to object since they'd have no reasonable grounds for opposition. As the proposed infirmary dealt with matters of public health, Captain Hammond was sure he could garner support from the State Sanitary Commission, as there were presently no existing medical facilities available to the local Chinese. He believed he could make the case that this might present dangerous complications if, as had happened before in 1887, another epidemic of influenza or smallpox should arrive off the deck of some foreign ship. The biased reality might have gone unspoken of in better circles, of course, but it was a sure bet that the county-run hospitals would never open their wards to poor Chinese regardless of the public danger. As in the past, poor aliens would be sequestered under guard, with minimal care offered to alleviate their suffering, and nature allowed to take its heartless course. This too had come to pass before, and the consequences were too shameful to be recounted in refined company.

After long appraisal and consideration between husband and wife, Captain Hammond went to his bank and made arrangements to purchase the old warehouse on behalf of Hammond, Macy & Yee. It would later be transferred to the Macy Trust when the dust settled, but in the meantime Captain Hammond needed a warehouse.

After the Bellini houses had been dressed out to fit future needs, Lady Yee put her craftsmen to work making all the necessary repairs and modifications to the warehouse. Because the carpenters were Chinese, none of the locals ever found out just what their labors implied for the future use of the buildings. For that matter, the carpenters were never informed either. They simply worked from Lady Yee's drawings and recommendations, and every two or three days Captain Hammond would visit the warehouse, inspect the work, and report back the results.

Lady Yee, on the other hand, was careful never to be seen in the neighborhood of any of her projects. She preferred to manage her affairs at a distance by using intermediaries. Then, if called upon, she could publicly feign disinterest. Perhaps the word "public" was slightly misleading, since Lady Yee rarely went out in public for any mundane reasons, and when she did, she traveled veiled and dressed in black. Except for private excursions with her husband to see this or that sight, Lady Yee far preferred her gardens and orchards, her studies, and the company of her beautiful daughter. However, she was also familiar with the observation that familiarity generally led to contempt, and so chose to remain aloof to social contacts not of her own making. What little power she possessed to influence matters could only be maintained if she adopted a regal and unapproachable bearing. As her husband had humorously pointed out, it would serve her purposes far better to have people be in awe of Lady Yee than to have them believe she was just a uniquely intelligent and beautiful Chinese girl named Silver Lotus who had rebelled against all tradition and, in search of adventure, had married a barbarian Yankee. Lady Yee wasn't sure she liked the texture of her husband's appraisal, but she certainly agreed in principle, and acted accordingly.

Though work on the renovations of the new infirmary was almost complete, Lady Yee was halted in her efforts because she had no doctor to make the appropriate recommendations for equipping the examining rooms or the split ward, and she dared not inquire locally for fear of giving away her plans prematurely. And disappointing news was soon to follow in a letter she received from her father in Canton.

In short, Master Yee informed his daughter that fulfilling her request would be next to impossible for numerous reasons, but the most critical of these was the will of the state. Though the Chinese authorities appeared quite content to feed thousands upon thousands of indigent peasants into an international labor market whence few ever returned, allowing the scholastically elite and privileged elements—specifically well-educated engineers, surgeons, doctors, and foreign-trained military officers—to emigrate at whim was out of the question. Besides, as her father pointed out in his letter, it was next to impossible to convince a Western-trained Chinese doctor, who could command high sums for his services at home, to emigrate to California to care for poor fishermen and laborers at less than a tenth of what he could earn at home. If there were some mission-trained doctors who were spiritually disposed to such selfless ambitions, and there were a steadfast few, there were still plenty of impoverished peasants in China to look after, and one needn't travel far to find dispiriting want and disease at hand.

Master Yee closed by regretting he was unable to be of any assistance for the present. If, on the other hand, a slim miracle should occur, and a qualified person could be found who was amenable to the idea of bundling up his life and voyaging to California for the foreseeable future, he would send notice at once. Yet he warned her against holding out much hope.

This turn of events, though disappointing, hardly put a ripple in Lady Yee's ambitions. If she couldn't get what she wanted, she would settle for what she needed, which Captain Hammond observed was pretty much the same thing either way. He, in turn, had used his connections with the Three Corporations to try to help find Chinese fluent enough in English to be able to teach it to children, but so far that line of inquiry had come up empty as well. A good deal of money had been spent to feather nests for occupation, but so far the lure had failed to attract the appropriate birds, and the captain began to worry that their efforts would come to nothing in the long run. He feared the company would end up owning the best-dressed empty warehouse in Monterey County.

Lady Yee refused to be daunted by her current circumstances. She told her husband that she was confident her efforts would be rewarded, and predicted that one way or another she would get her precious physician and teachers before the new century was a year old. Captain Hammond had his reasons to doubt this, of course, but he'd learned over the years never to underestimate his wife's occasional fits of groundless optimism. She had an uncanny practice of sensing things others couldn't, so he let the matter drift by without comment.

All thought of their own problems melted away in the following days as an unseasonable series of torrential storms came charging in off the Pacific and caused a great deal of local damage. Giant waves, some forty-five feet high, came rolling into the bay like a herd of stampeding elephants trampling everything within reach. And reliable denizens of Big Sur swore they witnessed breakers eighty feet high crashing into, and carving off chunks of, the sandstone cliffs. They said the spray from the waves, like a winter fog, hung in the air with such density and duration that it made breathing difficult and even painful for a quarter mile inland.

The Chinese fishing villages, because of their proximity to the storm-driven tides and crashing surf, suffered most, but the whole county could point to fresh scars caused by some tentacle of the storm's ferocity. Luckily there were but few fatalities, though a great deal of damage had been caused to everything afloat. Many fishing boats had been broken and sunk, or deposited like beached whales high onshore. Piles of torn and tangled nets were mixed with glass floats, broken spars, sweeps, buckets, and all manner of maritime debris. Whole trees, roots and all, which had been torn from some local cliff in tenacious resistance to wind and erosion, occasionally punctuated the homogenous waste and destruction. The violent expressions of the storm's tumultuous passing littered every beach on Monterey Bay as well as shores far to the north and south.

As fate would weave circumstances, Captain Hammond was in the company of the harbormaster, Mr. Campion, at the height of the storm. The captain had gone to call on the harbormaster at his office to see if he could be of any assistance in helping vessels still in distress. When he arrived he discovered seven other boat captains eager to do the same thing.

It had been odd, considering how protective of his person Lady Yee had become since the birth of Macy, but the captain's wife had been the one to suggest that he volunteer his services. There were people's lives and livelihoods to think of, and she said he would be glad of it later. So there he was, with the gale pounding at the office windows, standing with seven rain-soaked seamen and waiting for Mr. Campion to come out of his office and suggest a course of action. However, from the height of the seas, and the gusting force of the winds, all present secretly doubted that anything afloat in such conditions could be reached for rescue to begin with. There was no ship in port large enough to do battle with the elements as they stood at the moment, and the weight of the surf and gale-driven waves precluded launching shore-based rescue boats should a floundering vessel require assistance. The situation smacked of forlorn hope and frustration, and several men voiced the opinion that perhaps they were wasting time on improbabilities, and they decided to return home to their families.

Captain Hammond and two other men remained behind warming themselves near the iron stove. Over time the captain had become well acquainted with Mr. Campion, and they shared similar interests in harbor and wharf improvements. In that vein, though he agreed that his presence was most likely of little use, he stayed behind as a gesture of friendship and support more than anything else. Suddenly a man dressed in dripping oilskins entered the office with the gale at his back. He carried a message to Mr. Campion's office, and then quickly returned and departed back out into the storm without a word to anyone else. The clerk delivered the note and a moment later the harbormaster came out of his office with a distressed expression and the posture of a man who has gone without sleep for too long. Mr. Campion looked somewhat surprised and pleased to see his friend Captain Hammond standing among the men in the outer office.

The two men greeted each other with expressions of friendly concern. Mr. Campion proffered a note page and said that until now matters had looked pretty bad, but now Mr. Campion's worst fears had come home to roost. A small cargo ship flying the Canadian flag had been driven up on the rocks off Point Lobos, and though there was no question of her sinking, the vessel was taking a dangerous pounding abeam from the high waves. Using a signal lamp, the captain of the stricken vessel had signaled the surfboat men ashore that he had six passengers and two injured crewmen who needed attention. He requested assistance getting them off the ship as quickly as possible, and by any means available.

Mr. Campion regretted that he was unable to take charge of the rescue efforts himself, as he dared not leave his post with weather conditions calling all his attention to worsening harbor damage. Then it suddenly occurred to him to ask Captain Hammond if he could see his way clear to go down to Point Lobos as his representative and assist the coast surfboat men to effect a rescue if at all possible. If a surfboat should prove too dangerous, then a run-line would have to be shot out to the ship and a rescue harness rigged to haul the injured crew and passengers to shore. However, as both Captain Hammond and Mr. Campion were well aware, this method of rescue could be very dangerous in the presence of iron-bound waves three fathoms high, sail-slashing winds gusting to fifty knots, and blinding rains. For people unused to a conveyance as precarious as a bosun's chair or a lubber's harness, the experience of departing a stranded vessel during a storm was as daunting an undertaking as any landsman would care to endure. When presented with the opportunity, most sensible people would disdain the pleasure except for the certainty of drowning if they stayed on board. In some cases, highly distraught or aged passengers being rescued in this manner had to be involuntarily tied into the harness to get them to shore without hurting themselves. Captain Hammond recalled hearing about one fastidious lady who jumped into the raging sea rather than suffer the indignity of being slung ashore like a bag of mail. She also lived to tell the tale, and probably went on to remind other young ladies of the advantages of propriety in all things to include life-threatening maritime rescues.

Perhaps it might be attributed to their natural stubborn tenacity, but the mule team that hauled the wagon of supplies, the captain, and three other men down to Point Lobos seemed almost invincible in the face of the driving wind and rain. Not even the thick mud and downed tree branches could impede their progress. While the lightning and thunder appeared not to faze them in the least, no self-respecting horse would have made the journey without bolting right out of the traces.

As they came abreast of the beach just north of Point Lobos, Captain Hammond noticed a definite slackening in the weather. The eye of the storm was coming onshore from the southwest. Just then the men in the wagon heard two cannon shots fired from the point, and they knew that the surfboat men had noticed the lull as well and had taken the opportunity to shoot messenger lines out to the ship without delay. These light messenger lines would, in turn, be fished to heavier cordage capable of supporting the weight of the people to be hauled ashore. One end of the line would be rigged to the highest accessible point aboard ship, and ashore the other end would be secured to pass over crossed poles fifteen feet high that were erected for the purpose. A block and tackle rigged to suspend the rescue harness acted as the trolley and was hauled back and forth by strong men at both ends. If the surfboat men worked quickly, the rescuers might succeed in getting the people off the stricken ship before the eye of the storm passed inland and the other side of the storm slammed into the coast with all the winds and rain assailing everything from the opposite direction, which, of course, doubled the chances of further damaging everything in its ravaging course toward the northeast.

Despite the trying inclemency of wind and waves, the surfboat men had made considerable progress by the time Captain Hammond and the wagon arrived. Some of the injured had been hoisted ashore and were presently taking shelter under a large canvas storm tent that had been erected by the rescuers. It afforded only minimal protection from the elements, as it was little more than a very large lean-to anchored to the rocks by stout ropes, and the canvas flapped about, giving off reports that sounded like distant pistol shots.

Captain Hammond reported to the captain of the surfboat crews and offered his assistance. He said he'd been instructed by Mr. Campion to deliver blankets, fresh water, and rations for the use of the survivors, and to help those who wished to find shelter in Monterey to make their way to town as safely as possible, storm and medical considerations taken into account, of course.

Though it took hard work, most all the passengers made it to safety ashore with their dignity only marginally tarnished, though soaked to skins that were mercifully intact. Then the eye's interlude passed and the opposite wall of the storm struck like a rampaging phalanx of locomotives, and the work of hauling people off the ship became too risky. The people left on board were not yet in any immediate danger. The ship had been driven up onto the rocks to a point that precluded fear of sinking, but the constant battering of the waves against the ship's port and stern might also preclude her from ever getting off the rocks except in pieces. Only time and providence could resolve such questions, but in the meanwhile the captain of the stricken ship had signaled that all those remaining on board were safe, sheltered, and warm for the time being.

While looking to the comforts of the distressed and bewildered passengers, Captain Hammond noticed at once that the huddled survivors comprised both wealthy-looking Malaysian traders from Singapore and Indians of high cast and stature from Lahore or possibly Pondicherry. The presumptive difference that always stood out for Captain Hammond was that wealthy Singaporean traders never traveled with members of their own families, just servants, while Indian travelers of means would cart along their whole clan if they could afford to. It was quite economical in some perspective. Poorer relatives took the place of servants, and their gratitude and loyalty were worth far more than gold could purchase.

It was four such passengers, crouched in the sand at the back of the canvas shelter, who drew the captain's attention in particular. There were two men and two women. The men wore remnants of Western clothes, while the women, despite the obvious inconvenience, were attired in traditional Indian fashion. One couple appeared middle-aged, and the other pair looked to be on the verge of adulthood. They huddled close to each other for warmth and reassurance, and the captain realized they were in fact a single family. Captain Hammond smiled and greeted them with a traditional Hindu blessing, which indeed surprised the family. Then he gave them all thick, dry blankets, cork-stopped bottles of fresh water, and bars of sweet fruit pemmican until hot rations could be obtained. Knowing Indian culture well, the captain assured the shivering family that the ration bars contained no beef or pork. He also assured them that all would be well, that they were now quite out of danger, and that shelter and food would be provided for them as soon as it was safe to transport them to Monterey.

The eldest of the family, a trim, bearded gentleman of impressive stature and appearance, spoke a very educated but clipped English, and while including all the traditional Indian embellishments, profusely thanked his benefactors on behalf of his whole family. The captain smiled and said that gratitude was always a welcome treasure, and then moved on to help the other passengers. The injured crewmen had already been seen to and made comfortable by the surfboat men, a traditional courtesy between professionals that allowed injured seamen precedence over healthy passengers.

As the captain moved about helping the other distressed and disoriented foreigners, they too were in turn surprised that this imposing and courteous barbarian could speak a few polite and consoling phrases in their own languages, and they naturally gravitated toward him as a sympathetic and intelligent figure they could trust.

The few local farmers who had heard the bells, ship's sirens, and cannon shots braved the weather, harnessed their strongest teams to their sturdiest spring wagons, and made their storm-hammered way to Point Lobos. They would help as best they could, but in the backs of their minds there was always the thought of possible profit from salvage washed from the holds of rock-spiked ships. For centuries, coastal populations had benefitted from the occasional serendipitous treasures disgorged from the bowels of broken ships. Tradition said it was their just due for risking life and limb to help rescue and shelter survivors, but the practice would always be burdened by the darker connotations that recalled the predatory habits of ship-breakers and false-light pirates.

One of these local men came in tow behind the surfboat master, who, in turn, approached Captain Hammond and addressed him by name. It appeared there was a slight confusion about who was supposed to carry the survivors back to Monterey, but once this was addressed to everyone's satisfaction, the captain went back to looking to the injured sailors' comforts and preparing them for rough transport. It was then, as he kneeled next to one such man, that he felt a slight tap on his shoulder. When he looked up, he saw the Indian gentleman whose family he had assisted when they first came ashore. He appeared rather surprised and expectant simultaneously and began with a sincere apology for interrupting such important work, but he had heard the other officer address him as Captain Hammond, and he wished to know if he was the same Captain Hammond who had once commanded the trading schooner *The Silver Lotus*. The captain rose to his feet with a curious expression and answered in the affirmative. The Indian gentleman smiled broadly. He said that he didn't believe the captain would remember him after all this time, but they had, in fact, been introduced in Pondicherry. He was then known as Surgeon Major Atman Neruda of the Indian Army. He quickly recounted how, at the insistence of the captain's very persuasive wife, he had been dragooned (he used the term humorously) into treating three members of the

195

captain's crew after they'd been pointlessly assaulted by an inebriated pack of junior officers in British uniform. Dr. Neruda recalled that they had been introduced when Captain Hammond had called at the military infirmary to collect his men and pay their bills of care.

Captain Hammond thought for a moment. He did indeed remember the affair, and the kind Indian officer who had taken such pains to see that his men were treated with care and courtesy. There was a short pause while Dr. Neruda waited for the obvious to occur to Captain Hammond. When it didn't, he went on to remind the captain that when they first met, he did so in his capacity as a trained surgeon, an army doctor of long standing. If the captain needed a doctor to look after the injured hands until they reached hospital, he was prepared to offer his services. He said that his son-in-law was also a qualified doctor, and his wife and daughter were both university-trained pharmacists. Dr. Neruda said they were all in debt for their rescue, and thus more than happy to be of any help deemed necessary. With a sad expression he said that he had made the same offer to the captain of the stricken vessel, but that officer had been drinking and was in a foul mood, as might be expected. He had spurned the doctor's offer by implying that his men would not take kindly to being treated by a black man.

Captain Hammond shook his head with pity and

said if the captain of the ship had been any kind of proper seaman, his ship wouldn't be hanging on the rocks at that moment. But once the die was cast for good or ill, all offers of assistance, from any quarter whatsoever, should have been graciously accepted. He apologized for the thoughtless and dangerous conduct of a fellow captain and promised to have a word with the gentleman, if the imposter lived long enough to make it to shore.

Just then, one of the injured crewmen lying upon the earth spoke up and said no one had consulted him about his captain's decision, but now that he was beached and broken, he felt obliged to fend for his own interests. He almost begged Captain Hammond to allow the foreign gentleman to see to his fractured shoulder and arm before some butcher lopped it all off for lack of skill.

The captain professed to have no authority in the matter. He smiled and said that under the present circumstances, maritime tradition dictated that stranded seamen were always free to seek medical help where they could find it. The captain of the ship was still obliged to direct the ship's purser to make good on the bills.

Dr. Neruda nodded to the captain and then motioned for his family to join him at the task of dressing the men's injuries and making them more comfortable. The doctor apologized to Captain

Hammond for being so ill prepared, but all his instruments and medical supplies were still aboard the ship with their luggage. He asked what medical stores were available, and the captain had the first aid chest turned over to the doctor and his family.

The southwestern arc of the storm proved no less ferocious and cantankerous than the northeastern pass, and the canvas emergency shelter flapped about so violently that it had to be secured again and again. In any event, it only barely passed muster as a suitable shelter for so many people. But while the height of the storm raged overhead, moving the injured seamen by wagon was all but impossible, and the other stranded passengers were none too anxious to test their fates in open wagons with the winds gusting to forty miles an hour, with the frightening report of snapped tree limbs to be heard from all points. Having survived one disaster by the most precarious conveyance imaginable, most believed it was safer to stay where they were, huddled under the tormented canvas. To brave further unknown hazards elsewhere was not an alternative any of the survivors wanted to explore.

Captain Hammond agreed in the main, but he knew that arrangements would have to be made to accommodate the beached survivors, as well as the rest of the crew when they came ashore. It was obvious to almost everyone now that only a qualified salvage company could pull the spiked ship off the rocks without sinking her, and this would not require the services of the present crew. The accident would most likely cost the shipping company an appreciable fortune in salvage, lost revenue, damage claims from shippers and individual victims, and so forth. It was a certainty that whether the captain was at fault or not, his company would hardly be anxious to give him another ship until after an exhaustive investigation had determined the cause of this grounding, so in effect, he would be beached as well, perhaps for a short while, perhaps forever.

Captain Hammond borrowed a storm lantern and used a provisions crate as a desk. Kneeling in the sand under the whipping canvas, he wrote out a short report for the harbormaster, Mr. Campion, and numbered the casualties and survivors for whom shelter and rations would have to be found. He appraised the present condition of the ship as salvageable, barring further disasters, and the well-being of those remaining on board the ship good, barring the same. He stated that he would send the first wagonloads of survivors to town only after the storm had moved inland. He surmised correctly that the roads would be in very poor condition, washed out in critical places and generously littered with broken trees and other debris. It might take two days or longer to travel only ten miles, and a road crew with a four-mule team and a bucksaw squad would most likely have to clear the way first. The captain's only material request was to have a further supply of food and fresh water sent to Point Lobos by mule train if possible. He was sure the roads would no longer be passable to horse-drawn wagons.

As he wrote his report, Captain Hammond occasionally looked up and watched Dr. Neruda and his family working with the injured seamen and other survivors. The doctor's daughter had ingeniously fashioned a small oven from a large square ration can and six flat stones. She used small curls of wood deftly shaved from crate planking to fire the stove, and these she could whittle up at a wondrous rate with a sharp seaman's knife. Soon the oven warmed the stones and spread a reassuring glow to all those who came near. Using another ration can, she began to prepare a strong soup from the tinned meats and vegetables brought by Captain Hammond. The captain was captivated by her dexterity. Her husband seemed no less capable, while the doctor's wife acted as pharmacist and accurately dispensed medications where needed.

Suddenly Lady Yee's words came back to him. She had said he would be glad that he went, and it immediately occurred to him that she had been right. She needed doctors and nurses, and here they were, as if by destiny's call. He penned a note to his wife instructing her to have the big house prepared for occupancy as soon as possible. He said he believed that Guan Yin, goddess of mercy, had answered Lady Yee's humble supplications with compassion, wisdom, and a sense of the unique, as was her custom. He would send more information when time allowed. This note he folded and sealed with a request that Mr. Campion send it on to his house as quickly as possible. He then gave the report to one of the surfboat men along with five dollars to cover his expenses, and asked him to take one of the mules and make his way to Monterey and Mr. Campion. That done, the man was to lead the supply train back as soon as conditions permitted, and to report the state of the roads along the way.

The worst part of the storm passed inland about eighteen hours later, but the rains continued unabated for another day, and by that time everyone concerned was worn to a nubbin and weary to the bone. Tempers were running hot, and the injured were suffering the most alarming distresses from the elements. Dr. Neruda informed the captain that these people needed sheltered care as soon as possible and suggested that they be moved to the closest dwelling until they could be transported to a hospital. The doctor and his wife would look after the injured, while his son-in-law and his daughter would remain there to look after the others.

Captain Hammond thought this a reasonable

suggestion and approached one of the ranchers who had brought his wagon team to the point. It was sheltered in the trees across the road with the other animals and wagons. The rancher's name was Silas Gilpin, and Captain Hammond offered him twenty-five dollars to shelter the injured and ill survivors until transportation could be arranged. Mr. Gilpin said he would shelter them for nothing if they could make the journey of a mile and a half to his ranch. In fact, Mr. Gilpin said he'd just finished building a new hay barn, and it was tight and dry when he left. It could shelter all the survivors with room to spare, and there was plenty of fresh hay for bedding. And though he offered his barn gratis, he said the twenty-five dollars would be helpful in paying to feed all those hungry souls, as he would have to slaughter a pig or two and some chickens, but he believed he could cover the rest in fresh bread and root vegetables, if the captain could supply blankets and medical necessities.

Captain Hammond was so taken with Mr. Gilpin's honest generosity that he gave him forty dollars from his own pocket to cover all his expenses, to include the hay used by the survivors for bedding. In six hours' time all the victims of the disaster were comfortably sheltered in a new barn that smelled of milled wood, dried hay, and fresh paint. Dr. Neruda and his family continued to look after the well-being of their patients, which became easier with the availability of warm shelter, vegetables, hot food, and plenty of fresh water. Mrs. Gilpin brought a small iron trail stove, which was set up in a cleared space at the center of the barn. However, only Dr. Neruda's daughter was allowed to tend it, as she had already demonstrated her skill with fire. She knew how to generate the most heat from the least amount of fuel and yet produce less smoke and ash by forcing those elements to burn as well. It was a practiced technique unknown to most Europeans, but well understood by most all Asians. With the added heat, Mrs. Gilpin found a way to dry all the blankets from the beams of the hayloft. Within a short while the whole company was as comfortable as circumstances would allow, but certainly much drier, warmer, and far more contented than they'd been since the ship ran aground on the rocks two days previously. Tempers cooled, mutual sympathies resurfaced among the stranded passengers, and Captain Hammond at last believed that he had done all he could. After leaving a letter for Dr. Neruda, he borrowed one of Mr. Campion's mules and rode back to Monterey. His earlier assumptions about road condition proved painfully accurate, so he knew that no wagons would be passing either way for a few days yet. He would make his report to Mr. Campion and then go home to his beautiful daughter and his eerily perceptive wife.

10

CAPTAIN HAMMOND arrived home on Tuesday afternoon unannounced. He had been away for almost six days. Six days in the same torn, damp clothes that now looked like the captain had been dragged all the way home through the mud by an indifferent and callous mule. Not wishing Lady Yee to see him in this deplorable state, he bypassed the front door and went around to the back of the house and entered through the pantry hall, which also led to the large washing room with its water heater and polished copper bathtub. He called for old Lu Chen, the houseboy, and told him to return with a clean suit, fresh linen, and polished boots. After that, he was to inform his mistress that her husband had returned and would attend her when he was once again presentable.

Old Lu Chen grinned at his master's appearance, gave a crusty laugh, and said Lady Yee already knew. She had informed the servants at noon that the captain would be returning a few hours before sunset. She had instructed them to have the water heater fired up and fresh clothes hung in the washroom cupboard. The captain's shaving stand and mirror had already been brought down, and his razors were stropped and waiting. Captain Hammond just rolled his eyes to heaven, sighed, and muttered something under his breath about "the Almighty's gift of patience," and then he sent Lu Chen on his way and retired to the peace, warmth, and civility of a hot bath.

The washroom was a relatively large space, with a polished flagstone floor pierced in several places with small grated drains. The space on the left side of the room was devoted to the laundry, with two sets of enameled washtubs set against the wall. The other side of the room, which was separated by waxed shoji screens, contained the large copper bathtub, a bureau containing towels and facecloths, and a Chinese cabinet for hanging clothes. In the center of the room at the back stood a large water heater, which consisted of a forty-gallon brassbound copper tank perched above an iron firebox that used charcoal for fuel. A metal chimney and flue ran up through the roof, and copper pipes serviced both the laundry and the bath. Fresh cold water was fed into the system from the stone water tower adjacent to the house. The captain was delighted to see steam rising from the escape valve on the tank and that the room had been well warmed by the heat produced by the firebox. Captain Hammond smiled to himself, locked the door, and began stripping off his torn and mud-caked clothes. He saved only his old battered officer's cap and seaboots; the rest he threw in the waste bin to be incinerated or used as rags.

As the distant mission bell sounded evening mass, a scrubbed and refurbished Captain Hammond presented himself to Lady Yee in the parlor. His wife found it impossible to maintain a matronly composure, and she rushed into his arms. She professed to have suffered no real fear for his safety personally, but admitted that she had somehow allowed little Macy's constant concerns to seep through the cracks like a chill draft. Just then little Macy came dashing into the parlor like a miniature tornado of bayberry curls and Chinese silks. She was only steps ahead of Li-Lee, as usual, and full of bright squeals and laughter. She ran up and embraced her father's leg as if it were a tree. This was safe ground, and no one but her father was allowed to touch her once she reached sanctuary. The captain laughed, reached down, hoisted his daughter up to his hip, and asked for a kiss. He received three in return, but also a demand that he never go away again when the storms came. He said he thought that was a pretty good idea as well, but in this case there were people in danger, and sometimes other people had to help them to safety. He was just one of those people helping. To make up for his absence, he promised to read her a very special story at bedtime. Macy put her finger to her head in thought for a moment, and then magnanimously agreed to the lopsided compensation, but only if he agreed to use his funny voices. He agreed if she in turn would do just what Li-Lee wished her to do. Macy nodded and turned to follow Li-Lee out of the room.

Lady Yee waited until they were alone, and then led her husband to the settee and prepared a special blend of tea for them to share. She asked no questions about his adventures or hardships. Instead, she quietly enjoyed his presence, talked about small things like Macy's aversion to thunder, and waited for the captain to open discussion on the urgent Guan Yin note that he had seen fit to pen at the height of the storm. She didn't have long to wait.

Captain Hammond began by saying that among the survivors of the wreck he had surprisingly come upon an old acquaintance, someone who held detailed memories of his previous dealings with Lady Yee from years before. With a slight grin, the captain said this person had been of substantial service to her on their last voyage to India, Pondicherry to be exact.

Lady Yee thought for a long moment, and said her husband must be referring to that interesting Surgeon Major Atman Neruda of the Indian Army, the kind Hindu doctor who had taken such good care of the crewman who'd been brutally assaulted by those gold-braided British thugs near the docks. Lady Yee blushed to admit that she had given that poor gentleman a difficult time because of the military association with the British, who were not a popular people with the Chinese at the best of times.

Captain Hammond was again struck with the concrete impression that he was once again doomed to always know anything only after his wife knew it first. He had long ceased to show any amazement, and kept a disinterested expression.

Lady Yee asked after the major, and the captain filled in all the particulars, at least the ones he knew. He said there hadn't been much time for pleasant conversation in the middle of the storm, but the doctor and his family appeared highly educated and very competent medical practitioners in the Western sense. After all, Dr. Neruda had spent nineteen years in the Indian Medical Services, and must have been considered highly qualified to have achieved the exalted rank of surgeon major. The captain remembered once being told that such a rank in the Indian Army was notoriously difficult to achieve, especially in the medical corps, where a field surgeon was also required to have a thorough knowledge of ayurvedic medical practices, a principle that should have been copied by the British medical corps. But such was the racial and cultural bias that the British preferred to die in stalwart, patriotic ignorance rather than bow to ancient and proven medical procedures to lessen the suffering of their soldiers.

Captain Hammond reassured his wife that he

had made neither proposals nor promises to Dr. Neruda about anything concerning her project. But she was in dire need of a professional medical staff, and it seemed that they had literally washed up at her feet like a chest of rare jade. The captain smiled and said that in light of past association and acquaintanceship, he had simply offered Dr. Neruda and his family a place to stay until their baggage and goods could be retrieved from the grounded ship, and arrangements made for the continuance of their journey, if indeed that was what they wished. But for the present the Neruda family possessed only the clothes on their backs and fifty pesos in Mexican gold. The captain believed there was no better time to put one's best foot forward, if only to demonstrate honest gratitude for past kindnesses. He said the family would most likely be arriving with the party of injured men sometime the following day, depending on the roads. He would see to it that a surrey brought them to the big house on the other side of the property. In the morning the captain would go to Holman's store and purchase adequate garments for the men, but Lady Yee would have to go through her substantial collection of silks to provide material for traditional saris for the women.

He should have become accustomed to it by now, but Lady Yee's ability to absorb important news as though she had heard it all before, or always knew that such-and-such would come to pass just as she thought it would, still managed to rankle the captain just a little. Nothing ever came to her as a surprise or a shock. She simply nodded and went on as though she invariably knew where the road would eventually lead.

Lady Yee didn't bother to remind her husband that she had told him he would be glad of his service in the crisis. She didn't need to. But she had acted immediately upon receipt of his note. The house had been seen to, the beds made, and the fireplace and stoves charged with dry wood and tinder. Ah Chu would see to their food, unless they chose to prepare their own, in which case the kitchen had been well stocked. She would see that the water heater was fired before they arrived, and that they were supplied with fresh linens and flannel towels. Once they were well rested and attired in respectable clothes, Lady Yee would hold a celebratory dinner in their honor, and then let Guan Yin guide the course of events.

In the meantime, Lady Yee spent every effort to let her husband know how happy she was to have him back at her side, and how proud she was of his gallantry and courage. Her sentiments were like a soothing balm to his weary soul and aching joints. Her honest and sincere appreciation always made him feel better about everything unseen and unknowable. She always knew where to cast the anchor and bring all to rest in calm waters, and her quiet assurance in all things had become his refuge as well.

The next day, after turning their patients over to hospital care, Dr. Neruda and his family were taken to the newly refurbished guesthouse, where everything had been made warm and comfortable for their arrival. Captain Hammond was there to greet them, and did all in his power to make them feel at home. Lady Yee had instructed Ah Chu to prepare several rich vegetarian courses in the Indian fashion. These were delivered accompanied by heaping bowls of steamed rice and a box of fine teas.

Dr. Neruda and his family were stunned by the captain's hospitality and the profound kindness that allowed for a family's dignity to be held in such high regard, as evidenced by the new clothes the captain and Lady Yee had given them. The silks that Lady Yee had supplied from her own collection particularly impressed Mrs. Neruda and her daughter, and they hoped that the captain would convey their sincere appreciation to his bountiful and generous wife. Captain Hammond left the houseboy to look after the family's needs, and said he would return to visit them the following afternoon once they'd enjoyed hot baths, clean clothes, a few good meals, and a full night's rest. They could talk about more important matters on another day. He assured them that he would do all in his power to see that their goods and baggage were retrieved from the stranded ship as soon as possible. In the meantime, the captain assured Dr. Neruda and his family that they were welcome to stay as his guests for as long as necessary. When he left them, it was in a cloud of blessings and praise for his generosity and compassion. Captain Hammond humbly stated that in fact his brilliant wife had instigated everything at hand, and they could thank her personally when they met again.

When Captain Hammond returned to Lady Yee, she was in the midst of sorting through business documents that pertained to her proposed infirmary. She needed to compile an ironclad proposal that would pass muster with the city fathers regardless of public objections. Her focus rested upon the money the city would save in public services and the costs related to treating the poor at public expense. Not poor white applicants, mind you, for they seemed quite acceptable as recipients of the public largess, but rather poor Chinese, who were not. As the captain appeared, she began to question him about Dr. Neruda and his family. She assumed her husband saw them as a possible answer to her medical staffing problem, even though the question had never been broached to Dr. Neruda. She was curious to hear her husband's opinions and reasoning.

Captain Hammond grinned to himself. He could sense the maw of Chinese convolution open before him like a tiger pit, and he had no intention of even testing the trigger. He flatly stated that whether or not Lady Yee and Dr. Neruda ever came to terms was really none of his business. The scheme was totally hers from start to finish. It was her money that had given it blood, and her drive that had supplied the bone and muscle. This was all hers to command. He had simply taken the opportunity to repay an old debt to a man that had been cruelly unfortunate in his choice of ships and was cast upon the mortal shore of a strange land. As far as he was concerned, the matter ended there. If Lady Yee chose further association with Dr. Neruda, that was strictly her own affair. He had conducted himself according to his own codes, and he stood on their merits and motives.

Then, just to stir up the waters for his own amusement, the captain continued as though casting the observation off as an aside. Besides, he quipped, he seriously doubted whether tradition-bound peasant fishermen, Chinese, Portuguese, or even Filipino, would allow themselves to be examined, or prescribed to, by an Indian Hindu using ayurvedic medical guidelines and Western surgical practices. Indeed, he doubted if even the tong masters and village elders could be brought around to the idea, so the whole matter, to his way of thinking, was only marginally possible and speculative at best. The captain then called for his dinner and left Lady Yee to ponder his words. He knew full well that the surest way to charge Lady Yee's cannon was to tell her something was either impossible or improbable, and then sit back and watch the fireworks. The captain never tired of her intricate machinations, enigmatic though they sometimes were. It was like watching a fine magician pulling a long parade of colored silk handkerchiefs from a silver coin perched between forefinger and thumb.

EARLY THE NEXT DAY, Lady Yee took Ah Chu aside for a long conference in the kitchen, and then announced to her husband that she was preparing a small feast for their Indian guests that night, and the captain was instructed to carry her handwritten invitation when he stopped by to see Dr. Neruda after breakfast. The captain nodded in a distracted manner, and continued carefully spreading strawberry jam on a small piece of buttered toast. This morsel he then presented to an expectant Macy, who seemed thoroughly delighted with the whole performance.

When the captain arrived at the guesthouse carrying a basket of fruit from Lady Yee, he found Dr. Neruda on the front porch reading a small volume of French poetry. On seeing the doctor refreshed to his normal state of presentation, Captain Hammond had to admit that he was a rather dashing-looking fellow. He was of medium height, with a clipped black beard cut close and combed in military fashion. His black hair shined like polished silk without a hint of grey at the temples. He looked to be a man of late middle age, but he showed no signs of aging. He appeared strong, centered, and sure on his feet, and all his gestures, no matter how incidental, were graceful. His English was excellent, though his discourse was sparse and to the point, and lacked the flights of hyperbole that English-speaking Indians were so fond of.

The doctor smiled when the captain appeared and welcomed his host with warm sentiments of gratitude. He invited the captain to sit in the shade and called for his wife to please serve tea to their host. The men spoke in a slow, friendly, almost familiar manner common to those who have shared a traumatic experience. They talked of incidental matters for a few minutes, and then Captain Hammond asked permission to pose a few questions on behalf of his wife, Lady Yee. He confessed she was a woman stoutly rigged for curiosity, albeit benevolent in nature and creative in response. Dr. Neruda laughed and promised to keep that in mind. It was another point on which husbands held common ground most of the time.

Captain Hammond asked where the Neruda family was bound when their journey was so rudely interrupted by bad seamanship. "The jagged rocks of Point Lobos were, even as an expression of heaven's will, an unfortunate terminus at best."

Dr. Neruda thought for a moment, then stared off toward the bay, now calm and serene with low rolling swells being the fading signature of the departed storms. When he spoke the doctor seemed slightly at a loss, as though viewing the past like a dream. Then he shook himself free and said they had been on their way to Vancouver. He had been told that the harbor city was home to a small but affluent Indian enclave comprised mostly of aging ex-military officers who had remained loyal to the British Raj during the Sepoy Rebellion of 1857. Later, when their loyalty proved a liability to their personal safety, their futures came into question. Their defeated sepoy enemies, now driven underground, assassinated some loyalists and dangerously harassed others. As a result, a grateful British Raj allowed many retiring Indian officers and their families to immigrate to other parts of the British Commonwealth. Some went to South Africa, some to England to educate their sons, and some traveled to Vancouver. They applied their pensions and bonuses to starting businesses and sent their children to Western schools. Many children had been born in Canada and were now comfortable with Western medical practices, but tradition still held the floor as far as the older generation was concerned, and they controlled the purse strings.

When Surgeon Major Neruda retired, he and his family at first traveled to Peru at the behest of the British Foreign Office. The British legation in Lima, like other embassies, was often the focus of local political frustrations, and required a substantial guard to protect its premises and residences from mob violence. For reasons all its own, the Foreign Office had assigned a hard-line, blood-in-the-eye contingent of Indian Sikh soldiers and Nepalese Gurkhas to protect their interests, and not even the most fervent Peruvian revolutionary wished to cross steel with these men. They prayed to ancient bloodthirsty gods and were ignorant of all mercy. It was even rumored they delighted in killing Christians. Of course this latter invention was absurd on the face of it, but the Peruvian rabble believed it, and that was all that mattered. Dr. Neruda had accepted the assignment of working as a regimental surgeon with civilian rank because it paid well and he could get his family out of India, which was suffering greatly from Muslim-Hindu sectarian violence. It proved an unfortunate choice, as things weren't that much better in Peru. After two important secretaries were murdered in a street ambush, the British decided to close its legation and sever all trade agreements until restitution was paid and security could be guaranteed. This eventuality was hardly going to bloom anytime soon, so Dr. Neruda resigned his post, gathered up his family once more, and decided to travel on to Vancouver at the suggestion of a fellow Indian officer who had relatives residing there.

The doctor said he had hoped to establish a small medical facility to serve the Indian community of British Columbia, but the unseasonable storms, and the teeth of Point Lobos, had interrupted their journey. And if, for any reason, they could not recover their property from the ship, the disaster would have cost them everything they owned. Their ready cash and personal wealth had been secreted away in a hidden compartment of their steamer trunk, which as far as he knew was still secured in their cabin. He feared their belongings would not remain unmolested, especially when a salvage crew climbed on board.

Captain Hammond said that as a sailing man he could certainly sympathize, and he was going to see Mr. Campion, the harbormaster, that very afternoon. Mr. Campion had a great deal of influence in these matters. But with the seas now calm, the captain was sure that something might be done to retrieve their goods from the ship. He promised to do the best he could to resolve matters in their favor as soon as possible.

To change the subject, the captain asked after the doctor's family, and their roles in his plans for

Vancouver. Dr. Neruda smiled and said they were indispensable to his work, and they all labored as a team. The doctor's wife, Nandiri, was a university-trained compounding pharmacologist who specialized in ayurvedic as well as Western pharmacopeia. His daughter, Indri, was a hospital-trained surgical nurse who also specialized in convalescent nutrition, and his son-in-law, Chandra Din, took his two medical degrees in Paris and focused his studies upon bronchial diseases and skin disorders, both sadly commonplace in India.

The doctor said that poor Chandra was the one person who really got dragooned into this dangerous adventure. His son-in-law was deeply in love with Indri, and had been since they were children. He would not be parted from her for any reason whatsoever. Indri, on the other hand, though she worshiped Chandra, very pragmatically viewed her parents as superior scholastic mentors and medical professionals with volumes still to teach her, and she would not be parted from them either. Dr. Neruda laughed gently and said that dear Chandra, who was an extremely talented and dedicated physician in his own right, and certainly a creature of keen practicality, had courageously bowed to the inevitable, as husbands sometimes must, packed his instruments and books, and come along. Dr. Neruda said he was always so pleased to see how wonderfully Chandra and Indri worked together professionally. They always engendered the greatest confidence in all their patients, and sometimes that, he said, was as critical as proper medication when effecting recovery.

Dr. Neruda took a moment to choose the right words and finally declared that it was in the disposition of most native Indians to place the greatest confidence in the old established family concerns, and medicine in particular required reputable credentials to find acceptance in traditional Indian enclaves abroad. In short, the doctor and his family would always find much greater success together than apart, and so custom dictated they stay and work as a group regardless of circumstances. The doctor chuckled and said that medicine in India was very much a family-to-family affair. According to Dr. Neruda, by virtue of Hindu philosophy, the relationship between doctor and patient verges on the sacred. But sadly, he said, this fact had a tendency sometimes to run afoul of pure science, good medicine, and even simple common sense.

Captain Hammond admitted he would be hard-pressed not to agree. He had experienced many cultures and found parallels almost everywhere. Cross-cultural bias, mutual suspicion, and fear usually created barriers to the adoption or adaptation of positive innovations that might have come to light from those far foreign parts where barbarians dwelled under the rule of demons. And knowing the Chinese the way he did, he would never draw against the idea that suffering and death were altogether preferable to altering the tenants of long-established custom when it came to something as intimate as submitting to medical examination and treatment, especially for Chinese women and their children, and with this recollection Captain Hammond suddenly realized that there was definitely a fly in the ointment as far as Lady Yee's ambitions were concerned.

Mrs. Neruda came out on the porch with a fresh pot of tea. Captain Hammond appeared distracted for a moment, but then he rose, thanked the doctor and his wife for their kindness, and said that he was obliged to conduct other business that morning. Before leaving, he presented the doctor and his wife with Lady Yee's handwritten invitation for dinner that very night, which Dr. and Mrs. Neruda accepted with humble pleasure.

11

WHEN HE RETURNED HOME, Captain Hammond went in search of his wife. He found her harvesting flowers in her garden. These fresh and vibrant blooms, according to her, were destined to dance anew in her Ch'ien-lung vases and decorate the dinner table that evening. When he at last managed to focus her complete attention, the captain said he believed the whole experiment might come to nothing as far as the Neruda family was concerned. He shared his sudden foreboding that the Chinese fishing families, and the other Chinese laborers, would not willingly submit to Indian doctors of either sex. The cultural differences were too vast, he said, and the forms of medicine practiced too foreign. He was reminded that peasants of any land usually proved to be the most hidebound of traditionalists, and the most difficult to persuade when it came to any form of novelty.

Lady Yee could not help but laugh at her husband's sincere but ill-informed concerns. She said that the impediments he predicted were already accounted for in her plans, and she believed that the right approach to both parties, finite as they were, might nullify centuries of pointless tradition where health was a principle, and not a custom. As for medical practices, Lady

Yee took a mock pedantic stance and told her husband that a substantial portion of Chinese medicine came to China from India and the ayurvedic school of healing and health. Like much that was admirable about China, advanced Indian medical sciences followed in the wake of enlightened Buddhist teaching, or so the great scrolls record. But Lady Yee observed that the Chinese had been sailing on trading voyages to India centuries before that, and as her husband knew only too well, good health in a sailor is more precious than coins to his captain. Indeed, Lady Yee stood on her conviction that though Chinese medicine had made innumerable independent contributions to the art of healing, its roots were nurtured in the rich soil of ayurvedic tradition, so in principle, tradition and custom were being served to a higher order. If all the greatest emperors of China found it wise and expedient to pay high bounties to keep Indian doctors, surgeons, and even astrologers on their household staffs, then what was once enlightened behavior on the part of a son of heaven would always be adopted by others, if not for obviously pragmatic reasons, then vanity as a matter of court fashion. Either way, the truth, medically speaking, remained the truth, and if the empire's people remained healthy as a result, then all prospered from the Indians' contributions, especially the sons of heaven. In the end, Lady Yee persuaded her husband that she had already taken all possible cultural objections into her calculations and would play out the cards she was dealt. She wasn't vain enough to believe she couldn't fail, of course, but she always preferred to set her sights on optimistic horizons.

Lady Yee's dinner presentation later that evening was a surprise even for Captain Hammond, who thought he'd become used to such flights of culinary indulgence. She didn't do it often, but when Lady Yee chose to entertain at their table, her respect for her guests was always translated into exceptionally prepared food. But the captain had no idea that his wife's demon familiar, agent provocateur, and chef, Ah Chu, knew how to prepare such a variety of exotic Indian foods properly. Not that the captain was any kind of connoisseur in such matters, but he did recognize genius and artistry when it fell on him, and Lady Yee was always a marvel when mustering the forces of surprise. Dr. Neruda was not the least to be impressed either. Mrs. Neruda was beside herself with compliments and gratitude, and her daughter and son-in-law were equally vocal in their praises and sentiments of appreciation. Dr. Neruda freely admitted that they hadn't enjoyed such complex and beautifully prepared Indian cuisine in their three-year migration.

Over dinner, Lady Yee posed a number of polite

questions concerning the doctor's journey west. She had listened carefully to what her husband had reported to her, and so avoided the embarrassment of asking repetitive questions. She seemed more interested in their fields of study and their ambitions in Canada.

Dr. Neruda revealed that after many turbulent years in the British Indian Army, and having witnessed all possible categories of mass violence, both sectarian and military, and having also experienced the blatant and pointless inhumanity displayed by all parties concerned, he had finally determined to take his family to a part of the world where they could fulfill their callings as medical practitioners without living under the looming threat of violence for their efforts.

The doctor also confessed that in India, mythology, religion, and inflexible superstition in many cases ran contrary to sound medical practices, and one was forever obliged to invent mythological reasons to justify straightforward procedures, and in this regard the poor were always far more conservative than the well-to-do. Only Indian expatriates far from home seemed to honestly appreciate the skills and education the Neruda family brought into their culturally isolated communities. The doctor confessed that even his exalted rank and position in the Indian Army seemed to reassure these middle-class immigrants. He said they would allow precepts of

Western medicine to be practiced, of course, but only by Indian doctors who were qualified in traditional methods as well, and it was understood that Indian doctors comprehended the spiritual ramifications of their prognosis, diagnosis, and projected cures. But he bemoaned the fact that in India, regardless of the need, or nearness of death, Muslims would never allow themselves to be treated by Hindu doctors, and no self-respecting Hindu, even on the verge of discovering "the eternal mystery," would tolerate the ministrations of a Muslim physician, no matter how gifted and famous that man might be. In short, Dr. Neruda believed they could accomplish more good outside India, and his family shared his opinions.

Lady Yee openly sympathized in all the particulars, and especially with the medical needs of Asian minorities in foreign lands. She modestly mentioned her own efforts to start a medical facility for the local Chinese and reflected on the rigidly conservative inclinations of her own compatriots when it came to matters of traditional medicine. In that regard, she supposed there was little difference between their two cultures. Dr. Neruda agreed, but added that the sectarian inclinations toward violent expedients made matters almost intolerable for many people, and the Hindus were certainly no strangers to the dagger and the garrote either. The doctor shook his head sadly, and mentioned in passing that there was even a Muslim crewman aboard their ship who seemed to go out of his way to be rude to the doctor and his family whenever the opportunity presented itself.

It was then that the distant doorbell was heard to ring, and a few moments later the aging houseboy entered the dining room, bowed to Lady Yee, and apologized for the interruption. He carried a note for the captain on a small silver platter and said that there was a messenger waiting at the door for a reply.

Captain Hammond apologized to his guests for the interruption, took the note, and after reading it asked his guests to pardon his absence for a few moments. Then he rose from his seat, bowed to Lady Yee, and followed the houseboy to the front door. When he returned, Captain Hammond announced that he had good news. His meeting with Mr. Campion that afternoon had borne fruit. The harbormaster had used his influence, and it had been arranged to send a steam launch to retrieve the survivors' baggage from the stricken ship the following day. However, the captain noted that timing was a factor, and though the seas and swells had calmed considerably, off-loading the baggage was a feat that could only be accomplished at high tide if the ship's cranes were to be of any use. That tide would be at flood at 3:47 the following afternoon, and Captain Hammond's services had been requested to help supervise the transfer on behalf of the passengers. The captain blushed slightly and said it seemed that they had chosen him as their unofficial ombudsman, and Dr. Neruda's family happily seconded their choice. And in that vein, Captain Hammond said he would need to know the cabin numbers the Nerudas occupied and a description of the baggage they left aboard. Unfortunately, any goods stored in the ship's hold would have to wait to be unloaded until the ship was kedged off the rocks and brought into the bay for repairs.

The company rejoiced at the news and applauded the captain's efforts on their behalf. Then, as a perfect addendum to their celebratory feast, Ah Chu entered wearing his formal whites, bowed to Lady Yee, and presented the table with an elaborate jungle spectacle of sculpted fruit and custard-filled pastries molded and decorated to represent exotic birds. Even Captain Hammond was somewhat taken aback. He was usually required to settle for a simple rice pudding flavored with dates, a fruit tart, or a segmented orange laced with gingered honey, and he couldn't remember when he'd ever been confronted with a feathered dessert course that stared back at him from a pineapple perch.

The next morning, Lee Woo, the perennially drowsy stable boy, harnessed up the shay and drove Captain Hammond down to Mr. Campion's office overlooking the harbor. The fog was just beginning to rise off the bay, and the weather held a promise of bright sun and calm winds, which the captain hoped would make the off-loading exercise all the more rational. Once the ship was pulled off the rocks, the odds changed.

On arriving at Mr. Campion's offices, Captain Hammond had the dubious pleasure of meeting the captain of the stricken ship, and sadly his opinion of the man only slipped further down the scale. The officer's name was Sigmund Malakoff, and he claimed Estonia as his homeland, though something in the way he spoke English made Captain Hammond doubt his veracity. The man was in his late fifties, shabbily dressed, overweight, balding, and crude by nature. He looked disheveled by habit and spoke a fractured dockside English, supported by profanity in Hungarian and German. The spider's web of broken blood vessels on his cheeks and nose, his bad teeth, and the tremble in his hands spoke of a man who had long since left behind his amateur standing as a tippler. The general odor of cheap vodka seemed to cling to his clothes like an oily mist. It was obvious to everyone present that the Estonian captain, now that his company had beached him with prejudice to await further investigation, had become totally disengaged from all interests except those relating to his own situation. To everyone's surprise and distress, Malakoff claimed total indifference to the fate of his ship. He seemed even less troubled with the fate of his injured seamen. As far as the vodka-laced Estonian was concerned, since he no longer held command, the company could go get stuffed. The owners could shoulder the burden of the ship, the passenger liability, and the crew, and then go to the devil.

Captain Hammond was not in the least surprised to find that he had taken an instant dislike to this dangerously ignorant and blatantly self-righteous dipsomaniac. It seemed that even the ship's first officer, Mr. Atwood, who had since been placed in command by the vessel's owners in Vancouver, found that treating his ex-captain with even a shadow of civility was a forlorn exercise at best. Mr. Campion finally lost his temper and became enraged by Malakoff's attitude and manner. He angrily backed the man to the wall and threatened to have him immediately charged and arrested for criminal negligence. And he reassured Malakoff that he had the maritime authority to do just that at any moment he wished. The Estonian was suddenly taken aback. He blustered and stuttered at the harbormaster's effrontery, but seeing the determination of Mr. Campion's expression, Malakoff then squealed out an insulting sequence of ludicrous excuses, and despite the cool temperatures he began to sweat like a boiler-room stoker. He was at once deflated but not humbled.

He chose to remain intractable and couched all his replies with thinly veiled sarcasm.

Captain Hammond, Mr. Atwood, and several others watched with growing concern while Mr. Campion slowly began to lose all patience with the recalcitrant and unrepentant Malakoff. All at once the harbormaster threw up his hands in despair, pierced the air with a curse, turned on his heel, and disappeared into his office muttering something about duty and common decency. When he once again emerged, Mr. Campion was hefting a big navy-pattern Colt revolver and waving a pair of ship's manacles. He motioned for two of his burly harbor men to approach. From three feet away, Mr. Campion lifted and pointed the heavy Colt at Malakoff's head with both hands shaking with anger, and then he declared that the heathen was under arrest for criminal obstruction of an ongoing maritime rescue. Malakoff instantly puffed up like an enraged toad. Again Mr. Campion backed him to the wall while the man unleashed even more desperate flourishes of indignity and stuttered objections to violated prerogatives. But before he could finish his disjointed protests, Malakoff had been shackled by the wrists and bum-rushed toward the door on his way to the sheriff's lockup. Mr. Campion called after his men to respectfully inform the sheriff that he would prefer charges within the hour, and that bail should be denied pending judicial considerations of further charges.

Captain Hammond and the other men present were deeply impressed by Mr. Campion's courage and strength of character. His diminutive stature, receding hairline, and spectacles suggested a rather reticent warrior who disdained unseemly confrontations at all costs. But the witnesses were caught wrong-footed and found they were now well beyond appropriate comment. Captain Hammond saw at once that Mr. Campion was obviously not a man to be taken lightly, and despite his diminutive size, with a big navy Colt in one hand and righteous indignation to fire his boilers, he came off as ten feet tall and divinely buttressed with the vision and courage of a latter-day Diogenes.

Captain Hammond had sent word to the ship's passengers to respond with a list and description of their baggage, their cabin numbers, and so forth. And at two o'clock that afternoon, he boarded an ocean steam tug that had been sent down the coast to assist in the salvage operations.

Captain Hammond was to be accompanied by Mr. Atwood, who as acting captain would order the remaining crew ashore and then stay on board with two volunteers, so that the ship could not be claimed derelict by the salvage company; Mr. Campion contributed five iron-backed stevedores to help wrestle the passengers' baggage on deck.

From there the goods would be lifted in cargo nets and slung over the side with the ship's stern cranes. At the flood of high tide the tug would creep up to the port-stern portion of the ship, take on the nets, and then back away. The salvage company would also send their men on board to make a full hull inspection, and appraise the situation from an offshore perspective as well. The tug's captain would send out a boat to sound the seafloor to the stern of the ship and determine the best place to sink heavy kedge anchors, which in turn would be cabled to the steam winches on the ship's deck. Then, after due deliberation, and with bids and counterbids flying about like stock tickets, the salvage company and the owners would decide upon the best and safest way to pull the vessel off the rocks, hopefully without tearing out her bottom and sinking the poor freighter on the spot, an unacceptable outcome for everyone, especially the residents and tourists who cherished Point Lobos for its rugged natural beauty. The last thing anyone wanted to view was a rusting hulk sticking up out of the waves waiting for the sea to do what the salvage men couldn't. None of the locals were willing to wait that long, and there was already wild talk of blasting the derelict to smithereens with dynamite. This, as Captain Hammond pointed out to a local rancher, would only cause even greater damage to the seal rookeries and nesting sites by distributing noxious materials and garbage everywhere.

The steam tug approached the stranded ship around three o'clock, and the jolly boat transferred Captain Hammond and his men to the vessel shortly after. With cabin keys acquired from the purser at Mr. Atwood's orders, Captain Hammond, his stevedores, and various crewmen who had remained on board soon had the entire passenger compartment covered, and all the listed trunks and baggage were accounted for. The men then assembled the collection on the rear deck to await transfer to the tug.

At 3:47, exactly at flood tide, the tug crept up to the port-stern quarter of the ship and took the cargo net full of baggage in exchange for the salvage appraisers and engineers. She then used the cargo nets to bring aboard Captain Hammond, his men, and those remaining crewmen who had not been sent ashore before. This time the only people to remain aboard the ship representing the owners were the acting captain, Mr. Atwood; the chief engineer, Mr. Pennywhite; the purser; and the Filipino cook, who was too frightened of heights to ride the cargo net to safety.

As far as Captain Hammond could appraise the situation, everything went pretty much as planned, and by six-thirty that evening the tug was back in harbor, with the passengers and their baggage reunited at last. The captain made his report to Mr.

Campion and then hired a teamster and his wagon to cart Dr. Neruda's trunks and luggage up to the guesthouse. The captain rode with the wagon and was surprised to find his guests not at home to accept delivery of their goods. He had the wagon unloaded and the Nerudas' baggage placed in the house, and after paying off the teamster the captain walked home through the twilit orchards entertaining modest ambitions of a long hot bath, clean clothes, and a good meal served in peace with his family.

But the captain soon had to admit that the best-laid plans usually come apart in the planning stage, and so he was slightly annoyed, but not altogether surprised, to discover through Li-Lee that his wife was entertaining a few gentlemen in the formal parlor, and Dr. Neruda and his family were also in attendance. Captain Hammond had no wish to present himself to strangers in his present state of dishevelment, so he sent the maid to bring him clean clothes and boots, and then made his way unannounced to the bath. The captain didn't waste any time speculating about what his wife was concocting in the parlor. He knew he would find out about it sooner rather than later, and besides, the things Lady Yee could get up to were usually more colorful than he could imagine anyway, so he sat back in his beautiful copper bath and let the hot water soften the knots in his arms and legs.

12

WHEN THE CAPTAIN joined his wife just before dinner, after her guests had departed, it was instantly obvious to him that whatever he was feeling good about most likely now paled beside what she was experiencing. For the first time in memory, Lady Yee displayed an indelible smile that not even her vaunted inscrutability could modify or hide. Her expression was punctuated now and then by a slight, almost involuntary chuckle, which she politely hid behind her sleeve like a schoolgirl.

The captain pretended not to notice and recited an abbreviated gazette of the day's activities out at the ship, which ended with his delivery of Dr. Neruda's baggage and trunks to an empty house. As almost an afterthought he asked where the Nerudas had gone. It wasn't as though they were socially in demand after so short a time, and there was no sight of them about.

Lady Yee smiled and said that, at her personal request, the Neruda family had been invited to dine with Master Lao Key of the Boa Chen Key Company. This immediately got her husband's attention, and he flashed a rare look of surprise. The Neruda clan had barely been ashore seventy-two hours and they were already enjoying the hospitality of a man who was well-known for his highly secretive and mantled habits. Most everyone who had done business with the Boa Chen Key Company over the years, including Captain Hammond, had never met the man. Master Lao Key and his company controlled more than fifty successful mercantile and trading interests between Monterey and San Jose, and yet it seemed there were only about six people in all of California who could pick him out of a crowd. And it was said, in jest, that his wife and children were not among their number.

Lady Yee didn't wait for her astonished husband to ask further questions. She knew that he hated having to drag things out of people one detail at a time, and he was not particularly fond of surprises. He came to these tendencies naturally from long practice at sea.

Over a cup of tea, Lady Yee explained that she had for some time been in contact with various tong elders, local Chinese entrepreneurs, and various concerned businessmen who depended upon Chinese labor for their success. She said these interests had shown concern for the same problems, and had committed to making modest financial contributions, but only when the medical facilities and the infirmary were established and functioning. None had shown the least interest in financing a pig in a poke, and with empty buildings and a dearth of adequately equipped medical staff that's just what her schemes appeared to be on the surface. In polite terms they were saying that they didn't believe Lady Yee could manifest such an enterprise, much less contrive to have it function with the professionalism and certainty expected in the medical field. After ringing for the maid and requesting that dinner be served in fifteen minutes, Lady Yee continued. While the captain had been occupied rescuing the passengers' baggage and goods, she had taken the opportunity to interview Dr. Neruda and his son-in-law in some depth. She also had a marvelous conversation with Mrs. Neruda and her daughter later. Based upon an idea of their wants and wishes, and taking into account an unknowable future in Canada, she had offered them a contractual position to open and run the infirmary. There would be no need for them to seek out clients, and those patients who could afford to pay would be encouraged to contribute toward the upkeep of the infirmary, which would benefit all in turn. For those who could not, then perhaps a gift of goods or services would suffice. Lady Yee had agreed to finance the whole operation for three years, and that included not only salaries but medical supplies, linens, and food for patients. She then grinned and confided to the captain that she already had a scheme in hand to eventually farm out a majority of those costs to the very people who doubted her ability to harness such an extravagant and unusual agenda. Lady Yee's proposed financial responsibilities in the matter didn't concern the captain in the least. His wife was a very wealthy woman in her own right; in fact, the captain believed that if she called upon financial backing from her esteemed father, she could probably buy and sell the late Leland Stanford once or twice. But that aside, Captain Hammond was still concerned that the cultural and racial bias inherent in the conservative nature of the principal parties involved would, as it always had, derail the course of enlightened self-interest. It was the captain's opinion that traditional Chinese attitudes and prejudices would remain the most volatile hindrance to success. Without the full support of the tong masters and village elders, not to mention the more successful business elements within the Chinese community, one could easily end up with a medical staff, a functioning infirmary, and no patients willing to submit themselves to the care of foreigners.

When Li-Lee quietly announced dinner, Lady Yee took her husband's arm, smiled reassuringly, and guided him toward the door. Captain Hammond took his place at the head of the table. He kept silent while the soup course was served. He had almost finished his abalone chowder before he allowed his wife the pleasure of elucidating the details of her apparent success.

Lady Yee began by saying that her father, who

was a sage in his own right, had encouraged her to understand that the only truly imposing barriers between cultures were those constructed to service either fear or jealousy, or both. With everyone either grasping for what the other fellow had, or fearing that person's possession of some coveted technology, and subsequent influence and wealth, there was little room or patience for negotiation and compromise. She went on to say that both fear and jealousy were very personal emotions, and few people would admit to suffering the negative effects of either one. "Such goading emotions are always difficult to pin down," she said, "but relatively easy to manipulate if one knows what to do, and to whom to do it." Lady Yee went on to observe that most of the world's greatest warriors, leaders, and criminals have used this same principle for centuries. The Chinese were past masters at stirring up the masses using these methods. But then, she joked, unlike Europe, the Chinese had always enjoyed a substantially greater peasant population to inflame.

Apologizing for the digression, Lady Yee continued by pointing out that the greatest of all personal human fears is bonded at the hip with thoughts of mortality. And within that scope of abysmal trepidation there crouched the even darker menace of a painful or lingering illness that would eventually end in premature death because no serious medical care was forthcoming from any quarter. Barring deeply concerned relatives touting traditional folk remedies and voicing tearful petitions calling upon heaven's mercy for a cure, the end is almost preordained. Lady Yee recalled there was an old saying that she learned from her father's grain steward when she was a child: "The poor must die because it costs money to live. If dying cost money the poor would be immortal." Lady Yee set down her spoon, tamped her delicately rouged lips with her napkin, sat back in her chair, and stared out through the walls of the house to the black-water shanties and derelict junks along the Pearl River. She disavowed the tears forming in her eyes and went back to her meal.

Lady Yee said she believed that the aforesaid fears and trepidations were common to all mankind, and as far as she could intuit, impoverished was impoverished whether you were a Mongol, a Mexican, a Malaysian, or a Nantucket Yankee. But above and beyond that consideration, there floated a noxious cloud of self-righteous inflexibility when it came to the well-being and health of the working peasantry. The city fathers of the county certainly wanted none of the responsibility and expense entailed in looking after Chinese immigrant labor, documented or otherwise. It would cost tax dollars, and they were honest in their assessment of the odds against being reelected with such a proposal attached to a plank of their party's agenda.

The captain's wife took strength from her husband's patience and continued with her usual grace. She explained that in addressing each party's fears and concerns, she had discovered that each had three things in common. The first, as always, was the burden of expense and liability. The second thorn, mutual cultural suspicion, attended the first, but with an underlying fear of isolation as well. For instance, the various village elders and tong masters demonstrated their own racial bias when it came to the people dispensing the medical care. For most of these gentlemen, modern medicine had much in common with secretive temple rituals, and like all mystery-mantled wizardry, only the select few were allowed to know the secrets. Everyone, everywhere, she said, was suspicious of secrets, and distrustful of those who used secrets to manipulate others. Sadly, this same misgiving clouded poor people's acceptance of modern medical practices as well. It made little difference that Dr. Neruda was from India, she said. For all it mattered to the village elders, the Neruda family might as well be natives of Antarctica. Lady Yee was not pleased to report that, as expected, the elders' only consistent objection to their practice of medicine was that they weren't Chinese. Lady

Yee smiled and said she was inspired to politely remind these antique gentlemen that the Buddha wasn't Chinese either, and yet his teachings still held the power to enlighten and guide the soul.

Captain Hammond thought it was about time he said something just to keep his hand in the game, but he was at a loss for anything more constructive than a question. He set aside his plate, sipped his chilled tea, and asked his wife just how she had planned to nullify these impediments, especially now that she had already contracted for Dr. Neruda's services for three years.

Lady Yee appeared to look inward as she spoke, as though addressing an unseen presence. It was as if she were speaking to the powers of ancestry and soliciting their approval. The captain had experienced these charming soliloquies before. His wife often arranged her thoughts out loud, and once he came to understand how she tailored her ideas, her husband happily indulged the practice. It gave him occasional insights about the workings of her mind, but that too could be misleading, as she often changed and adapted her ideas before putting them into practice. This tactic gave her an edge that was totally beyond censure. She told you what she might do, and then did or didn't do it, whatever she was pleased to consider most expedient to accomplish her goals. The only consistency the captain could depend upon was his wife's total unpredictability. Happily, he always found this side of her nature most entertaining, and he lived with the assurance that whatever she chose to do, Lady Yee had the greatest good in mind. In that particular, Silver Lotus was the most philanthropic and generous of creatures, a trait not common in most people, regardless of origin or cultural influences.

Lady Yee waited until after the maid had cleared the fish course and served Ah Chu's hearty potage of wild boar, spring onions, and oysters. It was one of the captain's favorites, which instantly pinched him between hunger and curiosity. He set the lid back on the steaming terrine and looked at his wife with a slightly ravenous expression that begged for brevity.

Lady Yee simply pointed out that it was only natural for certain elements of society to express feelings of anxiety and trepidation with anything out of the ordinary, especially if they felt they might become liable at a later date for any mischief done. Lady Yee said that removing the causes for fear and the justifications for concern from the equation had changed all the values. All the contrary elements lost their moral potency, or at the very least, the desire to impede that, which at its core, was a reasonable, charitable, and responsible endeavor, and worthy to exist for its own sake. With that, Lady Yee concluded by serving her husband his dinner. She said no more for the present. She knew that once the captain had taken the edge off his appetite, his curiosity would wander back of its own accord like a distracted puppy.

When the captain had eaten his fill, his wife launched into her explanation. She set aside her plate and leaned forward for emphasis. She told how she had sent their lawyer, Mr. Bishop, to see the mayor and the city fathers, primarily to assuage any fears they might have about the Chinese infirmary. Lady Yee acknowledged that anything novel or strange was always fertile ground for concern in a small town. The first thing everyone always wanted to know was how this or that would impact their own well-being. A bit selfish perhaps, but there were always those benighted souls who believed that being on one's guard against exotic influences was a responsibility they could ill afford to surrender to the general public. Of course these same people were also deeply concerned with the subject of public and private liability. Public funds were not to be imperiled, or even requested, if it came to that. Lady Yee went on to explain that she had, through the offices of J. W. Bishop, Esq., representing Hammond, Macy & Yee, assured those potential critics that the infirmary project was fully funded by private donation and established in a location that would hardly impact residential sensibilities. She had Mr. Bishop explain in detail that the health of the laboring Chinese had a substantial impact on the economics of the region, and since there were no public facilities willing to attend to these people, it was a matter of public interest and safety to take up the slack privately. All that was required of the city fathers was a permit to open the doors. They would not be solicited for any further assistance, or any special considerations, and regular weekly reports would be made to the department of public health and sanitation concerning any outbreaks of communicable disease or unusual medical situations that would affect the public at large.

The captain said he believed his wife might have pressed the point a little too closely. The city's elected were jealous of their prerogatives, and usually dug in their heels when lectured about matters they were ill prepared to master by themselves. Their motto seemed to be "When in doubt, say no." They usually cared more for their reelection than for public advancement, but that was true almost everywhere, which gave inactivity a kind of traditional basis to lean upon when called to account, if ever.

Lady Yee bowed her head and said she found their accommodations quite reasonable. Then she pulled an official city use permit out of her billowing sleeve and slid it across the table for her husband's inspection. He looked at the document and asked if she had been as successful with her own compatriots.

It was Lady Yee's opinion that the Chinese elders needed the same assurances, but she made a further accommodation that seemed to secure their majority support. She had promised to have Dr. Neruda and his family train appropriate candidates from each of the fishing villages in rudimentary health care and first aid. This was to include all midwives. Those applicants who proved talented and dedicated would be given more advanced medical training. In this way the general health of the villages could be monitored, and if the case required it, the patient could be moved to the infirmary for more intensive care. And in that regard, Lady Yee had instructed Mr. Bishop to purchase a used one-horse army ambulance from the Presidio, and then have it refurbished at Mr. Bentley's coachworks. In that way, Dr. Neruda could transport seriously ill patients to and from the infirmary without relying on the necessity of using hired transport.

It was Lady Yee's ability to engage and involve the village elders in matters relating to their own health that gave them the confidence to endorse her proposals. They felt from the beginning that Lady Yee was an ally in cultural and traditional matters, when in fact she knew precisely how to use such agendas as served her own goals, and bowed to the rest as so much cultural plumage.

Such things served a purpose to be sure, but they also often served to justify inaction when imagination and ardor were lacking, and the captain knew that Lady Yee had little patience with inconvenient and superstitious impediments, nor could she abide those who claimed to know heaven's will from ancient magical sources.

Lady Yee had set about the whole enterprise with the intention of giving those very same venerable elders and tong masters credit for the whole idea. Since their social and political positions rested upon acquiring reputations for good works and civic responsibility, she saw no reason not to award them the recognition and acclaim. The captain knew well that public praise and appreciation meant virtually nothing to Lady Yee. By insisting others take the credit, and without incurring either expense or liability, she effectively dragooned them into becoming stewards of the enterprise whether they wanted to or not. Any attempt to hobble the welfare of the people now would be seen as traitorous to their offices. Lady Yee said that for women, getting men to do what was right and natural was easy, as long as you exalted them with praise and adulation for thinking of it first, and doing it so well. She reminded her husband of the ancient dictum that proclaimed that to be celebrated was to be made a tool of other people's expectations, and Lady Yee confessed that she much preferred the cloaked occupation of playwright and puppeteer. She said she had learned something from watching her father's mistakes. And she had determined that there was more power and influence to be gained from invisibility than from notoriety, no matter how well intentioned the endeavor. Jealousy, envy, and even hatred always cruised back and forth liked sharks hunting in the wake of celebrated personages. And if that noteworthy person just happened to be a woman, then she stood the same chances of escaping with her reputation unscathed as a wounded tuna trailing blood in the foam. Lady Yee told her husband that she was convinced that in this matter, as in other aspects of life, navigating a safe and creative course between such culturally divergent interests and desires required management from the shadows. As far as she was concerned, the less her name was mentioned in connection with the venture, the better for everything all around. In that same vein, she had instructed that the infirmary be dedicated to the immortal mercies of Guan Yin, and titled appropriately with no other reference, no matter how modest and well meant, to herself. She smiled and said this also precluded any of the other godfathers from naming the infirmary to reflect their own sponsorship or participation. She had even forced them into a position of modesty as well. No one of right mind would dare suggest superior precedence over the goddess of mercy.

The captain let out a hearty laugh, slapped the table, and raised his wineglass to toast the "queen of the shadows." Then he smiled sweetly and said it gave him great peace and satisfaction to know that Lady Yee was his wife and partner, and not his competition. To which Lady Yee replied that she was luckier than most Chinese women. She'd had the good fortune to marry for love, and in the bargain she acquired a husband who was enlightened enough to appreciate the fine art of accommodation. The captain was about to respond with equal sentiments of affection when the conversation was suddenly interrupted by Macy, once again narrowly escaping the clutches of Li-Lee, who came running into the dining room with her little arms outstretched to her father in supplication. It was a customary petition to be taken up in his arms and onto his lap. His arms were safe ground. And every time her father took her up, she would instantly look back to see if her pursuer had been halted. Satisfied that all was well, she'd giggle and kiss her father on the cheek. It was his traditional reward for faithful service. She really loved this game, but it only reminded the captain that his little Macy was really her mother's daughter in almost every particular.

13

THE NEXT TWO WEEKS were rather hectic by normal standards. Lady Yee supervised almost every detail from her parlor or her gardens. She held conferences with Dr. Neruda and his wife about the purchase of all necessary medical supplies, surgical instruments, and medicines, as well as food, linen, laundry, and sanitation facilities.

Lady Yee and the Nerudas made out long, well-considered lists, and Mr. Bishop sent out reams of orders under the company letterhead. A Chinese cook and kitchen boys were hired under Ah Chu's expert supervision. A qualified stableman was employed to look after the carriage horses and ambulance mules, as well as the shay, the spring wagon, and the ambulance. He was to be paid extra for driving services. He too was given a young assistant to help with the heavy work, and a feed boy to portion out grain and hay to the animals, and make sure the water troughs were kept clean and full.

Lady Yee knew better than to involve her husband in the minutiae and made sure he was disturbed as little as possible. He had his own business matters to attend to, and they had been set aside for far too long. At the same time, something perplexing transpired that brought his attention back to the recently stranded ship and the fate of the crew. Mr. Campion had kept the captain informed about the vessel and her condition. The salvage company had successfully pulled the tub from her snare, and after some patch repairs to her bottom, the steamer was deemed sound enough to be towed back to the harbor and anchored offshore until permanent repairs could be made. It was everyone's hope that they would be made soon. Everyone in town wanted to see the stern of that ugly old bark disappear over the horizon. She was considered bad luck all around, and the whole town wished she would continue her voyage to Vancouver as soon as possible. However, there were some inconvenient problems to address first, and not the least of these was the erstwhile captain of the ill-fated ship, Sigmund Malakoff. Malakoff was only held in custody for three days, which was the legal limit without a judge's order, but he was released with a stern warning not to leave the county, pending further investigations in which his testimony would most certainly be required. Malakoff's response to this new situation was typical of him; he snuck back aboard his old ship and rifled the contents of the ship's safe, to which he had the only key. Then he simply disappeared like morning fog.

The acting captain, Mr. Atwood, had not known where to find the key, but after consulting with the ship's purser and comparing paid cargo invoices, it was judged feasible that Malakoff could have easily absconded with as much as fifteen thousand dollars' worth of currency. Only a full audit would reveal the true scale of the loss, but the problem caused by the theft had far deeper consequences, for without the money to pay the crew, purchase coal, and provision the ship, much less pay a deposit on the salvage fees, the battered old freighter was going nowhere. The owners were contacted in Vancouver, but as yet they had done nothing to solve the situation.

And there was one other rather troublesome detail. As it turned out, even if the funds had been available, the men were all demanding to be paid off and released. They wanted nothing more to do with the ship, which they declared haunted by the ghost of their missing shipmate. They said they could even smell death belowdecks, and that was a sure indication that the man's ghost was close at hand. Every tar worth his pint knew the omens and what they meant. They wouldn't sign on with that ship again, even for a bounty of twice their pay. At the same time, the beached crewmen were not about to allow a bunch of sea scabs to steam the vessel out of the bay until they had been paid off. They had even hired a local lawyer to file an injunction on their behalf. In any event, the whole business was fast becoming a tricky predicament for a good number of people. Between the ship's grounding and salvage, Malakoff's theft of the ship's funds, the inability of the owners to satisfy their responsibilities, and the protests of the crew for back pay and release, it was easy to see how this situation might get out of hand. All of this only clouded the fate of the poor passengers, who were pretty much left to their own devices since the ship's owners had become so unresponsive. Their care had fallen to lesser civic institutions and local church charities. But some survivors had tired of the waiting and general ineptitude, so they had found the money and means to continue their journey. All those that chose to depart did so voicing stern intentions to seek legal redress from the shipping company as soon as possible.

The resulting collision of legal and personal interests amounted to warrants being broadcast far and wide for one Sigmund Malakoff on charges of grand theft and escape to avoid arrest. The pitiful old freighter swung on a shallow anchor in the harbor, manned only by Mr. Atwood, the cook, and a Japanese cabin boy. The fate of penurious crewmen and passengers remained unresolved, and there was hot talk of applying to the courts to impound the vessel to satisfy the growing claims of debt, and in that regard, the salvage company and their lawyers would most certainly stand in first position, leaving the others to fend for themselves.

It fell to an exasperated Mr. Campion to call

again upon Captain Hammond to assist in untangling the mess. The captain had gained a fair reputation as a gentleman who knew how to get things done. His wealth and striking reputation passed for qualifications in and of themselves, and complimentary stories had already spread about his astute handling of the survivors' situation. Even though he was considered a relative newcomer to Monterey, the local gentry had begun to look up to him.

The first thing the captain did was to interview the crew about their complaints and objections, but he heard nothing he hadn't already known from Mr. Campion. He already knew the status of the remaining passengers, at least those who remained behind due to a lack of funds to travel on. Before Malakoff had made off with the ship's funds, Captain Hammond had hoped the company would authorize the use of some of that money to recompense and assist those people, but it now appeared that they were making themselves hard to find. This turn of events persuaded the captain that perhaps the beached crew had a reasonable point in seeking a legal injunction, which in a sense would place the vessel under arrest until such time as all debts were satisfied. If the owners failed to fulfill their legal responsibilities, then the ship and its cargo would be sold to the highest bidders to cover all debts so far incurred. Captain Hammond arranged for a meeting with the city's attorney to discuss the legal ramifications of such a proposal.

In the meantime, Lady Yee moved her own project along at a marvelous pace, and all without ever leaving the comforts of her home, the company of her precocious daughter, and the beauty of her orchards and gardens. People came and went with messages and requests, and Lady Yee sent them on with her latest instructions. Captain Hammond likened it to Emperor Hadrian building his great wall across rain-swept England while pleasantly ensconced in sunny Rome. And by the standards of even the more affluent citizens of Monterey, Lady Yee was spending a fortune on her project. The cost of surgical instruments, medical apparatus, examination tables, hospital lamps, medical and hygienic supplies, and complex pharmaceutical compounds, not to mention a full stock of traditional Eastern medicinal herbs, would have financed a small farm, so to avoid public comment Lady Yee kept all her accounts and expenses secret. But even by her husband's own estimation, Lady Yee could endow ten infirmaries a year, for the next ten years, and still not make an appreciable dent in her personal fortune, which kept growing exponentially under her astute supervision. She kept poor Mr. Bishop and his two legal clerks very busy doing business exclusively on her behalf. If indeed there was such a thing as a lawyer who truly earned his salt by the sweat of his brow, it was J. W. Bishop. He was driven to impart his best efforts, not just by his avowed admiration for his employer, or the generous retainer, but also by fear of failure. But in that regard he was not alone. Though moderately forbearing when it came to most human foibles and weaknesses, there was something about Lady Yee's character that disdained all tolerance for failure in matters as mundane as business affairs. Life held enough disappointments that came unbidden; there was no reason to increase the negative prospects inherent in most business propositions by not planning ahead to adjust for most every eventuality.

The Guan Yin infirmary ceremonially opened its doors for the first time on the Saturday after Easter. Appreciating the Chinese tradition of appropriate dedication for anything of public or private value, Lady Yee arranged for a modest celebration to be held to mark the occasion. All the tong masters and village elders were invited to officiate, and Lady Yee paid for two Buddhist priests to come down from San Jose to crown the endeavor with their prayers and blessings. She even invited a renowned Confucian scholar to put his oar in the water. As arranged, he called for civic support to promote the general good. He reminded his audience that public dedication to the well-being of all souls was, in itself, a public virtue, and worthy in heaven's eyes. And since some of the local Chinese had converted to Christianity, Lady Yee also arranged for Father Escobar from the mission to attend and add his blessings. Captain Hammond was sure that if his wife could have found any village fishermen of Jewish faith, she would have employed a rabbi as well.

Despite the fact that the dedication ceremony was a rather colorful and noisy affair, with cymbals and drums crashing in syncopation with minor fireworks, gongs, and prayers, very few Monterey citizens knew anything about what had transpired. The location of the infirmary, in what was generally a workshop and warehouse district on the north end of town near the railroad tracks, precluded a wider audience. In fact, aside from a few disinterested warehouse guards who were trying to nap, and a minor parade of curious junkyard dogs, the Chinese celebrants had the streets to themselves. Saturdays were always pretty quiet in that part of town, which was why Lady Yee had chosen the date specifically. Though to forestall any charges of impiety or oversight, she did authenticate her choice with the help of her very accommodating Taoist priest, who declared the date auspicious for some esoteric reason no one could really quite fathom. But it hardly mattered in the long run, as there was a bounty of food, music, sweetmeats, and rice wine to appease any and all celestial objections.

Perhaps the oddest detail concerning the dedication ceremonies was the fact that Lady Yee did not attend, nor did she encourage her husband to do so. She insisted that it was important to avoid being thought of as a patroness. Public gratitude on any scale, she said, was always a fickle and dangerous business. Instead she thought it best to encourage the Chinese of Monterey to think of the infirmary as their own by right, not as a gift from a wealthy compatriot. With proprietary interest nurtured among the people, buds of concern, support, and protection might be expected to bloom. Lady Yee fully expected the people to eventually come to understand the necessity for such an institution, and then prepare for the future of the infirmary on their own.

In lieu of her own presence, Lady Yee sent the Taoist priest to represent the infirmary and to introduce Dr. Neruda and his family in the most glowing tones possible. He was instructed to remind his peasant audience that, like the teachings of the venerable Buddha, the great principles and tenets of Chinese medicine came first from India, birthplace of all the true medical arts. The priest was to convey the fact that every enlightened Chinese emperor in history had insisted that his household maintain a retinue of learned physicians, pharmacists, and surgeons from India. And now the fishermen, laundrymen, and railroad coolies of Monterey were to be afforded that same luxury through the abiding blessings of Guan Yin.

Captain Hammond talked to Dr. Neruda at length after the ceremony. They shared a few glasses of sweet apple cider and toasted cheese in the gardens, and then they watched the sun set over the bay. It was evident from the doctor's natural modesty that it had been a good thing he spoke no Chinese. The effusively gilded introduction that Lady Yee had composed for the priest would have caused him considerable embarrassment. Dr. Neruda expressed surprise at the enthusiastic response the priest's introduction received and the warmth of the greetings he personally garnered as a result. The doctor almost blushed when recounting the gifts that poor people brought. Those who could afford it presented the infirmary with boxes of rice, or dried fruit, or crocks of anchovies preserved in oil. Some offered signed promises to deliver fresh fish every month, or so many pounds of crabs. Since the Neruda family were all vegetarians, and happiest with their own traditional cuisine, all these gifts would be used to feed the patients and the staff, which now numbered six employees, four Chinese and two Filipinos. Lady Yee hired the Chinese women to be taught the skills of practical and surgical nurses and midwives, while Mrs. Neruda and her daughter were to train the two Filipino ladies as medicinal cooks. Learning the ayurvedic art of cooking for those suffering disease or injury was a priority, and the Nerudas placed much emphasis on diet and nutrition.

Thanks to Lady Yee's foresight, two of the new staff happened to be male and female cousins named Yah-Joon. Both were born in Santa Cruz, attended school there, and spoke excellent English as well as Cantonese. Lady Yee hired them especially to act as medical translators as well as nurses. One of them would always be present at every interview and medical examination. It was hoped this would make the uncertain patients feel all the more comfortable and unafraid.

Of course, Mrs. Neruda would examine the female patients exclusively and then consult with her husband in his role as chief pathologist. This cultural adaptation went a long way toward convincing the local Chinese matrons that their modesty would remain unsullied. However, Mrs. Neruda would still find it necessary to resort to the use of Chinese patient dolls to help diagnose the older women. These dowagers were anchored to more ancient traditions, and were always accommodated respectfully as a result. It was Lady Yee's conviction that these venerable grandmothers were the true power behind so many little thrones. If they were satisfied with the treatment they received, then they would press for others to seek treatment from the same source, especially where their grandchildren were concerned.

Lady Yee knew all this in advance, to be sure, and politely insisted that Dr. Neruda make every effort to see that his potential allies were not overlooked in any fashion. The doctor instantly smiled with appreciative agreement and nodded. And in that same vein, he modestly suggested that the infirmary make gifts of fruit to the older patients to help their digestion. Lady Yee thought this a marvelous idea, and from then on Dr. Neruda and Lady Yee seemed to be taking their text from the same pages. She said she was in a position to supply, when the harvest season dictated, a goodly crop from her own orchards, and the excess beyond personal use could be sold at market to purchase whatever foodstuffs or spices that were not readily available locally. She said her husband maintained excellent professional contacts with Chinese trading houses in San Francisco. She was convinced that he could easily acquire whatever esoteric goods the doctor might want. He need only submit a list of his requirements.

Dr. Neruda smiled, bowed, and introduced a rare note of levity. He said that if the Indian Army had been blessed with Lady Yee as a commanding general, the British Raj would have long since packed up and gone home to their cold, damp little island. Lady Yee caught the mood and responded with the observation that perhaps the British stayed in India primarily because they didn't like their cold, damp clump of rock. That was the first time Lady Yee ever heard Dr. Neruda laugh. Happily, it wasn't the last.

14

IN THE MEANWHILE, matters seemed to be arcing from bad to worse where the wounded freighter was concerned. The owners hadn't attended to their responsibilities, and even Mr. Atwood, the acting captain, was now so angry that he threatened to take his two remaining men, cut the anchor cables, and abandon the ship. This action would, of course, legally allow the salvage company to rush in, secure the vessel, and claim sole salvage rights. In fact, Mr. Campion had heard a rumor that indicated the Mercury Pacific Salvage Company had already secretly offered Mr. Atwood, and the full crew, eight thousand dollars to do just that. Mr. Campion, who had read the ship's manifest, believed her cargo of zinc and tin ingots, as well as the three thousand tanned hides and two hundred barrels of tallow, was worth at least five times the salvage offer. And then, of course, there was the market price for the ship, either afloat or as scrap, but either way there was a healthy profit to be had.

By way of personal depositions, Mr. Campion and Captain Hammond supported the claims of the crew and survivors, but the only way for Mr. Atwood and his two men to leave their posts was to have the vessel impounded by the courts to satisfy the debts. This also meant debts owed to the city for the support and housing of the survivors. If the salvage company got a chance to tow away the ship, no agency in American waters would ever see her afloat again. No one in Monterey really minded that eventuality as long as they got paid first. However, Mr. Campion and the crew were sure of one thing: The ship couldn't possibly leave the bay under her own steam. The Mercury Pacific Salvage Company had conveniently off-loaded the freighter's coal bunkers to lighten the ship before hauling her off the rocks. But with that chore came the added harvest of being able to fuel their own ship's massive engines free of charge. Even when in port, these oceangoing salvage tugs consumed a handsome portion of coal just keeping their boilers warm enough to facilitate a speedy departure. The first tug to arrive on any given station was always given the contract. And somewhere out on the bay was a big, soot-black, oil-streaked salvage tug just waiting to pounce on the hapless old freighter. Captain Hammond likened it to being stalked by professional game hunters, and he too ascribed to the belief that without timely legal protection, the odds weren't very appealing for anyone save perhaps the salvage company.

While the business of the ship's disposition seemed to drag anchor, Lady Yee's efforts were quickly rewarded. She had believed that it would most likely take a few months before the Chinese communities along the coast would take to using the infirmary with confidence, but Dr. Neruda was reporting full patient lists within ten days of the doors being opened.

The doctor was also pleased, and somewhat amused, to report that his wife, Nandiri, had become quite a favorite with the older Chinese patients. She often gave them especially fortified tinctures of ginseng root, gotu kola leaves, licorice root, and reishi mushroom caps. This simple concoction made the ancients as chipper as starlings because it regulated their systems and gave them sounder sleep and more endurance. And though compounding the tincture required expensive ingredients, and a complex series of steps that demanded exactitude and precision, the tonic was sold to the more elderly patients for a mere five cents per pint. Each bottle contained sixty daily doses, which made it the least expensive maintenance medication in any market, and far more effective than the patent medicines the people sometimes were encouraged to purchase by itinerant drummers with extravagant claims. Dr. Neruda also reported that three healthy babies had been born, a broken arm and a broken foot had been set, and an old fisherman with advanced pleurisy had suffered a minor heart attack but was resting comfortably in the infirmary. However, his prognosis was not very positive, and his relatives had been told to stay close at hand in case matters turned worse. The Nerudas had also treated two patients with allergic skin disorders, one fisherman who'd had a poisonous stingray barb driven deep into his calf, and a four-year-old boy who had suddenly shown signs of seizures with no apparent cause. Dr. Neruda was happy to report that all their patients, save one, were on the mend, and aside from a minor case of pneumonia, there had been no reports of any communicable illnesses from any of the fishing villages in the previous two weeks.

Mr. Campion, now totally frustrated by all the delays, sought to bring the matter to a head by petitioning the city attorney to seek an injunction that would effectively impound the ship until such time as the owners satisfied her debts. Whereas the beached crew and passengers were facing a drawn-out legal process hampered by a lack of funds, the city attorney and the harbormaster wielded influence that got the judge to sit up and take notice.

The process by which a ship was impounded was as old as maritime law itself. In one sense the ship was literally arrested by the authorities. A court officer, or a federal marshal, would go aboard the vessel in question and seize her registration papers, commissions, logs, cargo manifests, and flags of national origin. This last detail was purely ceremonial, since maritime tradition held that a ship without colors could not sign on a legal crew or leave port without the court's release. Before departing the ship with the skeleton crew, the freighter would be thoroughly inspected, her cargo affirmed, and her holds sealed. A deputized guard would then be left on board, to be relieved every second day, and the harbormaster would see to it that the security of the anchorage and the ship's cables were inspected regularly for drag or wear. The rest was up to the courts and maritime law.

Captain Hammond now felt himself well out of the picture and was quite content to be so. The whole business had taken up a great deal of his time and energy, and though he'd once visited Mr. Campion's office for social reasons, he put the ship's fate out of his mind and hoped that was the last of it. However, barely two days later, Captain Hammond received another urgent request from Mr. Campion. An unforeseen complication had arisen in the matter of the impounded ship, and Mr. Campion requested the privilege of an unofficial consultation.

As far as Captain Hammond was concerned, there appeared to exist some universal principle that determined no man should enjoy a full meal at home undisturbed by the outside world. This was affirmed by the fact that hand-delivered messages always seemed to arrive at mealtimes. However, this time the captain was determined not to be manipulated by circumstances and sent the doorkeeper away with the envelope until he called for it. As it turned out, the business was hardly time-sensitive.

Mr. Campion was somewhat distraught when the captain arrived. He motioned to be followed, then quickly closed his office door for privacy. With a voice tinged with exasperation, he sat his guest down with a glass of strong port and proceeded to tell Captain Hammond a very grizzly tale indeed.

Mr. Campion said that all that the court had required had been done. A marshal had boarded the ship with two deputies and secured all her papers and flags. In this they enjoyed the complete cooperation of Mr. Atwood and his men, who were overjoyed that the court had seen fit to protect their rights and wages.

But then something very odd happened. Mr. Atwood mentioned to the marshal that the black gang and ship's engineers, who were now all onshore, had complained bitterly that the ship was haunted because they could smell the ghost of the man who had been lost during the storm. Mr. Atwood took the marshal aside and confirmed that there was no one aboard except himself, the cook, and the cabin boy, but he had made an inspection of the engine room the night before, and in fact the cloying smell of death was anything but illusory. He hadn't mentioned it to the cook or cabin boy, because they were pretty well spooked already, but there was something definitely decaying down in the engine room. After a short search of the obvious hiding places, nothing was found and Mr. Atwood barely escaped the deeply fetid atmosphere without losing his supper. He described the debilitating odor as akin to death tinged with coal dust, machine oil, and raw sewage.

Mr. Campion wisely chose brevity to explain the rest. He told Captain Hammond that the marshal, commensurate with his duties to inspect the whole ship and its cargo, had all the deck hatches and ventilators opened, especially those that accessed the engine room. Within moments the marshal experienced that same sickly odor for himself. Once the atmosphere belowdecks had somewhat cleared, and with the overhead deck hatches propped open, the marshal and his men masked their lower faces with wet bandanas against the stink and initiated a thorough search. With the air of a man who hates to hear his own words, Mr. Campion described how they at last pulled up the heavy iron engine-room deck plates and discovered a dead man in the bilges. Sadder yet, there wasn't really that much of him that the rats hadn't gotten to first. The cause of death couldn't be disguised, for the marshal and his men saw a large rusting blade still protruding from the victim's skeletal chest.

Mr. Campion raised his arms in frustration and rolled his eyes to heaven. He bemoaned the fact that this whole crazy business now also involved a homicide, which would definitely cloud matters all around as far as the ship's disposition was concerned. Mr. Campion verbally rebelled at the thought that the one person who should be held responsible for creating this mortal train of events, and the only character with any explanations worth hearing, the darkly elusive Sigmund Malakoff, had taken to his heels with truly professional dispatch, and was now nowhere to be found, at least not under his own name and description. One might think this fact alone would, of course, place Malakoff in the prime position as chief suspect in the homicide, except for one thing: There wasn't the least hint of a motive or opportunity connecting the two men. Crewmen who had already been interviewed by the city attorney's office had stated that Malakoff and the missing crewman had never been seen speaking. Not one man could even hint at a sign of discord between the two men. This line of testimony made everything that much more confusing for poor Mr. Campion, and he desperately wanted Captain Hammond to reinterview the crew and passengers once more to help determine the truth. Due to his reputation for balanced and equitable judgment, Mr. Campion trusted Captain Hammond. If anybody knew how to avoid the snares of public expectation, which was always so freely broadcast by the uninformed, it was Captain Hammond. And there was one further fly in the ointment. The crime had taken place aboard a ship of foreign registry, albeit stranded on American shores. The incident would therefore come under the scrutiny of federal authorities very shortly. In fact, Mr. Campion and the sheriff of Monterey, Mr. Winslow—along with the state marshal who had impounded the ship and made the grizzly discovery—expected to be interviewed by federal attorneys any day. The legal problems inherent in the case would now be compounded. A matter that should have fallen under the jurisdiction of state courts might now easily be made to wait upon the machinations of higher authority, and that could take years. The ship's creditors might have to cool their heels, and in the meantime the people of Monterey would have to look at the rusting old steamship anchored out in the bay, a painful reminder of an extremely unfortunate incident made all the more tragic by murder and mayhem. Something would have to be done about that ship. As a sign of his blossoming frustration, Mr. Campion even spoke of using his authority to condemn the freighter as a navigational hazard and then having the unsightly derelict towed somewhere else less conspicuous. However, he well knew the crew's lawyers would object and immediately petition for a stay, so he didn't press the matter.

In his subsequent interviews with the crew, the captain really didn't learn anything new, but one disturbing fact did resurface to disturb his thoughts. He had discounted it earlier, but since the missing deckhand had been found murdered, he was forced to examine the information from a new perspective. Several men had recounted that there was something odd and disturbing about the way the dead man had tormented and insulted the Indian doctor and his family whenever he got the chance. But when Mr. Atwood heard of it, and called the crewman to account, the man angrily said it never happened, and swore the Indian faker was making it up because the crewman was a Muslim. In any event, Dr. Neruda chose to let the matter rest even though other crewmen said they overheard further incidents of the same kind.

Captain Hammond found it almost impossible to credit the idea that the man he knew as Dr. Neruda, a strict vegetarian Hindu who didn't even swat at flies, a man sworn by profession to care for the injured and ill, and a trained surgeon of proven caliber, could resort to cold-blooded murder to avenge a lowly deckhand's insult to his nonviolent religion. The whole idea seemed too far-fetched at best, but what would matter most was the reaction of the federal marshal's office when they eventually encountered the same testimony. The captain wondered how he should address the situation, especially as Lady Yee had invested so much time and effort in the doctor. This was not the kind of thing she would allow to rest without a thorough examination and explanation.

That very evening after dinner, Captain Hammond invited his wife into his study, and with his notes spread before him on the desk told her in detail about the murder and the crew testimony concerning the victim and Dr. Neruda. Lady Yee listened very quietly, showed no emotion whatsoever, and then asked only one or two incidental questions. When her husband had answered these to her satisfaction, she thanked him for the information and quietly departed.

Despite her superficial calm and almost indifferent demeanor, the captain knew that Lady Yee would now loft all sail and race to disarm all potential adversaries before a legal confrontation interfered with her own agendas. Yet he instantly perceived that Lady Yee thought the idea of Dr. Neruda acting the role of a murderer for religious defamation totally absurd on the face of it. But he also knew she would have to admit that they lived in a world where even groundless accusations caused great mischief and misery to innocent people all the time. She would have to find a way to forestall such an eventuality before any serious damage resulted, and to that end, Lady Yee quietly disappeared into her own sanctum next to the garden parlor, and she didn't emerge until after midnight.

The next morning at breakfast Lady Yee asked her husband if he had a copy of the crew list. He said he did. Then she asked if it also included the crewmen's country of origin. Again he answered in the affirmative. Then she asked if the missing Malakoff had left behind any papers or private logs after he rifled the ship's safe and escaped. The captain said that if any such papers existed, they would now be in the possession of the arresting state marshal, Mr. Sanchez, who, in turn, would be obliged to give them over to the presiding court upon request. Then he smiled and, accurately predicting her next question, told his wife that he might be able to talk Mr. Rice, the city attorney, into letting him see such evidence, if it existed, but he seriously doubted he'd be allowed to take it away for Lady Yee's personal examination.

Before the captain arose from the breakfast table, Lady Yee passed over seven elegantly hand-addressed envelopes. She politely requested that these missives be delivered to Mr. Campion, the harbormaster; Mr. Atwood; Mr. Rice, the city attorney; Mr. Sanchez, the state marshal; Mr. Winslow, the high sheriff of Monterey; and Dr. Neruda. There was also an envelope formally addressed to Captain Hammond. When her husband asked what they contained, Lady Yee said they were invitations for high tea on the following afternoon.

Captain Hammond went to his own small trading office near the customshouse and called in a bicycle messenger to deliver Lady Yee's invitations. Dr. Neruda's was sent to the infirmary, where he spent most of his time. Then the captain sat back to read his own invitation. He had no idea what the other letters contained by way of instruction, but he was asked to locate Mr. Atwood's cabin boy, Jojo Toyuka, and have him brought to the house no later than five-thirty the following afternoon, and this seemed odd since the invitation explicitly said that tea would be served at four.

Later that same afternoon, Captain Hammond paid a call on Mr. Campion at his office. There he discovered that Lady Yee had politely requested that the harbormaster bring along any and all papers relating to the fugitive captain, Sigmund Malakoff. And when Captain Hammond later accidently came across Sheriff Winslow, he discovered that Lady Yee had requested the sheriff to bring any reports he might have concerning the missing sailor, now presumed to be the murdered man recently discovered in the ship's engine room bilges. After a short discussion, Captain Hammond presumed Marshal Sanchez would also have received a similar request concerning the ship's papers and manifests now in his custody.

The city attorney, Mr. Rice, made a point of stopping by the captain's office. He was a little confused by his own invitation, as it requested the recipient to bring along an estimate of the ship's financial liabilities as listed in the court injunction, and he couldn't quite fathom what that had to do with the fate of the dead man, as it was obvious he had been killed about the same time the ship fetched up on the rocky teeth of Point Lobos. The captain, though mildly amused, commiserated. But he did say that Lady Yee practically invented social frugality, and that he'd never known her to waste so much as a breath of air, thus he was duly persuaded she had something significant to contribute, and suggested that simple compliance was the fastest way to arrive at a solution to the mystery. Besides, he said with a laugh, Lady Yee would see to it that her maniacal chef, Ah Chu, jumped through burning hoops of custard buns and spun sugar to impress her guests. Her teas were always the choicest blends, and her brandy punch was a heaven-bestowed nectar. Mr. Rice said he'd be proud to attend.

Before returning home that evening, Captain Hammond sought out Mr. Atwood at the French House. There he discovered that Lady Yee had requested Mr. Atwood to bring any private logs he may have kept. She knew from long experience

277

that first officers aboard ship often kept their own detailed journals. They never knew when they might be called upon to face official examination. It was considered better form to pen a complaint than voice one. Written private sentiments, no matter how scathing and vitriolic, could not be considered mutinous unless broadcast to other members of the crew to effect a change in command. With so many uncomfortable hours to fill, and so little satisfaction to be had, one would hardly be surprised to see the length of some of their private logs. Captain Hammond often recounted the story of a deck officer he once knew who was so at odds with every ship he sailed on that his journals often ran to four and five volumes of bitter complaints and criticisms. However, no matter how he might have seethed and scathed in private, while on duty he always remained the most amenable, polite, and competent officer imaginable.

Captain Hammond confided that he had been given instructions to find the cabin boy, Toyuka, and see that he arrived at a certain time. Mr. Atwood offered to attend to that detail on the captain's behalf, and even suggested that the cook, Mr. Beal, might be interviewed as well. He had supposedly known Malakoff the longest and might be encouraged to say a few enlightening words if approached properly. The captain agreed, but said he thought it best if Toyuka and Beal came separately, and were kept apart until after they were interviewed. Again, Mr. Atwood said he would attend to it, and so Captain Hammond thanked him and went home to dinner.

That night the captain decided not to mention what he had learned from the other recipients of Lady Yee's invitations. He knew that when she was ready to tell him anything, she would make a solid point of it. Until then he decided to avoid any discussion of her plans on the grounds that what he didn't know wouldn't keep him awake that night. He did, however, ask whether she had spoken to Dr. Neruda recently, and she said she had not, and would not talk with him until after he had been interviewed by her other guests. Lady Yee admitted that her professional relationship with Dr. Neruda already tainted her as biased on his behalf, and she wished to avoid any suspicion that she had prompted him to say one thing or another. She had hoped her husband might visit the good doctor in the morning and reassure him that all would be well, and that nothing would transpire to injure his dignity or reputation. Nonetheless, it was important for him to bring the documents she suggested, just in case the obvious called for support.

The next day the captain paid a call on Dr. Neruda at the infirmary, and found him not in the least concerned about anything beyond treating a squid fisherman who had been badly burned when his old iron fire basket collapsed. Nothing else seemed very important by comparison, but he said he would wait on Lady Yee that afternoon as requested. He appeared confident that whatever Lady Yee had tabled, he was to have the benefit of it, so he saw no reason to concern himself further.

Though he said nothing, Captain Hammond was privately very pleased that his wife had the power to inspire such secure feelings of assurance in people, and he fervently hoped she could replicate the sensation for her expected guests. If not, then he feared that perhaps someone might be facing a rope, and he sincerely hoped it wouldn't be Dr. Neruda. Nonetheless, the captain was well aware that religious intolerance and subsequent violence were a blade that cut in both directions. And though he had come to like and respect Dr. Neruda in the short time he had known him, the captain was modestly aware that he was by no means fluent in the subtleties of spiritual turmoil and hostility when it came to Asian religious conflicts. Indeed, aside from the fact that it seemed a constant all over the world, religious bloodletting was an aspect of human affairs that he found almost incomprehensible. If it had been a matter of one distinct religion going for the throat of a diametrically opposed philosophy, it might have been marginally comprehensible, but the truth made even less sense, for it seemed that Christians murdered Christians with the same enthusiasm used to kill Muslims, and Muslim sects appeared to delight in murdering each other with the same fervor usually reserved for the destruction of Christians. And sadly, the same could also be said for Buddhists, Taoists, Hindus, Sikhs, Parsis, and even Jews. They all appeared capable of destroying members of their own faith as well as those who bowed to a different deity altogether. It had come to Captain Hammond over years of experience that the world's religions formed the foundation for some of the most irreligious and criminally insane conduct ever devised by mankind. The idea of burning human beings at the stake because they refused to acknowledge a different version of the same deity had always seemed like complete madness as far as the captain was concerned. And sad as he was to admit it even to himself, Captain Hammond wouldn't have been in the least surprised to discover that Dr. Neruda had indeed killed his tormentor. History was replete with such incidences of moral lunacy, particularly when it came to religious conflicts. He intended to wait upon the truth with an open if somewhat skeptical mind, regardless of Lady Yee's instincts to the contrary.

15

THE FOLLOWING AFTERNOON found Captain Hammond playing host to all those who had received Lady Yee's invitations, save, for the moment, Dr. Neruda. Guests had brought a folio of one kind or another, and each seemed loath to be separated from his parcel. However, they were soon too distracted by the culinary wonders that Ah Chu had assembled on the sideboard to focus on much else. Along with four varieties of rare tea and two kinds of coffee, Captain Hammond was pleased to present his own contribution. This was a seductive and inscrutable concoction that went by the dubious title of "Russian punch." Though the more exotic ingredients included pomegranate and peach nectar, the whole recipe was a secret that depended upon the moral authority of calvados and pear brandy to make its point. If any potable could be said to replicate a wolf in a sheep's fleece, Russian punch would fit the description quite nicely. It was the captain's bemused contention that his secret punch could leach the meanest motives from the world's greatest misanthropes and transform marginally moral men into archangels. The concoction was always served in small glass cups to avoid accidental inebriation. The captain balanced the portions to warm the cockles of the heart and nurture fellowship. Intoxication, he knew, would have the opposite effect.

The captain temporarily took the head of the table and seated Mr. Campion, Mr. Rice, and Mr. Sanchez to his right, and Mr. Winslow and Mr. Atwood to his left. The chair at the opposite end was reserved for Lady Yee, who had not put in an appearance as yet. She had thought it best to let the men loosen up a bit before putting them through their paces. And there was nothing Ah Chu's marvelous creations could not amend for the better, though she did take the captain's Russian punch into account when timing her entry.

As the men discussed the fate of the Canadian ship and the possible whereabouts of the villainous Malakoff, a small silver bell sounded, and Lady Yee made her entrance. All the men at the table stood up at once. Captain Hammond was as surprised as his guests to behold his wife attired in a beautifully tailored azure gown cut to reflect the latest Eastern fashion. Her long, luxuriant hair was cunningly dressed to rival any Gibson girl illustration. Her subtle elegance was set off by an intricate gold hair comb. It was set with a spray of finely polished lapis lazuli stones in the shape of a cresting wave. Lady Yee never dressed in this manner, and her husband found it quite alluring and seductive, and so too did the other gentlemen at the table, for all eyes remained on her for the next hour and a half. Captain Hammond knew his wife had planned all of this some time ago. She never let any detail go begging for attention, or wasted a potential asset, and in that regard she had, in fact, accomplished her ends, for all the men in the room, including her husband, paid very close attention to her every word.

The liveried houseboy held his mistress's chair, while the maid poured her a cup of tea. She toasted her guests with a warm smile and put them at their ease with a humorous and self-deprecating reference to the fact that you could always dress up a gamecock to look like a goose, but it still couldn't swim. Then she told a funny story that was a little more pointed toward the issue she ultimately wanted to address. She laughed and said that one day in the willow park, an old monk approached her father and told him about a sage pig that was owned by a farmer in the provinces. In all seriousness, this holy man said he'd heard from a very reliable source that this unusual animal dressed in saffron robes could dance on his hind legs playing bells to the time of any music, always prostrated itself in front of the statue of the Buddha, and never ate a morsel on feast days. The old monk thought this must be a very remarkable pig indeed, and solicited Master Yee's opinion.

Her father responded by saying that the pig wasn't all that remarkable, but the story about the pig was. For in fact the tale of the pious pig was an ancient piece of agrarian mythology when his great-grandfather told the story as a joke sixty years before. Lady Yee said the old monk looked deflated and slightly embarrassed until her father reminded him that they had both just been blessed with a clear and present teaching. Rumors, he said, even stupid and moronic rumors, live far longer than pigs, whether pious or not.

All the guests laughed at Lady Yee's story, but they soon noticed that she wasn't smiling, and so their laughter suddenly died away. Taking no notice, Lady Yee went on to say that more reputations were ruined by baseless rumor than by the truth. And though she had no interest in hobbling the truth, she had a vested interest in gutting a few rumors that had come to light, and she begged her guests for the opportunity to hear their opinions on one particularly dangerous story that was presently making snares for the innocent.

Lady Yee reminded her audience that the previous year Mr. Winslow's campaign for reelection for sheriff was considerably impaired by a ridiculous rumor that he was taking money to look the other way when it came to smuggling. Luckily, Sheriff Winslow's broad reputation for irreproachable character and evenhanded though strict enforcement of the laws crushed the rumors and silenced those who spread them. Those same dark forces were at work when Mr. Rice was appointed city attorney, but again these politically motivated rumors were subdued by more virtuous and intelligent voices insisting the truth was otherwise, and the general public was happy to agree. Nonetheless, Lady Yee took pains to point out that there wasn't one person in public service who was immune to dark characterizations or attacks aimed at personal integrity. Lady Yee said jealousy and envy parented many insidious evils, not the least of these being defamatory rumors calculated to hurt not just one innocent person, but a whole class of innocent people.

The table remained quiet while Lady Yee refreshed herself with a sip of tea. She nodded to thank them for their patience and continued. The case, she said, that most preyed upon her mind at present happened to include the interests of everyone seated at the table, and she confessed that if matters got out of hand, many people would ingenuously suffer the consequences.

Lady Yee produced a small sheaf of notes in her own hand and laid them on the table for reference. She pointed out that the unfortunate case of the grounded ship, as bad as that had been, had now been amplified in consequence by the discovery of the corpse of a missing crewman supposedly murdered with a knife and hidden under the engine-room bilge plates of that same ship.

Lady Yee looked about the table and asked whether everything she had just said was substantially correct. All the men nodded, so she continued with a preamble to a question. Looking at her notes, Lady Yee said that according to the ship's crew roster, the name of the dead man was Clausa Vuychek who, from all officer reports, seemed a rather unsavory fellow who claimed Bosnia as his homeland and the Muslim faith as a birthright. Again, all the men nodded their heads and voiced agreement. Then Lady Yee asked whether during their investigations they had come across crew statements to the effect that the late seaman Vuychek had gone out of his way to be pointedly rude to a Hindu passenger and his family, claiming their "filthy" religion to be anathema to the will of the true God and his profit Muhammad, or like sentiments of similar absurdity and ill grace. Again, all agreed. Lady Yee then went on to ask whether it had been suggested to any of them that perhaps this man, Dr. Neruda, might have been responsible for the death of Vuychck. The reasoning being that the murder might have been religiously inspired as an act of sectarian vengeance for insults suffered. Everyone agreed that they had heard various thin versions of the same story, but as yet no one had stepped forward as the author of the claim. But as Marshal Sanchez pointed out, the odd thing was that nobody particularly faulted the doctor if indeed he had killed Vuychek. It appeared the Bosnian Muslim lacked for friends among the ship's company. Some men said he was morbidly crazy, others said he was simpleminded and just plain mean, but nobody really cared about him one way or another now that he was dead. And certainly none of the crew would venture their own futures to make unsubstantiated claims in court. Especially in an outspoken defense of a man they neither liked nor trusted.

Lady Yee said she appreciated all that and more, but even the faintest accusation of violence and murder spread at the feet of a doctor sworn by profession and the Hindu faith to preserve all life was in itself a very dangerous wound to the truth, and one that would taint the confidence of those who needed those skills the most. She confessed that a goodly number of people would go without medical services if people of stature and influence did not actively deny these rumors. To that end, Lady Yee had taken the liberty of inviting Dr. Neruda to take tea. She said he had also kindly agreed to submit to an informal interview by the gentlemen most concerned in the outcome of this case of homicide. She declared that it was imperative that her guests satisfy themselves as to the man's innocence, or else compile charges capable of standing up to close scrutiny. Anything less would severely cripple endeavors to bring modest medical care to the Chinese laborers and fishermen of Monterey.

As if on cue, a distant bell sounded, and a

moment later Dr. Neruda was shown into the dining room by the houseboy. He was warmly greeted by Captain Hammond and seated in his place at the head of the table. Dr. Neruda looked very trim and dapper in his new suit. His beard and handlebar mustache were closely groomed and brushed in the military fashion. This lent the doctor a further air of understated authority and professionalism. The dark tone of his skin and piercing black gaze appeared to have little influence on the audience since the doctor's educated and skillful use of English was quite disarming. He also possessed a self-deprecating sense of humor that passed for sincere modesty.

Having made polite introductions all around, Captain Hammond made sure Dr. Neruda was served tea, and then went to sit by Lady Yee at the far end of the table. There he would be in the shadows and out of the way, which seconded the fact that he really had nothing more to say in the matter. His wife had mastered the helm with no help from him, so there was no reason to interject so much as a sigh. Like the rest of the men at the table, he would just have to sit back and wait.

Out of respect, Lady Yee addressed Dr. Neruda first. Though she had sent him a short letter outlining what she expected from the meeting, and the reasons for which she felt it was imperative that the doctor be as candid as possible, she also chose to reiterate her motives for the benefit of her other guests. She was determined to avoid even the scent of collusion between parties on either side, and so she even divulged what she had written to Dr. Neruda the day before.

Lady Yee went on, and with nods of agreement from the other five men concerned she told the doctor that this gathering was by no means an official interview, but it had just as important a purpose as far as the people of Monterey, and especially his future patients, were concerned. She declared it her studied conviction that the virulence of destructive rumors and gossip could only rarely be quashed at the root level, and then usually through the mechanisms of a formal trial. Informally telling the man in the street that a circulating rumor is fallacious and preposterous will have little or no effect upon the tides of gossipmongers who delight in such detrimental twaddle. On the other hand, the common citizen is loath to disbelieve or discount the local men of prestige, power, and influence in their midst. If these good people took up truth and put it about that such-and-such a tale was absurd and totally without merit, then other sober and honest people would adopt the same opinion, and a crisis in confidence might be averted. She asked Dr. Neruda's patience for the sake of the infirmary. The doctor nodded and said he would do all he could to satisfy her august guests' curiosity on any subject they pleased, if it would satisfy the needs of the situation at hand.

Lady Yee signaled for her maid to serve more tea and then asked Marshal Sanchez, as the highest state law officer present, to begin the questions. As an old family *californiano*, Mr. Sanchez smiled with modesty at the recognition of his right to first place.

Marshal Sanchez ran a finger under his mustache and asked a few details about his passage aboard the Canadian ship. Then he reached into a portfolio and withdrew a rusted triangular-bladed dagger ten inches long from tip to guard. This he placed in the middle of the table in front of Dr. Neruda and asked if he'd ever seen such a weapon before.

The doctor took one look, nodded, and said he had seen hundreds, if not thousands, of such blades. It was a military dirk, carried by almost every enlisted soldier in the British Indian Army. They were stamped out by the case in Lahore and other places, and of relatively poor manufacture. He added that the soldiers usually ruined what little temper they had by lashing the blades to sticks and using them as cooking skewers. Marshal Sanchez then asked if Dr. Neruda had ever owned such a knife when in the service, and the doctor immediately shook his head in the negative. He said he wasn't acquainted with American military traditions, of course, but in the

British and Indian armies, doctors and medical staff were forbidden to carry arms of any kind. It put them at greater risk of execution if captured. Dr. Neruda picked up a folder he had placed next to his chair and withdrew an aging photograph. It showed three Indian officers in field uniform posing for a formal portrait. He handed this to Marshal Sanchez and continued. He said that he was the officer in the middle, and easy to spot because his uniform was dark blue with green piping and high-collared, whereas the other two officers were attired in khaki with their collars turned down. They also wore gun belts with dirks and pistols in plain sight, while the doctor wore no belt at all to indicate that he carried no weapons. He asked the marshal to note that the officers' dirks were of a finer design and manufacture. If he had felt the need to own such a weapon, he would have acquired an officer's blade, not a cheap blade made for enlisted men. The doctor confessed that, on the other hand, he did own a fine collection of surgical blades. He had several amputation knives that were fourteen inches long and so extremely sharp that they could neatly bisect an eyelash hair lengthwise. And while they were marvelous instruments for saving lives, they were not designed to withstand the rigors required by a contested murder, as the blades were brittle and easily broken.

The marshal took back the knife, put it back in

his case, and asked the doctor if he knew the name of the dead man. The doctor said that despite the man's uncalled-for comments, they had never been introduced, nor did the fellow ever volunteer his name. But since he had no intention of making a formal complaint to the captain, who was already well-known for being unsympathetic toward his passengers, the doctor didn't bother to inquire as to the fellow's name. The doctor said it was obvious to him that the man was possibly demented, if not worse, and showed particular signs of being the product of inbreeding.

It was here that Mr. Rice begged to interject a question, and Marshal Sanchez surrendered the floor. The city attorney said he was at pains to understand why the sailor's outright hostility, albeit in the form of insults, didn't particularly disturb the doctor or his family.

For the first time Dr. Neruda found a reason to laugh. He went on to say that when it came to the art of delivering insults and curses, there were eight-year-old beggars on the streets of Indian cities who were better qualified to do the job. The addle-pated Bosnian crewman couldn't even qualify as a starter against Indian street vendors, who could lace together twenty withering curses, punctuated by an equal number of brilliantly composed insults, and deliver the whole train in one breath, and then, within a blink of an eye, launch right into another lengthy assault. No, the doctor said with a smile, the foulmouthed and befuddled crewman wouldn't know a sepoy from a Sherpa and thought he was talking to a Sikh. The doctor said he assumed this when Vuychek said he knew the Indian carried a blade, but was too great a coward to use it. The doctor chuckled again, and said he thought the poor fellow could be forgiven for being confused. India had always been mother and home to many different kinds of religion, and its people spoke over a hundred different languages, which made matters even more bewildering to the ignorant. Dr. Neruda then apologized for the digression, and said he had really paid no more attention to the addled crewman than he would have to a demented street beggar.

And then Dr. Neruda surprised everyone by saying that in fact he had felt truly sorry for the man, as he had obviously been the tormented tool of somebody even more abusive than himself. Dr. Neruda remarked that in India, mental diseases were well documented, well understood, and in some cases treated very successfully. But sometimes, figuratively speaking, one came across a snarling, dangerously psychotic "yard dog" that had been beaten too many times to bring back in the house. No amount of affection, attention, or medical consideration, aside from a lobotomy or heavy opiates, could make it tame and civil ever again. It was very sad, he said, but the helplessness of the sailor's condition and his obviously predictable future, though most distressing to contemplate, were inevitable from a medical point of view.

Dr. Neruda paused, and with an iron-bound expression that was unmistakably serious, looked each person at the table in the eyes for a moment, and then closed by saying that "no reputable physician, licensed by virtue of binding oaths sworn to qualified witnesses, could possibly be convinced that killing an apparently mentally deranged person was a remotely rational course of action toward resolving religious questions of self-justification." When the doctor next looked around the table, all eyes were cast low, and only Lady Yee met his gaze and nodded.

Just then Li-Lee silently slipped from the shadows, approached Lady Yee, and leaned down to whisper something in her ear. Lady Yee nodded, tapped her husband's arm, and indicated that she was leaving for a few moments, and then silently withdrew so as not to disturb the interview. The maid led the way to the kitchen where Lady Yee was introduced to Jojo Toyuka, the fifteen-year-old Japanese cabin boy. He sat happily eating Chinese custard tarts under Ah Chu's watchful gaze. The boy appeared quite contented and composed, and didn't seem to care where he was as long as he was being fed so well. Lady Yee told him why he was asked to come and about the men who were going to ask him questions. He didn't appear the least disturbed by any of it, and though his English was broken and he relied here and there on pidgin or maritime slang, he had a forthright manner, and could make himself understood to Lady Yee's satisfaction.

On the way back to the dining room Lady Yee asked Li-Lee what had been done with the ship's cook, Mr. Beal. The maid said that he was enjoying his pipe and a bottle of beer out in the garden under the grape arbor. He knew to wait there until called. Lady Yee voiced her approval and resumed her seat without drawing attention. Her husband cast an inquiring expression, but Lady Yee simply returned her attention to the interview.

Dr. Neruda was answering a question posed by Mr. Campion. He was saying that as a Hindu, he had vowed to care for all sentient life. His people ate no flesh of any kind and refused to kill even insects. This interested the harbormaster. He asked how, if they didn't kill flies, they eliminated these pests from hospital wards, surgeries, and morgues. Dr. Neruda said that for centuries, just as now, they had captured them in honey or fruit-baited traps made of glass or pottery, and at night they took the traps outside and released the detainees. And though he said the flies came to no harm in the traps, it did seem that the tree frogs and rock lizards always gathered about to celebrate the mass release.

Next Sheriff Winslow took his turn, and politely asked Dr. Neruda if he had any reason to suspect that any other person on the passenger list had suffered indignities at the hands of this man Vuychek. The doctor said that he and his family did not fraternize with the other passengers except at meals, and even then people tended to avoid conversing with the dark-skinned foreigners in their midst. If Vuychek had extended his vituperation to others, no one took the opportunity to discuss the matter with Dr. Neruda. Then he volunteered that the same was also true of the ship's company in general, with whom he had even less reason to be on conversant terms. He had no reason not to assume that other members of the crew shared Vuychek's opinions about race, and he chose not to test the waters. He closed by apologizing that he had no further information or opinions that would reflect on the fate of the dead man. Then the doctor posed an unexpected question of his own. He asked the seated gentlemen whether Clausa Vuychek had received a proper burial under Muslim rites. Mr. Rice said the answer, sadly, was no. There were no Muslim clerics to officiate at such proceedings, and nobody else knew what was required. There were a few Asian Muslim families scattered around the county, of course, but no mosques to speak of, and no time or money to go in search of such niceties. The man was technically indigent, and his body was buried in a potter's field under a numbered marker. Under the circumstances, that was the best that could be expected.

There was an uncomfortable pause as this information sunk in, but since there seemed to be no further questions, Lady Yee took back the mantle of hostess and speaker of the house. She confirmed there was nothing else, and asked her guests to allow Dr. Neruda, who had been most patient, to return to his family and his work. All five men immediately concurred, and in turn each thanked the doctor for his cooperation and his candor. In parting, they all heartily, and somewhat self-consciously, wished him good fortune in his new life in America.

Captain Hammond looked over at his wife, and the expression on her face told him at once that she believed she had won her point with a wide margin. She had been totally convinced that once these men had met and talked with Dr. Neruda, any lingering doubts as to his complicity in the death of the unfortunate sailor would melt away. The doctor's self-deprecating good manners, obvious compassion, and religious devotion to nonviolence all spoke of a man incapable of murder, especially for something as trifling as a few religious insults.

Even though Lady Yee felt sure she had

accomplished her primary goal, she now believed it was time to uncork the genie and see where the spirit led. Any trail that focused popular speculation in a direction away from Dr. Neruda and the infirmary was all that was required. And since Lady Yee was certain that the doctor was innocent, she was also convinced there was a trail to be found that led in another, and more promising, direction. To that end, Lady Yee asked her guests' indulgence while two more people were called to speak. She said that having enjoyed many years at sea on her husband's ship, she had come to know a few facts that were, in the main, incontrovertible when it came to life at sea. And the most particular of these was that the cabin boy and ship's cook knew more about what transpired aboard ship when it came to the crew and officers than did the captain or the owners. In that vein, Lady Yee said she had asked both the cabin boy and the ship's cook to attend this meeting. But first she asked the indulgence of the gentlemen present to be allowed to ask her questions first. They, of course, were free to ask whatever they pleased before the interview was terminated.

When Toyuka entered with the maid, Lady Yee put him at his ease once again by saying he could remain standing if he liked, as they would only keep him a few minutes. The cabin boy seemed content with that, and so Lady Yee continued. She asked him if the dead man, Vuychek, had any enemies among the crew, enemies who would not be displeased to see him dead. The cabin boy laughed and said everybody hated Vuychek. When Lady Yee asked the reason why, Toyuka looked incredulous for a moment, as though the answer was well-known to all. Then he caught the gist of her question and said Vuychek was a bad man, crazy, mean, and he was Malakoff's spy. He was also a liar and sometimes tried to blackmail other crew members over minor infractions. Lady Yee took this to mean that Malakoff and Vuychek were friends, but the cabin boy soon disabused her of that assumption by saying the captain hated Vuychek worse than the crew did. When Lady Yee asked why, in that case, the captain hadn't gotten rid of the troublesome deckhand, Toyuka said he did special jobs for the captain when they were in port. He ran secret errands and such. The cabin boy suggested that perhaps Vuychek was too valuable to part with. Toyuka said it was difficult to make sense out of it all, since the crew generally hated Malakoff every bit as much as Vuychek. They were seen as an evil pair of bilge demons, but the ship paid well and fed well, so people kept quiet. Lady Yee asked if there was a basic reason for the bad blood between the captain and Vuychek. Again the cabin boy laughed at the question. He said Malakoff often called Vuychek a thieving two-faced Muslim dog. The captain was overheard to say that at home in Bosnia, such despicable characters would have been taken up and sold to the mines as pit ponies.

Suddenly, with apologies to Lady Yee, Mr. Campion interrupted and said he was given to understand, by the captain himself, that he was a native of Estonia, not Bosnia. Toyuka just shrugged. He said he wouldn't know one place from the other. He'd never been out of the Pacific trade. Then Mr. Campion, who harbored the greatest distaste for Malakoff, tried to officially confirm a detail that he had only suspected. He asked the cabin boy if Malakoff liked to drink alcohol, and this elicited the loudest laugh of all from the boy. In his broken English, Jojo Toyuka said the captain had a powerful thirst for Polish water (vodka), but he never saw the man really drunk on duty. But he did say the captain always carried a silver flask in his coat, and used it whenever he took one of his pills. Lady Yee took back the floor and asked the boy what kind of pills the captain used, but Toyuka said he didn't know.

Marshal Sanchez took a turn, showed the dirk to Toyuka, and asked if he knew whom it belonged to. The cabin boy took the knife, looked closely at the base of the grip, and handed it back to the marshal. He said the knife belonged to Vuychek, the dead man. When Marshal Sanchez asked Toyuka how he knew this, the cabin boy said that all crewmen mark their possessions, especially their knives. Vuychek, according to the cabin boy, and seconded by Mr. Atwood, could neither read nor write. He used a simple crescent moon and a star symbol as a signature, the same sign crudely scratched on the base of the dirk's handle. This news caused a quiet sensation of whispers all around the table. But since there were no further questions, Lady Yee summoned the cabin boy to her side, gave him a five-dollar gold piece for his time, and told him there were more tarts waiting for him in the kitchen. Toyuka thanked Lady Yee and looked at the men seated about the table. When Lady Yee quietly asked what the problem was, the boy asked why they were all so sure Vuychek had been murdered. Toyuka said he'd once known a bosun's mate who tripped during a bad storm and accidently drove his knife through an artery in his leg. He was dead in eight minutes. Then the cabin boy leaned closer and whispered to Lady Yee behind his hand. He said he didn't really understand what crazy Vuychek was doing in the engine room, as the chief engineer, Mr. Perez, especially hated him. Perez was one of the men who had been so badly injured during the collision and sent off to the hospital in San Jose. Toyuka said that the black gang sometimes talked of feeding Vuychek to the boilers. The boy whispered that even the captain had told Vuychek to stay away from them. But then Toyuka said they were all good men, and wouldn't have really killed Vuychek, at least not aboard ship. Then, from long custom, he bowed to Lady Yee, and disappeared toward the kitchen and the promise of more custard tarts.

Lady Yee was now sure she had accomplished her ends as far as Dr. Neruda's reputation was concerned. The focus of suspicion and speculation had been rightly focused on other quarters, but his name and motives still hung in the ether. She decided to gamble on the ship's cook as the next most likely person to have an interest, and therefore an opinion, about the matter at hand. Lady Yee confidently smiled to herself. Li-Lee had told her that Mr. Beal had consumed two bottles of dark beer in the garden, along with three pork pastries and a half pot of strong mustard. It was to be hoped that Mr. Beal would be in a very relaxed and loquacious frame of mind by now.

With this thought in mind, Lady Yee decided to set the helm on a more rewarding course. She asked her guests to indulge her one last time by allowing the ship's cook to answer a few questions. By now the second serving of Captain Hammond's Russian punch had taken full effect, and the gentlemen in question would have allowed Lady Yee to conduct a Mexican bullfight in the parlor if it would have been of some assistance.

The ship's cook was a slack-jawed, raw-boned, loose-jointed Cornishman of an indeterminate age somewhere between forty and sixty. His straw-colored hair was sparse, and his mouth was set in a permanent scowl that appeared even more sinister when he found occasion to smile, which was seldom. For a cook, his lack of bulk spoke of a man not overly fond of his own food, and his darkly wrinkled skin indicated that perhaps he had once been a lowly deckhand.

Mr. Beal was shown into the room and stood, cap in hand. His eyes were generally cast downward, but he had a way of looking out of the corners of his eyes that gave Lady Yee the impression of a chameleon. He spoke in a clipped Cornish manner that rarely intoned intent. In fact, his voice displayed no emotion whatsoever, and what passed for humor rested in what went unspoken, which challenged interlocutors to complete the jest for themselves.

The county sheriff was the first to speak this time. He had gained some momentum under the influence of the punch and was feeling the weight of his office. Once seeing Mr. Beal, who looked somewhat like a refugee from a road gang, Sheriff Winslow took on an authoritative tone. He demanded to know where Malakoff had gone. Mr. Beal only shrugged and said he hadn't a clue. The sheriff then asked who had killed Clausa Vuychek, and the cook again answered that he didn't know, but he added that the news hardly saddened or surprised him. Then he was asked if there was any bad blood between the cook and

Vuychek, which caused Mr. Beal to chuckle. He said Vuychek never got in his way about anything. The cook grinned and said the rat didn't dare fool with the man that cooked his food. Mr. Beal declared he knew a dozen ways to make a sailor wish he were dead without actually killing him, at least most of the time.

Lady Yee could see this line of questioning was leading nowhere, and begged permission to interrupt with some questions of her own. Sheriff Winslow nodded. She told the cook that having read the crew registry, she was aware that the only men who had stayed under Captain Malakoff's command for any appreciable length of time were Mr. Perez, the chief engineer; Jojo Toyuka, the cabin boy; Clausa Vuychek, a deckhand; and Thaddeus Beal, the cook. Lady Yee went on to say she thought this showed remarkable loyalty to a man who had been variously characterized by members of his own crew as villainous, dangerously unqualified, basically crazy, habitually intoxicated, perpetually angry, unjust, and uncivilized. She wanted to know what had inspired Mr. Beal's constancy to such a figure.

The cook looked at his cap for a moment, and then met Lady Yee's disarming smile. He said he remained with the ship for the best of reasons, because she paid well and fed well, and Malakoff stayed out of his galley. This peaked Lady Yee's interest, and she asked what the captain liked to eat. She was surprised when Mr. Beal said he had no idea, as the captain only cooked for himself in a makeshift galley next to his quarters. It was always kept locked, and the cabin boy cleaned the dishes and pots, and was warned not to speak of it. Mr. Rice, feeling his punch, asked, half in humor, if Malakoff, like Vuychek, was afraid he might be poisoned. Mr. Beal very slowly turned his head to address the city attorney, and after locking eyes, calmly said he thought that a very reasonable assumption on the captain's part, but in fact he believed there were other more personal reasons to which he was not privy. Then Lady Yee interjected another question that caught her guests off guard. She asked Mr. Beal just how devoted Vuychek was to his Muslim faith, to which the cook simply laughed and shook his head. The dead man was all bluff and bluster. In fact, the cook testified he had never known Vuychek to go into a mosque, or bow toward Mecca in prayer, or indeed do anything remotely religious. Mr. Beal grinned and said that as a Muslim, much less a human being, Vuychek must have been a miserable disappointment to Allah, as well as his parents, if he could remember who they were. This drew a slight wave of laughter from the gathering.

Mr. Beal seemed very pleased with his ability to draw a laugh from such an august audience, and might have gone on to further quaint Cornish jocularities had not Lady Yee struck first. She drew back their full attention with a little silver table gong used to call the maid. And when she had centered Mr. Beal's full attention, and using her utmost authoritative manner, like an officer speaking to the crew, she asked him pointedly what kind of pills Malakoff took repeatedly, and what he drank from his flask. Without waiting for an answer, Lady Yee went on to warn Mr. Beal not to bother lying to her, as she had ten years as second-in-command of her own ship (which was stretching the truth without breaking any covenants), and that she could smell a bilge-born prevarication from over the horizon through a dense fog (which was certainly the truth as far as Captain Hammond was concerned).

Mr. Beal started to nervously play with his cap as he looked at his shoes. After a moment, he said he knew nothing of that. He lived and worked in the galley, that was all, and he'd never even seen the inside of the captain's cabin, much less observed his habits. It was here that Mr. Atwood rose to call Mr. Beal a bald-faced liar. He had personally seen Malakoff and Beal trading words in the food stores locker on several occasions, and had witnessed the cook taking steaming pots of something that smelled odious to the captain's cabin at strange hours of the watch.

Mr. Beal found himself caught between two contrary waves, and nervously explained he had often issued out stores to the captain, the food lockers were part of the galley, and yes, on occasions he had boiled up large batches of a strange concoction using ingredients and a recipe given to him by Malakoff himself. When Lady Yee inquired what those ingredients were, Mr. Beal said gingerroot, licorice root, cinnamon sticks, willow bark, comfrey, honey, and a quart of apple cider vinegar.

Lady Yee suddenly smiled and nodded her head. It was obvious to her husband that she now believed she had most of the parts in play, and was only waiting for the obvious answers to come from the cook's lips without hints from her. After a moment, Lady Yee returned to her original stern demeanor. She asked Mr. Beal what Malakoff drank from his flask, and after a few stutters the cook admitted it was Polish vodka. But when asked about the pills the captain took so often, Mr. Beal insisted he knew nothing about them. He said only Vuychek knew what the pills were, because he was the one that Malakoff always sent ashore to get them. And as he had said before, Vuychek and he were not on familiar terms.

Then Lady Yee saw her mark, softened her approach, and said she believed Mr. Beal to be an old hand with long experience of the world. And old hands know things without being told. She said that under the circumstances, she'd be quite surprised if an old sweat like Mr. Beal, who'd been, after all, with Malakoff for years, hadn't formed an opinion on the matter.

Mr. Beal fidgeted with his cap for a moment, looked at his shoes again, and mumbled something under his breath that no one could hear. Lady Yee encouraged the cook to speak up. Mr. Beal said he believed Malakoff was an opium eater, and had been for some time. He said he'd heard that Malakoff had once suffered a serious injury to his spine, and that he suffered from debilitating sciatica at times. Because of this, and a diet that the cook believed was most probably simply meant to accommodate ease of digestion and passing waste (the latter because of a dangerous form of constipation suffered by all opium addicts), the cook came to believe the captain was eating opium. And also because he always chased it with a swallow of vodka, which every sailor knows makes the drug work faster. But Mr. Beal swore on his mother's grave that he and the captain never once had words concerning any of this.

Lady Yee smiled like a contented cat. She asked the gentlemen present if they had any more questions, and Marshal Sanchez again produced the rusted dirk and showed it to Mr. Beal. The marshal asked if he had seen it before, and Mr. Beal smiled and replied that he had four just like it in his galley, only his were in better condition. When asked who might have owned the knife, the cook shook his head and said he wouldn't know, but he was sure there were at least three men aboard who carried blades like it. Such items were easily available in any port in the Pacific. Captain Hammond took the opportunity to confirm this fact by interjecting that such knives were a common Indian export. The manufacture was cheap, to be sure, but the Indian steel was good and kept a keen edge and the leather scabbards were well greased against seawater. He said his own crewmen sometimes carried them, but in general professional seamen working sail preferred more utilitarian multiplex knives, models with three or more blades of different sizes. The fact that the blades folded into the handle precluded gutting oneself accidently, which may or may not have been a factor in the present circumstances.

Lady Yee smiled at her husband's timely interjection, and asked the other guests if they had any further questions. Only Mr. Campion showed some concern for the craggy old cook, by asking what he planned to do now. Mr. Beal smiled a crooked smile and said there was good work for cooks in the railroad camps, and he looked forward to working where the threat of drowning wasn't such a constant hazard, and where the cookhouse didn't pitch around at all angles.

Lady Yee thanked Mr. Beal and passed him a five-dollar gold piece. The houseboy was called to show the man out, and then all fell quiet for long moments while the men at the table pondered what they had heard that afternoon. Lady Yee took advantage of the pause to unobtrusively leave the table. She parted without saying a word. None was necessary. She knew full well, men being what they are, that every detail of what had passed that afternoon would be common knowledge in a few days. But she also knew that the blood-scented hounds of idle speculation and dangerous gossip had been turned from Dr. Neruda and were now encouraged to course on a more promising trail, one salted with dark possibilities and with a very promising perpetrator to liven suppositions all around. After all, Malakoff was a fugitive who had escaped custody and remained at large. But to Lady Yee's way of thinking, though she personally refused to offer judgment either way without proof, any scent that led opinion away from Dr. Neruda and the infirmary was useful and providential. By the time the authorities got their hands on the elusive Malakoff again, all sentiments to the contrary would have moved on to greener pastures, and Dr. Neruda would have been all but forgotten.

While on her way out of the room, Lady Yee nodded to her husband. This was a signal to serve the guests brandy and cigars, listen to their opinions if they cared to voice any, and then to see the gentlemen safely and quickly to their conveyances.

16

DURING DINNER THAT NIGHT, Captain Hammond gave a short account of the comments put forward by Lady Yee's guests. Mr. Campion and Mr. Atwood were of the opinion that Malakoff was at the heart of the matter, and probably the murderer. The city attorney and Marshal Sanchez kept an open mind as to guilt, but agreed that Dr. Neruda was totally above suspicion, and Mr. Winslow, the city sheriff, agreed that the Indian doctor couldn't possibly be involved in such an inbred sequence of events stretching back over years, and was, in fact, just another innocent victim dashed on the rocks of Point Lobos by the drug- and alcohol-induced incompetence of ex-captain Sigmund Malakoff.

Lady Yee didn't dwell on her victory in any fashion. Instead she remarked that she and her husband had something more important to celebrate. Captain Hammond looked surprised for a moment. He couldn't believe he'd missed the date of an anniversary or a birthday. Lady Yee smiled and passed him a small, ornate silver box, which when opened, revealed a tiny scroll of gold paper. The captain carefully unrolled the paper and read a calligraphic greeting from heaven. Below was a simple declaration, which announced that in seven and a half months Captain Hammond would become the blessed father of a new son and heir.

The captain, who was usually prepared for almost any emergency, found himself speechless once more. With tears welling in the corner of his eyes, he looked up at his beautiful wife and moved his lips, but nothing came out. And when his voice did return, all he could think to ask was how she knew it would be a son. Lady Yee simply laughed indulgently and shook her head. Captain Hammond recovered his dignity and agreed it was a ludicrous question. Then he gently kissed her hand, leaving behind a single tear like a jeweled drop of dew. He raised his glass of wine in gratitude, and toasted their mutual good fortune. With an unaccustomed emotional break in his voice, the captain vowed that he would endeavor to always be worthy of her sacrifices on his behalf. Then something else occurred to the captain and he smiled. He wondered what Macy would think of having a little brother. Lady Yee laughed and reassured her husband that as far as their daughter was concerned, the whole matter of credit for the idea of having a little brother was hers in the first place. The little imp would simply assume that she had gotten her own way once again.

Within the week Captain Hammond was happy to report that as far as Monterey County was concerned, "the Hindu" was forgotten altogether.

313

In less than seventy-two hours, the hounds had picked out another scent, and they were baying for Malakoff's blood. The papers reported armed farmers and orchard men patrolling their barns, ricks, and outbuildings at all hours, and townsfolk took to locking their cellars and carriage houses. In no time at all, Sigmund Malakoff inherited the mantle of every evil from childhood bogeyman to Blackbeard the pirate and beyond. There wasn't a case of chicken theft, stolen apples, or purloined pie that wasn't laid at his door. And as everyone knew, fugitive murderers were the most dangerous of criminals. They were men who would not balk at the most horrendous and villainous of crimes. But that being said, there still wasn't a person in or out of authority who had the slightest idea where to lay hands on the miscreant. Sigmund Malakoff had disappeared into the Monterey fog and was gone to all save the inventors of popular myth. And there must have been a numerous herd of such people, because Malakoff had been spotted in a score of unlikely places including a seminary in Carmel.

All of these matters ceased to be of any interest to Lady Yee almost immediately. The infirmary was her only real concern, and it was gaining in popularity with the Chinese all the time. Dr. Neruda's wife, Nandiri, and his daughter had become particular favorites among the Chinese women, especially those who were giving birth for the first time. And Chandra Din, the doctor's son-in-law, was embarrassed to discover that all the elderly Chinese ladies were flirting with him and laughing about it afterward.

Dr. Neruda and his family had already begun teaching a few promising candidates a rudimentary course of medical practices, mostly aimed at dealing with health emergencies or injuries. The biggest teaching hurdles were overcome with the help of dedicated translators, who were always young American-born Chinese. And as foreseen by Lady Yee, as soon as the infirmary became acceptable to the ancient and mysterious sisterhood of grandmothers and great-grandmothers and great-aunts and so forth, the men were encouraged, for the sake of the family, to submit themselves for proper medical treatment of illness or wounds. Midwives were instructed on sanitation, fishermen were taught how to bind injuries properly, and children were taught how to clean themselves and their food.

Provisions never seemed to be a problem because most people were constrained by economics to pay in kind. As a result, there was always an abundance of fresh fish and fruit, garden vegetables of every description, eggs, chickens, and of course, rice. One old man, whose life had been saved with proper medicines, took it upon himself to deliver two hundred gallons of fresh springwater every other day. And though he had long since discharged his debt, he kept up the practice because he saw there was need of it, and he was inclined, he said, to gain merit for the life to come. All other necessary supplies were purchased in bulk by Hammond, Macy & Yee and delivered on a regular schedule. But the greatest indication that the infirmary was doing well came from the fact that it was no longer a topic of conversation in Monterey. The mechanism worked so smoothly that it became all but invisible in the fabric of the town. Even the used army ambulance was painted a bright Chinese blue to avoid its more somber connotations. The city fathers, always so tender to the barbs of the public touch, were grateful to be shunt of a humane responsibility for which they had no mandate, no funding, and no interest. However, the county sanitary commission showed its interest by sharing surplus medical supplies, and various small charitable organizations contributed blankets, bandages, lamp oil, and stove wood. A local Salinas brewer, who used Chinese labor, contributed a hundred gallons of 180-proof clear grain alcohol to help sanitize surgical equipment. The fishermen even established a kind of informal tithe, by which on common agreement the last two fish caught on any given day would be set aside as the freshest of the catch, and sold to help buy medicines for those who could not afford them. Lady Yee could have funded all this herself without the slightest financial burden, but she felt it was important that the Chinese make the infirmary their own, and the best way to accomplish that was to allow them to make meaningful sacrifices commensurate with their own interests and appreciation. She insisted, however, that the same modest profile be maintained, and in fact there were few white residents of Monterey County aware that such a thing as a Chinese infirmary even existed. Perhaps the most notable changes over a period of time were too subtle for most to take note of, but if one happened to spot a fisherman with a broken leg mending his nets, it might be noticed that he had been fitted with a modern plaster cast and not two boards tied together with rag line. And when he walked, it was with the help of a real crutch and not a driftwood stick. A woman with burns from a kitchen fire could depend upon medicines and fresh bandages every few days. But intrinsically, the most wonderful thing of all as far as the Chinese elders were concerned was the lowered mortality rate among women in childbirth, infants, children, and even the elders themselves.

As soon as Lady Yee was confident that the infirmary could manage on its own, she went on to focus exclusively on another extremely important project, namely giving her husband a healthy son on or about August 1. This was the date she had decided was most auspicious for a son to be born.

Captain Hammond was later proud to say that she was off schedule by only two hours. But she had cause, since there was a full moon and strong tides, which sailors believe influence such things. So at the stroke of two o'clock in the morning of August 2, Lady Yee gave birth to a strapping boy that weighed in at eight pounds, eight ounces. Mrs. Neruda and her daughter were in attendance, but there were no real complications to contend with. Dr. Neruda had a more difficult time keeping the prospective father calm and collected, but by far the most excited and exuberant member of the reception party was little Macy who, in a very proprietary fashion, had decided she had waited far too long to get her promised baby brother. With Lady Yee's blessing, Captain Hammond named his new son after his long-deceased father. The child's birth certificate read Nathanial Yee Hammond. However, this wasn't good enough for Macy, who used part of her mother's name and for some inexplicable reason began calling her baby brother Silver, and, just as inexplicably, the nickname stuck. Soon everyone called him Silver, everyone except his mother, of course, who would only bend as far as Nathan, and disallowed Nat altogether. Even Captain Hammond gave in to Macy and began to call his son Silver, but Lady Yee suspected he liked the connotation as well as the sound of Silver Hammond.

The following months were creative and rewarding. The captain purchased a steam dredge, which proved a very profitable investment, and Lady Yee chartered a small private school for Chinese girls. There was room for only twelve students at a time, but they were instructed in a broad range of skills, and worked hard at improving their English. Macy was growing by leaps, and already showed promise with languages, speaking Chinese and French. In turn, Macy also thought it her responsibility to teach her little brother a thing or two, which sometimes backfired in amusing fashion. Little Nathan somehow picked up Macy's favorite phrase, "baka," the Japanese word for "stupid," and to Lady Yee's complete chagrin it was the first word her son ever gave voice to. It backfired on Macy too, because it eventually became Silver's nickname for his sister when he was angry with her, which, as time went by, was often.

Another dramatic curtain suddenly arose about nine o'clock one night while Captain Hammond was in Salinas on business. He had promised Macy, who was turning four and suffering from a cold, that he would be home before midnight with a special birthday present.

Lady Yee sat up with Macy. She was coaxing her daughter to sip ginseng tea and honey to alleviate her cough when Li-Lee entered the nursery and announced that a Mexican boy at the gate was the bearer of a very strange message, and the houseboy was at a loss to know what to do. It sounded like there was a man dying in a cart. Lady Yee left Macy in the care of Li-Lee, gathered up her cloak at the front door, and followed the houseboy and his lantern out to the road. A rickety canvas-covered mule cart waited with a barefoot Mexican boy wearing a worn serape and a straw hat. In broken English he said there was a man in the cart who was coming close to meeting God. He had paid the boy's father ten dollars to bring him from Gonzales to Monterey. The man was in great pain and in search of some Chinese princess who had an infirmary for poor people.

Lady Yee took the lantern, drew back the rotting canvas tail flap of the cart, and spied a man wearing patched overalls and crude farmer's boots, and splayed out on a bed of old straw covered with a tattered blanket. The man's hair and beard were graying, long, unkempt, and, like his face, soaked with sweat. His parchment complexion made him appear ready for the morgue, and only his eye movement, shallow breathing, and twitching hands gave testimony to life. The man was obviously in agony, and it appeared that if he had originally purchased clothes that fit, then he had lost a great deal of weight very quickly.

Lady Yee instantly ordered her houseboy to run and fetch Dr. Neruda. He was to tell the doctor to bring strong medicine for acute pain. In the interim, Lady Yee asked the Mexican boy why he had come here. He said the sick man had spoken of a place in Monterey that had doctors for poor people who couldn't afford medicines. The boy said he had no idea what the man was talking about, but by asking people along the way he narrowed it down. They had been on the road for three days when a Chinese washerwoman told him to seek out where Lady Yee lived, and they would know what to do. The boy was obviously exhausted and hungry, so Lady Yee rallied Ah Chu out of bed, told him to feed the boy, and then find him a place to rest. She reassured the youth that his cart would be looked after and his mule sheltered, well watered, and rewarded with fresh oats.

Though it seemed to take forever, a half hour later Dr. Neruda appeared with his son-in-law, Chandra Din. A cursory examination told the doctor that he might not have a patient for long. He administered an injection of heroin to alleviate somewhat the man's pain, but it was obvious that aside from a terminally diseased and tubercular spine, which must have caused him excruciating spasms, the man was suffering from the effects of a mortal opium withdrawal, complicated by advanced malnutrition and dehydration. He said the man would have to be taken to the infirmary if anything was to be done at all, but he feared there

321

was no time to send for the ambulance and a stretcher. Just moving the patient from one conveyance to another could kill him. By now all the servants were awake and converging to be of assistance. Perceiving that the boy's mule was jaded to the bone, Lady Yee told her stable hand to fetch one of their own mules, prop up the cart yoke, and then switch animals. Dr. Neruda agreed that it would be best to give the patient another injection, leave him where he was, and take the cart to the infirmary. Chandra Din had already called for fresh water, and was coaxing the half-conscious man to suck the fluid from a small sponge. As soon as the mules had been switched over, Dr. Neruda and Chandra Din headed the cart down the hill toward the infirmary a mile and a half away. In parting, the doctor asked Lady Yee to send word to their wives about where they had gone and why, and this she agreed to do at once.

The cart had been gone but thirty minutes when Captain Hammond returned home. His business happily completed, Macy's father had purchased a German-made doll for her birthday. In an aside to his wife, the captain said he hoped Macy would take to tutoring the doll and give her poor little brother a break. As soon as she saw her new doll, Macy became oblivious to all else, and Lady Yee had an opportunity to tell her husband what had happened.

The captain suddenly looked perplexed, and he

had to ask his wife to repeat herself to make sure he hadn't misheard her words. Captain Hammond's instincts told him there was something odd afoot, and he said he would change his clothes and go to the infirmary at once.

Lady Yee went to the kitchen to have Ah Chu prepare sandwiches and coffee in a hamper. She sent word to the stables to have a fresh horse harnessed to the captain's shay and kissed him on the cheek as he went out the door. The big parlor clock began to chime the midnight hour just as the garden gate clanged shut, whereupon Lady Yee returned to the nursery where she spent the rest of the night looking after Macy. She had placed Nathan's cradle in her own room, so as to avoid exposure to his sister, and Li-Lee rested on a cot nearby. She only disturbed her mistress when the baby required feeding, which thankfully wasn't often.

Captain Hammond found his way down the darkened streets that linked the warehouse and workshop districts. Residents were few, but the bouncing carriage lamps and jingling horse tack attracted the interest of various guard dogs chained to warehouse gates to give watchmen warning of strangers. The only lights burning in the whole district came from the infirmary. The captain let himself in and found Dr. Neruda, Chandra Din, and a Chinese nursing student still working on saving the inert man. Chandra Din explained that the patient had been in such excruciating agony that they had been forced to administer chloroform just to cut away the man's filthy, lice-infested clothing and clean and bandage his ulcerated spine. He added that while he was under the influence of the drug they were also compelled to clip away his matted hair and beard, which were equally infested with vermin and filth. The man was resting more peacefully now that the opiates had taken effect, but the pain was ever present just under the surface.

Captain Hammond asked if he might see the man, and was truly shocked at the sight that awaited him. He called Dr. Neruda to his side and asked him if he recognized the man. The doctor nodded. It wasn't until they had cleaned the man up somewhat, and cut away his mountain of flea-infested hair, that it gradually occurred to him that with forty-five extra pounds on his frame, the dying man would look a great deal like Sigmund Malakoff. But one thing was obvious. According to Dr. Neruda, the dying man had been addicted to opiates for many years, and had recently come to grips with terminal malnutrition, which was a very painful way to expire, with or without opiates.

It all seemed rather odd and fateful. Whereas the captain might have expected to find an anchor-framed sea captain, he discovered instead a withered old man on the cusp of death. Whatever he might have done, he was paying for his crimes with prolonged suffering that would shame a Persian executioner. Perhaps it was because they were both men whose lives had been forged from the same types of experiences, or because they shared the common bonding of courage and terror that casts the sailor's lot in life, but Captain Hammond could not find it in his heart at this moment to be anything but compassionate. The man before him, now clipped like a dying prisoner from a Dickens novel, looked to be in need of kindness and patience, and Captain Hammond felt obliged by maritime tradition to deliver both.

The captain asked for a chair, and then sat quietly by Malakoff's bedside for an hour. Then suddenly the patient awoke for a few moments and called an unknown name. He spotted Captain Hammond sitting next to him, smiled slightly, and rolled over his extended hand as if offering his grasp in greeting. The captain gently took Malakoff's hand and felt a weak but intentioned grasp. He was also instantly aware of the struggling pulse coursing just beneath the parchment skin. Malakoff smiled and closed his eyes once again.

As Chandra Din and the nurse rested on nearby cots, Captain Hammond remained seated holding Malakoff's withering hand. The two kerosene lamps had been wicked down to a golden glow, and the details of the room seemed to shimmer in a netherworld half-light. Then, while Captain Hammond's thoughts were far away, something strange and unforeseen happened. First he heard the sharp hooting of two owls from close by, and then after a slight pause, the deep chime on his pocket watch marked the hour like a clarion. At the last ring of three bells in the morning, Malakoff suddenly came awake with a renewed vigor quite unexpected in a man bartering for his last breath. He asked for water, so Captain Hammond held the cup and glass straw to ease his drinking. And then out of all expectation, Malakoff, who by now recognized Captain Hammond, decided he wanted to talk, and though his voice was weak and strained at times, the old seaman talked with purpose for over an hour. Even Dr. Neruda and Chandra Din stirred themselves to come witness this bright, last flickering of Malakoff's guttered candle. Captain Hammond asked for pencil and paper to take notes, and Chandra Din thought this a wise idea and did the same. In the meantime, Malakoff appeared most content when he could speak directly to Captain Hammond, and grasp his hand. This made note-taking difficult, but not impossible.

The dying man needed no encouragement to speak. He pleaded that knowing the end was near, he had come back to confess to his complicity in the grounding of his ship, and his part in the partially accidental death of his distant cousin, Clausa Vuychek. He wept when he said that he had always tried to be a faithful son of the mother church, and he could not allow others to suffer for his own failings and misdeeds. Now that he was coming to his end, he wanted to meet God's all-seeing judgment with a conscience cleansed of all lies, and he begged Captain Hammond, as a fellow officer, to see that when the time came, Malakoff's broken frame would be interred in consecrated ground. The captain agreed without a moment's hesitation.

Tears welled in Malakoff's eyes once more, and he said that life had dealt his family the worst of crossed allegiances. The majority of his clan practiced the Greek Orthodox faith, but a wealthy minority were Muslim mountain folk, who were held in low regard for historical religious reasons, but tolerated because of ancient common ancestry. He had inherited such a cousin in Clausa Vuychek. He said that sadly this fellow, who was only made known to Malakoff through written introductions from relatives anxious to see the man off on the high seas, was of very limited intelligence. Unfortunately, his lack of wit came bundled in a very nasty and aggressive package of dangerous habits. He made enemies everywhere, and depended on Malakoff's connections to keep him safe. He said Vuychek had virtually no idea how he affected people, and didn't seem to care one way or the other. He often appeared marginally crazy, and talked to himself in hushed tones a good deal, but that was all there was to it. Malakoff chuckled dryly and said there were old salts everywhere, before and aft the mast, who were just as crusty, addle-pated, and strange, but they stood their watches in good order, and justly earned their salt, bread, and vodka.

Malakoff asked for more water, but before he spoke again he closed his eyes, as if the darkness helped him to recall the sadness without tears. Finally he said that Vuychek had slowly become a necessary link in a chain of evils. Malakoff confessed that after being struck in the spine with a loose-flying crane block, he found the pain in his back could sometimes verge on the unbearable, and could even incapacitate him for days. He said he most feared being paid off and beached if his employers came to know of his incapacity. To ingratiate himself with his distant cousin, and possibly gain by it, Vuychek ventured into the more nefarious precincts of any given port to purchase high-grade opium for the captain's use. Malakoff said that at first he was very grateful to Vuychek. After all, it wasn't the kind of thing he could go off and purchase for himself. He couldn't possibly allow anyone to witness him buying opium from some back-alley Chinese drug peddler. The opportunity for blackmail was too great. Within limits, the opium worked its dark magic, and because he believed he was fast becoming indispensable, Vuychek started to dabble in a little darkness of his own. In fact, he slowly and very subtly became the blackmailer Malakoff had feared all along. It all started in small ways, but as the years and months passed Malakoff came to understand that he had been harboring a viper more dangerous than the opium. Though he now took full responsibility for placing Vuychek in temptation's path, and then nurturing his criminal acts because of his own frightful needs, Malakoff was also of the opinion that Vuychek, born to an evil sect, took to sin like a bear takes to salmon. The dying man swore that his cousin would have found the road to hell and perdition on his own merits, but because he was mentally ponderous, and morally myopic, it would have taken him longer to accomplish his ends without Malakoff's prompting and threats. The old captain digressed for a moment, and his mind seemed to wander back to a vault of regrets. Then he said that among opium's more insidious side effects, besides a radical adjustment of diet and bowels, was the fact that it imparted to the user a false sense of intellectual superiority, while at the same time harnessing the victim to a horrendously dark temper leading to unaccountable fits of pique concerning meaningless trivialities. Malakoff at last opened his eyes, picked out Captain Hammond specifically, and said that all these evils had come together in one blow the day his ship ran aground off Point Lobos. He said the engineers, black gang, and oilers had deserted the engine room when it appeared the ship would break up on the rocks. They refused to return to their duties until they were satisfied the bottom of the ship hadn't been torn out. Malakoff said he swore a blue streak up and down, and told them off for the cowards they were. Then he grabbed Vuychek, who was every bit as frightened as the others, and taking up a lantern, forced him to accompany his captain down the narrow companionway ladder into the still-smoking stink and darkness of the engine room. Once below, Malakoff ordered Vuychek to start pulling up the heavy metal floor plates that gave access to the bilges. Now, as every seaman knows, all ships' bilges carry some water, but most deckhands never see a bilge, except in port, and then only rarely. So under the given and very dire circumstances, the presence of even normal amounts of seawater sloshing around in the bilges hoisted Vuychek into a complete blue panic. So much so that he completely forgot to whom he was talking. He screamed a demand to be allowed to leave at once, but even before the captain could agree, Vuychek pulled his knife and threatened Malakoff with death if he stood in the way. According to the captain, matters might still have been salvaged amicably if Vuychek hadn't gone

one step too far. From a well of abject fear he drew his biggest blade and violently declared that in any event he was going to tell the owners that Malakoff had been drunk and drugged at the time of the accident. This last threat shortened Malakoff's burning fuse considerably, and he went from angry to infuriated in one snap. When a sudden wave pitched the ship's hull up off the rocks momentarily, Vuychek stumbled forward slightly, but before he could regain his footing, Malakoff saw his chance and kicked Vuychek's legs out from beneath him. Vuychek went down on his face, gave a stunted cry of pain, moaned piteously for a moment, and then was still.

Malakoff shook his head sadly at the retelling. He said he leaned down to turn the faker over, and was almost pleased to discover that Vuychek had fallen on his own blade and driven the dirk halfway into his sternum. He said the look of surprise on Vuychek's face would have been laughable were it not for the blood that began to gush from the wound when he tried to pull the blade out. And even then, with death at his shoulder, he again threatened Malakoff with exposure, prison, and disgrace. This last assault sent the captain over the edge and down into the dark pit he now occupied. He said his opiate-braced temper could tolerate no more betrayal. So rather than help poor Vuychek, who might have been saved, he stood up and with soul-damning fury and invective placed the sole of his boot on the handle end of the dirk. To the shocked and almost voiceless pleadings of his cousin, Malakoff stepped down with all his might and drove the blade down to the hilt like a marlinspike. His anger enjoyed watching the blood froth in bubbles from Vuychek's mouth as he exhaled his last breath with a mucous-muted moan.

Malakoff told Captain Hammond that he was so angry that the question of the body didn't even occur to him at first, but when it did, he expressed his driving indignation by kicking Vuychek's still-twitching frame down through the open bilge hatch. The body crashed with a splash in the oil-slicked water four feet below, and Malakoff confessed his drugged fury was so great that he even rejoiced at the thought of the feast he had just tabled for the ship's rats. This last declaration seemed to have exhausted the captain. He laid back, closed his eyes, and began breathing deeply with the resurrected torment from the pain in his spine.

Dr. Neruda came out of the shadows to stand by the other side of the bed. He felt for the patient's pulse, and then gave Captain Hammond a sad look that spoke of impending finality. But just when all seemed over, Malakoff breached consciousness like a sounding whale and continued his narrative as though nothing had happened.

Reaching out for Captain Hammond's grasp,

Malakoff confessed that he had secretly returned to the ship after he had escaped jail, but he had only done so to retrieve his secret strongbox, which contained his opium, his papers, his money, and his gun. It was only then that he realized that he would soon need to buy more opium, and the ship's purse looked like a viable bank, so he rifled the ship's safe and departed. He cried and confessed that, even at this juncture, the fate of Vuychek's body didn't concern him in the least. Fate had moved matters way beyond such mundane concerns, and besides, there were rats in the bilges that outweighed small dogs, and they would devour anything living or dead, and this included tick soap, insulated wire, candle wax, gunpowder, and ship's tar. The dead man's bones might ultimately be discovered at the bottom of the ship's bilges, but Malakoff was confident that nothing else would remain to tell the story of Vuychek's betrayal or his complicity. But now he knew he could not escape his crimes, and wished to make some small restitution. Malakoff reached for a greasy leather cord around his neck and pulled forth an equally worn leather string pouch.

Chandra Din whispered to Captain Hammond that they had left the talisman in place believing it had some religious significance to the patient. He said that he had known people to go into shock when such things were discovered missing. Malakoff tried to break the leather thong free but hadn't the strength. Dr. Neruda reached in and unobtrusively cut the greasy thong with scissors. When the purse came away, Malakoff's weakened hand passed the item to Captain Hammond. The oily pouch was the size of a quail's egg, and Malakoff begged Captain Hammond to use the contents to make whatever restitution was possible. Then the dying man closed his eyes and sounded into the depths of his own plummeting dreams. Reaching for Malakoff's pulse, Dr. Neruda voiced his professional contention that full consciousness would never return. Chandra Din compassionately suggested that Malakoff, having now relieved himself of a soul-sinking burden, felt free to surrender his own life in penance. Within moments of this last sad prognosis, Malakoff exhaled with a sigh of relief and then expired, still holding Captain Hammond's hand.

For unspoken reasons, perhaps linked to ancient maritime tradition, Captain Hammond remained to help prepare Malakoff's body for burial. When that was done, he climbed back into his shay, and as dawn rose over the eastern hills pushing back the rolling banks of morning fog from the bay, the captain rode off to leave word with Marshal Sanchez and Sheriff Winslow about what had recently transpired at the infirmary.

Captain Hammond had seen people die before, of course, but never quite in these circumstances.

He found himself deeply affected by the old man's struggle, not only with a painful death, but also with his own conscience, the latter contest possibly being as close to an act of contrition as he ever came. Still the captain was haunted with the simpler questions. Given the fact that Malakoff certainly had the funds to escape as far away as he liked, why did he chance hiding so close to his pursuers, and in a native environment where he would be obviously out of place? If you're a fox, you hide among foxes, and if you're a seaman . . . Well, perhaps not. The captain remembered that every harbor official in California had been wired Malakoff's description. He tried to imagine what kind of life the man had been reduced to living, but it almost didn't bear rational contemplation. Captain Hammond had already seen his share of opium addicts in the filthy, waste-bound alleys of numerous harbors. The victims' general physical and mental decay was never something that drew interest beyond possible pangs of pity or waves of gratitude that the situation wasn't reversed. Yet, for a man like Captain Hammond, it remained a worthwhile question to wonder the why and wherefor of a man like Malakoff. The variety of possibilities was emotionally and religiously endless. Luckily, Captain Hammond had long since determined to set the imponderables of life aside for later reflection. But one way or another, the captain knew he would always include the image of the expiring Malakoff within his personal catalog of indelible images. Captain Hammond recalled an old whale hunter who once told him that beating the odds was never a matter of knowing the complex answers to big questions, but rather being innocently curious about the simplest answers, and knowing a falsehood at a reasonable distance. The captain smiled at the recollection and rode on, working this simple logic toward some sense of balance worthy of the night's events.

17

WHEN LADY YEE next saw her husband it was almost noon, and they shared but a few words by way of explanation of what had happened because he was in the company of Marshal Sanchez, Sheriff Winslow, and Mr. Campion. They came in separate transport and gathered under the broad garden veranda to take coffee and a light lunch, and discuss what had transpired. Lady Yee thought it best to remain unseen. She knew she would be told everything eventually, but she wasn't particularly anxious to hear the sad details just yet. She also thought it best to let her husband take the lead, as she wished to avoid being called as a witness during the inquest. She believed the less the public heard about the infirmary, or its part in the Malakoff business, the better for all concerned.

After his guests had departed, Captain Hammond went looking for his wife and found her in the orchard pruning the Japanese pear trees she loved so much. She culled every bloom and potential fruit with the skill of a surgeon, leaving behind only those examples that promised eventual genius.

Macy and Li-Lee were having a little tea party of their own in the shade of a nearby apple tree, and the baby slept soundly in his special basket, which was securely suspended from a low tree branch within reach. Since they couldn't be overheard, the captain sat down on a fruit box and told Lady Yee every particular of the sad story. He related Malakoff's detailed confession and his sincere deathbed desire to make some restitution. However, he said, the poor man died with an estate of two dollars and ten cents.

Captain Hammond reached into his vest pocket and handed her the little leather purse on its thong. He said he had shown the item to the other men, but they couldn't make any sense of it. The stained leather purse held a worthless white stone the size and shape of a quail's egg, with no more weight than any beach pebble of the same dimensions.

Lady Yee examined the white stone carefully in the sunlight. Then she smelled it, and even tasted the surface. With a perplexed shake of the head, she scratched the surface with a little pruning knife, and then smelled and tasted the stone again. Suddenly she looked up and smiled. She called to Li-Lee to mind the baby, and then walked toward the stone potting shed that was built into the orchard wall. Captain Hammond followed and watched, but said nothing. On the workbench in the shed, Lady Yee arranged a small glass jar and a six-inch square piece of thin rag. She took a can of mineral spirits from the shelf and poured an ounce into the jar. Then she placed the stone in the center of the rag, and pulled up the edges to create a pocket that was then twisted to reveal the shape of the egg. This she tied off with a bit of string and immersed in the mineral spirits to soak. When the captain asked what she expected to happen, Lady Yee was frank and said she hadn't a clue. For all she knew there might be a chemical reaction and an explosion, but she doubted it. To be on the safe side she suggested they go back out into the gardens and wait for a while. The captain just followed his wife into the sunlight. He was soon so distracted by Macy's insistence that he become the guest of honor at her tea party that he forgot about all other matters for a while.

Later, just as he had finished his third cup of imaginary tea, as well as a command performance of "The Owl and the Pussycat," Captain Hammond heard his wife call to him from the potting shed.

Lady Yee stood at the door of the shed holding the jar of spirits with the stone still suspended within. Upon closer examination, Captain Hammond noticed that the clear spirits had become milky. With the air of two inquisitive children, husband and wife sat down on the shed's stone steps, and Lady Yee pulled forth the stone still tied in its rag. When the stone was unwrapped, it was noticed that the surface of the egg had become densely wrinkled, and part of that surface material clung to the rag in spidery strands. Captain Hammond and Lady Yee looked up at each other with identically quizzical expressions. Then Captain Hammond withdrew his little penknife and handed it to his wife. She in turn pressed the blade into the surface of the stone, and to their surprise the white skin split like the leather shell of a turtle's egg, and in doing so revealed a bright, blood-crimson stone that they both knew immediately was a ruby, and as the afternoon sunlight revealed, not just any ruby, but a flawlessly cut and polished ruby without scratches or imperfections of any kind.

Captain Hammond seemed confused by the shape. Who, he asked, would cut such a fine stone without facets? Lady Yee recalled that there was only one nation that, owing to ancient Christian symbols of rebirth and regeneration, venerated the egg as a religious icon, a nation whose wealthy masters could afford such stones. She smiled and said the ruby was obviously cut in Russia for a czar or church prelate. She mused that it had not been cut in facets because it had once been part of a larger arrangement that emphasized the egg shape to make a symbolic point. Perhaps it was a center jewel from some royal ceremonial regalia. She naturally assumed the stone was stolen, of course, but she cared little. She also assumed that if Malakoff had painted it with white lead, he didn't want it discovered either, which also led her to believe it was a valuable jewel.

Borrowing a handkerchief from her husband, Lady Yee gave the ruby egg a final cleaning, and then rubbed the gem on either side of her nose. The fine facial oil imparted a lustrous sheen to the stone. But it was only when she held it up in the bright sunlight that the true magic of the ruby became apparent; the sunlight entering the gem seemed to converge at the heart of the stone and created an animated, fiery core of ruby light that was almost hypnotic.

Captain Hammond and his wife remained seated on the stoop admiring the scorching brilliance of the gem. Then, after a few moments' reflection, Lady Yee asked whether fifteen thousand dollars in compensation for the ship's survivors and crew would help Malakoff's soul rest any easier. Lady Yee said she didn't mean to include the owners of the ship, of course, as those skinflints would most certainly recoup their losses from the insurance companies. Besides, Mr. Atwood had long since signed on another crew and steamed the battered old freighter north, much to the visual relief of everyone on the bay. But there were others, she said, who had been marooned and left behind in strained circumstances, including Dr. Neruda and his family. They had all paid premium prices to travel like cattle just to escape from political violence, and they would never see their money again if they waited for the ship's owners to soften their hearts. Besides, there were debts owed to the city for taking care of those people. The city fathers would be very pleased if Captain Hammond could find a way to recompense the public coffers as well.

Captain Hammond thought about this for a moment, and said he believed that was an excellent idea, but where were they going to find somebody with fifteen thousand dollars and a desire to own a ruby egg? Besides, they would have to get a professional appraisal to secure a buyer, and that could take months if not years, and then the word would be out. If the gem were stolen, the owner would be well within his rights to demand its return, and then no one would see any profit, and they would be out expenses.

Lady Yee suddenly looked up and said she would buy the gem for fifteen thousand dollars, and she didn't need a professional appraisal either. She had grown up around precious gems, and she knew from the manner in which the stone had been cut and polished, and how it transmitted light and color, that it was not only authentic, but also almost perfectly flawless. She was convinced that such a rare stone, cut in such an unusual shape, could only have been the work of Russian or French jewelers, commissioned by Russian royalty. Though she did point out, this didn't mean that the Russians hadn't stolen the rock from its original owners, who were most likely Turks. Then Lady Yee laughed and said she even knew a way to turn a profit on the transaction.

This last statement amused the captain, and he asked how his wife planned to accomplish that. She said that was simple. She would sell the stone to her father for twenty thousand dollars. Captain Hammond laughed, but observed that her plan smacked of familial disloyalty. He asked how her father was to see any profit at that price. Lady Yee said that was the easiest part of all. Master Yee would turn around and sell the ruby egg back to the Russians for twenty-five thousand dollars. That, she thought, would even entertain Malakoff's ghost. Captain Hammond just shook his head. He had married into a remarkable family, but he found that trying to stay ahead of the wave was usually an exercise in frustration. He handed the ruby egg back to Lady Yee, and they rose to walk back to Macy's tea party. Then suddenly Lady Yee stopped and cocked her head as though listening for something. She looked up at her husband and asked whether he had ever discovered what had inspired the man Vuychek to torment Dr. Neruda with insults. The captain said he didn't really know for sure, but he didn't believe Malakoff had instigated the incidents. Rather, he wagered a theory that Vuychek, like all ignorant people, was triggered by the oldest and most backward reasons possible: the color of the man's skin and the name of his god. Lady Yee took on a curious expression and asked what kind of skin she had. Her husband smiled, and bent to kiss her on both cheeks. With a twinkle in his eye he said Lady Yee had very expensive skin, which he prized above all else. But he reminded her that one could never place a true value on something that has no equal. There was nothing to compare with the incomparable. There was only one Silver Lotus, he said, imparting another kiss to her forehead, and she was unique in all the world.

The next day, Captain Hammond went to visit the little onion-domed Russian Orthodox church on the distant north end of Monterey. It sat on the banks of willow-lined Fremont Creek, embraced by a small forest of willows and blooming dogwood, and in the main was a lovely prospect all around. After a formal introduction, Captain Hammond met with the presiding cleric and arranged to pay for the funeral and burial of one Captain Sigmund Malakoff. Captain Hammond even commissioned a small stone to mark Malakoff's grave.

When Mr. Campion ultimately learned of this generous and selfless act, he sent Captain Hammond the most complimentary letter imaginable, and invited him to sit on the board of the harbor commission. Captain Hammond was of a mind to modestly decline this honor, but Lady Yee convinced him to accept as a means of helping others, while at the same time affirming his own reputation as a man capable of shouldering public responsibility. The financial remuneration was only ceremonial at best, and so Captain Hammond agreed to serve without pay for as long as he was needed. This consequently led to further invitations to participate in public service, but the captain chose to maintain an attitude of enlightened disinterest, especially in holding any position of authority, since these usually came with implied political allegiances that required more than gratitude to sustain. He far preferred to labor in the public interest on his own terms, in his own time, and using his own methods and means to accomplish his ends. Lady Yee understood precisely how he felt. The captain had been in sole command for too many years to abide decisions made by consensus, and he wasn't one to join clubs, committees, or social movements, no matter how well intentioned their motives or goals.

The passing of Malakoff brought a long spate of peace and quiet that allowed Dr. Neruda the time to place the infirmary on an active footing. He and his family proved very dedicated indeed, and they soon had everything working relatively smoothly, at least for a mechanism fashioned to deal with the turmoil of injury and illness, birth and death. Within a short while, aside from approving and paying running costs, Lady Yee found the infirmary worked quite well on its own and required no further supervision. She was now free to focus on other projects that had since taken her interest. She also felt that it was now extremely important that both her children learn to speak and read civilized Chinese, and not the slang dialects they were exposed to by the servants, gardeners, and stable hands. In this endeavor she trusted herself alone to accomplish the task properly. And that would take her full attention for a while.

For the next few years, under the captain's deft guidance and Lady Yee's intuitive commercial instincts, Hammond, Macy & Yee thoughtfully moved from one modest success to another, growing in assets and wealth. And though Captain Hammond had now resolved, at the loving insistence of Lady Yee, to do all his sailing on Monterey Bay aboard his custom-built thirty-foot catboat, the company nonetheless now controlled substantial or at least a majority interest in eight modern steam-powered freighters, chartered mostly to the lucrative coastal lumber trade, but sailing as far as Panama and Peru for rarer woods.

But like his wife, Captain Hammond's greatest pleasure and the focus of his happiest discipline were the needs of his daughter and son. The captain, according to Lady Yee, was a complete stooge when it came to any whim Macy might envision, and if his three-year-old son, Silver, could have come up with a reputable scheme to conquer Central America using toy soldiers, his father would have backed him to the hilt. Though he adored Macy, and indulged her every whim, even Lady Yee was forced to admit that there was a very special, very powerful, and very mysterious bond between father and son. When the boy was teething or ill, the only arms and voice that gave him any true comfort or relief were his father's. On occasion, Macy, who felt she held precedence where her father's interests were concerned, went into fits of sibling jealousy when she felt her little brother was receiving attention that should properly be hers. However, their father possessed diplomatic skills worthy of a French courtier, and always somehow managed to calm the troops and then inspire a resurgence of laughter, patience, and affection in the ranks. This was just as well, since Lady Yee freely confessed she had no proficiency at disciplining her own children and was grateful that her husband possessed the ability to maneuver them into channels of acceptable behavior without resorting to harsh words or threats. It was his contention that hurt feelings rarely inspire children to behave properly toward each other, whereas praise and laughter had remarkable healing properties when it came to injured pride and the tarnished ambitions of disappointed children. Though it sometimes piqued her own motherly pride, Lady Yee had to admit that her husband had the insight and patience to bond with his children in a very creative and yet orderly manner. He never raised his voice, never criticized, and never threatened. He also knew how to make them laugh by telling wonderfully silly stories, and often joined in their games, regardless of his personal dignity. Sadly, Lady Yee always felt she lacked these necessary skills, and though she adored her children, and they worshiped her in turn, she continued to believe that somehow she was not doing enough to make them happy. Captain Hammond laughed at her self-assessment, of course, and said she was talking halfpenny nonsense, and Lady Yee in turn would smile gratefully and pretend to believe him.

18

IT WAS LADY YEE'S unerring aptitude for unraveling the intricate skeins of the human mystery that led her to become once again involved with Sheriff Winslow and Marshal Sanchez in two mysteries that involved homicide during the commission of a theft. The first was the murder of a Chinese, and the second was a murder by a Chinese, and in both cases whites were involved, so the public demand for resolution was high.

The first case involved the brutal murder of an elderly Chinese craftsman, a fine wood carver of high local repute. His name was Master Chow-Ing Wah, and Lady Yee knew him primarily because he had carved the beautiful gold-leafed characters honoring Guan Yin that hung above the entrance to the infirmary. He had also contributed a marvelous little statue of Guan Yin that he had carved from a single piece of rose coral. To Lady Yee's great distress, Master Chow-Ing Wah had been found beaten to death in his cottage workshop. His property had been thoroughly ransacked in search of something of value.

The crime inspired Lady Yee to do her own research into the circumstances surrounding the old man's murder, as she was aware that the Chinese would never reveal anything to the authorities out of fear of becoming a target for the murderer or of being accused of the crime themselves. With this in mind, Lady Yee set out her own subtle web of inquiries to collect any information that might drift by. Like a hunting anemone, she let her tentacles wave through a cloud of irrelevancies until something significant swam within reach. And that is just what ultimately transpired.

Through Nandiri Neruda she learned that an elderly woman who had been a patient at the infirmary said she was the murdered man's cousin. According to Nandiri, the old woman was a creature of nervous temperament and vivid imagination, a very distressing combination in the elderly. She had come to see Mrs. Neruda because she was so fearful about the death that she hadn't slept for three days. Her distress was taking a definite physical toll, so Nandiri compounded a sleeping draught that seemed to work quite well. Lady Yee decided to send her familiar, Ah Chu, to interview the woman. Lady Yee saw to it that he carried a hamper full of gastronomic delights aimed to pamper the elderly palate. She also included a half-pint jug of a rare Chinese plum-wine brandy. This volcanic spirit was so powerful that tradition dictated it could only be consumed from cups the size of pinky thimbles, and even then the portion was deemed more than adequate. When Ah Chu returned, he bore information that Lady Yee knew at once was critical to the mystery.

She immediately penned a note to Sheriff Winslow inviting him for tea that afternoon. She promised strawberry custard tarts and critical information as inducements. Sheriff Winslow, who had formed a high opinion of Lady Yee's abilities during the Vuychek business, was fascinated to learn that the murdered man had once been an exotic pearl broker who had spent many years on the coasts of Arabia and the Red Sea. After serving two years in a Turkish prison for supposedly smuggling pearls, he escaped to Egypt. To feed himself in Alexandria, Chow-Ing Wah took work in a wood carver's establishment, where he learned he had considerable untapped skills of his own as an artist. He also learned it was safer to travel as an itinerant craftsman, burdened only by his chest of tools, than it was to travel as a pearl broker, whose burden virtually everyone wanted to relieve him of.

Lady Yee told the sheriff that the victim's aged and very distant cousin lived close by, and she had sworn that Chow-Ing Wah had come to Monterey from Seattle ten years before. Once settled, he had set up a small shop carving decorative elements for other furniture makers. He made a modest living, disdained all thoughts of marriage as too expensive in time and money, and seemed to want for nothing important. Lady Yee then smiled and suggested that, despite all evidence to the contrary, perhaps Master Chow-Ing Wah hadn't really set aside his deep interest in pearls after all. The killer had gone to great risk to thoroughly search the dead man's property. She said they could only assume the murderer had found what he or she was looking for. With this in mind, Lady Yee went on to suggest that Sheriff Winslow put out the word to be on the lookout for anyone trying to sell or trade in pearls, for she was honestly persuaded that the old man had been murdered for profit and nothing else. Lady Yee convinced Sheriff Winslow that Chow-Ing Wah, being Chinese to the core, would have set aside something valuable to see himself through old age and infirmity. What else could this consist of but pearls?

Sheriff Winslow left Lady Yee with warm sentiments of gratitude and assurances that he would act on the information at once. Matters soon fell into place when a rough-hewn Portuguese seaman was arrested in Moss Landing. He had gotten uproariously drunk at a popular local cantina, and it was noted that he drank only the best and most expensive spirits. When the cantina owner refused to take a large misshapen pearl as payment for the seaman's food and drink, the Portuguese assaulted him and then tried to escape. He was restrained by some of the other customers, and then arrested by the local deputy. It was then discovered that the seaman had a large stash of pearls in his possession, and Sheriff Winslow was contacted immediately. The man was then rearrested for the murder of Chow-Ing Wah, a crime to which he later confessed. He didn't really have much choice in the matter, as the silk-lined leather purse holding the pearls carried Chow-Ing Wah's personal chop stamped in cinnabar.

There were two odd codicils to this sad incident. The first was the fact that the Portuguese was the first man ever to be hanged for the murder of a Chinese in Monterey County. The second odd circumstance appeared in the guise of Chow-Ing Wah's distant cousin and now heir. The old woman begged Ah Chu for an audience with his mistress, and Lady Yee agreed. It was only then that Lady Yee learned that Chow-Ing Wah's cousin had gained possession of the pearls. But the poor old woman said she didn't need pearls, she needed money to live on. She had no idea how to liquidate the gems without being cheated, and she feared that now that the pearls were blood-cursed, someone would murder her as well. Then she blushed and modestly confessed that she really didn't think they were worth very much altogether, for they were far too large and grotesque in shape, and no two were alike in any respect including color, and though admitting complete ignorance on the subject, she said she wasn't sure whether they were really pearls at all. They certainly didn't look like pearls she'd seen depicted.

Lady Yee politely asked to see the gems and was stunned by what greeted her eyes. The old lady placed the silk purse on the table and slowly poured out twenty-five of the largest and most shaped baroque pearls imaginable. Some were the color of fine pink coral, while others reflected tones of azure blue, soft sea green, silver black, and translucent gold. The sizes and shapes were indeed bizarre and unattractive to the untrained eye, but Lady Yee knew from the first instant that there were court jewelers in Moscow, Brussels, and Paris who would sell their own children to possess these magnificent and unique natural sculptures. Once in gifted hands, they would become the torsos of golden mermaids or diamond-haloed cherubs in repose, or perhaps even set in some priceless piece of royal regalia. However, Monterey wasn't Paris, and taking these to market would involve some expense and time. Local appraisal of their value would be meaningless, since no one in California would know what to do with them.

Lady Yee knew she was treading a slick deck, but her instincts told her that, despite the fact that she knew little about baroque pearls, and colored pearls specifically, she might see her way to a profit if she helped the old woman simultaneously.

Lady Yee asked how much money the woman needed for the gems, but the poor woman had no idea of their value. She said she needed at least sixty-five dollars a month to support herself, her widowed daughter, and baby grandson, but more money would certainly be helpful. Lady Yee suddenly realized the poor woman's problem. If by some impossible act of perverse justice the old woman should find some buyer to give her the full value in cash, she wouldn't have the slightest notion of what to do to protect the money besides burying it under the hearth, and her personal possession of such wealth would only attract acts of fraud, theft, and possibly worse, especially if her darker fears were made manifest.

Lady Yee served the old woman honeyed tea and sweet rice custard, and while she indulged with delight, Lady Yee made a detailed written inventory of the pearls, noting their sizes, shapes, and colors. While doing this, her mental abacus simultaneously clicked away. Lady Yee constructed an enlightened and honest offer, one worthy of the old woman's needs.

When the old woman was quite sated with tea and sweets, Lady Yee calmly told her the truth. She said the stones were worth handsome money in some parts of the world, but not here, and that selling them on a world market would require a further investment in money and time. On the other hand, Lady Yee was willing to arrange a business contract that would, without fail, pay the heirs of Chow-Ing Wah one hundred dollars every single month for the next ten years, or two hundred dollars a month for five years. Lady Yee did this in the utmost confidence that her father would most certainly find a way to realize a modest profit commensurate with her investment. If an unforeseen monetary advantage came her way as a result of the ultimate sale, she would see that all concerned were rewarded according to their interest. That was her way with everything; either all profited, or none. She liked to quote her father, who said, "That which is equitable can be defended to the last, but that which is predicated solely on self-interest will soon wither, with loss and shame enough for everyone."

When the old woman heard Lady Yee's proposal, her eyes rolled up into her head and she almost fainted. And even after Lady Yee encouraged her to take some tea to clear her throat, the poor woman remained speechless for quite a few moments trying to find the words to frame a response. At last tears of frustration came into her eyes, and she cried that she could scarcely believe she would ever be the recipient of such generosity. The lives of her little family would now be spared the soul scourging of constant poverty and shame, and perhaps her daughter might still find a new husband.

Lady Yee was firm when she said this was not a matter of generosity but simply good business, and she expected to realize a modest profit from the exchange. She also told the old woman that, with thirty days' notice, she could adjust the amount of the payments up to as much as two hundred and fifty dollars a month, but this would also correspondingly shorten the pay periods. The total price to be paid for the stones was to be twelve thousand dollars. She asked the woman whether this arrangement was satisfactory, and the dear creature, now lifted to the heights of euphoria, said that satisfaction could not begin to describe her emotions. She said the prayers of a lifetime of struggle had at last been acknowledged by heaven's blessing, and as far as she was concerned, the agent of that miracle was Lady Yee.

The second incident involved the killing of a young Mexican bar maid in Gonzales. Eight people witnessed an unknown Chinese man strike the girl on the head with a heavy bottle. The blow killed the poor creature instantly, but the murderer escaped into the night with the other patrons racing out into the dark screaming for his blood. Marshal Sanchez said he expected a lynching if the mob found the man before he did, and he approached Lady Yee for help locating him. Even though she rarely left her own estate, Marshal Sanchez knew she could find out virtually anything that had to do with the Chinese communities. And he wouldn't have been in the least surprised to discover that her social connections spread way beyond that.

It took three days of diligent letter writing, but a week later Lady Yee was able to inform Marshal Sanchez approximately where to find the killer. However, she mentioned most earnestly that there seemed to be special circumstances involved. The man the marshal, and indeed half the male population of Monterey County, was looking for was a strange character known as Long Jimmy Wu, and from all the reports she had received from her Chinese correspondents, the poor man was totally insane, and most certainly delusional. Lady Yee had been told his condition had been brought on by a traumatic head injury suffered while working for the railroad. The man had no home to speak of, but when he was in the vicinity he usually slept rough out in the dunes on the north end of town; however, it was his habit to wander all over the county. People said he lived mainly on stolen orchard fruit, field produce, and the occasional purloined chicken or duck, but when it came to Jimmy Wu, no one was really certain of anything. He kept company with no one, only spoke to himself, and then only in the third person, and until now was considered relatively harmless, if somewhat distasteful to be around. Sometimes people would show pity and give him a few coins, but he only spent it on alcohol, which didn't affect him well at all. After consulting Dr. Neruda, Lady Yee advised Marshal Sanchez to take along three good men, as the strength of the insane could be remarkable. On the other hand, Jimmy Wu might decide not to be taken alive, so it was a situation primed for disaster either way. But in the main Lady Yee agreed that Jimmy Wu's only chance for survival depended upon the marshal finding him before anyone else did. An angry mob would most likely mop him down with hot tar and then hang him very slowly from a low branch of a tree. Such cruel and unjust punishments had been applied to the Chinese before, and for lesser crimes than murder. But at this juncture Dr. Neruda made his own suggestion, and one that he predicted would avoid hardship and injury all around. He proposed that Lady Yee's chef prepare a food basket containing items such as pickled fish and salt-cured meats. Of course, with this thirst-inducing ration, a quart of rice wine should be included. Dr. Neruda volunteered to taint this potable with enough sedative to put a man to sleep for twenty-four hours, and thus allow the marshal and his men to carry away their prisoner on an ambulance stretcher without the least question of injury to anyone. Ultimately, Long Jimmy Wu would awake already under restraint in a closed cell, which would save even further violence for all parties.

Marshal Sanchez, who still carried several bright pink knife-wound scars from an earlier confrontation with a livestock thief, thought this was a marvelous idea. However, getting the bait to the nest was the critical question until Dr. Neruda suggested that Lady Yee's houseboy take the basket and then innocently walk among the northern dunes until, hopefully, he came across Long Jimmy Wu. If their man was discovered, the aging houseboy was to say the people in the village had sent the food, and then noting the location, he was to return to the marshal and await events.

All was agreed to in principle, and Marshal Sanchez felt confident enough to propose an attempt of the scheme that very evening. He said he would return at five-thirty with three deputies. He politely requested Dr. Neruda to accompany them, just in case someone ended the evening needing medical attention. The doctor was happy to comply, and Lady Yee felt this was an appropriate precaution considering one could never quite predict the conduct of the insane, whether sedated or not.

Lady Yee instructed Ah Chu to prepare a food basket as directed, and then she retrieved a bottle of rice wine and gave it to Dr. Neruda. He poured off approximately half the wine into a simple stoneware crock and mixed in a half pint of some clear liquid of his own concoction, then recorked the neck. He smiled and said that just because Jimmy Wu was crazy, it didn't mean he was also stupid. Quality rice wine in a fancy glass bottle would certainly inspire suspicion.

Together, Lady Yee and Dr. Neruda spent an

hour rehearsing the houseboy on his part. This was important because he was the only one who could translate for the doctor and Jimmy Wu, should that ever become necessary. To secure his enthusiastic support, Lady Yee promised her houseboy a twist of black Turkish tobacco and a Mexican gold piece. The aging houseboy happily agreed, and to Lady Yee's amusement, he entered into his role with high theatrical enthusiasm that needed paring down to be credible.

Marshal Sanchez arrived exactly on time, riding aboard a horse-drawn Black Maria. Three armed deputies, two on horseback and one driving, accompanied the marshal. Dr. Neruda and the houseboy were invited to sit in the back, where they could ride in greater comfort, and where they would not be seen in the company of the authorities, a situation that might spark erroneous gossip.

An hour after their departure, Captain Hammond returned home from a three-day business trip to Salinas. He was dusty, dirty, angry, hungry, and in a bad mood generally. Not being able to find the houseboy to take his horse did nothing to improve this. He told Lady Yee that on his return it had grown dark, but he hadn't yet stopped to light the lamps. An unseen limb recently parted from its parent tree had snagged his rear buggy wheel and instantly shattered four spokes. The captain had been obliged to abandon the rig at a farmer's house a half mile back along the road. He was then introduced to the discomfort and humiliation of riding the buggy horse bareback the last ten miles. It all wouldn't have mattered that much to him, he said, except that he had been wearing his very best suit, and it now smelled of horse sweat. Lady Yee decided to say nothing about recent events until her husband had bathed, changed, and been well fed, and maybe not even then, depending on his disposition.

Happily, Ah Chu served up the captain's very favorite Nantucket oyster stew, followed by a plate of boned sand dabs grilled in butter and flanked by a side of pickled prawns, which the captain adored. Lady Yee was grateful to Ah Chu for his perception, and was pleased to discover that her husband had forgotten all about his suit and had moved on to relate a couple of amusing stories about a Greek banker he had met.

Lady Yee believed her husband's mood had lightened to a degree that made it possible to broach the subject of Long Jimmy Wu and the missing houseboy, and as dinner tea was served she began to share the happenings of the last few days. As usual, Captain Hammond could only shake his head in wonder at the complex adventures his wife was prone to attract. She was like a lodestone for acts of social chaos. The captain had heard about the killing in Gonzales, of course, but he had no idea his wife had been consulted about the matter by the authorities, or that she had discovered the possible whereabouts of the perpetrator and then arranged for Dr. Neruda and the houseboy to help subdue the mentally deranged culprit. Every new and distressing detail Lady Yee revealed brought the captain ever closer to counting up the possible liabilities his wife's contributions might have incurred.

Lady Yee had almost finished explaining her actions when the door's bell chimed, and a moment later the aging houseboy, now somewhat disheveled and emotionally spent, entered the dining room and softly announced that Dr. Neruda requested a short interview before he returned home. Lady Yee nodded and sent the old fellow to the kitchen to have his supper. Captain Hammond immediately rose from his seat and went out to the hall to invite the doctor in for a cup of tea.

When he entered the room, Dr. Neruda approached Lady Yee, pressed his hands together, and bowed his head in respectful salutation. He declared that her foresight had most certainly saved one man's life, and possibly more. The doctor was happy to report that everything had come to a surprisingly peaceful conclusion, and Long Jimmy Wu was now safely in custody, a situation, he said, that seemed to please Jimmy Wu every bit as much as it did Marshal Sanchez and his men. Lady Yee didn't quite know how to respond, so she just smiled and bowed her head in turn.

Captain Hammond seated the doctor and directed the maid to serve him tea. The doctor described how the party had stopped in a stand of pines at the edge of the dunes where they couldn't be observed. As twilight fell, the marshal sent the houseboy off with the food basket to search out Jimmy Wu in the high, grassy dunes that ran between the shore and the road. This was where Lady Yee had been informed the man could be found at night. She had been told that he felt safe there because he could hide between the dunes and kindle small fires that couldn't be seen at a distance.

The doctor said the party waited with confidence, but nothing seemed to work out as they had planned. Twenty-five minutes later the houseboy returned still carrying the basket, but he surprised everyone when he said he had found Jimmy Wu. He said the man didn't want the food. He told the houseboy he was dying and didn't need it. When the houseboy asked what ailed the man, he replied that he was being eaten by the darkest demons and there were round-eyes that wanted to kill him. He didn't know why. The houseboy, who was nobody's fool, told the man it sounded like he needed a wizard who could drive away evil demons, and protect him from the round-eyes as well. When Jimmy Wu begged to know if there was such a person, the houseboy said there was. He told Jimmy that he knew of a very wise healer from India who knew all about demons. He wasn't a round-eye, but he was very important, so he could protect Jimmy from people trying to hurt him. The houseboy said the wizard lived close by, and he would fetch the healer if Jimmy wished him to. The houseboy reported that Jimmy Wu began to weep, moan, and tear at his hair. He begged to be relieved of his torment before the demons ate him alive and took him to hell. He pleaded with the stranger to bring the wizard at once, but not to be surprised if all he found was a bloody pile of bones when he returned. He said he could feel the demons eating his body. When the houseboy once again offered the food basket, Jimmy Wu said he couldn't eat because it infuriated the demons that were gnawing at his guts. Then he clutched his head, cried, and begged for the Indian wizard to come and save him.

There was no doubt that Dr. Neruda had the undivided attention of his audience, so he paused to sip his tea and order his words to avoid misunderstanding. The doctor said that Marshal Sanchez was not happy about letting him walk off into the dunes without protection, but the doctor prevailed by saying that after years in the army he was sure he could look after himself. However, he needed the houseboy to guide and translate. The little man was not overly enthusiastic about going back, but when the doctor explained that people's lives depended on his skill, he bowed to his better nature, picked up the basket once more, and led the doctor out into the dunes as the last light faded in the west. In parting, he cautioned the marshal to be patient and wait for his return. He didn't want his new patient, who was obviously delusional, believing that more demons were coming after him. His reaction would most assuredly be violent, and therefore counterproductive all around.

The doctor suddenly went silent, and an expression of profound sadness clouded his features. When he spoke again there was a catch in his voice. He said that in all his years of service he had seen just about every injury and disease mankind is heir to. Most of these could be managed, if not cured, with proper care. But he said that those poor people who suffered mental disorders or insanity were the most distressing to him because, aside from sedation and close confinement and possibly even restraint, there was nothing that medicine could do to alleviate their suffering, and that was exactly the situation he now faced with Jimmy Wu. The doctor said that he had rarely seen such a pitiful case of paranoid delusion and dementia, which, sadly, usually ended in suicide or murder. He said that Jimmy Wu showed all the classic symptoms of a man tormented to the point of violence by advanced mental illness, and this, he said, was hardly surprising considering the size of the indented trauma on the back of his head, a deep concussive wound that had obviously gone untreated at the time of the injury.

When the doctor and the houseboy came upon Jimmy Wu, he was thrashing about, crying, begging his demons to leave him in peace, and Dr. Neruda said it was a good thing that he wasn't Caucasian, because the man appeared almost as terrified of white people as he was of his soul-consuming demons. After a pause, Dr. Neruda said the man looked almost relieved when the houseboy introduced the doctor not by name, but as the healer wizard.

The doctor said events went a little slowly at first, mostly due to the need for translation, and in many cases interpretation, but he finally convinced his new patient to drink some of the drugged wine, which he seemed to enjoy. Within twenty minutes his spirits had calmed to a point that made semi-rational discussion possible. In his role as demon-chasing wizard, Dr. Neruda finally convinced Jimmy Wu to talk about his demons. His patient said the devils inhabited everything and were everywhere. He recited a long, detailed litany of demons that he seemed to know by name. He said they dwelled in the soil, in the grass, in the trees, in the stones, and in the night sky. Even the air was thick with them when the fog rolled in, and they were all bent on destroying him. He said they always talked to him and never gave him any peace. And sometimes they made him do bad things he didn't want to do.

With the administration of more wine, Jimmy Wu grew calmer still, and the doctor believed he'd at last become pliable enough to absorb and act upon authoritative suggestions. Knowing the effects of the drugged wine, the doctor said he asked if the demons were talking to him now, and Jimmy Wu found it pleasantly curious that they weren't. Dr. Neruda told his patient that he could indeed drive the devils away for a while, but they were bound to return unless Jimmy Wu protected himself with secret magic. When his patient begged to know how to save himself, Dr. Neruda confessed he was caught off guard. He'd been thinking on the run, as one must do with mental patients, and he really didn't know what to say that would sound plausible. The doctor reminded his hosts that mental aberration does not imply stupidity; in many cases the reverse is true. Mentally unbalanced people can be unusually intelligent and logically geared.

The doctor then smiled and said that suddenly something oddly fortuitous and feasible occurred to him. He told Jimmy Wu that no demon, no matter how powerful, could stand the presence of iron, and thus could not pass through doors or windows guarded by iron bars. This protection also extended to the white devils that were after him. He slowly convinced his patient that he knew of a fine stone building where he would be safe, well fed, and warm. As a fortunate afterthought, he told his patient that he could even arrange for a wagon with iron bars to protect him on the way, and armed men to see that none of the white devils harmed him in any fashion. And to seal his safety from the demons, Dr. Neruda told Jimmy Wu he would travel along and accompany him safely to his destination.

Dr. Neruda sat back and wiped the weariness from his eyes. Then he smiled to himself and told his hosts that at the very moment he told Jimmy Wu that he would protect him, the full moon suddenly appeared out of the clouds and brightly illuminated everything in sight. Jimmy Wu took this as a sign that the wizard had driven off all the demons, and he instantly agreed to accompany the doctor anywhere, as long as it led away from his tormentors.

After encouraging his patient to finish the wine, Dr. Neruda said he and the houseboy guided a stumbling and sleepy Jimmy Wu back to where the marshal was waiting. The poor man soon fell fast asleep in the Black Maria even before they started out for the jail in Monterey. The doctor rode with him all the way, and for safety's sake saw to it that he was placed in a cell alone. The doctor informed Marshal Sanchez that he believed it might be best to keep the prisoner partially sedated until the court could make a medical disposition. It was obvious that Long Jimmy Wu could not possibly be prosecuted, thus the only alternative would be commitment to the state hospital for the insane.

When Dr. Neruda at last concluded his narrative, he slowly declared that it was all indeed very sad to acknowledge, especially after everything that had been done to save the man's life, but based upon a cursory examination of Jimmy Wu's initial head injuries, done while he was in a drugged sleep in the wagon, Dr. Neruda had come to believe that there was nothing that could possibly be done to save the man from his inevitably painful death, which, from all indications, would occur very soon.

Lady Yee at last spoke up, and with uncharacteristic emotion pleaded to know the reason why. After a sip of tea to moisten the tension in his throat, the doctor said he had found definite signs that beneath Jimmy Wu's original skull injury, which had not healed correctly, there was now evidence of a large tumor pressing on the base of his brain and protruding down into the neck. Without further examination he couldn't be certain, of course, but since there were no surgical procedures that could possibly deal with the problem one way or the other, he gave Long

Jimmy Wu less than two months to live, and considering his mental state, that figure could prove generous.

After a few moments to allow this information to distill, Dr. Neruda rose from his seat, thanked his hosts, and said it was time he returned to his family. But in parting, he observed that despite the ethics of his profession and his religion, he now believed that perhaps a well-aimed bullet from a marshal's gun might have saved suffering all around. Yet, with that said, he was still inspired by Lady Yee's compassion to see that Jimmy Wu was cared for till the end. This, he said, had kept his instincts for empathy kindled, and he would look after his patient until the court directed otherwise. He was contracted to care for the Chinese of Monterey, and he would do his best to fit reality to the model set forth.

Before he departed, Dr. Neruda bowed to Lady Yee and generously attested that the Hammonds' houseboy had been indispensable in bringing the whole affair to a peaceful conclusion. He suggested that his efforts be acknowledged. Lady Yee affirmed that those arrangements had already been seen to. However, upon the doctor's kind recommendation, she determined to amplify the agreed compensation and reward her faithful servant with a new suit of clothes and a hat.

19

DESPITE THE CAPTAIN'S insistence that she no longer become embroiled in civic upheavals, social calamities, or police business of any kind, Lady Yee's reputation as a person of influence, insight, and perspicacity still hung in the air like a battle flag. And in a town like Monterey, anonymity was a rare commodity usually reserved for drifters, saddle tramps, and seamen on shore leave. While she diligently sought to remain in the shadows, and was never seen out in public, Lady Yee's repute and celebrity seemed to grow of their own accord. Anything remotely remarkable that transpired always brought with it the question of whether Lady Yee might be involved in one way or another, and for most people a lack of denial was as good as a yes vote. As a result, people slowly began to send her petitions for help with their problems, and it wasn't just the Chinese who sought her wisdom and advice. Because of her exotic background, her beauty, and her great wealth, Lady Yee was not seen as occupying the same stratum as other Chinese. She was thought of as royalty, and therefore acceptable to all but the most socially rigid and racially intolerant denizens of the upper crust. Thankfully, they were few in number, mostly rich ranchers who prided themselves on pure and legitimate strains of everything from draft horses to children.

Even though he knew his wife had done nothing to personally encourage this tide of petitions and requests for help, Captain Hammond began to feel that something had to be done to stem the flow of expectations or there would most assuredly be trouble down the road. With this in mind the captain set about making his own plans.

Captain Hammond had recently purchased controlling interest in a newly launched steamship that had been purpose built on the River Clyde as a grain freighter. The owners had sailed the 230-foot ship all the way to San Francisco before running out of money and patience with each other. It was all a matter of being in the right place at the right time, but Captain Hammond knew a profitable and timely opportunity when it cleared the horizon. So with the help of a San Francisco investor as a junior and very silent partner, the captain purchased the ship at the asking price. His actions had been inspired by a burgeoning tragedy thousands of miles to the west.

Mainland China was at present suffering through a third year of widespread drought. Even the great rivers flowed at record low depths, making navigation all but impossible in some places. The suffering and privation soon spread to every level of Chinese society. The captain's father-in-law, Master Yee, had written several letters describing the disaster, and said that for the first time in living memory the rich and the poor were eating from the same bowl, grateful for every noodle and grain of rice. He related that food imports were woefully inadequate and selling at black market prices, which only increased the suffering. Russian grain was neither easy to come by at the best of times nor easy to transport, and it only rarely made it all the way to the eastern cities. And while grains from the Americas were always of high quality, they were also too expensive after costs, and because the present political system was in tatters, importers demanded gold or silver paid on the barrelhead. As matters worsened, shipping costs had become almost predatory, leaving Master Yee, a respected grain factor in his own right, to heartily regret that so many swine were feeding at the trough of this calamity. He surmised that there had to be a way to break the cycle, but it was beyond his power of insight to come up with a solution.

Then, one rainy night a few weeks later, the captain awoke from the effects of a strange dream, and suddenly he knew the answer to Master Yee's problem. After a little consideration, Captain Hammond was surprised that he hadn't thought of it before. The next morning he informed his wife that Hammond, Macy & Yee was going into the grain-exporting business. The primary market would be China, of course, and their factor would be Lady Yee's father. The captain pointed out that because of the close familial relationship, Hammond, Macy & Yee could easily afford to do something no other exporters and shippers could match: finance the cargo, sell it at reasonable market prices, and extend credit to Master Yee until such time as the cargo was liquidated. If in turn he could find brokers willing to pass on the savings to people of like mind, then more would benefit and perhaps other companies would find it necessary to modify their need for broad profits. Captain Hammond also added that, unlike the other companies, they could also afford to take their profits in goods like teas and silks and porcelains, with a full line of credit guaranteed by Master Yee's company. The scheme had several advantages, but the most interesting one seemed to be that, with the ability to sell quality grains at reasonable prices, Master Yee would become a local hero, venerated for his honest dealings. Of course this would only attract more customers, but one way or another, Hammond, Macy & Yee would make reasonable profits as it always had in the past. But there was also the spiritual profit that comes from doing something necessary for the benefit of others.

LADY YEE was very impressed with her husband's plan. And as a sign of her support, and to honor her father's lifelong generosity, she insisted on financing the first cargo herself. So with approvals all in hand, Captain Hammond went looking for another ship, and found one.

The captain's new ship had originally been christened *The Baltimore Eagle*, which considering her utilitarian lines, deck cranes, and bluff appearance, sounded rather pretentious and inappropriate to Captain Hammond. Waiting until certain modifications had been made to the vessel's accommodations, and without bothering to inform Lady Yee, the captain rechristened the ship *The Silver Macy*. Though they were his children's names, he knew everyone would ask him just what a Macy was, and why was it made of silver. The whole idea made him chuckle with the humorous possibilities, though he knew that Lady Yee would not be amused he had used her son's nickname, yet he felt that *The Nathanial Macy* sounded almost as pretentious as *The Baltimore Eagle*, and only appropriate for an old Nantucket whaler.

Contracting a grain cargo proved no problem at all, and since it was all California grown, the costs were quite reasonable. The Sacramento delta was awash in rice, and plains-grown wheat was fat kernelled and abundant. Lady Yee recommended that spare cargo space, if any, might be filled with dried fruits, beans, peppers, and ginger, as well as shelled almonds, pecans, and pine nuts, all capable of withstanding long storage while still retaining their food value. Lady Yee also suggested they play fast and loose with the Chinese salt monopoly, just as it had been done for years by the local fishermen. She believed they should purchase a hundred cases of dried squid, which was traditionally packed in shore-panned sea salt. In China the product would be taxed a duty as dried squid, and a blind eye turned to the fact that the salt, now rosy-pink and flavored like dried squid, was a far more valuable and useful commodity than the squid itself. The two products were then sold separately on the general market, garnering a double profit. She also believed that a thousand gallons of purified peanut oil would find ready buyers. If these items were sold at normal prices it would cause a sensation, and Lady Yee's father would garner public praise from all quarters as a man of modesty and generosity, for without a cash layout, he could also afford to allow his creditors time to profit first and pay later, thus increasing his reputation, customer lists, and client obligations.

Captain Hammond was persuaded that his wife's cargo recommendations were truly insightful, until he learned that the original suggestions had come from her familiar, Ah Chu. However, this only confirmed that Lady Yee had consulted experts before voting, so he acted upon each detail to the best of his ability, knowing full well that if his cargos satisfied Chinese needs and tastes, profits and honor would soon follow.

But there was something Lady Yee didn't know. Early in their deliberations, Captain Hammond had told his wife that he had no intention of commanding the ship himself. Despite his long experience at sea, he acknowledged that steamships were a queer breed that required the judgment of officers who were familiar with their capabilities, limitations, and in particular, their maintenance and fuel requirements. Just knowing how much coal to carry could make the difference between profit and loss, and the captain confessed that he was too old a dog to be learning that many new tricks in so short a period of time. On the other hand, the captain never said he wasn't going on the journey, and this is where his secret plans to extricate Lady Yee from her growing web of obligations came into play. Aside from the captain's cabin and the officers' quarters, *The Silver Macy* had four generous staterooms to accommodate either supercargo or paying passengers. Captain Hammond ordered that the two portside staterooms be combined to make one large suite, while one of the starboard cabins was to be split in two and the other reconfigured to accommodate two very special bits of supercargo.

Despite the fact that he was always reasonable, accessible, and usually open to suggestions made by his wife, Captain Hammond came from a lifetime of command, and in that regard he remained jealous of his prerogatives. In small matters he was amenable, but when it came to important decisions he was still master of his own vessel, and Lady Yee had long since realized that objections were not only useless, but in a deeper sense disrespectful. Nonetheless, the captain wondered just how his wife would react when he presented her with his real plans.

After seeing the children to bed and telling them a story, Lady Yee retired to the parlor and found the captain, hands clasped behind his back, pacing back and forth in front of the fireplace with an unlit pipe clenched between his teeth. She knew from his posture that he had something important to announce, and the thoughtful furrow on his brow meant he was ordering his words. Lady Yee was perplexed, but she quietly sat down, picked up an open volume of poetry she'd been reading, and waited for her husband to surface from his ruminations. After a minute or two, the captain took the pipe from his mouth, turned to his wife, and without preamble of any kind announced that they had two weeks to pack their trunks and close up the house. Now that the children were old enough to travel, the captain believed it was appropriate for the family to return to Canton for an extended visit. He declared it was time for his wife to present her children to their grandparents and aunts, and he was sure the rest of the extended

Yee clan would want to put their oars in the water as well.

Captain Hammond was not remotely prepared for his wife's reaction to this sudden revelation. Lady Yee threw aside her book, leaped to her feet like a girl, produced a happy squeal like Macy at full gallop, and rushed into her husband's arms. She kissed his cheeks repeatedly with little tears welling in her eyes. Finally, holding her husband close, Lady Yee enthusiastically professed that she loved him more than life itself, for he had just made manifest her fondest ambition and a dream that had haunted her for the past three years. She tearfully confessed that, considering her parents' age, she secretly feared never seeing them again in this world, and that they would never hear their devoted daughter personally voice her sincere expressions of gratitude and fidelity for all the gifts they had given her. Lady Yee went on to admit she had wanted to speak of returning home for a visit on any number of occasions, but there always seemed to be affairs of more immediate importance to attend to.

The captain kissed his wife and said that pleasing her gave him boundless satisfaction, but he was also happy to note that the journey would serve so many other worthwhile purposes at the same time. And though it went unspoken, by this he also meant extricating Lady Yee from the net of public expectation that had bloomed in the wake of her civic transactions. Then the captain paused, thought of something, and smiled. He told his wife that perhaps it would be a good idea if she immediately wrote her father a letter to say they were coming. Otherwise, he said, there was a good chance that the Hammond clan might arrive in Canton before the letter. He was pleased to say that the new ship was quite fast, even fully burdened, and they would only stop for fuel twice on the most direct route possible. Ships carrying mail under contract stopped off in numerous ports.

Captain Hammond had been fortunate in his selection of a master for *The Silver Macy*. While in San Francisco, he had made the acquaintance of the well-known Captain Christopher Penn. This intrepid officer had begun his career as a nine-year-old powder monkey aboard a Confederate commerce raider. They had been at sea when Lee surrendered, so in the company of other Confederate naval officers and seamen, he escaped west into the Pacific aboard an unsurrendered cruiser. Knowing they could hardly escape notice for long, and needing to avoid close inspection, they disguised their cruiser as a Spanish warship, and flew the royal standard for good measure. Then, as if to thumb their noses at the Union ships that were doubtlessly out searching for them, they sailed their small warship all the way to the Philippines and sold it to the Spanish Navy. Though they dared not interfere during the rebellion, the Spanish had always been fairly sympathetic to the Confederate cause. Captain Penn had said that the Spanish also enjoyed the humorous aspects of the transaction, and even kept the ship's original name, *The Pensacola*. For the next forty years, Captain Penn sailed to every corner of the Pacific and became famous in Asian waters as a man all self-respecting pirates should avoid like the pox.

Captain Penn had recently resigned his last ship due to a disagreement with the owners and was looking for a new berth. Captain Hammond was quite drawn to the man's professional demeanor and good sense. His manners were chivalric, and his reputation for honor and decency irreproachable. He also possessed a robust sense of humor, and loved quoting long passages from the works of Mark Twain. Captain Hammond, who had a good eye, liked the man at once, and offered Captain Penn command of *The Silver Macy*. After inspecting the ship thoroughly, Captain Penn said he would take command on condition that he could hire his own crew and choose his own officers. When that was agreed, Captain Penn signed on for an initial three-year contract, with an option to renew if the position proved lucrative enough.

Before leaving Monterey, Lady Yee made sure that Dr. Neruda and Mr. Bishop were reading from the same text when it came to finances, so there would be no interruption in essential services or salaries. She made her houseboy the nominal caretaker, but hired a Chinese woman to cook and keep the house clean. She also made a point of keeping her three Japanese gardeners employed at full salary to look after her fruit orchards and extensive gardens. She placed Mr. Bishop in overall charge of all the property and, with the exception of Dr. Neruda, the infirmary, and its employees, power to hire and fire as he saw fit. She also ensured that there remained no outstanding debts owed to local tradesmen, and made certain her bank knew its obligations to be paid out on her behalf. She spent the rest of the time crating away special treasures for storage in the bank's vaults and seeing that the family packed only those garments required for the journey west, for she strongly intended to have new and better clothing made for everyone once they were established in her father's compound in Canton.

Three weeks after making the first announcement of his intentions, Captain Hammond, Lady Yee, and their two children were comfortably installed in their staterooms aboard *The Silver Macy*. They were accompanied by Lady Yee's maid, a new children's nurse named Sing Joon to help lighten the burden on Li-Lee, and, of course, Ah Chu, who insisted that he was the only one qualified to cook for the family, especially the children. Lady Yee agreed in principle, and the captain acquiesced, knowing that any objection would only cause ill feelings all around.

The new nurse slept in the children's cabin, while Ah Chu and the maid occupied the newly split quarters next door. Captain Hammond and Lady Yee occupied the expanded double stateroom across the way. The passenger accommodations, though limited, had all been furnished with the most modern conveniences possible, including electric lights and fans, gimbaled beds, and water closets. Lady Yee was quick to confess that their stateroom was far more comfortable than the old captain's cabin aboard *The Silver Lotus*. And being a large and bluff steamship, it afforded the added luxury of not requiring one to live at unnatural angles all the time. Lady Yee even came to appreciate the ship's new name.

To the delight and surprise of all aboard, the outward-bound journey to the Hawaiian Islands was exceptionally smooth. Even Captain Penn was moved to regard the millpond surface of the ocean as something quite exceptional for so long a period of time and distance, and he openly wondered whether it presaged something less commodious, but in the end, nothing happened. The sky remained cloudless and a vivid blue, the breezes wafted gently from the southwest, the sunsets were clear and bright, and the ocean swells remained almost unnoticeable. All these elements together allowed *The Silver Macy* to log very good course speeds despite being fully burdened with cargo and coal. This made for a happy ship all around. Even the captain and Lady Yee found the experience broadly nostalgic and quite romantic. In the evenings they would sit alone in the stern, hand in hand under the bright stars, and talk of their many adventures under sail. But this was unique, as it was the first time Captain Hammond had ever enjoyed the experience of being at sea as a passenger, even though Lady Yee had noticed that every time the ship's bell was struck, her husband winced like a retired fire horse.

But it was the children who had the very best of times. Macy and Silver were totally convinced that the whole expedition was just for their benefit, and in a sense it was. Within two days, Macy and her little brother had endeared themselves to every man in the crew, and these hardened tars took turns watching over the children when they played on deck. Sometimes these salts even joined in games of tag or blind man's bluff. Then Macy somehow formed a special attachment for Captain Penn. She insisted she liked the way he talked, and she thought him very amusing.

This fact seemed to both flatter and frighten the

captain, who had never spent any time around children. But Macy persisted in her affections and devotion, and completely won the old sailor's heart. Suddenly, and when conditions allowed, Macy was permitted to go up to the bridge and stand with Captain Penn. Together they marveled at the vast schools of leaping dolphins that sometimes accompanied the ship for great distances, and also the flocks of flying fish that were determined to stay in the air for as long as possible to avoid becoming a dolphin's supper. Macy appeared to love it all, and she bubbled with clever questions that Captain Penn always patiently answered. In fact, Lady Yee became used to finding her daughter in the company of Captain Penn, and was surprised to discover how much her daughter learned every day about her new environment. On the other hand, little Silver became the darling of the deck officers, who went out of their way to arrange for all his amusements.

The ship laid over in Hawaii for three days, adding coal to her bunkers, taking on provisions, and allowing the crew a short while to stretch their legs and purchase personal items onshore. The children were allowed to play on the beach, collect seashells, and wade in tide pools that were clear as glass. Ah Chu had a particularly rewarding time visiting the local markets. He came back aboard ship with a splendid variety of fresh fish, fruits, vegetables, and herbs. Soon, even Captain Penn chose to eat with the Hammonds, rather than the other way around, as tradition dictated.

Though the ship made two more short landfalls, the journey to Canton continued as a swift and smooth affair by all sailing standards, and the Hammond family arrived in the hectically busy harbor of Canton on a beautiful spring morning six weeks later. After the relative tranquility and refreshing ocean breezes of the past few weeks, the raucous sounds of constant activity from the shore and the fetid odors of garbage mixed with the exotic smells of a thousand kitchens were all a bit overwhelming, though the children seemed to enjoy every moment of the insanity. Lady Yee told Macy that Canton was a remarkable conglomeration of cultures and peoples. Long before any European had ever set eyes on the city, the old harbor on the Zhu River in Guangdong province had been crowded with trading vessels from Hormuz, India, Java, Korea, Sumatra, and all points in between. An early Arab presence was still represented in the city's population, and their trading houses and banks had been some of the most successful in China.

Captain Penn anchored the ship, raised the appropriate signal flags, and waited for the Chinese customs and harbor officials to take notice to send out a launch to check their papers and cargo manifests. Patience was required as the harbor was so busy that it sometimes took many hours or even days for those officials to get around to paying a call. In the meantime, the ship was considered to be in a state of quarantine, and no one was allowed to come or go until the vessel had received permission to stay and off-load.

The harbor officials finally found time to come aboard in the late afternoon, and they were truly surprised to be introduced to the renowned Master Yee's daughter and son-in-law. As a mark of respect, the officials immediately sent one of their men ashore to find and inform Master Yee that his ship had literally come in, and in more ways than one, it appeared. *The Silver Macy* was then cleared to unload its cargo as soon as dock space became available, but there were no promises when that would be accomplished.

Upon hearing the news of his daughter's arrival, Master Yee sent a small army of porters and carts to the harbor. A bobbing fleet of sampans sculled out from the shore with all manner of goods to sell the barbarians. They nudged up against the ship like children awaiting a treat. A very handsomely appointed river junk came alongside as well. It had been sent by Master Yee to convey his daughter's family upriver to his small estate. The junk also brought written instructions informing Captain Hammond that a pilot would be sent to guide the ship to the company docks, where the cargo would be transferred to Master Yee's adjacent warehouses.

There were still a number of important details to be worked out concerning the ship and its cargo, and Captain Hammond felt obliged to see his part played out with caution and diligence. It was a mark of respect for his father-in-law. To his way of thinking, that included witnessing the transfer of goods personally and securing an accurate warehouse receipt for every pound of cargo unloaded. Though it went unspoken, Canton, like all Chinese ports, was a complex of interconnected commercial warrens where goods magically disappeared like smoke if one wasn't extremely diligent. This was why every warehouse in Canton employed at least a dozen guards around the clock. With pressing obligations in mind, the captain sent Lady Yee, the children, and the servants on ahead. He knew Master Yee would be anxious to greet his daughter and meet his grandchildren, and there would be plenty of time for the captain and his father-in-law to speak later.

Lady Yee was not quite prepared for the elaborate reception her father and mother had arranged for her homecoming. Every Yee relative for a hundred miles seemed to be in attendance with small gifts of welcome. How they knew just when she would arrive was a mystery, but she suspected they had been in the neighborhood for weeks living at her father's expense. Her father was almost moved to tears when his grandchildren greeted him affectionately, but respectfully, in almost perfect Cantonese.

The family reception, which lasted for two days, also included Lady Yee's two older sisters and their six children, as well as numerous little cousins from all quadrants of the clan. Lady Yee was pleased that after shy introductions and a bit of sniffing around, the children were all soon laughing and chasing each other around the compound like a pack of clumsy puppies. And now that there was need of it, Macy slipped into speaking Cantonese most of the time, and like all children her age, absorbed new phrases like a sponge.

Early the next morning, Master Yee boarded his private junk and sailed down the river to his wharves and warehouses in the harbor. Captain Hammond greeted his father-in-law with all the deference and formality expected of a Chinese son-in-law of a great khan. This amused and pleased Master Yee very much, who in turn complimented his barbarian son-in-law by saying that he had been blessed with lucky and talented relatives. After a ceremonial tray of tea and traditional exchange of small gifts, Master Yee joined his son-in-law in overseeing the off-loading of the grain. He was anxious to test its quality and appraise its market value. Master Yee was especially pleased with those items on the manifest that his daughter had personally suggested, and set aside the tea chests of salt-packed squid for special repackaging and sale at a later date. Though he intended only a modest profit on the sale of wheat and rice, he intended to make up the difference with squid-flavored salt, which was considered a delicacy. The dried squid, which was of very fine quality, would also show a reasonable return.

It was important that *The Silver Macy* take on a new cargo as quickly as possible and speedily return to San Francisco. An idle ship costs money. Captain Hammond had prearranged for three full shipments of grain to be taken on in California, but return cargos from Canton were a matter of catch-as-catch-can. A purchasing agent like Master Yee or Captain Hammond would use discretion, along with a sound understanding of their markets, and then make a choice from what was available. Leaving Canton with empty holds was out of the question. Happily, Master Yee knew this would be the case, and, subject to Captain Hammond's approval, he had arranged something special. With the tacit approval of friendly customs officials, Master Yee had recently purchased a confiscated cargo of raw Malaysian rubber, copra, and coconut oil, and at cut-rate prices. To this he added five hundred bolts of tent-grade Indian waxed canvas and a hundred cases of local Chinese porcelain, chosen for durability and the quality of workmanship. The latter came to Master Yee as partial payment of a long-standing debt, and the canvas came directly from a British naval warehouse in Singapore. All this he gave to his son-in-law on credit, as repayment for the credit extended to him on the grain.

Even with a credible force of stevedores and the use of the ship's steam cranes, it took two full days to warehouse the grain, and then another three days to take on the new cargo, which had to be carefully stored based upon bulk and weight. Of course, special care had to be taken with the porcelain, for though the pieces had been carefully packed in paper and rice chaff, and then placed in chests, it had to be loaded last, as near to the center of gravity as possible to avoid excessive movement or pounding during bad weather.

Captain Hammond had determined to remain with the ship until she was ready for sea again, then he would surrender *The Silver Macy* to the tender mercies of providence and Captain Penn. It would be three months before they would meet again, weather permitting. The day before the ship sailed, Lady Yee came downriver with the children. They were anxious to see their father and say farewell to Captain Penn and the crew. Lady Yee had even thought to bring gifts of fruit and sweet pastries for everyone aboard. Even the ship's cats were included with a small basket of steamed herring. After taking on bunker coal from barges, Captain Hammond said goodbye to his ship and wished Captain Penn a swift and easy voyage. Then he sailed back upriver to his father-in-law's compound to be with his wife and children for a well-deserved rest.

MASTER YEE had leased a handsome little compound just east of his own property for the use of Captain Hammond, his family, and servants. He employed other servants as well to look after the property and do all the cleaning. It was all rather elaborate, and Captain Hammond was moved to admit that, compared to their modest life in California, and certainly by American standards, they were living in veritable luxury twenty-four hours a day. He worried that the children would become spoiled, and worse still, that he would become spoiled and, like the lotus-eaters, never want to leave. Lady Yee smiled and said that was the prerogative of all grandparents. A desire to keep their grand-children close can sometimes inspire great expense and secret manipulations. It was to be expected, not to be feared. She said her father was simply doing what Chinese grandfathers do whether they have money or not. Spoiling grandchildren, she claimed, was one of those ageless privileges, and as far as she could discern, one shared by all mankind.

During most days Lady Yee visited with relatives, worked with the children on their lessons, and saw to her husband's comforts, while Captain Hammond spent much of his time with

Master Yee studying the intricacies and formalities of Chinese business practices. Buying and selling was an art form in and of itself, and gentlemen merchants prided themselves on observing certain courtly formalities. It was akin to bowing and complimenting your opponent before a duel, only in this case it was a duel of wits. And in that regard, Captain Hammond was amused to learn that the only people the Chinese held in high esteem for their trading skills were Arabs, Alexandrian Jews, and down-cast Yankee traders. They disdained most European jobbers as arrogant and stupid, and took unfair advantage of them whenever possible. They thought it only fair considering all the damage the Europeans had caused in the past. They liked the Yankees more or less, despite their lack of sophistication and subtlety, primarily because they always backed a fair offer with cash on the barrelhead. Master Yee was fond of saying that the Americans were not all that bright in business either, but they were scrupulously honest, loyal to their trading partners, and didn't dabble in Chinese politics, which made them the very best of a bad lot when it came to barbarians.

Captain Hammond was also surprised to discover that though there was a healthy market for his California-grown rice, the Chinese didn't enjoy eating it because it lacked the sticky consistency that gave the rice a quality they enjoyed. On the other hand, Yankee rice, once milled, made superlative rice flour, which was used in great abundance, and because of its high natural sugar content, brewers of rice wine and rice wine vinegar paid very good prices for Sacramento delta rice. Master Yee also introduced his son-in-law to the highly prized and extremely profitable Chinese markets for American tobacco, ginger, arrowroot, dried beans, and especially cured salmon, or native Indian smoked salmon. Mexican dried peppers were popular as well as American jerked beef and pork, which lasted months and was used in China to flavor foods, since fresh meat was expensive and difficult to come by for most Chinese.

Master Yee also presented his son-in-law to other prominent Chinese traders, which proved most helpful as he planned for future return cargos. Master Yee ensured Captain Hammond's social status and his line of credit as he had in the past. This allowed the captain to arrange to purchase goods without having to set out hard cash until he took delivery at the docks. In this respect, as well as others, Captain Hammond was once again to become the most privileged Yankee trader in Canton. As a barbarian, it was one thing to do business with the Chinese, but once a person like Captain Hammond was acknowledged as a member of an established family as prestigious as the Yee clan, then all the tides flowed in his favor. Still, it was important not to take undue advantage. The one quality all Chinese most admired was self-effacing modesty, especially in a wealthy barbarian, but one was still obliged to balance the books when it came to reciprocation, so it was critical never to overextend oneself when it came to asking favors. Captain Hammond found his education very enlightening, and he thoroughly enjoyed the company of Master Yee, who had a wry sense of humor as well as a faultless sense of the absurd, both necessary qualities for a man who was essentially a gambler on a very large scale.

The weeks passed into months with no notice of time except for the coming and going of cargos, which could be remarkably fast. The captain's first grain cargo was sold off in less than six hours, and Master Yee gained great face and respect for not gouging a starving market. Nonetheless, twenty-five tons of rice and forty tons of wheat couldn't be expected to go very far in a city the size of Canton, and Master Yee speculated that not much of it ever left the city proper. He suggested that perhaps the next cargo should be loaded onto junks and taken inland to be sold, but either way it was obvious that three shiploads of grain would hardly make an impression on the market. What they needed was twenty or thirty cargos of similar size every three months, but the cost outlay was prohibitive, even for Master Yee and Captain Hammond. And considering the great population of southern China, not even their concerted efforts would have made any substantial impact on the problem. Nonetheless, as profits slowly returned, Master Yee took advantage of his son-in-law's business connections in San Francisco, and arranged for a further three shipments of grain under the aegis of Hammond, Macy & Yee.

In the meantime, Lady Yee was proving quite a success in her own right. It was incumbent upon her to take the children and go about the countryside paying formal calls on all the venerable elders in the clan to hopefully garner their blessings. She tutored the children on how they were to address their relatives, and how they were to behave. She also arranged for them to present these elderly ladies and gentlemen with appropriate gifts as signs of filial homage. Little Macy, being an unrepentant showboat, handled her part with charm and dexterity, while her little brother had to be bribed into playing his part by being promised a ride on a wooly Asian dromedary that was kept at the Canton zoological gardens for just such a purpose.

In matters of business, Lady Yee also had surprising success. One night Captain Hammond and his wife were invited to an elaborate reception at the French legation. Since Lady Yee spoke fluent French, Captain Hammond thought it would be amusing to watch Lady Yee charm the "frogs" out of their ponds.

Captain Hammond arrived at the French reception sporting a handsomely tailored black silk suit that his wife had commissioned. Lady Yee wore what appeared at first glance to be simple black silk robes trimmed at the cuffs and the throat in red satin. But closer examination revealed that her black robes were intricately and elaborately embroidered with figures of dragons, cranes, and bats all done in black silk thread. Only the soft variations in light revealed their presence. Aside from her wedding ring, Lady Yee wore only her mother's intricately carved white jade bracelet. It depicted two entwined dragons with ruby eyes, and was worth more money on the open market than her husband's ship, cargo included. She wore her long, beautiful hair in the traditional Chinese fashion for a woman of her status, but two wonderfully pierced tortoiseshell combs secured the arrangement. The combs were decorated with rich amber temple lions rampant on a field of amethyst chrysanthemums. These gems also showed their best in the twinkling candlelight, and reflected deep inner fires every time Lady Yee moved her elegant head.

Captain Hammond, who had rarely ever attended a gathering of this caliber, and certainly never in the company of his wife, was truly amazed, and not a little disconcerted, to discover how much attention she was attracting. In fact, in a ballroom hosting a hundred fashionable and attractive women, Lady Yee seemed to be the only point of focus for most of the men present.

It was after a stylish buffet supper that Lady Yee was introduced to an elegantly dressed Russian gentleman by the name of Peter Carl Gustavovich. Small and personable, he appeared to be in his early sixties and claimed St. Petersburg as his home. The two communicated quite easily in French, and seemed at home in each other's company. Upon politely inquiring as to the gentleman's profession, Lady Yee received a rather disjointed response having to do with special commission work. Finally he admitted that he was in fact a designer of fine jewelry, and confided that he had been sent to Canton to purchase rare jewels for his wealthy patrons in Russia. Without a second thought, Lady Yee grasped her opportunity like a trout takes a mayfly. She modestly asked Mr. Gustavovich if he might be interested in seeing her collection of large baroque pearls. She enticed him further by describing the size, shape, and color of some of the bigger specimens in her collection. Mr. Gustavovich appeared more than just a little interested. Then Lady Yee baited the hook by discreetly casting her gaze downward, and hinting that the whole collection, excepting one stone, might be for sale, if the right price were proposed.

She invited the little Russian gentleman to take tea and view her trifling collection on Wednesday afternoon two days hence, while Captain Hammond went downriver with his father-in-law to inspect a ship they intended to charter.

With Ah Chu's assistance, Lady Yee entertained Mr. Gustavovich with a complete Russian high tea. Her tea was chaperoned, as custom dictated, by two female relatives and her maid, none of whom had the least idea what was transpiring before their eyes.

At the appropriate time in her conversation with the little Russian, Lady Yee withdrew a silk and satin purse from her copious sleeve and revealed the contents by pouring the pearls onto a red silk pillow. Mr. Gustavovich was almost dumbstruck. His eyes widened, he stuttered a few odd words in French, and while reaching for a jeweler's lens in his vest pocket began talking to himself in very rapid Russian. Forgetting all else, he carefully examined each pearl, and set each aside in separate piles based on size and shape. Then he did something rather odd. He casually began to take stones from various piles and arrange them together in strange patterns that had little or no symmetry. He asked which pearl was excluded from consideration, and Lady Yee picked out a large double-lobed pink pearl that looked very much like a heart. She said that she planned to have it mounted as a pendant for her daughter when she grew older. Mr. Gustavovich smiled and nodded his head. Begging his hostess's indulgence, he withdrew pocketbook and pen and began to make detailed notes. From another pocket he withdrew a small silver box containing a cunning little pocket scale and miniscule counterweights. With Lady Yee's permission, he weighed every pearl carefully and made a note of the weight next to a simple sketch of its shape and general size. When he'd finished this task, he carefully put the pearls back in their purse and handed it reverently back to Lady Yee. Then they finished their tea very pleasantly, and talked on several interesting subjects without mentioning another word about the pearls.

Just before taking his leave, and with many compliments over the care taken to make him feel at home, Mr. Gustavovich made a notation on the back of an engraved calling card and then placed it on the table between them note side down. Lady Yee left it where it was and politely escorted her guest through the flowering central court with its decorated fishpond and up to the gate. Here he thanked Lady Yee again and departed promising to repay the honor at his earliest convenience.

When she returned to her place, Lady Yee picked up the card, turned it over, and read the back. There was a figure written there beginning with an English pound sign. Dusting off her mental abacus, she translated the figure into

American dollars, and this time she was the one who looked surprised. If her math was correct, and it usually was, Lady Yee had just been offered three times what she had paid for the pearls in Monterey.

The one other person who seemed to derive great pleasure and some profit from being back in Canton was Ah Chu. He convinced Lady Yee to allow him to purchase new kitchen equipment. He then ordered custom-made woks, steamers, kitchen knives, and other cooking utensils. He said he intended to refurbish the kitchen in the Monterey house with goods fit for a lifetime of use, and only the best was worthy of Lady Yee's table, to say nothing of Ah Chu's considerable talents.

Ah Chu also invested some of his own money to purchase rare Chinese herbs and condiments not available in California. He knew by reputation a number of professional chefs who worked for wealthy Chinese families in California. They would pay top dollar for certain exotic items, like pickled stingray roe or Persian smoked oyster paste, but only if they knew the complete provenance of the product. In effect, it had to be delivered under seal, and there were only certain companies in China who were licensed to do so. Additionally, the buyers, who it must be assumed knew what they were purchasing, had to thoroughly trust the professional standing of the person who had originally purchased the goods. Ah Chu also knew they would trust another professional chef of status before they would trust a spice broker, for those men, not being cooks, were sometimes fooled by clever counterfeits. Ah Chu, who was nothing if not cunning, knew that he would gain great face and reputation if could befriend renowned members of his own profession, and the best way to do that was to create a network of amicable obligations based on mutual needs. But sadly he ran short of enough money to buy in bulk.

Lady Yee knew of his scheme, of course, as nothing ever really escaped her notice, and she kindly offered to loan Ah Chu the necessary funds to accomplish his purpose. However, she required the loan to be secured by his future wages, and this, she hoped, would force her minion-cook to pay extremely close attention to every detail of his transactions. She reminded him, in no uncertain terms, that he would be the only loser if he misjudged the needs of his proposed clients by so much as a misplaced cardamom seed. Ah Chu bowed with gratitude and signed the contract.

With Master Yee's many connections, Captain Hammond arranged numerous excursions for the family into the countryside and up the Zhu River. They visited many famous Buddhist temples and shrines, and sites of historical interest, but most of the time they preferred to travel to sites of great natural beauty. After six months in Canton, and with the application of regular study supervised by a paid tutor, Macy and Silver were speaking and reading Cantonese with surprising dexterity. It seemed that every day they absorbed more and more of the nuance and subtlety of the language. After a while they rarely spoke English except to their father, and he was away on business with their grandfather a good deal of the time. Every day, because they played with Chinese children, were cared for by Chinese servants, and tutored by Chinese teachers, Macy and Silver became more and more Chinese in manners, dress, and custom. Indeed, Lady Yee was hard-pressed to get them to keep up with their studies in English and history.

August promised to be hot, dry, and dusty, and people almost prayed for a monsoon, regardless of the danger, just to have fresh stocks of clean water, and possibly raise the level of the river to help bring back the fish. August 10 was also Macy's eighth birthday, and her grandfather had promised her something special. In fact, he took all the arrangements into his own hands and refused to share his plans with anyone, including his daughter. On the morning of her birthday, the maids dressed Macy in especially beautiful robes that her mother had commissioned. The garment was made of the finest black silk and intricately embroidered with golden dragons flying above blue cranes at rest, green turtles basking, and red fish swimming beneath silver water lilies. Macy loved it at once, and swore she would never take it off. She said it was magic, and she believed she could make magic happen if she wore the robes to the exclusion of all else.

The celebrations started early. Master Yee had arranged to have all the foods prepared in his own large kitchens and then delivered across the way to the captain's house, and Ah Chu happily volunteered to prepare all of Macy's favorite foods, including, of all things, ice cream flavored with all kinds of fruit syrups. An air of marked anticipation, punctuated by the strange sounds that could be heard coming from their grandfather's house, kept Macy and Silver on an emotional edge that their father found most amusing.

Guests began paying calls at ten in the morning, and the only ticket required was to bring a child. There was plenty of food and drink for all, and people were encouraged to indulge themselves, and even take food home to share with other family members. The central court and public rooms were almost overflowing with forty adults and as many children. Then suddenly, on the stroke of noon, the raucous sounds of crashing cymbals and blaring horns came from just outside the front gate of the compound. When a servant opened the gate, Master Yee entered wearing elaborate robes and carrying a long white staff.

Behind him entered three jugglers dressed as clowns and a man with a trained monkey that could do the most amazing gymnastics. Master Yee came forward and called out to his granddaughter to join him. Macy ran up, took his hand, and smiled up into his eyes. Then Master Yee announced that everyone was invited next door to enjoy a full circus of entertainments and refreshments. They led the way with all the other children laughing and clapping and following behind.

As it turned out, Master Yee engaged the whole Canton circus, and there were over sixty performers of all kinds in attendance. There were marvelous acrobats, and jugglers who could balance and toss about an amazing variety of things, including furniture. Macy was particularly drawn to a magician with an ominous-sounding name. He was titled the Great Wizard Yea-Wu Shoo, and he could do the most sensational things of all. He made the gymnastic monkey climb a rope and just disappear. He made plants grow, flower, and fruit within minutes. He made a dozen pheasants fly out of an empty basket, and made spirit money grow from a burning tea plant. The wizard possessed a full quiver of magnificent illusions, but he won Macy's heart when he had her magically float in midair out over the audience while seated cross-legged on a small Indian carpet and casting little wrapped sweets to the other children from a basket, as she floated about overhead. There was a man who had trained twenty white cats to do tricks, and another who could coax dogs to dance on their hind legs to music. Then there were more clowns, who jigged about and got into amusing situations.

The entertainments came to a close with a beautiful little fireworks display, followed by red and gold temple lions dancing to music and balancing on big gold balls. The general festivities ended at four, and the guests politely thanked Macy and her family for being honored with an invitation, and then departed, taking away small parcels of food and sweets for others less fortunate.

That same afternoon at five, Macy participated in a Chinese birthday tradition. In the company of about twenty Yee relatives and her parents, Macy went in a procession to the family shrine overlooking the river. Her mother had rehearsed the ceremony with her. She taught Macy how to make offerings and address prayers to her venerable ancestors, and how to petition heaven for the blessings so necessary to the survival of the clan and the nation.

The afternoon sun was soon shrouded in dark clouds that seemed to herald rain, but never delivered. It had been the same for many weeks, and if indeed there had been rain, it never reached the ground. The dry heat and dust remained unaltered, and the rain never materialized despite the presence of thunder and lightning on many occasions. It seemed the clouds' promise of rain would never be fulfilled, and this only heightened the people's deepest frustrations, and inclined them to believe that perhaps they no longer merited heaven's blessings or consideration.

Macy performed all the rites flawlessly. She clapped three times, thanked heaven for the privilege of life, and with her little hands pressed together in supplication she called upon the spirits of her Chinese ancestors to intercede with heaven on behalf of the family, the clan, and the nation. Then Lady Yee lit a bundle of incense for her daughter, and Macy placed the smoky fragrant sticks in an ancient stone bowl filled with black sand that stood in the middle of the ornate altar. She then reverently placed offerings of salt, rice, fruit, and wine on the altar, after which she stood back, bowed her head in prayer, and clapped three times again. Then Macy, as was sometimes her habit, did something that totally surprised everyone, and even shocked some of the elder members of the family. Her whole demeanor changed, and Macy stamped her foot like the angry mandarins she had seen at the Chinese opera. To Lady Yee's utter surprise and consternation, Macy proceeded to politely admonish her venerable ancestors for not petitioning heaven strongly enough to relieve the people's suffering. She said the clan had been blessed with great prosperity and influence, and now was the time to repay their debts. The people needed rice, and grain, and fish, and clean water, and none of this would come to pass without heavenly intervention, so she encouraged her ancestors to redouble their efforts on behalf of all the people, and not just the Yee clan.

There was a shocked, stunned silence. Without the least consideration that she had done anything either inappropriate or unworthy, Macy turned from the altar, walked up to her grandfather, bowed, and looked up at him with a sweet, innocent smile. Master Yee tried his best to maintain a stern expression, but he just couldn't manage it. Macy then took his hand and led him out to the covered veranda that fronted the shrine. The other guests followed silently, not sure of what to say. Then Master Yee looked down at his beautiful granddaughter and asked why she had spoken as she did in front of her ancestors. Macy simply replied that they were very old, and very tired, and needed to be awakened to the problems of this world, not heaven. She giggled and said that's the way her mother always spoke to her when she didn't want to get out of bed, or do her lessons properly. This answer so charmed Master Yee that he began to laugh, and the others chuckled self-consciously not knowing what to make of it all. Macy sensed their discomfort and disapproval, so she turned to her grandfather and cited an old Chinese proverb. She said ancestors and gods were always amenable, but like cats, you first had to get their full attention.

A gigantic lightning bolt raced across the sky from west to east, and quite uncharacteristically parallel with the earth. It was followed by a thunderclap so loud that it rattled all the buildings and frightened everyone. For a few moments the flash of bright light and the stupendous explosion of sound both blinded and deafened the party. And when they at last regained their senses, they looked up to discover the everdignified Master Yee and little Macy holding hands, laughing, and skipping up and down. It was raining, and it was a generous, sweet-tasting rain, and it continued to rain in this manner, on and off, for six full weeks. The monsoon rains had returned at last, after a drought lasting almost four years. This occasioned destructive flooding in some areas, but the people rejoiced all the same. Everyone worked together to clean out long-dry cisterns and clear irrigation channels. Runoff was judiciously channeled into enlarged duck ponds, stone reservoirs, fish hatcheries, and, of course, rice fields. And at last, to everyone's relief, the air was finally washed clean, and the breezes no longer smelled of road dust, garbage, soot, and dry manure.

To know the Chinese is to be certain that the story of the little girl who scolded heaven for its lack of compassion and brought back the rain was all over Canton in twenty-four hours, and possibly all over southern China in another week.

The Hammonds had been in China for almost a year, a generous family visit by any standard. The captain also confessed to being somewhat homesick. He longed for his home, the company of friends, and long conversations in English. As much as he enjoyed China, he enjoyed California more, and he believed it was time to go home. Thanks to Captain Penn's unerring seamanship and strict harbor schedules, *The Silver Macy* had made four round-trips, and a fifth shipload of grain was expected within six weeks. As a result, Captain Penn had earned himself a considerable bonus. The ship had performed flawlessly in all weather, and the engine ran like the proverbial Swiss watch. Every cargo imported into California had seen healthy profits, and a world glut of sea coal had reduced fuel expenses appreciably.

Though she had not voiced sentiments one way or the other, Lady Yee was very attuned to her husband's moods and motives. She had begun to sense his agitation and restlessness. She was therefore not in the least surprised when he announced at breakfast one day that they were returning to California on *The Silver Macy* in six weeks. Lady Yee simply said she would see that everything was prepared for their departure in good time.

For Lady Yee, the hardest formalities involved making farewell calls on her numerous relatives. To each she brought a small commemorative gift, and from each she received protests and tears. It was expected. Then one day Lady Yee received a note sent by one of her favorite aunts. It requested she come to tea the following afternoon. The note hinted that her niece might discover something of great interest and value. Lady Yee accepted the invitation, but mostly to take her leave. Old ladies thought the oddest things were of interest, and so Lady Yee expected little.

The next afternoon Lady Yee waited upon her aunt with a farewell gift. Then her aunt suddenly took the opportunity to introduce a newly arrived guest, a young man named Dr. Wei Chun of the Korean legation in Canton. The young doctor spoke little Cantonese, but was quite conversant in English and French. Lady Yee and the young man jumped back and forth between the two languages where necessity required.

After a course in traditional greetings and pleasantries, Lady Yee discovered that Dr. Wei Chun had begun his medical training under his father, a well-known Korean physician, when he was eight years old. Having shown exceptional promise in the field of traditional Asian medicine, when he was sixteen he was sent to study under the famous Dr. Su Wong Loo in Peking, where he received praise and honors. When he returned to

Korea, he was chosen by the government to be sent west to study Western medicine and surgery in Berlin and Paris, and when he returned to Korea five years later, he went to work for the government.

Canton was his third foreign legation posting. His nominal assignment was to look after the health of other high government officials, which he said was mostly a matter of dealing with their perpetual overindulgence in one vice or another. The work lacked all the challenges he had trained so long to master. Finally, he said, his contract was up at the end of the month, and though he had been invited to stay, he wanted to get married, and that was not allowed for low-level legation personnel, and anyway, in his present position he really couldn't afford to get married. He bemoaned the fact that his salary was almost ceremonial, and therefore close to nothing. The bulk of his earnings went to repay the government for its investment. He believed he could do better somewhere else, and was told that Lady Yee might be able to help him find a new position more suited to his education and ambitions.

Lady Yee looked over at her aged aunt and smiled like a cat with a sparrow. She asked Dr. Chun where he wanted to work, and he replied that it didn't really matter. He humorously added that he would live anywhere as long as it was relatively civilized, not at war, and not very cold.

All he really wanted was a useful medical position, at which he could make a living wage and support a family. Lady Yee asked if he had any objections to treating poor Chinese. He responded by saying that the human body had no nationality, and only marginal differences based on medical susceptibilities to certain diseases. One human was very much like another. If you could cure one, you might cure another, but the principal importance still lay with the cure, not the monetary wealth of the patient. In short, he would use his skills to save anybody who requested his services as long as he could still feed and shelter his family decently.

Lady Yee played her part with her usual charm, elegant patience, and timing, and promised nothing that might confuse the issue. She continued her understated interrogation with the aura of a concerned friend, which went a long way toward making the young man feel at his ease. They shared subtle jokes in French, and absolutes in English. She asked if the doctor might be willing to immigrate to another country if his economic needs were satisfied, and he said he would as long as his other requirements were met. Lady Yee modestly laughed behind her sleeve and said she would keep that in mind. Before the tea party ended, she told the young doctor that she would look into the matter, and if he were to come to her residence in two days she might just have a solution to his predicament. The young Korean doctor seemed amazed at Lady Yee's gentle confidence and concern, but she was Chinese, and in that regard he knew not to harbor unsupported presumptions.

Lady Yee told her husband all about the interview, and he encouraged her to strike while the steel was hot. He reminded her that Koreans were, in general, better engineers, scientists, and soldiers than the Chinese. He declared that it could be supposed that a Korean doctor may well show equal genius. At first Lady Yee thought her husband might be indulging a private joke out of affection, but then he laughed, kissed her on the forehead, and offered to loan her five hundred dollars in Yankee gold to secure the young man's contract at once if it pleased her.

When Dr. Wei Chun came to call he seemed quite disoriented, and Lady Yee decided to take advantage of this situation. When the timing was right, she asked him if he was willing to travel to California on a five-year contract, and he said that he was. Then she asked if he was willing to look to medical needs of the poor, and again he said he was. Lady Yee then proposed a yearly stipend that made the young doctor blink with disbelief, and she even offered to pay half a year's wages in advance so that he could send for his intended bride.

But there was one proviso: He had to be ready

to depart in four weeks, wife or no wife. Lady Yee then stated that she had a contract at hand, and upon signing, everything would be set in train, as it were. As an afterthought, Lady Yee asked about the doctor's intended bride, and learned that she was a trained midwife and nurse, with a particular genius for herbal remedies applicable to the perils of pregnancy. Lady Yee smiled and signed her part of the contract at once.

When Dr. Wei Chun departed he was carrying five hundred dollars in Yankee gold and a semi-humorous promise that Lady Yee would track him down if he betrayed her. The young doctor was so enamored of Lady Yee, as well as her generous offer of employment, that he would have battled his own family to please her. Happily, that test never came to pass, and Dr. Chun and his new bride returned to Canton five days before *The Silver Macy* was due to sail.

For Lady Yee, the hardest part of the preparations was taking leave of her parents and sisters. For Master Yee it was saying farewell to his grandchildren, and for Macy it was saying goodbye to her cousins. She was extremely happy in China and saw no reason to leave. She even asked if she might stay behind with her grandfather. And little Silver, who thought of his father's ship as his own, mainly because his name was on the stern, couldn't wait to get back aboard. The sailors had always spoiled him with constant attention, and he loved them all in return. The only thing that gave Macy any consolation was the fact that she would soon be reunited with Captain Penn, for whom she maintained a unique and profound affection.

Captain Hammond had to make special arrangements for Doctor Chun and his new wife, but that was soon taken care of to everyone's satisfaction. Finding space for Ah Chu's special cargo took some thinking, as it included a small flock of exotic Chinese geese and chickens that he hoped to crossbreed with their hardier California cousins. There were also ten large cases of cooking utensils, preserved foods, spices, and all the hardware necessary to construct an authentic Chinese baking oven and wok stove. Captain Hammond humorously bet his wife that her cook was about to go out on his own and start a restaurant using her money. Lady Yee took the bet as a sure thing. She said Ah Chu was far too lazy for commerce of any kind.

21

THE SILVER MACY left Canton on the morning tide two days later. Lady Yee's mother and father came to the docks to say a final farewell and to present Captain Penn with ceremonial gifts of wine, rare fruit, and fine silks. Master Yee gave each of his grandchildren a gold-mounted jade pi yao to be worn about the neck as protection. He gave his son-in-law an affectionate embrace, a few words of praise, and a silk envelope containing a bonded draft drawn on the Bank of England for sixty-two thousand pounds sterling. It represented just a portion of the expected profits from their mutual business ventures.

The ship cleared the coast in good time. The seas were kind and the winds gentle, but on the third night it began to rain heavily, and the seas kicked up considerably. It wasn't anything *The Silver Macy* couldn't handle, of course, but the passengers were nonetheless encouraged to stay in their cabins and avoid the slippery decks. Slowly the driving winds increased from the northeast, and Captain Penn decided that, with a full cargo and plenty of sea room, it would be better to turn his stern to the wind and go with the storm. It was easier than fighting waves he could not see. The heavy rains, though a godsend for the boiler collectors, made the bridge functionally blind. All the watch officers had to go on was the binnacle compass and the direction of the waves. To be sure, there were lookouts posted bow, nest, and stern, but they were no better off than the bridge officers. And then the ship's compass decided to change its mind and became decidedly fickle. A pocket compass, though affected by the iron hull, showed the binnacle compass to be far in error, and no one, considering the weather conditions, had the time to find out why. Repairs, if possible, would have to wait until the storm abated.

Then, at approximately four-thirty in the morning, *The Silver Macy* struck an obstacle substantial enough to throw the lookouts to the deck and the captain from his day berth behind the bridge. The ship shuddered like a bull, and then settled down to continue on course in the trough between the waves. At first no one knew what had happened, but the bow watch reported that he believed that in passing he saw the deck of a swamped fishing boat with broken masts but no sign of life. There didn't appear to be any damage to the ship until later a crewman reported that the bow chain lockers were flooded with seawater. There was no immediate danger, since the chain lockers for the anchors were separated from the rest of the ship with a watertight bulkhead, but the added weight in the extreme bows might cause the hull to hog and place undue stress on the box keel. Captain Penn ordered pump hoses lowered into the flooded lockers, but it was soon discovered that the iron hull had been breached at the waterline with a handsome three-foot puncture that staved and split two abutting iron plates. They could pump all they liked, but it wouldn't make the least difference until the breach was plugged and patched from the outside. There was too much anchor chain in the lockers to access the hole from within the ship while at sea.

There was some consternation among Captain Hammond's many charges, but he and Lady Yee managed to calm everyone and saw that they returned to their berths, where they would be safest during the storm. Then the captain donned an oilskin and went to the bridge to support Captain Penn in any way possible.

At exactly noon, the storm moved on and left *The Silver Macy* floating like a battered swan on a placid sea. It was then discovered that one of the compensating magnets on the compass had come loose and fallen to the bottom of the brass binnacle. When that was repaired, Captain Penn and Captain Hammond took sextant sightings and determined that they had traveled a very fair distance to the southeast, and that the closest station to effect repairs was a Dutch naval re-coaling and maintenance base on an impoverished jungle island off the northern tip of the Malaysian archipelago. Sailing directories considered the port pestilential and its harbor an anchorage of last resort, but *The Silver Macy* and her present cargo were deemed far more important than the weather or the scenery, and Captain Penn set course for Van Koop's Island at once.

The ship arrived eighteen hours later, anchored in the offing, and set up flags calling for a pilot. The harbor was empty of ships and almost looked abandoned. There were few people to be seen onshore, and those few appeared totally disinterested in the presence of the steamship offshore. Two hours later a boat approached with the harbormaster aboard. Captain Penn and the harbormaster communicated with voice trumpets. The ship was warned that the harbor was under tight quarantine due to an outbreak of malaria and cholera. The American ship would be permitted to anchor in the harbor to make repairs, but they could neither land people nor goods, nor allow locals to board with goods of any kind. They were permitted to purchase materials needed for repairs, but the ship's crew would have to take delivery from unmanned barges ferried up to the ship by the harbor tug. If there were men ashore willing to assist in repairs on the outside of the ship, and they agreed never to board or fraternize with crew members, that might be arranged, but otherwise *The Silver Macy* would have to be its own best salvation. The Dutch harbormaster said that the recent heavy rains had raised virtual clouds of mosquitoes, sand fleas, blackflies, and fleas. For those unaccustomed or susceptible, life ashore was a death sentence. Dr. Chun recommended that before the ship entered the harbor, all the ports be closed and insect netting be placed over the companionways. He also suggested that despite the heat and cloying humidity, all those not needed on deck stay below in their cabins and quarters. This particularly applied to the women and children. Captain Penn agreed and made the doctor's suggestions ship's orders.

It took four long days to effect the simplest of repairs. However, all the anchor chain had to be pulled from the bow locker so that men could descend below and buck the back of the hot rivets that secured the iron patch plate to the starboard side of the bow. And the conditions belowdecks were uncomfortable in the extreme. Insect netting purchased from shore had been doubled over the deck ventilators, but since there was no breeze to speak of, the atmosphere in the cabins and saloon was hot and humid to the point of claustrophobia. No one escaped the constant discomfiture, but it was the children who suffered the most. For the men working on deck it was even worse. Even though the ship was anchored out in the harbor away from the jungle, the very presence of warm-blooded creatures drew virtual clouds of biting gnats, and when they departed the blackflies took up the feast, and as the sun slowly set, millions of thirsty mosquitoes appeared to do their part to torment the crew. The men made hoods of mosquito netting and covered their exposed skin with thick layers of black engine grease, but neither would drive off the blood-sucking fog of insects. Captain Penn had smoke buckets set up near the bows, but the breezes blew the smoke away without bothering the insect population one bit. Dr. Chun suggested the men be given plenty of raw garlic to eat, as this seemed to make the victims' blood and body odor distasteful to biting insects. Luckily, there was plenty of that particular commodity on board. The cooks always placed numerous garlic bulbs in the potato sacks, vegetable bins, and fruit nets to prevent mold, and the process worked quite well. Captain Penn instructed the cook to peel numerous bulbs of garlic and had the crew swallow three or four of them like pills every few hours. It not only kept the mosquitoes from biting, it also somehow increased the men's stamina and endurance. The clouds of insects never really departed, however, and they got into everything, including the food and the paint used on the hull patch.

The Silver Macy left port almost the moment repairs had been completed. The paint hadn't even dried. Their departure occasioned jubilation all around. The companionways, deck hatches, and portholes were opened to air out the ship, and the passengers and crew came out on deck to relish the ocean breezes and take in lungfuls of fresh air that hadn't been used by everyone else first. The children played on deck in the sunlight, and Lady Ycc relaxed in the shade of her Chinese parasol and read from a volume of English poetry that Captain Penn had loaned her. To show his gratitude for surviving all that had befallen them, Ah Chu sacrificed two of his precious chickens and bartered with a crewman for a small freshly caught tuna. With these and a few Chinese vegetables, newly madc ricc-flour noodles, and fruit, hc produced a remarkably diverse feast for the Hammonds, Captain Penn, and the officers.

The next day the dark clouds again rolled in from the south, and it rained all day. Happily, the seas and swells remained moderate, and the ship continued to make good time on an even keel, allowing those who needed rest a peaceful, cradle-like sleep. But the next morning, hell once again came to visit.

Captain Hammond awoke and complained of aching muscles, a bad headache, fever, chills, and nausea. Lady Yee immediately scnt Li-Lee for Dr. Chun, but he was a long time coming because he was not to be found in his cabin or on deck. The doctor and his bride had, in fact, been forward in the crew's quarters since before dawn. They had been treating two other men who had come down with exactly the same symptoms. When Dr. Chun at last arrived, he made an immediate determination on treatment. He ordered that the patient be kept warm when chilled and cold-bathed when fever set in. He gave Ah Chu a big bundle of green willow bark and told him to brew it into a very strong tea. This in turn should be mixed with four parts water and fed to the patient on an almost continual basis to maintain hydration and help alleviate painful muscle cramps.

Then suddenly, Macy ran into the cabin and, unaware that her father was ill, rushed up to her mother in a panic. She begged her mother to come at once. With tears in her eyes, Macy said little Silver couldn't get up, and he was hot and all wet. Lady Yee immediately swept her daughter up into her arms and rushed back across the saloon to the children's cabin. Dr. Chun followed quickly on her heels.

After examining the little boy, Dr. Chun turned to a distraught Lady Yee and said the child was afflicted with the same disease his father had contracted, and the same as the two crewmen. There were several possibilities as to the cause, he said, but considering all the possibilities based upon conditions and the similarity of symptoms, he had ruled out typhoid and cholera because the patients showed no signs of dysentery as yet. The doctor said he believed that their last port of call held the answer, and led him to believe that the stricken had all contracted what the Americans called malaria. Treatment was limited, but in the case of all three possibilities, continuous rehydration was absolutely necessary. And it would be best, he said, if all the water was boiled for at least ten minutes, and then cooled.

Captain Penn entered the cabin with a distraught expression, and asked if there was anything he could do. Little Macy spoke first. With tears in her eyes, she begged her dear captain to help her little brother get well. Witnessing Lady Yee's distress, the captain reached out to take Macy into his arms, where he distracted her with calming reassurance that all would be well and a gentle reminder that she must remain strong and think good thoughts to help her brother. Then, speaking to Dr. Chun, he asked what help he needed. Dr. Chun asked if there happened to be any quinine in the ship's medical locker, and Captain Penn said he believed it was listed on the inventory sheet. The captain called for the cabin boy, gave him a key, and told him to fetch the medical chest from the stores locker in his cabin. When it arrived, the captain handed it over to Dr. Chun, and told him to make use of anything he liked. He then belatedly thanked the doctor for being so attentive to his crewmen. Dr. Chun nodded politely and said that in one respect fortune smiled, as the hoped-for remedy would be the same for one and all. This would save time and effort, though the patients would still need constant care. He suggested that the same arrangements be made to bring the stricken crewmen up into the saloon, and temporary berths be prepared for them there. He confessed that it would be easier for him to look after all his patients if they were in one place. The close proximity of the galley also made the saloon more convenient than the crew's quarters forward. Captain Penn agreed and said he would see to it at once. Then he handed Macy back to her mother and went off to give his orders. In later consultation with Dr. Chun, who showed signs of deep concern for his patients' recovery while they remained aboard ship, Captain Penn determined to make for Hawaii with all possible speed. He had plenty of coal and no qualms about using every rock of it if necessary. And if that ran out, he had no problem with burning anything else at hand, including the cargo if need be.

Dr. Chun's patients had become almost comatose, but between the doctor, his bride, Lady Yee's maid and nurse, Ah Chu, the cabin boy, and Lady Yee herself, everyone received relatively constant attention and care. The sanitary aspect of their ministrations was an arduous and continuous process, and to aid in this, Captain Penn had makeshift laundry barrels secured to the deck rails. He then had the chief engineer rig a steam hose on deck to supply them with hot water at will. Soiled clothing and linens were washed daily and dried in the cleansing sun. Since two of their number were among the afflicted, the crewmen were asked to volunteer to help with this distasteful chore. Every man aboard, including the black gang and the cook, placed their names on the duty sheet, and the deck officers took on nursing duties when off watch.

Dr. Chun saw to it that all his patients were cooled and bathed with compresses when feverish, and swaddled in blankets when chilled. This rotation of symptoms was more or less continuous, and they racked the patients' tortured bodies with constant pain in every joint and muscle. It was a small mercy, therefore, that they were almost beyond caring. The doctor spent many hours compounding medication from the medical supplies available. Though limited for his purposes, he found adequate supplies of quinine and aspirin salts, as well as tinctures of laudanum to help deaden the pain. Unfortunately, he dared not administer that kind of drug to a child, and instead relied on a traditional Korean herbal solution concocted from tiny dried mushrooms, and it seemed to alleviate Silver's suffering by degrees.

Little Macy was beside herself with tears of anxiety and fear. She begged to be allowed to help care for her little brother. Rather than thwart her need to help, Lady Yee set Macy to reading stories to Silver, and told her that despite the fact that he appeared not to hear her, he actually heard everything very well. Macy spent hours reading her storybooks, or just making up stories as she went along.

Captain Hammond's suffering almost broke his wife's heart, and she rarely left his side except to see to her son's needs. Dr. Chun was of the opinion that his elevated distress might be occasioned by a prior infection of a similar kind, perhaps years before. Lady Yee shook her head and stated that she had never seen the captain ill a day since they were married. She confessed that, like everyone else living aboard a ship at sea, he had suffered occasional bouts of indigestion, but nothing more serious. Dr. Chun then suggested that he might have contracted the illness as a child. But he said with some confidence that, with proper attention, the captain's natural strength of body and stalwart constitution would help him pull through the worst of the disease.

On the other hand, the doctor confided to Lady Yee that he was very worried about her son. His supply of reserve strength was limited due to his youth, and in the case of malaria, endurance was a critical factor. The heart could only take so much stress before it gave out from exhaustion. He encouraged Lady Yee to try to get her son to drink small amounts of strong beef broth at room temperature, and to administer it as often as possible to help keep up his strength, and he gave

Lady Yee a vial of herbal medication and told her to drink it and lie down before she fell ill from exhaustion herself. He would see to her husband personally. Captain Penn had offered Lady Yee his cabin, and so she retired there with Macy, drank the draft, curled up on the bunk, and slept for sixteen hours. Awake or asleep, Macy never left her mother's embrace in all that time.

Eight days after the onset of the illness aboard, Captain Penn sighted the harbor of Honolulu to the northeast. He anchored in the offing with six other ships, but rather than just await the arrival of the quarantine boat, the captain sent up distress flags indicating a medical emergency and requesting the services of a doctor. Then he fired the ship's signal gun twice to draw attention to his flags. Twenty minutes later the harbor captain's launch arrived with the appropriate officers and a quarantine doctor aboard. Once the patients were examined to be sure they suffered from nothing contagious, they would be allowed to transfer to the port hospital for further care. Dr. Chun was most helpful in convincing the authorities that his patients were suffering from malaria, and even showed them his medical logs and what remedies he had already applied. The port doctor concurred with all his findings, and within five hours all four patients were comfortably bedded down in clean sheets in a modern hospital ashore. Captain Penn arranged rooms for Lady Yee, Macy, and the maid at a nearby hotel. It too was very modern, and thankfully very clean. Ah Chu and the nurse were left aboard ship to look after things and straighten up the disorder. Dr. Chun and his wife stayed aboard as well, but they paid regular visits to the hospital and walked about the town for exercise, and to satisfy curiosity.

Captain Penn knew that, according to custom and commerce, his proper course of action now would be to restock his coal bunkers, take on water and food, and sail for San Francisco with his cargo, but he decided to ignore that for a while. Nothing on the cargo manifest was necessarily perishable, and as long as the crew could draw some shore leave to maintain morale, Captain Penn felt content to stay. He wanted his crewmen back, but he wanted his friends back more.

Lady Yee stayed with her husband and son as much as possible, but she could be found at night sitting by her son's bedside, holding his hand and whispering to him. In fact, she was doing just that the very night little Nathanial Silver Hammond died peacefully in his sleep. His heart had simply failed.

Having grown up in China, and in Canton particularly, Lady Yee was intimately familiar with infant mortality and the premature death of children from disease. In most instances the poor suffered the worst of it, and if cholera or typhoid was at the root, the numbers of dead children could be absolutely staggering. But even armed with this knowledge, Lady Yee was not prepared to acknowledge that her son was like other children. He was the son of Lady Yee, and no power on earth had the right to deprive her of his life. She cursed the gods, she cursed the plague-infested island, she cursed the sea, and she cursed herself for going back to China at all. Then she broke down completely and collapsed in tears by the side of her son's bed. The presiding doctor gave her a strong sedative and placed her in his care for her own good. Again Lady Yee slept for many hours, but when she awoke she seemed quite composed and lucid. She called for the doctor and made him promise not to mention the death of her son to her husband. She feared the news would only distress his mind further, and thereby weaken his condition. The doctor agreed that this was probably a very good idea, and promised to say nothing. She also insisted that the time wasn't right for Macy to know the truth either. Her invention was necessary, but rested on a jewel of truth. She told Macy that her brother was very ill, but he was now under the care of the most important doctor in the world. She said he would be away for quite some time, but all would be well in the end. Macy seemed to take this in stride, but it hardly dampened her curiosity about details, and Lady Yee was hard-pressed to invent plausible particulars.

Captain Hammond and the two other crewmen were declared ambulatory in about seven days, but none would say they were fully recovered. Captain Hammond was still very weak, and sometimes complained of sharp intermittent pains in his chest and legs. However, he did begin to eat a better diet, and after a while it seemed he was always hungry, which was taken as a good sign.

Captain Penn visited often, always bringing gifts of fruit or cold marinated lobster tails, which he knew his friends very much enjoyed. He privately conferred with Lady Yee about the arrangements to take her son's body back to California, but she confessed that until she informed her poor husband and daughter of the tragic passing of little Silver, she was at a loss to know just what to do. Captain Penn promised to look after any arrangements she chose to make, but he kindly advised her to inform her husband of the truth. He was not a man to appreciate evasion, no matter how well meant, and it was best he not hear of the sad tidings from some other source. Lady Yee agreed.

The news of his son's death left Captain Hammond speechless, heartsick, and stunned. He just sat quietly in his bed weeping and shaking his head for hours. He refused to eat or speak to anyone for three days, and slept only when exhaustion set in. His doctor administered a sedative, and when Captain Hammond awoke twelve hours later he had composed himself considerably.

Lady Yee harbored private fears of culpability, and though hardly pragmatic on the subject, she convinced her husband that the will of heaven rules the destiny of all mankind, and to kindly remember that he still had a beautiful, intelligent daughter who desperately required her father's love, strength, and compassion if she were to survive this tragedy spiritually intact. This last revelation seemed to gradually draw the poison from the captain's grief, and he once again became himself. He soon came to remember his place in the chain of dependencies, and even chose to take on the soul-rending brief of telling Macy what had happened to her little brother.

But then something quite remarkable happened. While Lady Yee and her husband sat together on the hospital's veranda pondering the very question of this painful revelation, Li-Lee brought Macy to the hospital for a visit. The maid had sent ahead an urgent note for Lady Yee saying that she thought it very important that she speak with her daughter. Li-Lee wrote that Macy had been deeply troubled by a very powerful dream the previous night, and though she wouldn't talk about it, she seemed deeply disturbed, and begged to see her father and mother at once.

Macy's parents were not quite prepared for what they saw when their daughter rushed into

435

their arms. She was not crying, but she looked as though she had suffered a severe bout of weeping. And there was also something very different about her deportment. She looked older, which was a shock, and she no longer moved with the animated rapidity of a child. Her gestures seemed more deliberate and gentle. Without preamble of any kind, Macy grasped her parents' hands and said she was sorry for it, but she had sad news to impart. Macy wiped away the edge of a tear, and said that little Silver would not be going back to California with them. Her parents looked shocked and understandably perplexed. However, without a pause to register their response, Macy calmly announced that last night her grandfather had come to her to introduce an imperial envoy of the Celestial Emperor. This messenger, she said, was made of many colored lights, was magnificent to look at, and was very gentle. The envoy informed her that Silver had been called to the heavenly court of the Celestial Emperor to fulfill his duties in the Jade Palace. Macy suddenly looked very sad, but she steadied herself and continued. She said Silver had been chosen because he was bright, innocent, kind, and brave. Macy looked up at her parents and said she knew this would make them very sad and unhappy, but they were not to worry, as the celestial messenger had told her that Silver was now among the immortals.

Lady Yee was more surprised by the expression on her husband's face than she was by Macy's pronouncement. His whole physiognomy seemed to melt with grief. He suddenly clutched his daughter to his breast and began to weep. He tried to speak, but could find no words at first. Macy begged him not to cry, but her father seemed not to hear her. In a few moments his despair found voice through his tears and bemoaned the passing of his beautiful son. As though speaking to the universe, he vowed to have his vengeance to assuage his broken heart. When Macy pressed her point and insisted that Silver hadn't gone anywhere, and that he was among the immortals, her father's distress almost fired his temper, and he insisted that no dream could change the fact that his son was dead. Macy pulled back and looked to her mother for support. Lady Yee, setting aside her own tears, nodded in agreement. Then she reached over and drew up her husband's face so that he could see her expression clearly. She was calm but very serious. She looked deep into her husband's eyes.

"It is true," she said. "What Macy has told you is the truth. It has the blessings of innocence and insight. She sees more clearly than we do, and to be angered by the truth won't change that."

Captain Hammond wiped away his tears and looked down at his beautiful daughter. "To be sure," he said, "I know she's right, just as you say, my dear. I apologize for doubting you, Macy."

Macy smiled and reached into her pocket and withdrew something, which she handed to her father. It was a small seashell of a type he had never seen before. "That's Silver's favorite thing in the whole world," Macy said. "Grandfather gave it to him, and told him it was for creating magic that would make people happy. Silver wants you to have it now, so you can make people happy too." Then she moved back into her father's embrace and said, "Would you like me to read to you, Father? I brought you our favorite book, *The Tales of Sun Wukong and His Journey to the West.*"

"Yes indeed, my darling Macy. I would like that very much."

The captain decided to take his son's body back to Monterey, and informed Captain Penn of his decision and his wish to keep the matter confidential. And though he by no means hardened his heart to his own grief, or that of his family, Captain Hammond assumed his wife's aura of dignified emotional restraint. And though he accepted all condolences politely, he never voluntarily spoke of his son's death again; like his wife, cold thorns of guilt haunted the captain like a red tide, and this sealed his lips and guarded his innermost thoughts from any and all inquiries.

The voyage back to California was a sad affair. Quite unexpectedly, Macy became somewhat morose, quiet, and unresponsive to almost everyone. Even Lady Yee found herself cut off from her daughter's inner thoughts, and Macy went from being a child of voluminous expression to one of guarded sentiments. The only people who seemed to be able to make the child laugh were Li-Lee, Ah Chu, and Captain Penn, and she stayed in their company as much as possible.

The Hammonds eventually returned to Monterey, but it was weeks before anyone but Dr. Neruda and his family knew of it. Dr. Chun and his wife were installed in the smaller of the two staff houses, and it was with great relief that Lady Yee discovered that the two doctors got on marvelously. They shared many of the same theories on medical practice, and both had grounding in traditional Asian pharmacopeia. Mrs. Neruda and her daughter warmly welcomed Mrs. Chun into the fold and did all in their power to make her comfortable. They tried to help explain all the mysterious incongruities of life in California. The women found it easier to work together than the men. A universally shared female history of cooperative efforts toward rational goals, and similar backgrounds in education and aspirations, bonded the three women from the beginning and made them a formidable alliance.

Soon after they arrived home, Captain Hammond and Lady Yee quietly buried the small coffin of their son by the west-facing wall of the fruit orchard. At Lady Yee's instruction, the gardeners had prepared a special grotto surrounded by fragrant roses transplanted from other parts of the garden, and a young flowering cherry tree was set nearby to someday give shade. Macy was not told any of this, however, as Lady Yee had determined that her daughter's memory of the events encompassing her brother's passing should remain foremost in her mind. The dream was true and must remain so. Thus, on the day of interment, Macy was sent off with Li-Lee and Ah Chu to enjoy a picnic at the beach, so that besides the captain and Lady Yee, only a Taoist priest was present to perform a modest ceremony. As she so aptly described it to her husband, they were in fact interring only a shell. "The creature that once lived within, though departed from us now, lives on in our recollections, and beyond that, as our Macy so adamantly affirms, now dwells among the immortals in the celestial halls of the Jade Palace, where he is also well-known and much loved. I hope the same thing can be said of the two of us one day."

Despite all attempts to maintain strict privacy, word did get out, and many private gifts and sentiments of condolence came in from the

Chinese community. Aside from that, few people in Monterey were ever aware that anything sad had happened, and the Hammonds preferred to keep it that way.

Macy was remarkably composed through it all. She seemed to have decided to follow her mother's example and said nothing that might reveal her true feelings. Her father didn't think this was necessarily a good thing for a child, but he had to admit that Macy was becoming more like her mother with every passing day, and he could think of no viable alternative to the inevitable. Macy spent many hours seated in her brother's grotto and could often be heard talking to him as though he were alive. This behavior bothered the captain at first, but Lady Yee gently reminded him that this was common practice in China, and Macy had just spent a year deeply immersed in Chinese culture. She said it was only natural to want to believe that someone you love can hear you speaking from beyond the pale. Her husband nodded and never mentioned it again.

It was obvious to everyone that Captain Hammond was not recovering either his health or his spirits with any appreciable ease, and Dr. Neruda and Dr. Chun made a studied point of attending to this problem. They adjusted the captain's diet and prescribed a number of herbal remedies that were aimed at balancing his digestive, respiratory, and adrenal functions. They also recommended an increased consumption of onions and garlic whenever possible. Bread was to be avoided at all costs, as well as spirits made from grain or corn, while rice and vegetables in any form were encouraged. And in that vein they even suggested that a cup of mulled rice wine in the evening would be very efficacious and soothing for the nerves as well as the digestion. But however brilliantly the two doctors might exert themselves to be of assistance, Captain Hammond knew with utmost certainty there was no medical solution to his disease, for it was a dark, guilt-haunted torment of the soul that leached away at his stamina, shivered his spirit, and hobbled his aspirations to a standstill.

The captain chose to be alone more and more, and he began to read a great deal. In fact, he spent whole days shut away in his study just reading his ever-growing collection of books. His choice of reading material proved eclectic. In one stack, Lady Yee noticed titles that included the works of Spinoza, Dickens, Marco Polo, Voltaire, Edmund Burke, Captain Cook, William Blake, Mark Twain, Lao-tzu, Walt Whitman, and Shakespeare, and three large technical volumes on hydrology, tides, and celestial navigation. And that was just one stack. New boxes of books arrived from San Francisco every month, and the captain had to call in carpenters to build new bookcases wherever space allowed. He even had cabinet bookcases constructed for the parlor.

When Lady Yee questioned him about this notable change in his habits, her husband replied that he had spent his entire life working and making money. As a result, he had never taken the time to study all that he thought was important for a man to know. He said they now possessed all the money they could possibly want or need, and thanks to Hammond, Macy & Yee, more money was being banked all the time, and without much effort expended to do so. That was enough. He frankly admitted that business now bored him, as did many other things deemed valuable to fashionable society. He declared that he no longer wished to go among such people, or even keep company with their standards and values. He said he preferred to stay at home with his family, and hopefully acquire the education he was never privileged with in his youth. He felt he had earned that right, and Lady Yee, who wasn't primed for an objection in the first place, heartily agreed. She knew it would take a long time for her husband to set aside his grief, and until then it was proper to allow him to go his own way. In all, she counted herself lucky that he hadn't chosen rum or opium as a remedy.

Life for the Hammond family settled into a sedate and private routine that admitted few people into the inner circle. And as Captain

Hammond retired more and more into his books, Lady Yee took his place directing Hammond, Macy & Yee in most of its business concerns. In fact, within five years, she was Hammond, Macy & Yee. Aside from the Chinese infirmary, which was now running on its own steam, she continued her support for selected local charities and civic programs. However, she accomplished these ends from within the protective shelter of the corporation, and allowed Mr. Bishop to take point in every case. These measures ultimately achieved their intended purpose, and since neither Lady Yee nor the captain was commonly seen in public, and never entertained public persons worthy of note, after a while most people in Monterey forgot all about the gallant Yankee sea captain and the exotic Chinese noblewoman who lived on the hill overlooking the bay.

22

LADY YEE had little faith in Western public education, and so she occupied herself with tutoring her daughter at home. By the time she was twelve, Macy could speak, read, and write in English, French, and Cantonese, with Mandarin mixed in. She had no lack of playmates to while away the hours of youthful magic, but she preferred to play with Chinese children similar to her cousins. It wasn't so much a matter of race as it was of cultural familiarity. The Chinese children knew the games Macy loved to play, and sang the songs she liked to sing, and knew the puzzle jokes Chinese children loved to share. She also loved to play with the Mexican children who lived in the neighborhood, and she learned a fair amount of Spanish on her own.

One day when she was thirteen, Macy decided to give a party for all her Chinese and Mexican playmates, and Lady Yee, though she had her doubts, agreed to supply all the food and entertainment. She, in turn, also prepared adequate entertainment for the parents of the invited guests. Lady Yee had not the least inkling of how the two peasant cultures would mix, but she decided to trust Macy's strong keel of compassion and innocence. She needn't really have worried, as unbeknownst to Lady Yee her daughter had generated great feelings of loyalty, not only among her friends, but among her friends' parents as well. And in the spirit of pleasing children, everyone contributed what amusements they could. Uncles, fathers, and cousins became magicians, musicians, and clowns, while mothers and aunts became singers and dancers. The captain said the festivities were the most unusual conglomerate of cultural contributions he had ever experienced. It was a most remarkable display of fellowship, he said, perhaps because the whole affair was focused on the children. But it came off handsomely in the end, and the captain complimented his daughter on her taste in friends. He later told his wife that he believed Macy could make her way in life anywhere in the world she chose to live. She was like her mother in that regard, and the captain was very proud of her.

DESPITE ALL THE EFFORTS focused on Captain Hammond's health, Dr. Chun had come to the conclusion that the malarial infection that had almost taken his life had in fact injured his heart muscle permanently, and was most likely the cause of his irregular heartbeat. Dr. Neruda, who confessed to no recent training in cardiac medicine, bowed to his colleague's superior knowledge in this field. The captain's condition only became a noticeable problem when he overly taxed his energy or kept long hours, which wasn't often. Lady Yee was apprised of the situation, of course, and did what she could to maintain a quiet, steady household routine. She saw to it that little frustration surfaced to tax his spirits or cause him undue concern.

As the months passed into years, Captain Hammond retreated deeper and deeper into his studies. He lost interest in most everything except his books, Macy, and Lady Yee. He seemed to be only truly content, and indeed sometimes even lighthearted, when he was in her presence. Macy could still bring a smile to his face, and she often spent time reading to her father when his eyes tired from the lamplight. He also slowly lost his interest in food, and it was all Ah Chu could muster to keep the captain's meals entertaining as well as wholesome. Mrs. Neruda and Dr. Chun carefully managed the elements of his diet, which were chosen specifically for medical reasons, and Ah Chu created as much magic as those elements allowed for. Still and all, the captain admitted to his wife that he only ate to keep the engine running. Nothing really tantalized his palate any longer besides fresh fruit.

Besides his reading, the one thing that gave the captain the greatest pleasure was sitting in the shaded gardens with Lady Yee on lovely afternoons. They would reminisce by the hour about their adventures and old friends. Macy often joined them because she loved these stories. She would sit quietly plaiting leaves of grass into chains from which she made complex love knots for her parents. Sometimes she would ask a question, but mostly she just listened and laughed when her father told a funny story. Though one would have to suppose that, much like her mother, she was operating on instinct, Macy was aware that her father was slowly slipping into the shadows of his own mind, and she often tried to entertain and comfort him. Yet she began to feel her efforts were becoming a fruitless exercise at best.

When she asked her mother what more she could do, Lady Yee just shook her head in resignation and tried to explain the problem as simply as possible. At fourteen, Macy well understood the true circumstances surrounding her brother's demise, but she preferred to ignore them in favor of her dream, which she often told her mother was as real as anything she had ever experienced. But like most children, Macy saw no logical reason why both aspects of the truth could not occupy the same space at the same time. It was therefore difficult for Lady Yee to think of a plausible way to explain to her daughter the real basis behind her father's slow withdrawal from those things in life that once gave him so much pleasure. Yet it was some months later, as Macy experienced her father's seemingly rapid decline, that she went to her mother and demanded an explanation of what exactly was happening to her father. It seemed, she said with tears in her eyes, that sometimes he didn't even know her anymore.

Lady Yee could see that the moment of truth had come at last, and after a few moments of thought she invited her daughter to walk through the gardens while she divulged what she knew. She walked hand in hand with Macy as was their habit, and then spoke to her as an equal.

"Men," she said, "are far too complex and varied to categorize with any hope of accuracy. Yet there is one aspect of their composition that makes some of them endearing and noble, which also allows for a flaw that most women can shoulder but that most men of conscience cannot. You see, my dear, though he never speaks about it, your father is deeply burdened by an abiding sense of guilt concerning your brother's death. You must know that as a ship's captain he has always been primarily responsible for the lives and safety of his crew, and to his credit, he has lost very few men except to unforeseen disease or natural accident. Each and every loss he has taken personally because he believed that it was his decisions that brought about their suffering. I don't believe that he ever contemplated that his own children would ever have to endure the privations professional seamen took as part and parcel of a profession universally marked for its danger."

Macy found it convenient to pretend to comprehend what her mother was so kindly trying to share with her. But her sentiments seemed to tell her they came from another plane and rested on mysterious logic that was denied to her by age or ignorance.

But slowly, sadly, and almost imperceptibly, the captain's condition worsened.

Only Dr. Neruda, Dr. Chun, and Lady Yee were fully apprised of the declining condition of the captain's heart. His youthful maritime bouts with yellow jack, and any number of other tropical fevers, had taken a toll on that organ.

When Macy had just turned sixteen, on a night broadly remarked upon for the size of the full moon over the bay, her beloved father, Captain Jeremiah Macy Hammond, died quietly in his sleep.

Though it dismayed her to the core to dwell upon the inevitable, Lady Yee had been prepared for this eventuality. However, despite her knowledge of her father's condition, Macy was not. Her grief brought forth all the tormented memories of losing her brother, and compounded the agony with the sudden demise of her father. Macy's spirit sounded into the depths of her sorrow. Like the great ocean whales, she dove steadily down in silence and tears until the black oblivion below enveloped her pain, and there she stayed. She didn't speak a word for days, and ate next to nothing for a week. Even Dr. Chun was at a loss to know what to do, but voted on the side of empathy, patience, and attentive indulgence.

Lady Yee's grief and distress were hidden from view by a delicate façade of pragmatism and emotional strength. Privately, she knew not how she would survive the loss of her girlhood Yankee hero, her first love, her husband, her life's companion, her children's father, and her best friend, and all for the want of a simple heartbeat. There were those frozen moments when she wanted nothing more than to throw herself into the sea and search for the emotional oblivion Macy was seeking. But at the core of her soul Lady Yee knew that spiritual cowardice garnered greater penalties than patient endurance, no matter how painful the transition from one form of existence to another. And that was exactly what had transpired. Lady Yee's world had dramatically altered its poles, and now her compass pointed toward unknown horizons and the unfathomable destinations of age.

As if to compensate for this shift in heaven's favor, a few days later all the fruit trees in Lady Yee's manicured orchards came into bloom at the same time. The gardeners were beside themselves with disbelief and trepidation, and being Chinese, they spoke of fairy enchantments. And though it was certainly very odd to have twelve different species of fruit tree flower simultaneously, it was still extraordinarily beautiful and fragrant.

Lady Yee took it as a sign of something special, and as yet undefined. To ease her spirits, she spent long hours in the flowering riot of pink, white, red, and lavender. She sat on a carved wooden bench that had been placed by her son's grave by her late husband. It had been commissioned especially for its location. In spite of all that had befallen her family, she knew that good fortune had jealous neighbors. She had been the child of privilege and wealth all her life, and she had married a man who had become very wealthy, and in turn she had become wealthy in her own right. She had done her best to see that a good portion of that wealth had gone to serve those less fortunate, but good works don't necessarily absolve dark karma, and she had long since learned that true justice was a cumbersome myth at best. The ways of fortune were capricious and irreverent in the extreme.

The waves of misfortune seemed to always break in threes, and Lady Yee was bracing herself against the inevitable impact of the third blow. Sadly, she hadn't long to wait. Two weeks after her husband's passing, Captain Penn came to pay a visit of condolence. However, his condolences concerned the death of Lady Yee's father, Master Yee. He had passed to the keeping of his ancestors at the age of eighty-six.

Captain Penn, who still mastered *The Silver Macy* on behalf of Hammond, Macy & Yee, had been in Canton when the venerable gentleman had passed away. The captain had even delayed his departure to attend the funeral as a matter of respect, and so that he could more accurately relate what had transpired to Lady Yee personally. He also carried letters from her family, as well as a sealed copy of her father's will. Captain Penn had also been instructed by her father's executors to guard and deliver a small wooden chest to Master Yee's youngest daughter, Lady Yee. He said the chest was secured with two locks, but he'd been given the keys.

Captain Penn, in turn, was truly distressed to hear of his friend's death. He said that Captain Hammond had always been a good friend and a generous employer. Lady Yee assured Captain Penn that business would continue as before, and that in the future he would receive an additional three shares' profit on every cargo. Though deeply saddened by the purpose of his errand, and the news he received upon its completion, Captain Penn was nonetheless very grateful for the generous increase in wages. He apologized for not being able to stay over a few days and visit, but his ship would soon be loaded with a cargo of farm tools and industrial goods bound for Canton, and he needed to return to San Francisco to confirm and sign the manifests, then take the ship to sea as quickly as possible. But he did ask if it might be possible for him to visit with Macy before he departed. He said she held a very special place in his heart, and he wouldn't feel right about leaving without saying something to let her know of his affection and sympathy. Lady Yee thought this was a marvelous idea, but warned Captain Penn that her daughter had taken the deaths of her brother and father very hard. She was no longer the happy child he remembered. She specifically asked him not to mention the death of her grandfather. That would be too much on the heels of her father's passing. She would tell her daughter when matters settled a bit. Captain Penn of course agreed not to say a word. Later, she saw the captain and Macy walking in the gardens, and Lady Yee was pleased to hear her daughter's still-gentle laughter now and then.

Lady Yee had the letters and chest from Canton taken to her study, and later that night, after Macy had gone to bed, she read them all. Her father's will was a rather painful but enlightening instrument. She had no idea that he was as wealthy and powerful as the document indicated. Large fortunes and extensive property were settled on all three daughters, but there was a codicil that secured Lady Yee's portion in bearer bonds, cash, and gold certificates. Since she no longer resided in Canton, properties that might have come to her by inheritance were either purchased by rich relatives or by Master Yee's company, and the equivalent value forwarded in the aforesaid manner. The two keys that opened the polished wooden chest were tied with a ribbon and secured to the last page of the will with sealing wax impressed with her grandfather's personal chop. Lady Yee remembered the chest from her childhood. It had always stood on a table in her father's study. The chest's two locks were a Chinese puzzle in themselves, and to disengage the mechanism the right key had to be fitted into the right lock, and then the two keys turned in alternate sequences of a few degrees at a time until the tumblers were heard to drop into place. If the proper sequence was missed, the whole process would have to be reversed and started again, or the keys could not be extracted from the lock mechanism. Lady Yee remembered every sequence as though she were a child again, and she had the chest open at the first try. Inside she found a letter from her father dated just a few days before he died, and below that, in large wax-sealed envelopes, she found bearer bonds, gold certificates, bank draughts, and five thousand pounds in English banknotes. At the very bottom of the chest, wrapped in waxed silk, she found three Chinese cash sticks. Each stick formed a spindle of sixty gold coins, each coin weighing a little more than one troy ounce of twenty-three-karat gold. These were never used in common trading, but were known as "bank sticks" and only used for large purchases or for transferring company wealth from one place to another.

Lady Yee also discovered a padded silk pouch. The pouch was segmented into eight separate pockets, and they contained eight perfectly matched pear-cut rubies. According to the Chinese invoice contained in the pouch, the stones were near-perfect and weighed almost eight karats each. A note attached to the inventory said that the stones were to be liquidated, and the money held for Master Yee's granddaughter as a wedding dowry, or, if she preferred, she could make use of the stones as she pleased.

Macy soon came to know of the passing of her grandfather from her own sources. She was saddened, to be sure, but the death of her father and brother had wrung the more demonstrative expressions of her grief from her expression. Master Yee's passing after so many successful years of adventuresome prosperity seemed appropriate in the scheme of things, whereas the other personal tragedies seemed somehow out of balance. In this regard, Macy seemed to become more like her mother every day, and though she never lost her sense of humor, Macy became more circumspect about those events in her life over which she had no influence.

The next day Lady Yee put her abacus to work, and compensating for currency differences, she did a detailed inventory of the chest. Aside from the gold cash sticks and the matched rubies, she appraised the value of the chest's contents at somewhere around seven hundred and eighty thousand American dollars. Counted together with her husband's legacy and her own personal fortune, this effectively made Lady Yee the richest and consequently the most powerful Chinese woman in the Americas. This was a fact that Lady Yee, like her late father, worked very diligently to disguise, and that wasn't easy. Her company traded in a score of foreign and domestic markets, and her company banner flew above four burly steam-driven freighters, two of which she owned, and two that she and her husband had chartered since returning to California. All four ships were set up for the grain and rubber trade, and Captain Penn was made commodore of the little fleet. California grains were shipped west to Canton, and Chinese silks, pottery, and finished goods went from Canton to Malaysia, where they were traded for raw Malaysian rubber, which came east again. It was an established circuit of loosely united trading factors that had been put together by Master Yee himself. He had arranged the lucrative triangle in gratitude for his son-in-law's extending such enormous amounts of credit on grain purchases. In fact, the circuit ran so smoothly that Lady Yee barely gave it a second thought. Mr. Bishop, who now kept residences in San Francisco and Monterey to facilitate Lady Yee's business interests, received, copied, and forwarded all pertinent documents by special messenger to her.

23

AS THE YEARS PASSED, there were those few occasions when Lady Yee was required to travel to San Francisco with Mr. Bishop on special business. She made a point of taking her daughter along as a means of introducing her to a wider world of society.

By this time, Macy had become a strikingly beautiful young woman. She had grown tall and well framed, and she had inherited her father's copper-bright auburn hair. Her long locks veritably sparkled with golden highlights when she walked in the sunlight. She possessed almost azure-blue eyes that were framed by arched lids that spoke of her Chinese ancestry, and she moved with a natural grace and confidence that reflected an ancient sense of purpose and dignity that was obvious to all at first sight. Indeed, whenever Macy entered a public room, all eyes, both men's and women's, turned to her. The strange thing was that Macy had no idea of her effect on people. In fact, she didn't think she was particularly pretty, though most would argue to the contrary.

Soon after her father died, Macy took possession of his study and his library, and began to read all his books. Seeing that this proximity to her father's favorite possessions gave her daughter some peace and happiness, Lady Yee made no objection, but she thought it best to employ a series of retired scholars to help tutor and guide Macy through the complex labyrinths of philosophy, history, science, and art that waited on the study shelves like jessed birds of prey. Macy's favorite teacher was an old Chinese gentleman named Quan-Hu Shu. He had once been the tutor for the children of a very powerful mandarin dignitary. He spoke four dialects of Chinese, as well as reasonable English and some French, but his avocation in later life had become the study of Arabic, Hebrew, and Greek. For reasons that Lady Yee was hard-pressed to explain to herself, much less others, Macy had taken a deep interest in the old scholar's studies, and asked to be taught to read and write in Arabic and Greek. Again, Lady Yee felt the distraction of study was far preferable to other methods of dealing with grief.

When Macy turned seventeen, Lady Yee decided it might help her education to be exposed to the broader world of fashionable society. She arranged to take two connecting suites at the stylish Mason House on Nob Hill in San Francisco. While there, Lady Yee and her daughter were invited to a celebratory birthday ball hosted by the Russian legation. It was to be a very grand affair marking the young czar's birthday, and everybody of importance or influence in the city was sure to be present. Lady

Yee stinted on nothing to see that her daughter was attired in the latest Parisian fashion for the occasion, and even allowed her to wear her great-grandmother's magnificent triple-rope choker of matched swallow's egg pearls. She added her own Persian-crafted emerald earrings and bracelets, which harmonized with Macy's eyes and complemented her sea-green satin gown.

Though she had always hoped for more from her adopted country, Lady Yee well understood that there was little real sophistication or delicacy entailed with present American courting traditions, and there was certainly no real subtlety to the ancient Anglo-Saxon or Latin practices of presenting eligible daughters to the gaze of an audience of eligible bachelors. In some instances, powerful families sought brides for their sons, preferably without complaint, for the sole purpose of financial or political connections.

Lady Yee knew the game well and had certainly circumvented all custom where Captain Hammond was concerned, so she knew her brilliant and willful daughter would always find her own way in the end. The one tactic Lady Yee had readily at hand was the illusion of great wealth, and the diffidence not to mind the appearance of great wealth. She adorned her daughter in the indisputable social armor of her day, wealth, and in such a regal manner as to declare to any prospective suitors that they had best be able to match and better the stakes, or simply stay away and save face. The rest of the process would take care of itself in due time, as it had for centuries past. But in all of that, Lady Yee was more than confident that Macy's keen intelligence, intuitive social equilibrium, refreshing Asian manners, and winning personality would eventually steal the wind from any competitive sails maneuvering on the same tack. And if that lacked impact, her daughter's sense of humor, sometimes wreathed in absurd Latin or Greek quotations, was bound to seduce the educated and baffle the ignorant, which always saved time in the long run. Macy, like her mother, had little patience with bigots or fools, but unlike most young people, she knew the fine art of keeping her opinions well guarded.

The czar's birthday ball was a marvelous success according to all who attended. Even the San Francisco papers touted the event as the most fashionable, well-attended, and socially complete gathering the city had witnessed since California became a state. However, this occasion was further honored by the presence of the diplomatic corps of eight countries, most attired in extravagant, gold-burnished versions of national uniforms. Some senior diplomats of the old imperial school sported cocked hats and egret feathers, but those of the highest rank, and therefore beyond all common comparison, were inevitably plumed in black swallowtail coats, starched white linens, satin cravats, gold and jeweled appointments, long evening capes, and tall silk hats.

Lady Yee, on the other hand, being a mother and a widow, was modestly but elegantly gowned in cobalt-blue satin, very subtly embroidered with flying cranes picked out with silver thread. She wore full-length white kid gloves, and a silver shawl made of the finest Chinese silk, edged in freshwater seed pearls the color of malachite.

Lady Yee usually prided herself on predicting most social eventualities, but in this case she had to admit that Macy was fishing in deep waters for the first time. So to cover those hidden eventualities properly, she saw to it that they were accompanied to the Romanoff birthday extravaganza by none other than her old friend and business attorney, Mr. Bishop. He in turn was so surprised and personally moved at being asked to fulfill such a gallant role on behalf of his longtime employer that he suddenly lost all sense of proportion, and went out and spent a month's earnings by commissioning the finest Italian tailor in San Francisco to reproduce the newest in silk formal attire including, to be sure, patent leather shoes, top hat, and an ivory-capped walking stick with his name inlaid with gold wire.

And though they were very touched by Mr. Bishop's almost boyish enthusiasm for the role assigned, both Lady Yee and Macy privately agreed, with forgivable laughter aside, that dear Mr. Bishop and his festive wardrobe were ill matched at best. Macy said it was like watching a man at war with his own clothes, and sadly, Mr. Bishop was the only fatality. However, though Lady Yee might smile behind her sleeve, she felt obliged to remind her daughter that their faithful escort was widely known and well respected in many important circles, and as the long-standing representative of Hammond, Macy & Yee, was acknowledged by every important bank and trading house in California and the Pacific circuit.

Lady Yee had chosen her escort with care. Mr. Bishop had always represented her interests, and it was most fortuitous that he was present the night of the ball, because as fortune favors the novice, Macy somehow managed to draw the undivided attention of the grandest-looking elk in the herd. He was young, he was almost theatrically handsome, and by all appearances he was very rich. He proved to be an honored scion of the Russian imperial diplomatic establishment, and was introduced to Lady Yee as Count Henri Pavel Volkofsky, special imperial secretary to the Russian legation from the court of the czar.

With Lady Yee's kind permission, the handsome young Russian begged every dance he could from Macy's card, and since Miss Hammond had only rarely been seen in such circles, she had many openings. Other young stags soon caught sight of Macy's undeniable beauty, grace, and apparent wealth, and they coursed to make their own formal introductions. However, the dashing young count proved truly dedicated. He very subtly pulled rank and graciously claimed all Macy's dances in the name of the czar, to whom he was proud to be distantly related. His grandmother, according to another guest, had been from a cadet branch of the Romanoff family.

At ten-thirty there was an intermission to the dancing, and an elegant little supper was served to various parties in small private dining rooms placed about the hall. The young count rushed to invite Lady Yee and her daughter to dine with his party. Lady Yee smiled as she immediately recognized that the fish was placing the hook in its own lip, and since she thoroughly trusted Macy's knowledge of the appropriate behavior required in such situations, she decided to let the quarry run with the line for a while. Thus Lady Yee graciously declined the young Russian's invitation on the grounds that she had prior social obligations. However, she said that Macy was free to accept if she chose to.

The young count humbly entreated Miss Hammond to join his party. He promised to personally return his guest to her mother at the conclusion of the meal. Macy looked at her mother for confirmation, and when she saw her mother's somewhat conspiratorial one-cornered grin, she knew that something was up, and she graciously accepted his kind invitation.

With Mr. Bishop to make all the necessary introductions, within three-quarters of an hour Lady Yee knew almost everything about Count Henri Pavel Volkofsky. Through various sources, she discovered that Count Volkofsky was the youngest of three sons of a prominent Russian diplomat who had held important portfolios as special ambassador to various troubled and dangerous postings, including the Levant, Korea, and Japan. None of these governments were particularly fond of Russia's historical encroachments, and keeping matters on an even keel required great diplomatic skill. Being the youngest son, Henri would not have inherited his father's title, but rather than allow his youngest son to enter the army or the priesthood when he was fifteen, as was tradition, his father sent Henri off to Paris with a French tutor to study international law, languages, and political history. The old count foresaw a diplomatic career for his youngest son. The name Volkofsky would be enough to gain him consideration in that field, while his older brother carried the title, ran the family's considerable estates, and paid court to the czar when necessary. The next youngest was a dashing major in a prestigious guards regiment in St. Petersburg. After eight years in Paris, young

Henri had gained a scholastic reputation second to none, and was already being courted by the foreign service, the court attorney's office, and the diplomatic corps. Sadly, on the eve of his return to Russia, Henri's father and two older brothers were killed in a horrific train wreck that many believed was the work of anti-czarist revolutionaries. The young man returned home to discover that he was now Count Henri Pavel Volkofsky, owner of vast estates of well-watered farmland and the master of twenty thousand souls in sixteen villages and towns. Since his poor mother had died of a lung infection eight years before, Henri was left in complete control of a very substantial family fortune.

Lady Yee also discovered that the young count had a dedicated following of people who praised him for numerous superior qualities. He was a gentleman born to the Enlightenment, and one who was uncomfortable being the absolute master of others. He had spent too long in Paris among illuminated minds ever to be content with a life in rural Russia, and to alleviate the pressure of administration the young count decided to lease a good portion of his arable land to the peasant farmers who worked the soil so diligently for generations. The saltworks, lead mines, and timber mills he turned over to his cousins to manage. They had been doing the job for almost a hundred years, and so Henri gave them a larger portion of the profits and allowed them to continue as part owners. He felt this would commit them to greater economy and secure their ongoing loyalty to his wishes. Henri then took over his father's palatial residence in St. Petersburg, and focused exclusively on installing himself in a favorable position with the imperial diplomatic corps. He had obviously succeeded in fulfilling his ambitions, and from all appearances with plenty of room to spare.

The young count was as good as his word, and he returned Macy to her mother after the supper. He regretted that Lady Yee had not joined them, and requested the company of both mother and daughter at a more intimate supper the following week. Lady Yee was pleased to accept, and without further comment sent Macy off to dance with her Russian count.

Lady Yee had no need to ask Macy whether she was enjoying herself, or if she found the handsome young count to her liking. Her daughter's sentiments on both subjects were reflected in the glow of her complexion, the grace of her movements, and the childlike sparkle in her eyes. When Macy was ready, she would tell her mother all about it. She always did.

Lady Yee spent the rest of the evening being introduced to various notables by Mr. Bishop. One introduction in particular was quite a surprise. An elder member of the Russian commercial legation introduced himself as Dmitri Ermolov. He was head of the trade delegation, and had known Lady Yee's father, Master Yee, when he was posted to Canton. At the time he had been in charge of the Russian fur and amber trade, and bartered ermine and mink pelts for jade and Canton silk, and Baltic amber for fine bone porcelain and other artistic luxuries. The old Russian and Lady Yee talked for quite some time about Canton and the China trade, a subject about which she knew a great deal more than Mr. Ermolov, as it turned out. However, it was from this lovely gentleman that Lady Yee discovered everything she really wanted to know about the young man who was paying court to her daughter.

Lady Yee knew that the young count would eventually have to stand up to Macy's father as a primary pattern of male prominence and grace, and that would not be easy. It was only natural that a girl would judge all other men by the standards of her father, good or bad, but in Captain Hammond's case that would represent a very long benchmark indeed. But there was a contextual problem. Lady Yee's predilection toward prognostication was now functioning in an analytical mode only, and though she secretly believed she might be addressing her future son-in-law, she also knew that Macy was a unique element, and one whose coefficients were sometimes highly unpredictable. Just when it looked like she might tack with the wind and steer the common course, she would suddenly come about and race off on her own, showing her heels to one and all as she charged past in the opposite direction. Nonetheless, Lady Yee knew her daughter well enough to believe that those instances were never the result of a fickle or childish temperament, or simply fits of contrary pique, but rather a sincere conviction that her safest and surest course was guided by a different star, and for Macy that guiding beam sometimes appeared in a different quadrant of the sky altogether. In point of fact, Macy's unique thought process and oblique train of logic were very much like her mother's, which must have come as something of a shock to Lady Yee when she finally figured it out.

Lady Yee smiled as she recalled that her own adoring and indulgent father Master Yee often said it would have been far easier to raise a platoon of boisterous and disobedient sons than another daughter like the Silver Lotus. He complained that nothing about her was in the least predictable. But he smiled knowingly when he at last met his new granddaughter, for he knew at once that Lady Yee would soon come to experience the same riveting confusion and consternation he had enjoyed as a parent of three intelligent, headstrong daughters. He saw it, as most elders do, as the inevitable balance of karma, and it had amused him to ponder the outcome.

Though she tried to keep an open mind to all the possibilities, Lady Yee was not quite prepared for Macy's undeniable attraction to the handsome young Russian who labored so hard to please. She could see the excited expression of romantic expectation in her daughter's eyes, and she was reminded of the first time she had met and talked with Captain Hammond. But of course, Captain Hammond was taller and far more attractive than the Russian count, at least to her way of thinking, but that was to be expected. The captain had been a yard-larking Yankee seaman of the old school, who towered over most men by more than a foot. His great mane of bronze-colored hair made him look even larger, and certainly more imposing. But in the main, none of that really mattered, because even Lady Yee had to admit that the dashing Count Henri Pavel Volkofsky possessed the most beautifully clear aquamarine-blue eyes she had ever seen. The honesty of his expression compounded with the liquid innocence of his eyes had the hypnotic lure of moral transparency.

THE DAY AFTER THE BALL, Count Volkofsky sent Lady Yee and her daughter a handwritten invitation to take dinner that night aboard a visiting imperial Russian cruiser docked in San Francisco Bay. If they could kindly see their way to accept the invitation, the count promised to provide the most comfortable transport possible. They were to be the honored guests of Admiral Prince Vesili Chekovich.

Every other day the count sent baskets of flowers and exotic fruits, as well as invitations to one fashionable event or another. With a natural gate of chivalry that Lady Yee found sincere and endearing, the attentive young count hosted mother and daughter at numerous theater parties, opera dinners, elite horse races, and elaborately fashionable picnics laid out under colorful canvas kiosks and broad awnings set up in private garden parks overlooking the bay. Lady Yee could easily see where matters stood, and though the count had said nothing formally on the subject of courtship, he seemed to be accomplishing his ends very well.

Macy, on the other hand, needed no boyish professions of romantic intent, because she knew instinctually that she was at the reins of the whole business, or at least that's what she believed at the time. Lady Yee knew better, however, and privately decided it was time to reel in some slack and see just how tenacious the count could be when snagged on a short line.

Without telling Macy beforehand, Lady Yee arranged to accept an invitation from Mr. Bishop to enjoy a steamboat excursion up the American River to the state capital, to attend a celebratory ball favoring the recent election of the new governor. They would be gone for ten days, and though she made no secret of their destination and intentions to the hotel management, she believed no purpose could be served by informing Count Volkofsky of their plans. He would have to discover those for himself, and then judge what to do with the information. It was just one of the hoops that Lady Yee had planned to test the dedication, endurance, and flexibility of her daughter's suitor.

As matters progressed, Lady Yee discovered that she might just as well have saved all the effort, for on the night of the governor's ball, Lady Yee and her daughter were greeted at the door by the Russian counsel general, Prince Magoyan, and the dashing young Count Volkofsky. Lady Yee was totally surprised to discover that the count was the person who had arranged for the Hammonds to be invited in the first place.

It appeared that Count Volkofsky had the will and the way to achieve his purposes, even to the extent of using his position to manipulate the offices of the governor of California. Romantically speaking, he was fearless, and even confessed to Lady Yee that no effort or expense of time or fortune was too extravagant if it helped convince Miss Hammond of the sincerity and enthusiasm of his sentiments. Miss Hammond, on the other hand, was in the throes of her own emotional gallop through the woods, ducking every contrary limb and circumventing every negative obstacle that appeared in her path. By the end of the evening, Lady Yee was securely aware that her daughter had fallen deeply in love with the handsome Count Volkofsky, and she had it on the viable authority of the aging and slightly inebriated Prince Magoyan that the young count was totally besotted by the beautiful Miss Hammond.

Upon hearing this, Lady Yee chose the better part of discretion over the fruitless gestures of maternal valor and sat back to watch love's labors sail on as they might. Her father had not been able to effect the least influence on her own choice of a husband, her beloved Yankee captain. She thought it only proper that she allow her courageous daughter the same sweeping horizon that she had once expected for herself.

24

THREE MONTHS LATER, Macy Yee Hammond was married to Count Henri Pavel Volkofsky in an elaborate Russian Orthodox wedding ceremony that was in part sponsored by the Russian legation as a sign of Russian-American compatibility. Macy, whose own spiritual philosophy was decidedly but unobtrusively Chinese, was philosophically pragmatic in the extreme. She happily converted to the Russian Orthodox faith to accommodate her purpose, but did so only when the count swore she would never be forced to practice any ritual she found incompatible with her own philosophy. He confessed that he was hardly a paragon in religious matters, and only went to church for weddings and funerals. He said that he had traveled too far, and seen far too much of the world, to be remotely impressed by the functions of either politics or religion, which, as far as he was concerned, represented the same beast wearing different hides to beguile the gullible.

After the wedding, the bride and groom escorted Lady Yee back to Monterey, where for ten days Henri was treated to the very finest meals Ah Chu's genius could create. The new family spent leisurely hours getting to know one another, and in the evenings Lady Yee held her new son-in-law enthralled with tales of her adventurous life at sea with her dashing Yankee husband, Captain Jeremiah Hammond. She took time to apprise Henri of the intricate family connections that still bound her daughter to very important people in southern China, clan associations with whom Hammond, Macy & Yee were presently doing very profitable business. She jokingly chided the young man by warning him that it was one thing to pass muster with her in America, but his biggest social hurdle would come when he was presented for inspection among the notables of Canton, where Macy had always been a particular favorite.

Before the couple departed, Lady Yee held a small reception for their Monterey friends and associates. It lasted quite informally for three days, and Ah Chu saw to it that the sideboards creaked under the weight of exotic and tasty things to eat and drink. The Neruda family and their professional associates from the infirmary were the first to pay their respects, and they all arrived bearing gifts. In all these simple gatherings, Lady Yee made a point of introducing her son-in-law as Henri Pavel Volkofsky. As an aside, she informed her darling Henri that most people living in California had migrated far to relieve themselves from the burdens of royal entitlements and prerogatives. Words like "baron," "prince," "count," or even "marquis" made Americans either frightened or envious. Both extremes were distasteful since they inhibited social honesty. She suggested, with an inscrutable smile, it might be best to be known and admired first, and titled later. Volkofsky enthusiastically agreed, and Macy loved him all the more for it. Soon it was known all over town that Macy Hammond had married a devilishly handsome young Russian named Henri Pavel Volkofsky. And as luck would have it, the groom had money, which was every mother's dream come true. Lady Yee's Chinese friends were of course most especially pleased with that last all-important sign of joss.

Two days later, Henri and Macy departed by train for Oakland, where they would be reunited with their luggage and then taken aboard two luxuriously appointed railroad salon cars for a journey to New York, from where they would sail to Europe in the grandest accommodations afforded by the White Star Line, and then proceed upon the leisurely and extensive cultural tour that Henri had promised Macy as a wedding present. Henri even promised to take her back to Canton to visit her relatives if she so desired. The whole idea of facing a battalion of Yees so unnerved him that he requested a letter of personal recommendation from his mother-in-law. Lady Yee laughed and said that document had already been sent many weeks before, and so far she'd not heard one word of protest.

Lady Yee did not accompany her daughter and

son-in-law to the departing train, and she showed no inappropriate emotion when they left. In fact, she immediately changed her clothes and accompanied Dr. Neruda on an inspection tour of the infirmary, which had grown somewhat since her departure to San Francisco. She spent hours each day confirming that her gardens and orchards were properly cared for, and her evenings were spent answering or initiating long-delayed correspondence. In short, life became rather quiet after Macy's departure, but that hardly made it uneventful, since the captain had long since failed to have an influence on Lady Yee's endeavors at certain improvements in the conduct of affairs, both personal and public. And she exchanged long, illuminating letters with her daughter as Macy traveled about the world with her husband.

Time passed quite agreeably for Lady Yee. She had no feelings of solitude or loneliness because she was always involving herself in any number of rewarding civic endeavors or working with Mr. Bishop to increase the flow of business. She wrote numerous letters to those she was pleased to refer to as her committee of correspondence, and in return received, through rather clandestine channels, private and pertinent news from everywhere one could imagine. It was Mr. Bishop's contention that Lady Yee knew more about what was happening in California and most of Asia than anyone in the Americas.

• • •

FOR THOSE FEW PEOPLE whose business concerned such things, it was an uncontested truth that the venerable Lady Yee was one of the most interesting people in Monterey County. The reason this fact was generally unknown to most citizens was the result of a concerted effort on the part of Lady Yee herself. She worked diligently to make sure that her name was never remotely connected to any philanthropic or civic endeavor in which she took a financial interest.

Those fortunate people who could claim to know the regal Lady Yee moderately well always thought it truly remarkable that anything she wished to come to pass always did, and sometimes in the most mysterious or coincidental manner. Though none would dare to ask, Lady Yee never voiced even the slightest explanation as to how these marvels came to be. It was as though her abiding confidence was always enough to manifest the result she wished.

Lady Yee still lived in a lovely stone house in the foothills overlooking Monterey Bay. She and her late husband, Captain Hammond, had purchased the property and its fifteen pine-crested acres from the estate of a wealthy rancher and farmer named Liam O'Sheen, and she lived there in what some people in town called "exotic Asian splendor." The large house was noted for its beautiful walled gardens, which contained numerous floral specimens from around the world. Others in town still spoke about the time when all twelve varieties of fruit trees in her orchards bloomed at once.

No one knew exactly how old Lady Yee really was, for she never appeared to age. Her hair showed no signs of graying, and the skin of her hands and face appeared free of any of those subtle discolorations that hinted at advancing age. There were few people still living who could remember when Lady Yee first came to Monterey as the young bride of the redoubtable Captain Hammond. No one really knew how Captain Hammond acquired his considerable wealth, but it was acknowledged that he'd been in the China trade for many years, most of the time in command of windjammers he owned and operated. And since anything having to do with Asia and trade implied great profits, most people just assumed he'd been highly successful in business and let it go at that.

When the good captain died suddenly of heart failure, it is said that Lady Yee inherited his entire estate. She then took her substantial wealth and went on to make many more sage investments that added considerably to her fortune. She owned a great deal more commercial property in Monterey County than anyone ever imagined.

All of her noteworthy accomplishments were not merely luck or happenstance; they were the creations of a remarkably creative and insightful intellect, and rather than weakening with age, Lady Yee's powers of perception and intuition only increased. The famous San Francisco jurist and writer Judge Duncan Haines faced her in a court case involving her late husband's maritime interests. After his clients lost the case, Judge Haines was overheard to say that Lady Yee made King Solomon look like a backcountry circuit judge. He declared she had a better legal mind than most of the political turnips warming the seats on the Supreme Court. He was so impressed that he later sought her out socially, and over the years they became good friends.

There were people in Monterey who were just as aware of Lady Yee's extraordinary powers of intellect and memory. She never forgot a name, or a face, or the place of first introduction. Her precise recollection of dates and figures seemed almost eerie. She could recall what she paid for a pair of black lace gloves when she was only twenty-two, and she could fix complex mathematics in her head by visualizing and manipulating an imaginary abacus. She knew to the penny how much ready cash she had at her disposal at any given time, and how much property she controlled, and what the rents were worth for each. These skills engendered broad admiration and deep respect, primarily because she was so meticulously unassuming and reticent when it came to praise or acknowledgement of any kind.

The Silver Lotus professed to believe that all things in her life were in the hands of a merciful god. She would always smile demurely and say that she "simply rode the back of the buffalo and played her flute to ease the journey."

No one quite understood what she meant exactly, but of course they weren't seriously fooled either.

Acknowledgements

MOST PEOPLE ARE NOT aware that a professionally published book is a complex team effort, and I don't mean just the physical book itself, for the creative process doesn't exist or bloom in a vacuum. Every artist, regardless of his or her medium of expression, stands in need of the support, creativity, and concern of others. My father once told me, and not in jest, that if I wanted steady and useful employment in a profession that was culturally necessary, and one that possibly offered the advantages of potential wealth, then I should avoid writing at all costs, and take up the study of drainage to become a plumber. He was right, of course. But like most children I didn't know sound advice when I heard it, so here I am. I seriously doubt that I shall ever become as wealthy as a successful plumbing contractor, but I'll wager that there are very few plumbers who get as much fun and enjoyment from their work as I do from mine. Even so, none of these blessings can be attributed to just one element or person. Indeed, it took the creative efforts, artistic sensitivity, openhanded generosity, and kindness of a goodly number of fellow travelers, family, artists, and good friends to bring this modest adventure to its present existence.

First in line to receive my sentiments of profound gratitude must be my wife, business partner, and the love of my life, Gail Knight Steinbeck. Her enlightened business acumen, industrious sense of detail, and most of all, plain hard work have been the driving force that has mastered the technical hurdles of getting my work into broad publication. Few authors are capable of dealing with the challenges presented by such tricky endeavors as contract analysis, payment schedules, and the subtle business manipulations that publishers have traditionally been so fond of employing with their authors.

Next in line for my sincere compliments and gratitude is my dear friend and editor Dan Smetanka. He has been creatively essential in the guidance of my work from the very beginning of my career as a published author. Only a writer of ineffable ignorance, made blissful by vanity and self-delusion, or an author of mind-boggling genius, who possesses an infinite brilliance of wit plus an unerringly objective sense of self-appraisal, should even try to go to print without the assistance and support of a really dedicated and experienced editor. In this regard I have been blessed with the detailed and precisely objective literary skills of Dan Smetanka. I can state without the least reservation that a great part of my success is predicated on one principle. I never argue with my editor. His vested interests are the same as mine in the end, and his knowledge of the tastes and interests of the book-buying public is indispensable. Over the years that I have known and worked with him, I have learned a number of highly significant lessons. The first among these is "just because I think it's good doesn't necessarily make it so." I have learned not to be precious about my work. In that regard writing is like sculpting in stone. With Dan's help and practiced sense of literary perspective, I keep chipping away at the marble because we both have every confidence that there is a book in there somewhere.

Every literary exercise, great or small, requires the support, both spiritual and material, of other people, and in that particular I have also been extremely fortunate. The backing of family and close friends has made this work not only possible, but also far easier than circumstances seemed to allow at the time. To quote an old Irish friend of mine, "Sometimes we all need a kindly hand up, and sometimes we just need a good friend to bribe the wolf at the door to come back another day." In that critical vein, family members have proved the truest guardians of my modest efforts. The fact that they are all, family and friends inclusive, very accomplished artists in their own right, might explain my survival and success as a writer. They all, without exception, organically understood and appreciated the challenges involved in bringing any creative endeavor to the public eye.

In particular I wish to acknowledge the kindness and generosity of my dear friend and niece (by marriage), Lindsay Hilton, an extremely talented graduate of the Berklee College of Music in Boston, and my darling nephew, the highly accomplished and internationally known composer and musician Johnny Irion. Both have been supremely supportive. The everyday world always appears more entertaining, and certainly more creative, when they come to nest for the holidays, or while on tour.

One of my oldest and dearest friends, Phillip Rosen, has always been my most stalwart ally, and for more years than I care to count, he has looked out for my well-being with grace, generosity, and a well-honed sense of humor.

It is often said that success has many parents, but in the case of this modest volume it is essentially true. And as far as this work is concerned, the generous godparents are Simon and Diana Raab. Again there was an empathy born of mutual interests. Simon is an outstanding, and intellectually courageous, painter and sculptor whose work enjoys an international audience. His wife, Diana Raab, is one of the few modern poets that I look forward to reading with loyal regularity. Simon and Diana are both, by any standard, extraordinary talents, and I feel quite honored that they count me as a loyal friend and worthy colleague.

Lastly, I wish to thank my father's granddaughter, Blake Smyle, her husband Jim, and their children, Nicholas and Hannah, for their love and filial concern. It took years of searching, but we have at last successfully managed to reunite our wandering brood. It is every artist's private glory to feel that he can leave something of intrinsic value to generations of his own family yet to come. Thanks to my audacious and talented niece, after years of believing I was the last of a lost clan, I now have a whole family once again, and I sincerely hope my modest efforts finds favor in their eyes, and perhaps provide a tickle of pride.

Center Point Publishing
600 Brooks Road ● PO Box 1
Thorndike ME 04986-0001 USA

(207) 568-3717

US & Canada:
1 800 929-9108
www.centerpointlargeprint.com